Without A NET

KIMBERLY COOPER GRIFFIN

NIGHT RIVER PRESS

Printed in the United States of America First Edition 2019

Edited by Jennifer Renton

Cover and interior design/layout by Matthew LaFleur

Night River Press
Denver, CO 80209
NightRiverPress.com

Without a Net
ISBN (Hardcover): 978-0-9972190-7-4
ISBN (Paperback): 978-0-9972190-8-1
ISBN (eBook): 978-0-9972190-9-8

Visit the author's website at
http://kimberlycoopergriffin.com to order additional copies.

Without a Net *is dedicated to Summer,
my favorite wife.*

Also by Kimberly Cooper Griffin

LIFE IN HIGH DEF

CHASING MERCURY

ACKNOWLEDGEMENTS

WITHOUT A NET **SPENT MANY** an afternoon torturing my writing group; Lake McCleary, Carrie Repking, and Beth Escott Newcomer. I'm grateful for your brilliant insight, inspiration, and precious patience while I figured out how to turn what was once a dark and brooding story into something that wouldn't drive my readers into a crippling depression. I miss writing with you wonderful ladies.

THANK YOU JENNIFER RENTON. YOUR editing magic makes my wandering prose stronger and clearer than I ever thought possible.

SKEETER BUCK, I'M GRATEFUL THAT we met in our children's kindergarten class. You helped me find the courage to publish my stories, and gave me a path to get it done. You rock!

SUMMER COOPER GRIFFIN, WITHOUT YOU I would be nothing. I owe you everything.

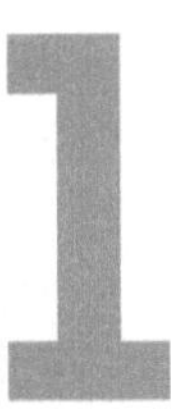

A SHARD OF GOLDEN LIGHT snuck around the edges of the closed bedroom blinds, making its way across the pillow until it pierced Fiona MacGregor's eyes through her closed lids. They fluttered, but did not open. She grimaced and pulled the comforter over her aching head with a groan. It wasn't the light that had woken her up, driving a brutal spike through her head. It was the delivery truck that sounded like it was rumbling through her bedroom. She tucked the covers against her ears as defense against the head-splitting sound and tried to summon back the black and empty nothingness of sleep. It was no use. The truck came to a stop outside her window with a piercing squeal of brakes. The engine idled with an uneven growl. Doors opened and slammed. Horns blared. Men's voices shouted an argument about double-parking. Every sound was an agony and all Fiona wanted was to drift away.

Any other time, the constant noise of the city was a comfort to Fiona, but at this moment, she'd do anything for the blissful sound of silence. As she took a bleary inventory of her body parts, pain registered from every sector. Especially her head, which ached with a fury she'd never experienced before. Her mouth tasted disgusting and the smell of alcohol exuded from every pore. Gingerly, she rolled from her back onto her stomach. Limp strands of her long brown hair stuck to the perspiration on her pale face as she pulled the pillow back over her head. Where was Mrs. Rickles when she needed her?

As if in sympathy, the truck noise stopped and Fiona slid back into a dreamless sleep.

2

"I CAN'T THANK YOU ENOUGH for letting me stay here, Aunt Vi," Meg Jordon said as she dropped a backpack near the front door of the third floor apartment. She was out of breath from running up the stairs. The moving truck had just pulled up and she'd directed them to a loading zone Aunt Vi had said they could use in front of the building across the street.

A middle-aged woman poked her crew-cut styled head out of the kitchen. "What can I say, Megsi? It's the least I can do for the daughter of one of my oldest friends."

As one of her mother's best friends, Aunt Vi wasn't Meg's aunt by blood, but by choice. Meg had known Vi her entire life.

"Well, I hope it's not an inconvenience. I don't have much. Most of the stuff on the truck is going on to Seattle."

"Not at all. It's a guest room, but most of my guests don't sleep there, if you know what I mean." Aunt Vi wiggled her eyebrows suggestively before her head disappeared back into the kitchen and the sounds of dishes being washed resumed. Meg laughed. She'd gotten used to Vi's ribald humor over the years. Besides, Vi's girlfriend Sherri meant there wouldn't be a stream of different women coming through the apartment. Or, so she hoped.

"Still, I owe you one," she said, as she added the apartment key Vi had given her to her keychain.

The sound of running water stopped and Vi came out of the kitchen, drying her hands on a dishtowel.

"The room is fully furnished so you should be comfortable."

"I'm sure I will. Anything beats the dorm bed I slept on the last three years. I'll only need a couple of boxes. Mostly clothes, books, and art stuff. The drivers from the moving company are parking across the street, like you said."

Aunt Vi moved the curtains and looked across the street. "Ah, yeah. I meant the loading zone a half a block up. But it should be okay if it's only a couple of boxes. By the time the old lady from the building across the street makes it out to yell at them, they'll be pulling away."

Meg joined her at the window. "Ooops! I could have sworn you said directly across the street!"

Aunt Vi laughed and ran her hand over her short hair. "I might have. At my age, you say a lot of stupid shit. Anyway, parking is one of the downsides to living in the city. It's always hard to find."

"That's what my mom said, so my Jeep is one of the things going back to Seattle."

Meg's cell phone chimed the receipt of a text message and she pulled it from the back pocket of her shorts. It was the truck driver.

Vi grabbed a couple of beers from the refrigerator and waved them enticingly at Meg as she read the message. She glanced up and shook her head. It wasn't yet ten a.m. and it was a little early for beer. She waved her phone and moved toward the door. "That was the movers. They're across the street and some guy is giving them a hard time about not having a permit for the loading space. I better get down there."

"Must be the old lady's son. They take turns yelling at people who get too close to their building. It's a perfect excuse to have a beer," Vi said, cracking both beers open despite Meg's protest. She handed one to Meg. "Cheers, Megsie. To being roomies!" Meg knew she had lost this battle, so she tapped the neck of her Blue Moon against the one in Vi's hand, and took a drink before she put it on the table next to the door and bounded downstairs to the moving van double-parked across the street.

3

THE ROAR OF A DIESEL ENGINE wrenched Fiona from her cocoon of sleep again, the metal against metal of grinding gears flaying her brain. Visions of flying out of bed and smashing windshields ran through her mind. She would have done it, too, had she not been dying from her self-inflicted misery of the night before. To make things worse, a piercing back-up signal started up, heightening her torture with the subtlety of a sledgehammer. Her own dry alcohol-infused breath threated to suffocate her under the pillow she was hugging over her head. She whimpered, praying for silence. The gods were either busy or ignoring her.

"Whaddaya think you're doing, ya fuck, ya? This zone is for residents of this building! Move your fuckin' truck, or I'm callin' the cops!"

The voice belonged to Harris, the son of her next door neighbor, Mrs. Rickles. How had a tiny, soft-spoken woman like her given birth to such a hulking, loudmouthed man? Fiona feebly attempted to throw her pillow at the window and pulled the covers over her head.

An indistinct female voice responded, but Harris wasn't having any of it.

"Oh, yeah? I've heard that one before. Fifteen minutes, my ass! Your driver has taken longer just parking this piece of shit. Get it outta here!"

The woman's voice responded again.

"I don't care, lady! Get it moved!"

The woman spoke again.

Harris must have liked the woman. "Okay. Twenty minutes. Not one minute more."

The rumbling of the diesel engine cut out and relative silence filled the room. Fiona sighed in relief. Normally she appreciated the territorial behavior of her next door neighbor, the self-appointed building watch captain, but today it only added to the number of decibels she was being forced to suffer through, making her cranky.

With silence restored, Fiona emerged from the covers and sat up in bed. Big mistake. It loosened her fragile grip on her equilibrium, triggering an overwhelming wave of nausea. She lurched out of bed and immediately tripped over the pillow she had thrown, before stumbling into the bathroom across the hall just in time to fall to her knees and re-experience the tapas she vaguely remembered enjoying at the bar the night before. The second time around wasn't as delightful as the first.

Wiping her mouth with the back of her hand, Fiona flushed the mess away but stayed close to the bowl, uncertain she was done being sick and too weak to move. Exhausted, she dozed with her head resting on the toilet seat, her body slumped against the cold porcelain and hard tile flooring, which felt surprisingly good against her hot skin through her cotton pajamas. A distant concern about her hair dangling in the toilet water nagged at the back of her brain, but it wasn't enough to initiate a reaction. She couldn't even begin to think about moving. Not yet.

Eyes shut, she drifted in and out of sleep with her cheek resting atop the toilet seat. Self-recrimination would come later; the effort of moving, followed by hurling tapas, had sapped what little strength she had. The warm embrace of sleep pulled her back in. Within minutes, a string of saliva was dangling from the corner of her slack mouth and the sound of her breathing was the only noise in the otherwise silent room.

"YOU ALL SET?" VI HOVERED outside the open bedroom door of the
guest room, which would be Meg's home for the next several months. "Is
everything comfy-cozy?"

"It's great," Meg smiled. "Very homey." She'd already gotten used to the
smell of Chinese food from the corner restaurant which permeated the
entire building. The bed she was sitting on was comfortable and the sparse
furnishings in the room were nice. Aunt Vi's spare room was perfect for her.

The moving guys had finished bringing her stuff up, making the room
feel like her own space already. The morning had gotten off to a rough start
with the argument between the movers and a jerk from across the street, but
she'd smoothed that over. Now, she was on the bed with her Mac propped up
on her lap.

Vi tilted her chin at the computer. "You getting ready to post something
on the social media about getting to stay with your crazy old Aunt Vi? You
need a selfie with me? I'm game. We can do this!" Aunt Vi smoothed the
sides of her crew cut hair and hiked up her chinos.

Meg laughed. "Definitely later. Right now, I'm checking to see if the
ICVA has sent the results of my exam yet. It's a compulsion. I look at the site,
hoping for results, at least a hundred times a day."

"Is that the vet test?" Aunt Vi walked into the room and peered around
to see the screen.

Normally Meg bristled at nosiness, but with Aunt Vi, it was different.

"Yeah. It's the International Council for Veterinary Assessment. The
licensing agency for all of North America."

"You're not worried about passing it, are you? You're the most smartest
person I know!"

"Not really," said Meg, honestly. She wasn't being arrogant. She had studied hard and knew her stuff.

"Good. Your mom told me you were second in your class. Cornell's no school for slouches from what I hear. I'm not an expert, I know. My education is only from the Navy."

Meg looked up from what she was doing. "Hey. Don't sell yourself short, Aunt Vi. You served your country. Right now, I'm more excited to see if I can call myself a bona fide veterinarian."

Aunt Vi sat down on the edge of the bed. "You still planning to go work with your other aunt?"

"Assuming I pass the licensing part, I'll have to take the Washington state boards. But, yeah, I'll go practice with Aunt Claudia in Okanogan this fall."

"Oakie-whatsit?" Vi scowled comically. "Is that a real place?"

Meg laughed. "Okanogan. It's in North Central Washington State."

Aunt Vi patted Meg's leg. "Well, I'm sure you'll pass and your less-favored aunt will be happy to have you join her. I know your mom would rather have you in Seattle. She's told me as much. It's been hard for her to have you and your brother living across the country."

"Okanogan is definitely closer than I am here. It's about a four-hour drive."

"What about CJ? Is he planning to go back home? Where is he these days?"

Meg shook her head. Who knew what CJ was up to? She was a little tired of people expecting her to know. CJ and she hadn't been close since before college, but just because they were twins, people thought they were two parts of the same person. "I'm not sure. He left Ithaca and went to Europe last year after he failed the bar. I know Dad expected him back a while ago. He's supposed to retest and join the law firm, but so far, all CJ has been interested in is partying. He calls Mom and Dad once in a while to check in, but with Grandpa's trust, he can stay in Europe for a long time before he has to worry about making a living on his own."

Vi shook her head and tutted. "You two are like night and day. I love him, but that boy sure needs some sense knocked into him."

Meg had to agree with Aunt Vi. She scrolled through her email and sat up with a start. Her stomach was suddenly full of butterflies. Actually, they felt more like bats, whirling and churning against her guts. "Oh! It's here. The email is here!" With a trembling hand, she moved the cursor over the message, but she didn't open it. "I'm so nervous. I don't know if I want to look."

"I thought you said you weren't worried."

"I wasn't until now." She stared at the unopened message. This was it. The point where her real life could be starting.

"So, what're you waiting for?" Aunt Vi asked. "Just open it. You got this."

Meg was surprised by her sudden jitters. She selected the message. The first line started with "Congratulations". She breathed out a huge sigh as the bats subsided. She'd done it!

"I passed!" She was officially a veterinarian. All the hard work and then the waiting. The moment seemed so small, sitting on a borrowed bed, staring at a computer screen. She wasn't one for over the top responses, but it seemed almost anti-climactic.

Aunt Vi patted Meg's leg. "Good job, Megsie! I knew you would do it. Your mom's gonna be proud."

"I should give her a call to let her know." Meg shifted her laptop to the bed beside her, picking up her phone. She couldn't wait to tell her.

Aunt Vi stood up. "Tell her I'll give her a call this—"

The front door squeaked open and a rattle of keys sounded from the living room. Aunt Vi's head swung around.

The phone rang in Meg's ear as she looked at Aunt Vi to see if she was expecting someone.

A woman's voice called down the hall. "Sorry I'm late, Love. My shift ran long."

Aunt Vi slapped her hand to her forehead but she was smiling. "I forgot Sherri was coming by after her shift at St. Anthony's. Say hello to your mom for me." She disappeared through the doorway, shutting the door behind her.

Meg liked Aunt Vi's girlfriend Sherri, and she felt rude for not going out to see her. The phone rang a few more times and went to voicemail. It was three hours earlier in Seattle, after all. Meg left a short message telling her mother she passed the exam and hung up.

She could hear Aunt Vi and Sherri in the living room but not what they said. It sounded a little intense, so she decided to give them some privacy and opened the laptop to read the letter again. Holy shit! She was a real veterinarian now!

5

FIONA WOKE UP WHEN HER left hand fell into the toilet water.

While she slept, she had somehow managed to wedge her body between the toilet and the vanity shelf. Her right arm, tucked under her head, was numb, and her neck had a kink in it from the unusual position. When she tried to move, she whacked her head on the toilet paper dispenser and found that her right hip, which was supporting most of her weight, had fallen asleep against the cool tile floor. As she extracted her hand from the toilet bowl and wiped it on her pajama bottoms, she attempted to force open her eyes, only to suffer the full effect of the pounding headache trying to shatter her skull. She needed water, but her traitorous stomach threatened to revolt at the mere thought of ingesting even that innocuous liquid.

She squinted into the too bright room. With shaking arms she slowly pushed herself up to sit on the edge of the tub. A nice warm shower was what she needed, but the spinning threatened to force her back onto her knees any time she moved. The mere thought of the effort that would be required to get into the shower thrust her forward over the toilet again. A whimper escaped her as she sat back up after another fruitless retch did nothing more than cover her body in a thin sheen of sweat and further abuse her already throbbing abdominal muscles. Her aching stomach didn't even have bile in it to bring up.

Fiona rose carefully and reached behind the shower curtain with a shaking hand to turn on the water. As soon as it was warm, she slowly peeled off her sweat-dampened pajamas and stepped over the edge of the tub into the stream of soothing water.

God, what a mess. She would never drink again. She managed to wash her hair and body, the smell of lavender giving her mood a welcome boost, until the water started to run cool and she forced herself to get out. Brushed teeth and fresh pajamas made her feel a little more human before she stumbled back to bed. She probably needed to eat something, but she wasn't going to chance it.

As she was about to drift off, the phone rang. She reached over and picked it up without opening her eyes. It was probably Mike checking to see if she was okay.

"'lo," she croaked into the phone.

"Hey, Sweetness," drawled the voice with a thick southern accent on the other end of the line. "Did I wake you?"

Christ! She rolled onto her back and slapped a hand over her eyes. Her head started to spin but she had to hold it together. She was supposed to be at work. She worked every other Saturday at the firm and this was the day. Shit.

"Oh, jeez, Twyla. I overslept." She peered at the clock. It was ten a.m. She was an hour late, but there was no way she was going in. "I think I might have food poisoning. I'm not feeling very well." She grimaced. She was a terrible liar.

"Food poisoning, huh?" The air quotes were apparent. Twyla wasn't buying it. "That's just terrible, honey."

"I was up all night being sick."

Twyla tsked. "Well, you take care of yourself, girl. I already talked to Gregory and he told me to tell you to take the day off. It's a gift for passing the bar exam."

Her eyes welled up. Gregory was one of the partners at the firm. Corporate law may not have been Fiona's dream job, but she'd lucked out being able to work with such an awesome team during her internship.

"You're the best, Twyla. Thank you. Tell Gregory thank you, too."

"I'll tell him, sugar. You just get better soon." There were those air quotes again and Twyla hung up.

Fiona let the phone drop onto the bed.

She closed her eyes and settled into the down comforter. As if on cue, the angry growl of an engine shattered the silence, followed by the excruciating back up warning that had originally roused her. The delivery truck must have finished its business. With a grinding of gears and a volley of backfires, the roar gradually faded into the general noise of the city.

Her last thought was to wonder how she was going to get back to sleep.

6

MEG'S FOOTSTEPS ECHOED IN THE stairway as she skipped every other stair in her descent from Aunt Vi's third floor walk-up. She glanced behind her to see if Aunt Vi had followed her out. She'd tried to slip out without disturbing her and Sherri, who'd disappeared into Aunt Vi's room, but the front door to the apartment had a nasty squeak.

Based on the argument she couldn't help but overhear when their voices had grown louder, Meg had discovered that Aunt Vi hadn't told Sheri that Meg was temporarily moving in with her. In fact, Sherri had questioned whether it was really Meg in the guest bedroom. Meg was debating whether she should step out of the room to prove it was her, when they took the argument into Aunt Vi's room. Now, pushing open the glass front door, Meg was happy to be free from the suddenly oppressive apartment. She hoped this wasn't going to be an issue.

After they'd dropped all of her belongings at the apartment, the movers had gone to get some coffee and it looked like they'd gone well past the twenty minute timeframe she'd negotiated with the angry man across the street. It looked they were done now and the van rumbled into traffic. The kid driving spotted her and waved from the open window. The way the truck's gears were grinding indicated he hadn't been driving for very long.

She shook her head. "Ease up on the clutch, kiddo," she mumbled to herself as the truck lurched forward, nearly stalled, and then jerked forward again.

She hoped her belongings would survive the drive cross country to Washington. Maybe she should have gone with the company with the brand name she recognized, instead of taking advice from Aunt Vi, who always "knew a guy" giving a great deal.

The man she'd talked to earlier was standing on the far sidewalk flipping the truck the bird. She laughed at the comedic performance as he added his other hand to the salute for good measure. A little old lady shuffled up to him and patted his arm. He dropped his hands and they walked into one of the garden-level apartments in front of the building.

The truck got lost in the traffic up the street and at just half past ten in the morning, the heat was already radiating off the cement in waves. She had a feeling that summer in the city was going to be hot. With a quick look up at the third floor of the building, she decided to go down to Helga's café to get an iced coffee. Maybe Taylor would be there. Meg was going to work at the shop for a couple of months while Taylor and her wife, Karma, went on a trip to Europe. It was a vacation for Taylor but a work trip for Karma, who was looking for "old world recipes" for a new cookbook she was writing. Meg knew they'd be awesome no matter what they were. Karma was a fabulous cook.

After the two block walk in the warm spring sunshine, the air conditioning in the homey café hit her with blessed relief. The shop was bustling with customers on this Saturday morning. Meg stood in line to order a drink. She loved Helga's. Indie rock music played over the competing din of customer conversations and the hissing of the giant espresso machines as they dispensed steaming drinks. Meg had visited the store several times before. It had a different vibe compared to her Uncle Arthur's coffee shop up in Ithaca, which was sleek and industrial, but she was sure she'd like working here. It may have been different if she needed the job, but since she was only helping out, she looked forward to getting to know the people from the neighborhood.

"Hey, Meg!" Taylor's eyes lit up when Meg made it to the front of the line.

Taylor was working the register but she rushed around the counter to give Meg a hug. Good thing no one had come in after Meg. Taylor's hugs couldn't be rushed.

"How was the trip down? You all settled in?" Taylor let go of Meg and adjusted the colorful head wrap holding back her nearly floor-length dreadlocks.

"The movers just left. I don't have much, so I'm as settled as I can be right now."

A customer came in and Taylor greeted them with a warm smile.

Taylor turned to the barista who was finishing up the order of the person who'd been ahead of Meg. "Noel, do you mind whipping up an iced

Americano for my friend Meg and helping Mr. Glugman while she and I chat?" Noel smiled and gave an agreeable nod while Taylor led Meg to an empty table near the window, stopping to say a few words to some customers along the way.

Taylor adjusted a few of the woven bracelets on her wrists. "Do you need a couple days to get situated?"

Meg shook her head. "I can start tomorrow if you need me."

Taylor relaxed into her chair. "Thank the goddesses, girl. You don't know what a lifesaver you are to help us like this!"

Meg was delighted she was in a position to help. "Hey, it's what friends do. Besides, I have time to kill before I get my license to practice in Washington and I wanted to spend spring and summer in the city."

Taylor tapped Meg's wrist. "Well, all I can say is you're doing us a big favor. Karma's been planning this trip to Italy for two years. When Thaddeus told us he was quitting to open his own comic book store and Gertie came down with the shingles, I was all, 'Holy guacamole, what am I gonna do?' Probably stay here. You're a lifesaver, girl. A lifesaver."

A woman in a barista apron Meg hadn't noticed when she'd first come in approached their table and placed drinks before them. "A large iced Americano for Taylor's friend. Here's your chai, Taylor."

Meg thanked her, and the barista nodded but didn't smile. Interesting. Maybe it was just the way she was. The woman's dark hair contrasted with her very pale skin, thickly lined eyes, and blood red lipstick. A small hoop nose ring decorated one of her nostrils and tattoos covered much of the skin on her arms. All black clothing finished the look. Even though the woman was several years younger than her, it was as if Meg was back in high school and one of the cool kids had just walked up.

"Who's this, Taylor?" the woman asked, hooking a thumb toward Meg. "This the one helping out while you're in Italy?"

Ah. Maybe she wasn't happy with Meg coming to help.

"Meg, this is Betty." Taylor draped an arm around Betty's waist. "Betty's been here forever. She can show you all the stuff you need to know. She'll manage the books. I can manage most of it remotely, but just in case a vendor calls and needs us to cut a check or something."

Meg felt the weight of Betty's stare. She reminded herself that Betty was young. Under all the makeup and hair dye, she couldn't be more than twenty-one.

"Nice to meet you, Betty."

Betty's stare grew less intense when she smiled. "Backatcha, Meg Jordan. Taylor said you can barista and do the register. It'll be nice to have someone start who I don't have to train."

Meg watched Betty's back as she walked towards the register.

Taylor held Meg's wrist. "Her bark is worse than her bite, I promise. I actually think she might like you."

"Could've fooled me," Meg said with a grin.

7

THE PHONE, SET TO VIBRATE, shuddered between the wood tabletop and the metal side of the lamp, splintering the silence. By the time Fiona's groggy mind realized what the racket was, the vibrating had stopped. She slumped back into her pillows with a moan. There was no way she was going to move. Whoever had called could wait.

Sinking back into sleep, her leaden body succumbed to the comfort of her bed. Sleep had almost reclaimed her when the phone began to vibrate again.

"Stoooooop," she begged.

With more effort than it should have taken, she rolled over and reached for the phone. It stopped vibrating before she could answer, but when she picked it up, she saw it was already after three. Damn! She knew she should get out of bed, but instead settled further into the pillows. To her surprise, she felt better. Kind of. Her head throbbed and it hurt to move her eyes, but the all-consuming fatigue was slowly dissipating. Best of all, the urge to retch her guts out was gone. In fact, she was ravenous. Trying not to make any sudden movements, Fiona lifted her phone and squinted at the display. Three missed calls from her best friend, Maureen. She better call her before she showed up on her doorstep. Her aching head could not deal with Maureen if she got riled up.

8

MEG WAS BACK AT AUNT Vi's. A long visit with Taylor to get the lay of the land at the coffee shop meant that it was now well into late afternoon. When she'd gotten back, neither Aunt Vi nor Sherri were in the apartment, which was a relief.

The day had turned into a scorcher, and while the air-conditioning units in the living room and Vi's bedroom were adequate for making most of the apartment comfortable, there weren't any in the guest room, which was at the very back of the apartment. It was stifling. Meg decided she'd rectify that as soon as possible. It was only spring and the heat would get worse when summer arrived. The small oscillating fan she'd found in the closet moved the hot air around, but did little to cool the room. She opened the window of her new room and noticed it opened to a fire escape. The detail delighted her, reminding her of countless movies she'd watched as a kid. She suddenly understood where her mother's nostalgia came from when she'd described her memories of New York City after Meg had announced she'd be spending the spring and summer here.

She padded out to the kitchen to find something cool to drink. Unsurprisingly, she found the choices Aunt Vi had were limited to tap water and beer. She grabbed a beer and went back to her room, where she picked up her sketchbook and crawled out the window.

The fire escape was an architectural piece of art, built out of decorative wrought iron with a century or more of scuffed black paint slathered on it. A small grill and an old metal folding chair were tucked up against the brick building. Meg smiled to think about Aunt Vi, who was built like a fireplug, climbing out the window. Meg unfolded the old chair and sat down. The ubiquitous scent of Chinese food competed with other cooking smells—pizza, barbeque, something fried. She'd visited New York City several times over the last few years in school, but having grown up on the outskirts of Seattle, she'd never lived in a large city before. The dense pulse of humanity beat all around her; people above and below her were all doing their own thing, not even aware she was there. It was a humbling thought. At first she imagined the feeling flooding through her was loneliness, but soon realized it was more like the feeling she got when she gazed at the stars and remembered how small she was in comparison to the infinite universe. But instead of feeling insignificant, she felt like a vital piece of the city. It may have been huge, but she was a part of it, contributing her own energy to the city's rhythm. This was the reason she'd decided to spend the spring and summer here.

As she took a sip of her beer, a cool breeze lifted the hair from her face. The heat was starting to break ever so slightly as the sun moved beyond the buildings. From her third-floor vantage point, she watched people on the sidewalks moving up and down the street. Helga's was visible a block from where she sat. A steady stream of people flowed in and out of the front entrance, a good sign, since late afternoon was typically slow for coffee shops, especially when the weather was nice.

Across the street, a woman in a red skirt and a tank top emerged from one of the street-level apartments and lifted her long brown hair from her neck before she set off down the sidewalk. Purpose marked the woman's stride, similar to many of the other people walking down the sidewalk. It was confident, no nonsense. She didn't pay attention to the people she passed and they didn't seem to notice her. Meg noticed her, though. She wasn't sure what it was from so far away, but there was something about her that made Meg keep watching until she disappeared into a restaurant. Meg wondered if the woman was joining friends.

Meg finished her beer as the sidewalk continued to fill up with people and the afternoon cooled into the early evening. Many of the pedestrians had the determined walk of the woman she had seen earlier. She wondered if she'd ever have that kind of New York attitude.

She picked up her sketchbook and started to draw.

9

"**SORRY I'M LATE.**" **FIONA DROPPED** her phone and keys onto the
Formica tabletop, gathered her skirt to her and slid into a tattered vinyl
booth in the Budget Diner. She had a hard time making eye contact with
her two closest friends, Josh and Maureen. Maureen looked fabulous, as
usual. Her red hair was down and looked soft and shiny. Josh, in his weekend
clothes, looked like he had just rolled out of bed. One would never guess
that during the work week he was a well-dressed attorney. The threesome
had gone to law school together at nearby Columbia University. The Budget
Diner had always been a favorite spot for studying, with unlimited refills on
coffee and cheap, but delicious, daily food specials. With the rigors of law
school over, it was now a habit to meet there.

"You being late is nothing new," Maureen said as she licked the spoon she
used to stir her tea before sitting it down on the edge of the saucer.

Fiona grimaced. She deserved it. "I know. I suck. Especially since I live
so close." The fake leather beneath her squeaked as she settled back in the
booth. Were they staring at her? Did they know anything about the night
before? Mike wouldn't have said anything. Would he?

The brief walk to the diner in the warmth of the spring air had helped to
blow away some of the haze of the hangover she had battled most of the day,
but the flickering of the diner's overhead florescent lighting wasn't helping
the headache she couldn't seem to shake. She was never going to drink again.
She ran her hand through her hair and picked up a menu, hoping at least
that the eye drops had erased the red from her normally clear hazel eyes.
She peeked over the menu and caught Maureen and Josh exchanging looks.
A feeling of paranoia swept over her. Were they judging her? She shouldn't

have come.

A waiter appeared suddenly beside her. "Hey, Fiona." He lifted a carafe of coffee. "Whatzit today? Coffee or tea?"

"Coffee's fine. Thanks, P." She smiled at him, flipping over the cup in front of her. P was short for something he wouldn't reveal, although Fiona and Maureen had been trying to guess since they'd started coming to the diner. "Percival?"

He rolled his eyes and shook his head as he topped off Josh's cup. Fiona lowered her menu, Maureen was back to innocently bobbing the teabag up and down in her cup, while Josh chewed on a hangnail.

"I'll be back to take your orders in a few. I suggest the Polish sausage over the snapper for you, Hon." P pointed to Josh with a wink and a jut of his hip before he wandered over to talk to a guy at the end of the counter.

"What are you smirking about?" Maureen looked over her shoulder to see what Fiona was looking at. "Oh. I think your diner boyfriend has a new man, Josh."

Josh looked over his shoulder. P wiggled his fingers in a wave and blew a kiss. Josh laughed and turned back to the table. He shrugged. "We decided we made better friends."

Maureen shoulder bumped him. "P doesn't want to be friends, and you know it."

Josh shrugged. "And as flattered as I am by the attention, he's not my type." Josh wasn't gay and P knew it, but it didn't keep P from flirting with him all the time. Josh didn't seem to mind, either.

Maureen picked up her spoon and aggressively stirred her tea. "You kill me. People basically throw themselves at you. Guys, girls, everyone in between. And you act like it's nothing at all."

Fiona watched the exchange with amusement. Maureen and Josh had always reminded her of a sitcom couple with their constant fake—but not really—bickering. Except they weren't a couple.

Josh slurped his coffee and put his cup down. "Hey, I appreciate it. I'm comfortable in my skin, is all. People vibe with it and relax around me. You should try it."

Maureen slumped back into the booth. "Who has time to relax? It takes an hour for me to get out the door. I wasn't blessed with Fi's naturally clear skin and effortless hair."

Fiona was taking a sip of her coffee and only sheer exhaustion prevented her from doing a spit take. Her? She knew some people thought she was attractive, but she'd always felt like a wallflower next to Maureen. She swallowed the warm liquid and was happy it settled in her stomach without issue. Maybe she would be able to have some real food.

"What does my skin have to do with anything?"

Maureen's shoulders relaxed. "Nothing. I'm just cranky today. I stayed out past my normal bedtime last night and had to get up early this morning because Robert had to get to the airport early. I guess I'm just jealous of the unencumbered freedom you two seem to have."

"Well, you *have* been in the same relationship since high school," Josh said.

Fiona yawned.

"Are we boring you?" Maureen asked.

Fiona tried to sit up taller. "I'm tired. I think I caught a bug or something."

Maureen studied her over the rim of her coffee cup. "Well, I didn't want to say anything, but you do look like shit."

What happened to the clear skin and effortless hair comment of a moment ago? She knew Maureen didn't mean it in a bad way. She smiled sweetly. "And here I was, thinking how lovely you look, as usual, with flawless face and hair."

Maureen glowed at the compliment. She waved her hand magician-like before her own face. "The magic of makeup, I assure you. Beneath the spackle is a different story. I'm running on four hours sleep over here."

Josh shifted in his seat to face Maureen. "Did Mr. Charisma keep you up all night? You two didn't stick around The Limerick very long. Did Robby pop a Viagra and use *his* magic wand?"

Maureen shifted to face Josh. "Yes, in fact Robert *did* keep me up all night. But not in the way you think. We got in a fight. And you know Robert, he won't let something rest until he's analyzed it to death."

Maureen's fiancé, Robert, was not one of Josh's favorite people. Fiona had never understood why. He was a bit of a stick in the mud, but it didn't bother her. Josh could barely stay civil around the guy, though.

Josh shifted back in his seat and smiled into his cup. "Trouble in paradise?"

Maureen glared at him. There was a whole story playing out in the silence, but Fiona had no idea what it was. Maureen and Josh had always been this way. She'd stopped trying to figure it out after their first year of law school.

Maureen swung her gaze across to Fiona. "Tell me about your night. I'm calling bullshit on the "caught a bug" thing, by the way. You're hungover. I'll bet my beloved Coach bag on it."

Fiona really didn't want to talk about last night. Not now, not ever. What a mistake.

Josh set his cup down with raised brows. "*Are* you recovering from a hangover, dearest Fi?"

Fiona hated that he was surprised; it made her feel like a dud. Yet the truth was, it wasn't like her to be hungover. She wasn't much of a drinker, but they'd all been out celebrating the results of their bar exam the night before. Under different circumstances she'd relish admitting to the hangover simply to prove she wasn't such a bore, but not today. Not after the Big Mistake.

She sighed. "A hangover would be a step up from the meat grinder I crawled out of this morning when I first woke up."

Maureen laughed. "I'm not surprised. I saw you and Mike do half a dozen shots before Robert and I left. I'll bet you could barely roll yourself out of bed at the crack of noon."

"More like an hour ago. I'm finally starting to believe I can eat something without it coming right back up." Fiona stopped trying to pretend she didn't feel like roadkill and pulled her hands down her face.

Josh signaled to P for more coffee. "I'm impressed. You finally let loose enough to have a little fun for once, eh, Fi? You must have kept the party going after we all left last night."

"Yeah, something like that." Fiona knew he wanted details, but she wasn't going to give them. She had a lot more introspection to do before she talked with anyone about what had happened.

P dragged himself away from the guy at the end of the counter and topped off their cups.

Josh flashed his most charming smile at him. "Can you leave the pot… Pasqual? Our Fi tied one on last night and needs a pick me up."

P shook his head with a smile and set the carafe on the table after topping them all off. He gave Fiona a teasing conspirator's smile. "Do you need a little something to doctor your coffee? I can bring you some Baileys or Kahlua."

They all looked amused and Fiona hated being the target of their ridicule. She waved him away. "I'm fine, thank you."

P laughed and went back to the counter to flirt.

Maureen shook her hair back. "Don't worry. It wasn't only you letting loose last night. I'd say aside from me and Robert, the entire group woke up with a headache this morning, including innocent little Josh over here."

Josh straightened his shoulders. "Hey, I was fine this morning. I didn't have anything more than my usual last night."

"If your usual entails a half dozen shots and as many beers, I stand corrected and in awe that you are not in some sort of rehab," Maureen said.

"Hardy-har-har." Josh rolled his eyes.

Maureen ignored him. "I'm not one to judge, though. I'd be hanging too if Robert hadn't scheduled a six a.m. flight."

Josh cast his eyes upward at the second mention of Robert. "Big surprise there," he said into his cup.

"What did you mumble over there?" Maureen asked.

Josh glared at Maureen. "I said, I may have drunk a lot, but I wasn't out of control. I think the occasion called for it."

"Can we stop talking about alcohol?" Fiona made a face. She still felt like shit and the conversation wasn't helping, but more than anything, she wanted to forget about last night.

Maureen returned Josh's glare. "Sure. But just for the record, I don't blame you for drinking yourself into oblivion, with Mopey Mike hanging all over you. My god, I love the man, but he needs to face up to a few things. First, he failed the bar exam because he wasn't focused. All he needs to do is regroup and retry. Plenty of people take it twice. Second, he needs to step out of the closet and shut it behind him. And, finally, he needs to stop letting people treat him like shit."

While Fiona agreed with all of Maureen's declarations, she felt a flare of shame at the last one.

Josh sat back in the seat. "I honestly can't believe he went out with all of us last night. Why would he want to hang out with a bunch of people celebrating something he failed? Besides, he should have known Charlie would show up with one of his bim—."

Maureen put a hand over his mouth. "I know you weren't about to name call a woman you've never even met."

Josh grabbed Maureen's hand and playfully bit the tip of her finger. "Oh, come on. If a woman would date Charlie, she definitely isn't an upstanding citizen."

Maureen pulled her hand away and smacked his shoulder. "Okay, I can't believe I'm about to say it, but I agree. Let's assume she hasn't seen his real side. He's good-looking and if you don't know him, he can be kind of charming. Maybe it was their first date. It doesn't mean she's a bimbo."

Josh waited for Maureen to turn back to Fiona before cupping his hands over his chest and mouthing the words, "total bimbo", to her.

Fiona closed her eyes and shook her head. She was with Maureen on this.

When Maureen turned to look at him, he gave her an innocent wide-eyed smile and rested his arms on the table. "Where'd you guys go after the bar?"

Fiona searched for an answer that would provide the bare minimum of information. "We planned to go home, but Mike didn't want to be alone when the Lyft we shared got to my place, so he talked me into going to Sylvester's."

"What a dive," Maureen groaned.

Fiona shrugged. "It's close."

Josh laughed. "Close to being a shit-hole."

Fiona couldn't argue. People only went to Sylvester's for the cheap drinks. "It's not that bad. Locals like it. Anyway, we ended up having a few more drinks, and then Mike walked me back to my apartment." What happened after was a disaster she was trying to forget. Some people forgot things when they drank. Not her. She remembered every pathetic and embarrassing detail, and she wasn't about to divulge any of it.

Josh shook his head. "I don't blame him for not wanting to be alone. I can't even imagine having to take the test again. You're a saint for hanging out with him. How's he taking it?"

Fiona traced a scratch in the Formica on the table. "Badly, which is expected."

Maureen tore her napkin in half. "I'm a terrible friend. I shouldn't have called him Mopey Mike. I'll call him later to check in. He was pretty hammered last night."

Josh leaned forward and looked around the table. "Missing the bar by two points. I know he wasn't the only one who failed from our study group, but being the only one out of us four... well, no one worked harder than him. I don't blame him for being devastated. I was surprised when he told us."

Maureen shook her head. "I felt guilty about celebrating in front of him, but should we have thrown a wake instead? I know. I'm such a bitch. You know what I mean, right?"

Fiona knew Maureen had a heart of gold, but she didn't often let it show. "Mike went out with us for his own reasons. Mostly to drown his sorrows with friends, I guess. But Charlie bringing a girlfriend was too much for him. He said that bothered him more than failing the test."

"Is that why you left with him? So he wouldn't be alone?" Josh asked.

Fiona didn't want to tell them Mike had basically begged her to leave with him. She probably would have anyway, but they didn't need to know the sad details. They didn't need to know how Mike had sobbed in her arms. "I'd already had too much to drink. And, honestly? I was pissed at Charlie, too. He's an arrogant ass. I never liked him for Mike, but I never thought he'd play games." Maybe if she hadn't felt so sorry for Mike, she wouldn't have done what she did.

"Fi?" Maureen waved a hand before Fiona's face and she realized she'd zoned out on them.

"Huh?"

"I just changed the subject. I said it was nice of your work to let you have the day off. Weren't you supposed to go in today?"

Fiona shrunk back into the booth seat. "I slept right through my alarm."

Josh looked astonished. "Perfect Fiona was late for work? Did you get in trouble?"

Fiona flipped him off with a smirk. "Ha ha ha. When I talked to them, Gregory told me to consider the day off a gift for passing the bar."

"My firm would have fired me." Josh thumped back against the booth. He was miserable in his job. While Fiona had gotten lucky with her firm, Josh had been equally as unlucky in his. The personal injury law firm he was at worked him like a dog and treated him worse. He'd hated it from the start, but he wouldn't leave. Fiona secretly thought he enjoyed telling the horror stories.

Maureen, who worked at her family's law firm, gave him a sympathetic look. She'd once told Fiona she'd never hire Josh because he acted like he was entitled to a position simply because he'd finished law school. Maureen thought his current gig would give him a little dose of reality. Fiona agreed.

Maureen patted Josh's shoulder and turned to Fiona. "Should we call Mike? See how he's holding up? Maybe ask him to come down and have a cup of coffee with us?”

Fiona wasn't ready to see him yet. Embarrassed was not a strong enough word. She wondered if she'd ever be able to face him again.

“He might want to be alone,” Josh said, unwittingly giving her an out. “I know I would.”

Fiona nodded, glad for an excuse not to see him. “That's probably true.”

10

"CAN I TELL YOU SOMETHING and you'll promise not to get mad?" Betty asked the question as she wiped the wand on the espresso machine with one hand and poured the steamed milk to make a leaf shape in the foam of the latte she had just brewed with the other.

"Are you ambidextrous?" Meg asked, avoiding the question. She was a couple hours into her first shift at the coffee shop and she still couldn't figure Betty out.

Betty winked at her. "The ladies seem to like it." She grabbed another cup, filled it with milk, and put it under the wand. She looked over her shoulder at Meg. "Are you going to answer my question?"

"First of all, no safe conversation has ever started off with a request to promise not to get mad." Meg took a break from dusting the mug display to face Betty. "And second of all, I don't know you. I suspect your idea of boundaries and mine are significantly different, so promising probably wouldn't be in my best interest."

Noel snorted from behind the register. "Smart woman."

Betty tossed the rag she was using at him. He batted it away with a laugh and turned to the next person in line, which stretched nearly to the door.

Meg was supposed to be learning the lay of the land and doing things like restocking, wiping down tables, and filling in at the register when Noel took a break, but one look at the line and she stepped up to the second espresso machine and took the next order. Betty glanced at her and nodded approvingly.

So far, Meg was pleasantly surprised by how well run the shop was, especially with Taylor out of town. She was most surprised by Betty. Despite the weird introduction the day before, Betty was mostly acting friendly this morning. She was also a hard worker and good with the customers. It was a nice change from most of the people Meg had worked with at her uncle's coffee shop in Ithaca, where it seemed she was the only one who put in any effort. Betty seemed to be wired the same way.

Once the line dwindled, Meg went back to dusting the mug display.

Betty held the metal frothing pitcher with both hands under the steaming wand. The loud shooshing of the machine filled the space. When she closed the valve, the noise abated. "Okay, no promise." Betty poured a shot of espresso into a cup and poured the frothed milk in after it.

So much for Betty forgetting her question.

Betty placed the cup on the pick-up counter and called out the name written on the side of the cup. "Now, I mean this in a kind way."

"Watch out when she says that," said Noel from his position at the register. "It normally precedes something you don't want to hear."

"Shut it, Noel." Betty glared at him as Noel pretended to shake in fear.

"That doesn't sound ominous at all," Meg laughed.

Betty broke her gaze from Noel and went back to work on the next order. "It isn't ominous. I totally didn't expect to like you, is all."

Noel laughed. "Betty doesn't like anyone."

Betty ignored him.

"Why?" Meg asked.

"To begin with, you're friends with the boss. I thought you were going to act all superior." Betty cleaned the steam wand with a new rag. "And you're a doctor. I thought you'd be all superior *and* not want to do any of the shit work."

Meg absorbed the statement. She appreciated Betty's candor.

"Fair enough, I suppose." Meg refaced all of the mugs she'd moved around. "But I wouldn't want to ruin a friendship by doing anything less than a good job for Taylor, even if I'm only filling in. As far as the veterinarian thing, I haven't started yet. I have the degree, but I wanted to spend time in the city through the spring and summer before I went back home to practice in Okanogan."

"You obviously know your way around a coffee shop."

"I worked in my uncle's shop in Ithaca while I was going to school."

Betty shrugged. "I admit I was totally judging a book by its cover."

Meg grinned. "If it makes you feel any better, I did the same thing."

"Interesting." Betty placed the order she'd prepared on the counter and folded her arms across her chest with an amused look on her face. "Tell me what you thought of me at first."

Noel, who had a break in customers, assumed the same position. "This is going to be entertaining."

Meg glanced from one to the other. She felt fenced in. "Is this a trap?"

"Not at all." Betty waved her hands impatiently. "Now go."

"Well, you've got that hard-core, rock-chick thing going on," Meg said.

"And?"

"There's a certain vibe you put off. A 'don't eff with me' vibe. So, I admit, I was a bit intimidated. I suspected you'd be more aloof and wouldn't be one to mince words."

Betty laughed. "I've never been accused of holding back, if that's what you mean."

"Don't I know it!" Noel said, turning back to the register to help a new set of customers.

"I feel like I passed a test," Meg declared, breathing out a sigh. Betty seemed pleased by the assessment, which was a relief.

"Nah. There's no test. I know I put off the vibe. It's part of the scene, you know? I actually am a "rock-chick" as you called it. My real job is guitar and lead vocals for a local band."

Meg smiled politely. How many aspiring singers and actors had she slung coffee with? Most didn't wear their stage make-up to work, though.

Betty shook her hair back as she tamped grounds into the filter cup. "It's called Magenta Morning. You've probably heard of us."

"I just recently moved here, so..." Meg wiped down the counter by the espresso machine.

Betty exhaled loudly and pointed to a flyer posted on the corkboard near the condiment counter. "There are probably a thousand of those posted all over Morningside Heights and a thousand more across the rest of Manhattan. You'd be blind not to see them. Our street crew is super active."

Meg squinted to see the poster across the room and recognized it. "Oh, yeah. There's one taped above the mailboxes in my building."

"It's me and four other girls. We've been playing together since seventh grade. Except Daphne, who plays cello and violin. She joined us a couple years ago. At first, she was one of our drummer Lydia's many girlfriends, but it fizzled as fast as all the others. Daphne stuck around, though. We enjoyed her company. Then she wrote a song for us and we liked it, so we asked her to play with us as a trial thing. The additional strings turned out to be a cool sound for us, differentiating us from all the other bands out there, so we asked her to stay on."

"The band is successful, then?" Meg picked up an empty cup and began to prepare a mocha.

Betty gave her another nod of approval. "We do okay. Gigging takes care of the rent. We're lucky, since New York is notorious as a pay-to-play city."

"Pay-to-play?"

"You gotta pay the venue to play there," Betty explained.

"That doesn't sound fair." Meg cleaned the wand on her machine.

Betty shrugged. "It is what it is. The venues need to pay their rent, too. It can be brutal for new bands. We were lucky because Sketch knew some people, so we didn't have to pay very often early on. Now, our reputation gets us into almost anywhere we want to play. Sketch is our base player. Sara plays keyboards. Sara is Noel's sister."

They'd finished with all of the queued up orders while they talked and there was a break in customers, so Meg rested her hip against the counter and watched Betty clean up after the last order. "You're telling me I'm working with a rock star?"

Betty smiled and nodded her head. "That you are, my friend."

"So much talent and humble, too, as you can see," Noel muttered as he walked past them to grab a new stack of large to-go cups.

Betty pretended she was going to squirt him with the whipped cream canister. Noel laughed and dashed into the breakroom.

"That's right. Run away, little man," Betty called after him. She put the whipped cream dispenser back and chuckled. "Things are looking good. We have gigs at least three times a week. We're getting ready to expand our tour. We have to figure out the logistics and I'll probably have to scale back working here, which I'm not excited about, but I guess I can't stay forever."

Noel snuck back to his place at the register as a new customer walked up.

Meg was intrigued. "Now, it's my turn to ask why *you* work at a coffee shop."

Betty finished wiping down her machine. "Medical benefits and flexible hours. Well, they're flexible when we're running full staff, which we aren't. I was happy when I heard you were coming to work here, until I found out it's only temporary."

"If we're being all honest with one another, it didn't seem like you were happy at all when you first met me."

Betty scowled at her. "I had to make sure you didn't get comfortable until I'd scoped you out a bit, made sure you were going to fit in. Good news. You pass." Her scowl morphed into a smile.

Meg couldn't help but smile back. She felt like she'd been accepted into Betty's inner circle.

Betty pressed grounds into the filter basket. "Hopefully Taylor will hire a couple more people as soon as she gets back, or I'll have to figure something out."

Noel handed them each an empty cup and they worked on their orders.

Betty was finished first and put the mocha she'd prepared on the counter while she eyed a guy texting as he propped himself against one of the middle support beams crisscrossing the open layout of the coffee shop. "Harpo, your mocha with extra whip is ready."

"Thanks," the guy said, dropping a dollar into the tip jar.

Betty winked at him. "No, thank *you*. He's such a cutie," she whispered over her shoulder to Meg.

Meg wondered if her gaydar was off. She would have sworn Betty batted for her team.

Betty must have seen the confusion on her face. "I'm attracted to the inner person, not the gender."

"Yeah, she especially likes the lower intestines and gall bladder," Noel quipped.

Betty threw a rag at him. "Didn't I already warn you to shut it, little man?"

Noel caught the rag and laughed.

Meg enjoyed the banter of her new workmates and laughed along, shaking her head. She began to switch out the bucket used to catch the processed coffee grounds. When she looked up, she saw a familiar face in line at the register. She couldn't place where she knew her from, though. From her unobtrusive place behind the espresso machine she watched the woman give Noel her order and then go stand next to the guy Betty had been flirting with.

Betty bumped her shoulder. "Are you done drooling over there." She consulted the paper cup in her hand. "*Fiona* needs her high-maintenance decaf, non-fat, two pump, extra hot, vanilla latte and you're standing in front of my machine."

Meg laughed and stepped aside to take the bucket to the composter in the back. The drinker of high-maintenance coffee had a beautiful smile.

✷✷✷✷✷

THAT SMILE WAS ON HER mind as Meg skipped up the three flights of stairs to Aunt Vi's apartment after her first day at Helga's. She knew she'd seen her smile before, but she couldn't place it and it was driving her crazy. Then it hit her. The Artful Bean! She'd seen her at her Uncle Arthur's coffee shop!

With the mystery solved, Meg thought about her day. It had gone well, but she was tired. She'd drastically underestimated the amount of work it was going to be, even though Taylor had warned her how busy the coffee shop was. Her feet were killing her and the muscles between her shoulder blades were on fire from slinging espressos for most of the day. She'd taken the register after Noel's shift was over, but Betty had switched positions with her because Meg was talking to the customers too much. How was she to know baristas in NYC didn't make small talk? At Uncle Arthur's café in Ithaca he'd encouraged the staff to be friendly. She got it, though. Helga's did ten times the business and it was always busy. They'd never get through the line if they talked to everyone. It was get the order, ring it up, and move on. Quick, quick, quick.

She keyed the lock on the door to the apartment and held the door with her foot as she pulled the key out. Out of the corner of her eye she saw movement in the living room.

"Hey, Aunt Vi." She dropped her keys onto the table inside the door. When she looked up, her face grew warm. Aunt Vi was sitting in the large chair in the corner of the room. Straddling her lap was a woman Meg had never met. Her blouse was unbuttoned and had slid off her shoulders so it was pooled around her waist. The woman pulled the shirt back up over her lacy pink bra with a slightly embarrassed smile. Meg, not knowing where to look, turned around and faced the door. "Sorry! I should have knocked!" She plucked up her keys and turned in a circle wondering if she should leave. Her feet hurt so badly, though! Finally, she started down the hall to her bedroom.

"Hey, you don't have to run off, Megsie." Aunt Vi sounded like her normal self, not like she'd just been caught having sex in the living room by her unsuspecting roommate. "This is your place, too. I'm the one who should be sorry."

Meg saw movement in the corner of her eye as Aunt Vi laughed. Meg stopped and stared at her hands. "Um…"

"Don't worry. We're decent."

Meg chanced a look. Both of them stood next to the chair. The woman's blouse was now buttoned up over her very ample chest. Aunt Vi tucked her polo shirt into her shorts. "I guess I'm not used to having a roommate."

"I got off a little early. I'll, uh…" She studied her shoes and glanced longingly down the hall to her room—anywhere but into the living room.

Aunt Vi cleared her throat and the woman giggled.

"Um, I'll, er, go to my room." She felt unable to string a coherent sentence together. "Uh, carry on."

Meg jangled the keys in her hand for no reason and fled to her room. She shut the door and leaned against it, totally embarrassed. Muffled laughs and steps across the hardwood floor preceded a door closing. They'd gone into Vi's room. Meg took the few steps across her room to her bed and with a great sigh, she fell onto it, covering her head with a pillow. What had just happened? She tried not to think about what she'd seen and didn't want to think about the two women in the room down the hall. Finally, she put the pillow aside and sat up.

The apartment was silent. They may have taken their business into the room for privacy, but she knew what they were doing. Meg picked up the keys she'd dropped on the bed and left her room. It was a little early for dinner, but there was no way she was going to hang around in the apartment after that.

As she passed the door to Aunt Vi's room she wondered what had happened to Sherri.

11

Two months later

Journal entry: Fiona MacGregor - June 26, my bed, my apartment,
Morningside Heights, NYC

Dear Mom,

I was writing in my journal but the words weren't flowing very well, so I decided to write to you instead. I hope you don't mind me doing this after so many years. It feels weird, though. I don't believe in a sentient afterlife, not like you did. But I can definitely understand why people in crisis turn to religion. The thing is, I need a little grounding right now. I wish you were here to tell me everything will be okay. I know you can't, though. And there's no way it's going to be okay. My life has gone to shit, Mom.

Sorry for the cursing.

But it has and I don't know what to do.

You know me. I've spent my entire life knowing exactly how it should go. You used to tell me to loosen up and not try to plan things out so meticulously. But I'm a planner. You know how it was supposed to go: finish high school with honors so I could go to a good college; graduate from law school; pass the bar; get a job at a great firm; make partner by thirty. Boom. Boom. Boom. That was the plan. You always wanted me to be a lawyer, too.

Mom, I was right there! I had it in my hands!

But I screwed up.

Guess I'm not as smart as I thought. I know you wouldn't ever say it to me, but I feel like a disappointment.

Life goes on. Isn't that what you always told me when stuff didn't happen the way I planned it? Don't obsess about the bumps in the road, you said.

But, Jesus, Mom, and excuse me for taking the Lord's name in vain, but how glib. Life goes on? What a joke! What life? I've been too busy my entire life planning and working for my future to have any sort of life. And for this? How did I let it happen? I studied and I focused and I was doing so well. I was on track. I was most definitely on track. Nineteen years of school, then months of studying for the bar exam. I was almost there. And then I blew it. Blew it big time!

This was not the plan!

Sorry for yelling.

I keep thinking about Aunt Corny. She used to say, "Fate doesn't always give you a warning when she decides to throw a curveball." I sure figured out what she meant the hard way.

I've heard it said countless times that things happen for a reason. Maybe it would be somewhat comforting if I actually believed in fate. But, honestly, I think it's bullshit. Goddamn platitudes aren't going to fix this, though.

Sorry about the language.

This is where I could use your wisdom, Mom, but that's not gonna happen. I'm writing a letter to my dead mother in my journal and I miss you so much I ache and my eyes burn from staring at these pages, trying to conjure up something—anything—that will help me plan my way out of this. But the answers refuse to write themselves. Where does it leave me? Sitting in the dark like some Emo kid, lamenting the details of my wasted life. Looking forward to a shattered future.

Fuck.

Sorry for the language, Mom. Sorry for the blasphemy. But more than anything, sorry for letting you down.

How did this disaster become my life?

I never wanted to let you down. I always thought I was smarter than this. What kind of idiot passes the bar exam on the first try, then goes and gets herself pregnant?

This kind of idiot, I guess.

Aunt Corny is right. Life goes on. Fuck my life.

Fiona read the words she'd written in her journal for the tenth time.

It didn't even sound like her, she thought dismally, as she looked at the sentences penned in her neat scroll. She closed the journal and tossed it onto her nightstand, scattering the seven pregnancy test wands she had carefully placed in a neat little row on the polished wood tabletop. She pulled her legs up onto the bed and dropped her head onto her knees. Her attempt at writing in the leather-bound book she hadn't cracked open in over five years had been a failure. Her entire future was on the line, and her words sounded like a poorly written indie blog. She never had been good at journal writing. At best, the act of writing her deepest thoughts felt arduous and manufactured. Trying to write the letter to her mother had helped, but it was little more than a stream of self-recrimination. Why was it so hard to find the self-awareness to get the feelings out, let alone explore them? The flood of emotion she felt threatened to drown her. God, she wished her mother were here. She missed her so much. For a minute, the ancient grief of losing her parents eclipsed the awful present. She cried with the pain she felt all those years ago when the loss was fresh.

She fell sideways, curling up in a tight ball on her bed. Self-pity consumed her. She needed someone to talk to. Someone to help her with solutions. For the first time in her life, she didn't think she could face something by herself.

It had been two and half months since that stupid night. She and Mike hadn't spoken since. With the bar exam behind them—at least for her—and no more marathon study sessions, they'd had no need to get together. But, the truth was, it had been the embarrassment that kept her from calling him. She assumed he had similar thoughts, since he hadn't called her, either. Now, she wished it was simply embarrassment she had to live with. This was worse, though. So very, very, very much worse than embarrassment.

Pregnant.

Holy crap.

She was pregnant.

Something she never thought she'd be. Ever.

Should she tell him?

Mike deserved to know, right? Or did he? If she took care of it, became un-pregnant—for some reason she couldn't even think of the real word, even though she was categorically pro-choice—would it matter if she told him?

The thing was, if he wasn't part of this whole mess, he'd be one of the first people she'd actually tell. If she told anyone. Despite the past couple of months, he was one of her closest friends, up there with Maureen and Josh.

But could she bring herself to tell her closest friends about this? She was terrified of being judged. Self-pity consumed her. Who would tell her everything would be okay? Would everything be okay? She couldn't imagine it. Her perfect life was ruined.

Stop it, she scolded herself. She would not feel sorry for herself.

Women got pregnant all the time.

Not women like her. She had her career to think about. What did this mean for her future? Her dreams of becoming a high-powered New York City lawyer were on the line. She had every reason to feel sorry for herself.

The question was: what were the next steps? Fiona had spent the better part of her life knowing exactly what came next, but now she found herself in the previously unimaginable position of not knowing. She felt like she was perched on a tightrope, without a net, teetering wildly.

She pulled the covers over her head and continued to cry.

12

MEG DANCED FROM FOOT TO foot, holding herself, praying for relief. She didn't even try to paint, although it had been a good distraction in the beginning. She'd had to go to the bathroom for a long time, but Aunt Vi and yet another woman Meg didn't know were at the end of the hallway doing God knows what, and she didn't want to deal with all the awkwardness. She should have gone earlier, when it had been only a faint need, but she'd been in the zone and the colors had been flowing perfectly. The urge to pee had tipped to code red at the same moment she'd heard Vi's bedroom door open. She'd gotten up and stood by her bedroom door, listening for the woman to leave. Now she'd been hovering there for several minutes, hopping from foot to foot, listening to the murmur of the two women's voices. She eyed an empty glass on her bedside table, both wishing she hadn't downed the entire lemonade and wondering if she should use it for more practical purposes.

How had she gotten into this situation?

Aunt Vi had the most active dating life Meg had ever seen. Since she'd walked in on Vi in the living room two months ago, she'd seen her with at least a dozen different women. Sherri continued to come over, too. Nobody talked about Vi's extracurricular love life.

Meg sat back down on her bed, crossing her legs to keep from wetting herself. When she heard a final laugh and the front door click shut, she leapt from her bed, snatched her bedroom door open, and bolted to the bathroom. Aunt Vi was also stepping into the bathroom, but Meg barely acknowledged her surprised face as she pushed her aside and lurched toward the toilet. She didn't even bother to shut the door before tearing her shorts down and sitting. Her shoulders lowered as she sighed in relief. Peeing had never felt so good.

"Hey!"

"Sorry! Emergency!" Meg said as she kicked the door closed in her face. A twinge of guilt hit her, but she pushed it away, justifying her actions as having been caused by Aunt Vi in the first place.

A few minutes later, she finished washing her hands and exited the bathroom, to find Aunt Vi leaning against the wall outside the door.

"It's bad for your bladder to hold it, you know. You'll start pissing yourself when you sneeze. Take it from an old fart like me."

Meg laughed. "I'll keep it in mind." Despite Aunt Vi's revolving door of conquests and unapologetic cheating on her girlfriend, Meg truly loved her.

Vi ducked into the bathroom as Meg went back to her room and to the painting she'd been working on right before she'd nearly peed her pants for the first time since kindergarten.

A few minutes later, Aunt Vi appeared at her bedroom door. Meg had kept it open after the woman left, in hopes of drawing in some of the cooler air from the living room. Vi had a bundle of sheets and pillow cases in her arms. Gross. "Do you have any towels or sheets needing a wash? I'm gonna run down to the laundromat and I have a little more room. Save you a trip."

Not having to lug her laundry up and down three flights of stairs and across the street trumped any queasiness of intermingling her sheets with her aunt's. "That would be great." Meg dropped the brush she'd been using into the cup of water next to the easel. She sorted out a couple towels and the sheets from her laundry bag.

"Holy crap almighty, it's warm in here!" Aunt Vi said when she stepped into the room to take the laundry. "We need to get you a window unit or something, kiddo!"

"I've gone to the hardware store and few places around here to get one, but they're all out everywhere."

"There's this new thing called the internet, my dear." Aunt Vi teased as she took the sheets Meg held out to her.

Meg lowered her head and stared at Aunt Vi with her arms crossed. "Very funny. I just haven't gotten around to it and opening the window usually helps. Until today."

"That's all about to change." Aunt Vi said as she walked to the door. "The city is unbearable without AC starting about now. I forgot how warm this room gets." She turned around to look at her before leaving the room. "I know a guy. We'll get you all set up."

Aunt Vi always had "a guy". It sounded so mobbish.

"Is this the same guy who sold you and Sherri those fake tickets to Hamilton?"

Aunt Vi's face clouded. She'd splurged on front row tickets the month before to celebrate her and Sherri's anniversary. They'd been so cute, Sherri all done up in a pretty dress with high heels and Aunt Vi in a stylish suit, complete with a bow tie.

"He's not gonna be ripping off anyone else any time soon," she said cryptically.

Meg laughed. "What? Did you send Kneecap Larry to see him?"

Kneecap Larry was a plumber over in Flushing that Aunt Vi and her mother knew from high school. The story in the family was that one of their friends had been verbally assaulted by a group of boys from a nearby neighborhood on her way home from school. Larry overheard the girls talking about it and took it upon himself and a tire jack to teach the boys a lesson. After all was said and done, he'd spent ten years in prison for busting all of their kneecaps. When he got out, he went to work in his father's plumbing business. A couple of years later, he married the girl he'd defended. The joke in the family was that anytime they needed retribution, they'd call Kneecap Larry to take care of it.

Aunt Vi raised a knowing eyebrow. "Worse. Sherri has a friend who works at the IRS. We got him audited."

"You're a scary person to piss off."

"Don't you forget it, Megsie. But never for you. I got your back, coming and going." Aunt Vi winked and turned to leave, but stopped and looked over her shoulder. "Oh, yeah. Sherri's coming over for dinner tonight. She wanted me to ask you if you'll join us. I'm going to try to fit some steaks on the little grill out on the fire escape. If it's okay with you that I go through your room, that is. Otherwise I can fry them up."

Meg tried to think up an excuse about joining them for dinner. She wouldn't be able to look Sherri in the eye without thinking about the parade of women Aunt Vi had brought to the apartment.

Aunt Vi shifted the laundry to her other hip. "Sherri thinks you don't like her since you hide away every time she's here."

"I like Sherri a lot." *I just don't like lying to her*, she thought to herself.

For good or bad, Aunt Vi was impervious to her thoughts. "Good. Because she's a keeper. It would be difficult if you didn't like her. You know, since you're like family, and all."

Aunt Vi made to leave again, but Meg couldn't hold it in any longer. "Can I ask you something?"

Aunt Vi backed up and faced her. "Anything, kiddo."

"Well, if you and Sherri are serious, well…um…" She wished she hadn't started. It was none of her business.

"Yeah?" Aunt Vi dropped her head and raised her eyebrows in expectation.

Meg suspected Aunt Vi knew what she wanted to ask. She moved from one foot to the other. "Well, normally when you're serious about someone, there isn't so much, um, well…" How could she be delicate? She couldn't. She had to be direct. "Is Sherri okay with all of your other girlfriends?"

Aunt Vi scratched the back of her neck. Meg felt even more awkward for having brought it up. When Aunt Vi finally answered, she wished she hadn't.

"You see, kiddo, not really. She isn't okay with it. But, what she doesn't see doesn't hurt her. Know what I mean?"

"Oh." It wasn't what Meg expected and her respect for her aunt took a steep dive. She'd struggled with being judgmental before she knew the truth, but now she knew. It made her a little sick to her stomach.

Aunt Vi repositioned the wad of linens. "I see the look on your face, kiddo. I know how it seems, but it's our deal. Sherri knows I see other women. She doesn't like it, and she doesn't ask about it, but she respects the way I am. I respect her by not telling her the details."

Meg wasn't sure how to process it. "Then why…" Meg started before she realized she should have kept her thoughts to herself. She stopped mid-sentence. It wasn't her business.

"Why do I see other women? Probably for the reason you think. I like sex, kiddo."

Merely thinking about it made Meg blush.

Vi shook her head and smiled. "Sherri made a decision several years ago to work the night shift at the hospital. And she works two jobs. It doesn't give us a lot of time to be together, let alone get naked and bump uglies, you know what I mean? She works twelve hour shifts, six and seven days a week, and she sleeps all day. I have my day job. So, rather than pick fights with Sherri about not getting enough intimacy, I get those needs met with a few friends."

Meg felt like she shouldn't judge, but she couldn't help it. Aunt Vi seemed to anticipate her thoughts.

"You're wondering why she doesn't give up the second job so she can spend more time with me."

Meg nodded. "It's none of my business, I know."

Aunt Vi laughed. "I'd rather you ask than making up your own version of our admittedly untraditional situation. She's working the second job so she can save enough money to retire early so she can quit both jobs and we can be together. Like I said, I know it isn't conventional, but it works for us."

"I understand." Meg lied. Even her first years at college hadn't been as active as what she'd seen of Aunt Vi's sex life. Meg needed a deep emotional connection with people she slept with. Aunt Vi called the women "friends". They didn't seem to do anything else but have sex. Was that all they were to each other? Fuck buddies?

"I'm glad we had this talk, Megsie. I didn't know how to bring it up and I'm not one to hide things. I am who I am. But I value your opinion of me." Aunt Vi pushed away from the doorjamb. "Oh, by the way, I've appreciated you being discreet about it with Sherri. I wasn't about to ask you to lie for me, because there's nothing worse than a liar in my book. But I do appreciate you not waving anything in her face. We have a good thing going and, like I said, she's good with not knowing what she doesn't know."

With that, Aunt Vi took the laundry to the laundromat and Meg returned to her painting as she tried to process what Aunt Vi had told her.

13

IT WAS THURSDAY, BUT IT didn't really matter to Fiona what day of the week it was. Almost a week had passed since she'd taken the pregnancy tests and she couldn't seem to lift herself from the funk she'd descended into.

Funk?

More like a massive depression, uncontrollable anxiety, hair trigger rage, and an endless stream of other debilitating emotions. Long hours spent at the office did little to help create a sense of normalcy about the awful new direction her life had taken. If anything, work had kept her from doing much personal introspection, which was both a good and a bad thing. At some point, she was going to have to face the terrifying facts of her situation, but for now she was standing next to the printer in her office, hugging a cup of decaf coffee, absently staring out the window.

Someone cleared their throat. She looked over her shoulder to see Twyla standing in the doorway. The copier had finished spitting out copies of a contract for a client she was meeting with later in the afternoon. Who knows how long ago they had finished printing?

Fiona didn't even have it in her to feel her normal self-consciousness around Twyla, who was always dressed to the nines with perfect makeup and freshly styled hair. Twyla could have passed as a fashion designer rather than the law firm's efficient office manager.

"Hey." She forced a smile. Everyone liked Twyla. Despite her carefully poised appearance, Twyla was one of the warmest, down to earth people Fiona knew.

Twyla held a stack of papers out to her. "Fiona, love, I found this in the breakroom." Her whisper conveyed her slightly faded North Carolina accent.

"It was in the refrigerator. The half and half was sitting on the counter next to the coffee maker."

Fiona sighed and looked into the cup of coffee she held. She hadn't even noticed there was no creamer in it. It was also the second time in as many days Twyla had returned something of hers she'd found in an odd place. The first one had been her cell phone, which she'd left on a cookie platter in a conference room after meeting with a client.

She took the file from Twyla. "Thanks. I didn't even know I'd misplaced it."

Twyla waved her hand in the air. "My mama used to tell me I'd lose my head if it weren't screwed on tight," she said with a wink. "You best be careful you don't lose your pretty little head, Miss Fiona."

"Yes, ma'am." Fiona gave her a genuine smile, the first she'd given in a week.

Twyla came into the office and sat on the edge of Fiona's small desk. "Whatcha, doin'? Gathering wool?"

How long had she been staring out the window?

Fiona looked at her watch. "I'm printing out contracts for the meeting with Margin Corp this afternoon."

Twyla gestured toward the machine. "You're gonna need to put some paper in the printer, then."

Fiona looked down and saw a single page in the tray and not the five copies of the thirty-six page document she expected. A red light saying the tray was out of paper was blinking on the digital display.

"Oh, for fuck's sake." She slammed down her coffee cup and grabbed a package of copy paper from the shelf. Normally, she watched her mouth around Twyla, but she was past caring about most things at the moment.

"You doin' okay, girly?" Twyla asked, rubbing her own stomach and nodding at Fiona's.

Fiona stopped what she was doing and stared at her. Did she suspect?

"Gregory noticed you were a little peaked, too." Twyla took the paper from Fiona's hands and cleared the alert on the panel.

"I've got a few things on my mind." Fiona used a few tissues from the dispenser on her desk to sop up the coffee she'd spilled when she'd slammed down her cup.

"Well, I'm a good listener if you want to share." Twyla filled the paper tray and shut the door on the copier.

Share what? That her life was ruined? She took a deep breath and let it out slowly. Twyla was only trying to help. "I'm good. But thanks. I appreciate it."

Twyla patted her hand. "Gregory told me to tell you you've been working hard this week, and you should leave at a decent time this evening and take tomorrow off. It's a half-day anyway, because of the holiday weekend."

"Holiday?"

Twyla glanced at Fiona's stomach again and moved toward the door. "The 4th of July, silly. It's Monday. Don't tell me you forgot. You're coming out to Brooklyn to watch the fireworks from our rooftop, remember? I'm making Mama's key lime pie. Hector married me for my pie." She paused at the door.

Fiona felt cornered. She wasn't ready to hang out with people, not with everything that was going on weighing on her mind. "Time sort of got away from me. I've got some stuff I need to do and, well, can I change to a maybe for your party?" She probably wouldn't go, even with the prospect of Twyla's amazing key lime pie. She had to do some thinking about her situation. Burying herself in work and staring off into space wasn't going to fix anything.

Twyla didn't seem surprised and turned to leave. "Sure, sweetie. Remember. I'm a good listener."

14

SWEAT DRIPPED FROM THE SIDES of Meg's face and ran in rivulets down her back. Shrugging off her small hydration pack, she keyed open the glass inner door to the apartment building. She held the door open with her foot as she lifted the bottom of her baggy T-shirt to blot her forehead. She'd caught her breath and she felt good, invigorated. The loop she'd taken around Morningside Park after her volunteer shift at the animal shelter had been short, but exactly what she needed. Being shut up in Aunt Vi's apartment all afternoon on her day off would have been suffocating, even if the day *was* a scorcher.

As the door clicked shut behind her, the door to the apartment closest to the main entrance swung open. An older woman with wispy white hair stuck her head out to see who was in the hallway. When she saw Meg, she stepped out and leaned against the doorframe in a casual pose of crossed arms and ankles. The shapeless housedress that hung off the slight woman made her arms and lower legs look like sticks. She shook a knobby finger at Meg. "You're dripping wet, young lady. Did you fall into a fountain while gallivanting around our quaint park?"

Meg smiled. "I definitely thought about it, Mrs. Skinner." She wiped the sweat from her forehead on the shoulder of her T-shirt. "It's a hot one today. I hope you're staying cool."

"I got no fat under this ancient hide. I'm always cold." Mrs. Skinner slapped her upper arms, and without pause she frowned and shook a fist at the ceiling. "I thought you mighta been that no good McCandles finally coming to fix my toilet." (Mrs. Skinner pronounced it "ter-let"). "I called him three days ago and he hasn't showed his mick face at my door yet."

Meg enjoyed Mrs. Skinner's oh-so New York accent even as she cringed at the casual use of the racist slur to describe the building's handyman. Despite Mrs. Skinner's derision, Meg liked him. He'd repaired the loose threshold to Aunt Vi's door and had mentioned how busy he was keeping up with all the work in the five-story, twenty-unit apartment building. If he'd heard the comments, Meg doubted he'd take offense. It was a New York thing to give people grief.

"What's wrong with your toilet? Want me to take a look at it?" It was probably the flapper and it needed the handle shook.

Mrs. Skinner made a motion with her hand. "It keeps on running. I jiggle the handle and it does nothing. It sickens me to think about all the water wasted, flowing into the sewers, especially with all those people in third world countries walking miles and miles to get a bucket of muddy water. McCandles replaced the dumaflache before, but it only works for a few days and then starts running again."

Dang. Not the handle. But now she was committed to at least look at it. "I can't promise anything, but I've fixed a few running toilets."

Mrs. Skinner studied her with squinted eyes, looking her up and down before she answered.

"You're not gonna try any funny business, are you?"

"Funny business?" What did Mrs. Skinner have in mind?

Mrs. Skinner pointed her bony finger at her. "You're one of those Lesbonese gals, am I right?"

"Lesbonese?" Meg knew what she meant, and under normal circumstances she'd have been angry about it, but Mrs. Skinner didn't seem to mean any offense by it. In fact, she seemed very matter of fact. If anything, Meg was amused.

Mrs. Skinner pushed away from the doorjamb. Meg was a good foot taller than Mrs. Skinner, but she still felt a flicker of intimidation.

Mrs. Skinner waved her in and followed her into the apartment. "It's the politically correct name for your type, if I'm not mistaken. We had other names for them back in my day. Not such nice names, so I won't repeat them. I got nothing against the likes of you, but I don't want you kissing on me or grabbing at my tuckus." Mrs. Skinner smacked her own butt and did a little shimmy as she led Meg to the bathroom. "I'm too old for all that. At 92, I'm too old for most things. Maybe if I was 20 or 30 years younger, I'd give it a go, see what all the fuss is about. God knows the men I've known weren't the prize catches they thought they were. Not even my Herbert, rest his soul. But right now, the greatest pleasure I get is a good BM and the toilet noise is making it difficult." Meg tried not to laugh at Mrs. Skinner's running dialogue. The neat apartment, although decorated in furniture from another era, was the exact floor plan of Aunt Vi's, so she knew where she was when the old woman stopped before a closed door. "I get all tense with the anger I have for that no good McCandles not doing his job in a timely fashion and my innards bunch up, stopping the movement, if you get my drift. Now, I'm all bloated up. I look like I'm in the family way." She held her hands against her stomach, pressing the house dress against her, and Meg nodded at the non-existent roundness Mrs. Skinner was trying to show her.

"I promise. There will be no funny business. May I open the door?"

"It's the only way you'll get to the toilet." Mrs. Skinner waved a hand toward the door.

Meg opened the door, turned on the light, and stepped into the small room. It had the same black and white subway tile covering the floor and half-way up the walls as Aunt Vi's bathroom.

"I don't hear it running?"

Mrs. Skinner squeezed past her and pointed at the plumbing behind the toilet. "I turned off the doohickey behind the works. I turn it off when I'm not using it. Not such an easy thing for a woman of my advanced years. I have to fold up a towel and put it on the tile to protect my ancient knees. The towel's right there on the counter, so you can use it when you turn it back on. Righty tighty, lefty loosey." Mrs. Skinner demonstrated with her knotty hands.

Meg dropped her hydration pack on the floor, spread the towel, and opened the water valve to the toilet. She stood up and lifted the top off the tank and peered in. The tank was empty and water was running in to fill it. She saw the problem right away. The chain that attached the handle to the flapper had a small tail on it which was under the flapper, preventing it from closing all the way. The water was constantly draining out. She reached down and tied it in a knot to shorten it and prevent it from obstructing the flap. As soon as the tank filled, the toilet stopped running. Meg explained the issue to Mrs. Skinner.

Mrs. Skinner shook her fist at the ceiling again. "Wait until I tell that no good McCandles a woman showed him up."

Meg folded the towel, washed her hands, and picked up her pack. "I don't think you'll have any problems with it running now," she said as she followed Mrs. Skinner from the tiny bathroom back to the front door. Mrs. Skinner kissed her fingers and flicked them toward the ceiling. "From your lips to God's ears, young lady!" Then she raised a finger as if she had an idea. "You wait right here. I have something for your trouble."

"Please, no." Meg watched her retreating back. "It was a favor."

Mrs. Skinner's voice shouted from the kitchen. "Nonsense. For your trouble." Mrs. Skinner came back. "Some nice peaches. They're the perfect ripeness. Not too firm. Not too soft. Some people like them with a little cream or soft cheese on them. Eat them any way you like them. They're yours." She pushed three peaches into Meg's hand.

Meg smiled. "Thank you, Mrs. Skinner. I love peaches."

"I didn't grow them," Mrs. Skinner said, as if Meg thought she had a tree growing in her first-floor apartment. "I got them from the wop market down on Fifth. Mr. D'Angelo's shop." Mrs. Skinner winked. "Now, he's a man who could interest me in some funny business, I tell ya." Mrs. Skinner opened the door and ushered Meg out of the apartment and into the hall. "I appreciate your fixing my toilet, young lady. I'd invite you to stay for some coffee, but all this talk about toilets has got my innards working, if you know what I mean. An old lady like me doesn't turn a deaf ear when nature calls. Come back and visit sometime."

The door shut and Meg shook her head as she took the stairs up to the third floor two at a time and let herself into Aunt Vi's apartment. The air in the apartment was stale. The window unit was cranking out air, but barely kept the room comfortable.

To Meg's relief, Aunt Vi was alone in the living room. She looked up from her book when the door opened.

"What ya got there, Megsie?"

Meg held up the fruit. "Mrs. Skinner gave me peaches for fixing her toilet."

"She's a sweet lady, that Mrs. Skinner. She gave me half a loaf of banana bread for changing the lightbulb in her refrigerator once." Aunt Vi folded the corner of the page she was reading and closed the book. Meg bit her tongue when she saw the page being bent. "She's a racist homophobe, but she's got a heart of gold. She'll ply you with food and talk your ear off."

Meg laughed. "So, I discovered. She's a character. She asked if I was going to grab her 'tuckus.'"

Aunt Vi raised her eyebrows. "I'm not surprised. She once asked me if I was trying to be a man."

Meg rolled her eyes. "What did you say?"

"I told her I was just trying to be comfortable."

Meg sighed. "She said a few colorful things, but I couldn't get a word in edge-wise. And I honestly don't think she would even understand if I did say something."

Aunt Vi nodded her head. "Yeah. I have to remind myself she's a dying breed. A generation of people who lived their lives segregated by unwritten social rules and archaic laws. No one keeps them appraised of societal changes in a way they can understand, so they cling to what they know."

Aunt Vi, for all her interesting ways, often shared insights that surprised Meg, even if she wasn't completely on target. "There are too many ugly people out there spewing their hatred, and they're not all elderly."

Aunt Vi placed her book on the end table next to her chair. "A lot of them only need to have a civil conversation with someone who isn't telling them they're assholes for using the wrong term for a person who isn't like them."

Interesting. She immediately thought of her twin brother, CJ, and then felt bad because he was the first person who came to mind. Growing up in Seattle and being raised by progressive parents meant that they had both been taught to be sensitive to social issues. Yet even though he knew better, CJ had always been contradictory and got pleasure from pushing other peoples' buttons. At first it had been funny, but as they'd grown up, he'd become mean. "Some of them *are* just plain assholes."

"True." Aunt Vi stood and stretched. She tucked her white tank under-shirt into her cargo shorts. "How'd your volunteer day at the shelter go?"

Meg smiled at all the puppy love she'd received. Oh, how she missed having a dog! She couldn't wait to get one once she moved back to Washington and settled down again.

"It went well. We spayed or neutered over forty animals. I did twenty on my own."

Aunt Vi's eyebrows rose. "Was it an assembly line or something?"

"Not at all, but the procedures are simple so you can get through them fairly quickly."

Aunt Vi went into the kitchen and Meg followed her.

"Do they have cats?"

Meg's ears perked up. "Quite a few. Are you thinking about getting one?"

Aunt Vi washed her hands. "Maybe I'll go down and check them out. I've been thinking about it."

"I'd love to go with you."

"Having an expert with me would be a plus." Aunt Vi dried her hands. "It's good you get to keep in practice while you hang out here for the summer. But are you getting to explore the city like you wanted to do? You spend so much time helping at the coffee shop and now at the shelter."

Aunt Vi took two beers out of the refrigerator, pried the caps off, and handed one to Meg. After two months with Aunt Vi, she'd finally understood it was her way of connecting with Meg. It was their little tradition, so she went with it now. The cold glass in her hand felt wonderful and she touched it to her cheek.

Aunt Vi took a sip.

Meg considered Aunt Vi's question. Her time in New York hadn't turned out to be what she'd imagined, so far. Not in a bad way. Just different. She'd explored all of the areas she'd set out to see—all of the touristy places and a few places locals had suggested—but she realized it wasn't as fun doing it on her own. It would have been nice to have someone to share it with.

"Pretty much. I've checked off most of my list as far as things to see and do are concerned. The main thing was to live like a local. Having a job and volunteering helps. I tried not to have specific expectations when I got here."

"Have there been any surprises?"

Besides the continuous line of women visiting her roommate? Meg stifled a laugh. She'd never say that to Aunt Vi.

"I guess I'm surprised at how easy it was to adjust to the city. I like the slower pace of Washington state, but I like it here too. I mostly see why mom talks about it so fondly."

"Mostly?"

Meg sipped her beer. "Mom always has this wistful nostalgia thing going on when she talks about her time in New York. I guess I expected there'd be more romance to it or something, if that makes sense."

Aunt Vi laughed. "Yeah. I think I understand. I've lived here all my life, so it's all I know. I wouldn't live anywhere else, but it's just a place to live. I work here. I have friends here."

Meg understood. Every time she came back to Seattle, she was blown away by the trees and water—things she never thought about when she was there all the time.

"Well, I *didn't* expect to spend so much time at the coffee shop. It was only supposed to be four weeks, while Taylor and Karma were in Europe." She took another sip of her beer. She was finally starting to cool down. "Don't get me wrong, I'd do it again." Taylor had to extend the trip when Karma was offered an unexpected chef's residency. And there was no way Meg could have left when Gertie came down with a second bout of the shingles when Betty was on tour down south. "Things will be back to normal in a week or two. I can leave the shop then."

Aunt Vi tipped her bottle at her. "I hope your friends appreciate all you do for them?"

"They do. Besides, I plan on letting them show just how much they appreciate me by letting them feed me." Meg patted her belly and laughed. She looked forward to going to their house for dinner. They were great friends. Then it hit her. The feeling she couldn't put her finger on. It was loneliness. She looked forward to going to Taylor and Karma's place, but she wanted what they had.

"As long as you get to do all the stuff you wanted to do when you came out here."

"I've seen all the touristy stuff—the Statue of Liberty, Times Square, Broadway, Chinatown, the ferry out to Coney Island—but it's kind of nice to see how the locals live. It was even cool to help Mrs. Skinner out. It was a very apartmenty thing to get to do. Much better than standing around someplace with a bunch of tourists."

"You take after your mother. She was the same when she came out here all those years ago."

"I'm not surprised." Meg liked being compared to her mom.

Aunt Vi looked her up and down. "What's the dress code at the shelter?"

Meg looked down at her running clothes, which were still sweaty from the run back to the apartment.

"My work clothes are in my bag. I took a cab to the clinic this morning and changed before I ran home."

"How far is it? It's over on the East side, right?"

Meg looked at her smart watch. "Almost five miles. But I ran through Central Park and I added a mile and a half by circling Morningside Park. It's pretty magical getting to run through the parks."

"You're crazy running in this heat."

"True. I could do without that part. I'd like to try it in the spring or fall."

"Well, you're always welcome to come back to check it out," Aunt Vi smiled.

15

HEEDING HER BOSS' DIRECTIVE, FIONA went home at a reasonable hour. Stepping out of the air-conditioned office, the heat of the City wrapped around her like a wool blanket. It was especially stifling in her business suit, sapping her strength as she walked the few blocks from her office to her apartment. She couldn't wait to change into shorts and a tank top.

She was peeling off her work pants when her phone rang. She was shocked to see Mike's name in her caller ID. It had been over two months. She debated whether to answer it, when the phone quieted after only two rings. Relief washed over her, but she was also a little disappointed. She liked Mike. Not in *that* way, but he was a good friend. But now it was back to the impasse they'd been at since the night he'd slunk out of her apartment.

She finished changing into shorts and was about to head toward the kitchen to figure out what to eat for dinner, when the phone rang for the second time. It was Mike again. She let it ring a couple more times to test his resolve before she answered it.

"Hi there, stranger." Maybe it would be less awkward if she acted like nothing had happened between them. Her false cheer sounded hollow in her own ears.

"Hey, Fi. I wondered if you'd answer." His familiar voice sounded a little strained.

"I was figuring out what to make for dinner." It didn't exactly answer his implied question, but it was an answer of sorts.

"Oh. Should I let you go to finish up?"

"No. I can heat up a bowl of soup and talk on the phone." She didn't want the hot food, but the nausea she'd been feeling didn't give her a lot of options.

There was an awkward pause Fiona filled on her end by selecting a can of chicken noodle from the cupboard and grabbing the can opener.

"So. Any plans for the long weekend?" he finally asked.

"Nothing exciting. Gregory gave me tomorrow off, though, so I get an extra-long break." She switched the phone to speaker so she could open the can of soup.

"Nice."

"Yeah." They'd never had a hard time talking before. She balled her hand into a fist and pressed it against her forehead, before reaching up to get a bowl from the cupboard.

There was another pause as she poured the soup into the bowl and put it in the microwave. She wondered if microwaves stayed in the food after you cooked it, and if so, if it would have any effect on the fetus. She noted these were thoughts she'd never imagined herself having.

Mike spoke, taking her out of her head.

"It's nice to talk to you."

At least he was trying. She should, too, but she honestly couldn't think of anything to say, except what was on her mind these days, and she wasn't ready to get into it with him before she figured out what she was going to do about it.

"Yeah. It is."

He sighed. "God, this is weird."

She laughed. "Yeah. It is."

He laughed. "More than a little weird, right?"

"Definitely more than a little." She rested her elbows on the counter and played with a strand of her hair.

"Um, is it okay that I called?"

"I'm glad you did." It was good to hear his voice.

"We saw each other naked." He blew out a breath at this, as if it had been a challenge to get it out there.

"Oh god, you went there." She covered her face with her hand. That night came back to her and she'd been trying not to think about it. They'd been drunk. Beyond drunk. She wished she couldn't remember the awkward, awful attempt at intimacy.

"I know. It just came out. It's like I had to acknowledge it, otherwise it would have been hanging there. You know?"

She pushed her hair back and closed her eyes. Would the shame ever go away? The repercussions sure wouldn't. "Yeah, I guess."

She let herself remember in the ensuing pause. The embarrassment was excruciating.

"I feel like I might have pressured you." His words were almost a whisper. At least she wasn't alone in her embarrassment and regret.

"You didn't. I was a willing participant." Afterthoughts didn't count once you'd done something you should never have done.

"Is that true?"

She heard the hope in his voice. He didn't need to feel like a predator on top of everything else. She remembered his clumsy kisses, his request to touch her breasts. She didn't know why she let him, but she did. Even though she'd never been with a man before. She liked women. She'd always liked women. It had been almost clinical, the way she'd experienced the whole thing. His actions weren't passionate. A quick hand on her breast, a squeeze, and then he'd moved on. She'd felt more emotion during a breast exam. She chuckled.

His voice was tentative. "What did you say? I didn't hear you."

She cleared her throat and the laughter faded immediately.

"Yes, it's true. It was completely consensual. Why would you think it wasn't?"

"Because you were crying."

She could almost see him grimacing and pinching the bridge of his nose the way he did when he was stressed out. He'd been the one crying. Had she been crying, too? "I'm sorry."

"Don't be sorry. I was crying, too."

"I don't remember." But she did. She had been crying because he was so sad. Not just sad—bereft. He'd failed the bar exam. His heart was broken because of Charlie. His parents would never accept him if they knew he was gay. His world was caving in on him and he'd been trying to pretend he could be someone else, when they were actually proving he couldn't. Her heart had been breaking for him, so when he'd started to kiss her, she had let him. She didn't know why she did, but she did.

"I didn't stop, though. I should have stopped." He sounded like he was crying now. "When I saw you crying, I should have stopped."

"Stop saying that. I never asked you to stop."

She hadn't, either. In fact, she'd done the opposite. When he hadn't been able to perform—maybe it was the alcohol, maybe it was because she wasn't a man, whatever it was—but when he hadn't been able to get it up, she'd helped him with it. And when it was all over, after an excruciating amount of time, they'd both laid there. He on top of her, motionless and tense, she beneath, wishing he'd move so she could close her legs. When he finally rolled off her, it was both in relief and embarrassment, their nakedness displayed in such an obvious manner. She'd pulled the edge of the comforter over herself and he'd gotten up and dressed without a word. She'd heard about this. When the guy just got up and left afterward. She'd wanted him to leave though. He'd stood by the side of the bed at first, moving his mouth like he wanted to say something, but in the end, he hadn't. She'd felt like shit, letting him stand there so uncomfortable. But she'd already done enough to try to make him feel better. She'd wanted him to disappear and never come back. She was sure he'd seen it in her eyes, her rejection of him. Another blow to his heart.

Now, here, they were talking about it.

"Can we chalk it up to experimentation? A drunken experiment and pretend it never happened?" He sounded like a little boy and it made her grimace. She was glad they were on the phone and not somewhere he could see her.

"Yes, please." She laughed but it was more of a bark. The humiliation remained, but a little of the tension had faded. "Maybe we can joke about it someday, but for now, let's pretend it didn't happen."

There was still the… But she couldn't think about it, let alone talk to him about it. Not yet.

"Oh, good." He sounded infinitely relieved. At least one of them could move on. "It was awful, wasn't it?"

"So awful." If there was a word more explicit, she'd use it, but her mind wasn't functioning well enough to come up with it.

"I've never had a more awful—"

"Mike…"

"Yeah?"

"We're pretending it never happened, remember?"

"Oh, yeah. What were we talking about?"

"Exactly."

They laughed a little and there was another pause, but this one wasn't as uncomfortable as the previous pauses.

"So, Fi?"

"Yeah?"

"I miss you. You wanna get some coffee tomorrow? I have to work, but I can take a break. We could meet at Helga's at ten-thirty?"

"Sure." It would be better than hanging around her apartment thinking about not thinking.

16

"UGH! TODAY HAS BEEN DEAD! I hate it when it's dead. It makes the day go by so slowly. I wish I was still on tour." Betty threw the rag she'd used to clean the steam wand onto the drip plate.

Meg was straightening up the scones in the display case. "It's the holiday weekend. Uncle Arthur's shop was always dead on the weekends before the 4th of July. Everyone's on vacation. It's hotter than fuck. No one wants coffee."

"I know. And I go crazy like this every 4th of July weekend. The band only has one gig this weekend, too. I'm so bored." Betty dragged out the last word like a morose teenager. Meg laughed. She actually liked the slower pace. It allowed her to talk to the customers a little more.

"Where are you playing?"

"At the Dockside in Hell's Kitchen. There'll be a few bands and then there'll be fireworks. We're playing on the rooftop terrace. It'll be pretty cool. You should come."

Meg had gone to see Magenta Morning a couple times, and one time she had hung out with the band after the show. It had been sort of cool to be considered part of the group at first, but she'd become uncomfortable when several fans had gathered trying to get the attention of the band members. It wasn't her kind of scene.

"Maybe."

"You say that every time."

Meg closed the case. "I mean it this time. I think it would be cool. I haven't been to Hell's Kitchen."

Betty wiggled her eyebrows. "You might meet a woman there. We have quite the lesbian following."

Meg pretended to consider it. "So tempting."

Betty picked up on it. "What? You haven't been on a single date since you moved to New York."

Meg rested against the counter. "It's hard to date when I know I'll be leaving in a month or so."

"By date, I mean fuck. You don't need to fall in love. Just have a little fun."

Meg looked around to see if any customers had heard. The place was deserted. "That's really not my thing."

"What is your thing, then? So far, all I've seen you do is drool over the woman with the boyfriend who comes in once in a while."

"What are you talking about?"

"You know who I'm talking about. The cutie you always flirt with."

Meg knew exactly who she was talking about. Fiona. Maybe it was her coffee order name, but she liked it. And her smile. She had a beautiful smile. Although she rarely smiled anymore. She'd never actually talked to her, but it was nice to think about her sometimes and wonder who she was, what she was like, what would make her smile again. She decided to make an effort next time Fiona came into the shop.

"I don't flirt."

Betty pushed her shoulder. "But you like her, huh?"

"I don't even know her."

"You can change that, you know."

Meg shook her head. "Like I said, I'm leaving soon. I don't see the point in it."

"And like I said, you don't have to fall in love."

A customer came in and saved Meg from having to respond.

17

FIONA SLEPT IN ON FRIDAY, hoping to escape her problems through sleep. It worked for a little while, but even so, she was still up by eight. When she got out of bed, she cleaned her apartment from top to bottom. It was a small apartment though, and she wasn't a very messy person, so it didn't take too long. After taking a shower, Fiona threw on an old hippie skirt, a well-worn Columbia University T-shirt, and a pair of flip flops.

She grabbed her keys and her sunglasses from the ledge near her front door on her way out. Her keys were on top of the journal she'd tried to write in. On a whim, she picked it up and decided to give it another try. She needed to figure out what she was going to do about the pregnancy. Maybe she'd stay at the coffee shop after Mike went back to work and she could come up with a plan. Decisively, she tucked her journal under her arm and began the short walk up the block to the coffee shop. The day wasn't too hot yet, so her plan was to find a quiet table on the patio where she could sit and think about her situation. Avoidance wasn't working. She knew if she focused, a plan would come to her and things would be okay. They had to be.

Fiona looked for Mike when she got to Helga's. She didn't expect to see him there yet because she was half an hour early, and she didn't. The sparse crowd in the normally bustling coffee shop was a welcome surprise. It was the Friday before the 4th of July weekend and most people had already left the city to get a head start on the three-day weekend. Holidays often came and went without Fiona giving them much thought, and even without her current crisis, she probably wouldn't have made any big plans. Maybe hang out with friends if they asked, but if it were left to her, she would have worked through it. Thanks to her boss, she was left with a large chunk of time to fill and she was at a loss. She was suddenly thankful for the coffee date with Mike, as brief as it would be. In a sudden and uncharacteristic bout of self-pity, it hit her again—she didn't have much of a life. Faced with everything else going on with her, the unsurprising, but depressing, knowledge reignited the funk she had hoped was lifting.

Preoccupied by her depressing thoughts, Fiona waited in the unexpectedly short line to place her order.

She recognized the new barista when she got closer to the register and a tiny bubble of excitement filled her stomach. Jeez! She really need to get a handle on her all over the place emotions. As usual, it felt like she'd seen her somewhere else, but she couldn't place it. She would have remembered if she had. It wasn't because she was so pretty—striking, really, with piercing blue eyes and dark brown hair, a look Fiona found arresting on anyone. It was more in the way the woman carried herself, so confident and amiable. She didn't chat with the customers, but she had a friendly smile for each of them. Fiona watched her wait on the customer ahead of her and she couldn't help but anticipate her turn.

"I see you checking her out," whispered a voice behind her.

Fiona spun to see Josh. He was almost laughing as he looked between her and the barista, nodding his head.

"Shut up!" She bounced against him with her shoulder. She was pretty sure the barista hadn't heard him, but she blushed. "I was not."

"Were, too. I don't blame you, though. I go two blocks out of my way to come here to see her. Café Joe's is closer to my office, but the coffee jockeys look like they were hired straight off the docks. Not so easy on the eyes, even if I leaned that way. You here by yourself?" He looked around.

"You're a pig. Seriously, I wasn't checking her out. I was looking at the menu behind her." She didn't know why she lied. So what if she checked out a beautiful woman? Either way, she knew how Josh could get, so she wanted to change the subject before the guy before her finished paying and Josh said something to embarrass her in front of the barista. "I'm meeting Mike here. Did your boss free you from the dungeon today, or are you on a break?"

Josh snorted. "Jared, The Prick, took the day off so I'm taking a long break. Actually, it's a normal sized break, but when you're used to getting no breaks at all, even fifteen minutes feels like a luxury. I'm gonna have to order and run, though. Bummer. I haven't seen Mike in weeks. Since the exam results came out. He's been lying low. I guess I would, too." He glanced at her T-shirt and skirt. "Anyway, you look mega-casual even for a Friday. You got the day off?"

"Yeah, my boss told me to get a head start on the holiday weekend. Little does he know I have no life. I'll probably run through cases from home."

"You have no idea how lucky you are, Fi. You'll tell me first if something opens up at your firm, right? I don't know how long I can take it where I'm at. Maureen's no help. She won't 'blend her personal life with her professional life', she says." He rolled his eyes.

Maureen always knew how to handle things like this. Unlike her. "Of course. You'll be the first to know." See? Like that. She didn't want to work with Josh, either. He was a good friend, but was one of the most entitled people she knew. Thankfully, she was fairly confident there would be no attorney positions available for quite a while. She'd taken the last slot, and before she was hired, it had been at least ten years since the last position opened up. The attorneys at her firm liked it there and were unlikely to move.

The guy before them shuffled to the other end of the dark granite counter where a woman with black hair and tattoos all over her arms delivered the drinks she prepared. Fiona stepped up to the register with Josh next to her.

"Fiona and Harpo, right? How are you two doing today?" The barista spoke to them. And knew her name. Fiona was surprised. The barista must have read the puzzled look on her face. She smiled her dazzling smile and shrugged. "It's a weird gift I have with remembering names. You're regulars."

Fiona laughed. "Ah, yeah." She looked at Josh. "Harpo?"

He smiled. "What? Josh is boring. At least she remembered me."

"Is Fiona your real name?"

The barista's question surprised Fiona. Not the actual question. Josh had admitted to making his name up. Rather that she even asked a question. New York City baristas were famous for their terse, less than friendly service. She got it. They sort of had to be to keep the lines moving. She'd ordered from the tattooed barista dozens of times and hadn't ever chatted with her. This one was always friendly, but she, too, had always been busy and had never chatted. Although the place wasn't slamming busy like usual, there were still a few people behind her in line, so Fiona was a little uncomfortable with the chit-chat. "It's a family name. We're Irish." Fiona glanced at the barista's name tag. "Dr. Coffee" was written in black marker on some tape. Not very helpful.

"Hey, me, too," The barista smiled. "Irish, that is. Part, anyway. I think there's some German and Persian in there, as well. So, what can I get you two to drink today?"

The weight of the past week lifted a little as Fiona gazed into the woman's beautiful blue eyes. They were arresting—the color of blue verging on violet, and almond-shaped. A dark rim around the iris made them stand out in vivid relief. Sun-kissed skin, a strong jaw line, and a chin with a slight cleft completed her nearly perfect face. A slight dimple on the woman's left cheek was almost too much. Dimples drove her crazy—in a very good way. She had to look away, but she couldn't.

"I'll have a large iced coffee." Josh pulled her from her reverie. She looked at the floor. How long had she been staring?

Fiona cleared her throat and looked up. The arresting eyes held her once again. "And I'll take a medium, decaf, vanilla latte. Hot. Not iced."

The barista held her pen over the cup. "Two pumps?"

"Yeah, how'd you guess?"

"Similar to the name thing. I remember drinks."

"That's pretty amazing." Josh flashed what he thought of as his killer smile. Fiona almost rolled her eyes. God. What was wrong with her?

The barista smiled at his comment but her eyes stayed on Fiona. "Will that be all?"

Fiona could only nod her head. She couldn't tell for sure, but was the barista flirting with her?

Josh handed some cash over before Fiona had a chance to get her card out.

She put her wallet away. "Hey, thanks Josh. I'll get you next time."

"Deal," he said as the barista handed him his change.

"Come back and see us again." The barista smiled at Fiona.

Fiona could only smile back and duck her head. Her cheeks grew warm and she hoped Josh didn't notice. They moved to the end of the counter. A few people loitered close, waiting for their drinks, and Fiona stole furtive glances at the barista, who kept the line moving. Fiona noticed she was friendly, but she didn't chat with any of the other customers.

"Not checking her out, my ass." Josh smirked. "And something tells me she liked your business better than mine, if you know what I mean."

Fiona ignored him and changed the subject. "Hey, last time we were here—when was it? Two or three weeks ago?"

Josh looked at the ceiling. "Three. Because I had a deadline and I was having a shit week and I begged you to take a break and meet me here to talk me off the ledge."

"Yeah. I assume everything worked out okay? I keep meaning to check in but it's been sort of hectic. Not to take the spotlight from you, but they haven't hired a new research assistant since they moved me to full-time attorney after passing the bar. So, I continue to do both jobs."

"God, I'd be happy with research assistant at this point. They haven't stopped dragging their asses on my promotion. The position should be mine. I'm internal and I kick ass for them. I swear to god, I'm this close to walking out," he said, holding his forefinger and thumb so close together they almost touched. "I'm positive I can get a position at a dozen firms. I don't know why I give them my loyalty. I'm a fool for believing them. In the meantime, I'm busting my butt to keep proving my worth to them."

"You took them at their word. And they *are* the best personal injury firm on the west side."

"Yeah. I think I'm done waiting, though."

"My advice is to pick a timeframe you're willing to wait and if runs out before you get the promotion they promised, you leave."

"Yeah. Maybe I should." He looked like he was seriously considering it.

"There was something else going on, too, when we talked. There was a woman you were seeing? You weren't dating and you called her unavailable, but you refused to give me details. You ready to talk about it yet?"

Josh's expression told her she'd struck a nerve. He looked like he was considering what to say, which was unlike him. He'd always been the guy telling her way more than she wanted to know about his sex life. Their names were called to pick up their coffee and Josh looked relieved.

"Oh, yeah. I'd love to talk, but I have to run back. I'm already beyond my break limit. Love you. Bye!" He kissed her on the cheek and he was gone.

Sighing, Fiona walked to the front door in search of a quiet table on the sidewalk patio. It was hot out, but the patio was in shade and she wanted to be outside.

The heat meant there were several tables open. Fiona took a seat in front of the café's multi-paned windows, far enough away from the front door so as not to be bothered by the in and out traffic. She faced the door so she would see Mike when he arrived. The table was placed in the dappled shade of a large elm tree and near an alley running between the old brick building housing the coffee shop and another brick building next door, home to an appliance repair store. Taking a cautious sip of her steaming latte, she thought about Josh and his sudden exit. She wondered what was going on there as she absently tapped her pen against the cover of her journal.

The journal reminded her she had other things to think about, but instead she watched the barista through the window. Her situation prevented her from pursuing any sort of relationship, but it was the first time in a very, very long while that Fiona had experienced anything close to the kind of attraction she was feeling. But anything beyond simple attraction wasn't possible. Despair about her situation enveloped her once again. She had to figure out what she was going to do.

Not for the first time, she thought about how her decision didn't affect only her. Fiona stared at the journal on the table and wondered how she would tell Mike about the pregnancy. Would it matter if she decided to get an abortion? Would she tell him if she did?

"Hey, Fi. You look like you're deep in thought."

Fiona looked up, startled, spilling a few drops of her coffee over her hand.

"Mike! Hi!" She wiped her hand on her skirt. The print would hide the stain.

Mike laughed and grabbed a few paper napkins from a dispenser on a nearby table. "I didn't mean to scare you. I thought you saw me."

Fiona accepted the napkins he offered and laughed, too. She got up to give Mike a quick hug, which was stiff and awkward on both of their parts. Fiona sat back down.

He pointed at the door with both hands. "I'm going to zip in and get a cup of coffee. Do you want anything? More coffee? A scone? A clean skirt?"

She laughed again. "No, thanks. I'm good."

Fiona watched him through the window. He shifted from foot to foot as he waited in line and chewed on his thumbnail. She'd seen these same quirks when they'd studied for tests during law school, and they'd gotten bad when he was going through his thing with Charlie. He was nervous. God. Her news was going to knock him for a loop. Her own nervousness spiked at the thought. How was she going to do it? While she struggled with the question, Mike came back.

"So, how have you been? You look radiant, as always." He slipped into the chair across from her.

"Lots of change, a few surprises." The nuance seemed to pass over him undetected. He didn't ask what she meant.

"Yeah. I know what you mean. Same here. Have you seen anyone since May?"

He said anyone, but he meant Charlie. She could tell. The hopeful look he always had when Charlie came up was glimmering in his eyes.

"I've seen Maureen and Josh a few times." She hadn't seen Charlie since the night at the bar, and wouldn't tell him even if she had. She had nothing nice to say about him. "Everyone's so busy. You missed Josh by five minutes. He was on break so I only got to talk to him for a couple minutes. He said to say hi."

The hopeful glimmer blinked out and Mike sagged into his chair. "I feel like I haven't seen anyone in so long. With work and studying, I've been pretty busy. How is Josh?"

"Good. Hating his job, as usual, and something mysterious is going on with his love life, but otherwise, same old Josh."

Mike sipped his drink. "And Maureen? She's called a few times but I've been awful and haven't called back."

"She thinks you're depressed. You should call her."

Mike played with the lid of his frozen mocha. "Yeah. I will. I had to, um, clear up things with you first. You know?"

She almost laughed. There was no clearing up some things. Some things left an indelible mark no matter how you addressed them. Speaking of addressing, how was she going to tell him their single pathetic encounter had gotten her pregnant? Now that was a mark that wasn't—

"Earth to Fiona."

She looked up from his drink. "Huh?"

"I asked what you've been up to since I last saw you."

"Sorry. I, uh, well… I've been swamped with work." She couldn't bring herself to tell him. "I accepted the position at Threadlocke and Guernsey, the same place I did research for."

"I knew you'd stick with T&G. It's a great firm. Have they given you any cases yet?"

She nodded. "I've actually gone to trial on a couple of them."

"I have dreams about going to trial." His voice was wistful.

She touched his wrist. "You will. Have you signed up for the next exam?"

He nodded. "I'll take it as many times as it takes to pass. I was born to be a lawyer."

Fiona sensed his uneasiness was starting to fade. Maybe she'd wait to tell him after they'd had some time to feel normal with each other.

"You must be in study group hell."

He played with the condensation on his cup. "It's not so bad. The group isn't as fun as ours was, but they're committed and I get a lot from it."

"What else have you been up to?"

He paused so long, she began to think he might not answer.

"Well, I don't want to jinx it, but Charlie called me."

She studied his face. He stared at his drink. "Oh yeah?"

"He wants to meet up and get a drink or something one of these days."

"Mmm hmm." She couldn't help but roll her eyes. "Or something."

He glanced up. "Stop. It isn't like that."

Fiona bit her tongue. She knew it wasn't like that for Mike, but it's all it had ever been for Charlie.

"Did he break up with the woman he was with?"

He frowned. "Jenna? No, but I think it's just a matter of time."

"Do you?"

"It's only a drink, Fi ."

"Mike…" she said dragging out his name.

"What?" He peeked up at her and looked away.

"Is it simply a drink for *you*?"

"Yeah. No. Yeah. No. Well, it's all it can be." He looked like someone was flicking a switch in him from ecstatic to woebegone over and over again. "He's moving back home at the end of the summer anyway. So, there's that."

"Will you be miserable seeing him if all he wants is a booty call?"

He looked like he was giving it serious thought, then he raised his hands and shrugged. "Probably. But I can't help it. I can't not go."

"I get it." She wanted to say more, urge him to protect his heart, not let himself get hurt, but she didn't. It was his business.

"Well, I'm glad we met up." He changed the subject. "I was worried we weren't going to be friends anymore. I'd die if we weren't."

"Me, too."

He seemed almost like his old self sitting there across from her. He was relaxed even as a balloon of dread expanded in her stomach. As the pause lengthened, the balloon got bigger. She had to tell him, but it was as if there was a physical barrier in her chest preventing her from saying the words. She shifted in her seat, but still couldn't speak. She shifted again and leaned forward, but the words remained out of reach. She sat back and then leaned forward again.

"Have to pee?" he asked with a laugh.

"I'm pregnant," she responded.

At least she thought she said it. She wasn't quite sure because the pounding of the blood in her ears was the only thing she heard and Mike was sitting there like a statue, the expression frozen on his face. She began to think time had stopped somehow and only she knew it. She lifted her hand to test the theory. Her hand lifted and everything else stood still. She suddenly felt like she was having an out of body experience except she was in her body. Then the smile dropped from Mike's face and was replaced with a confused expression. A hollow laugh followed.

"I thought I heard you say—" He didn't finish the sentence.

She cleared her throat. "I'm pregnant."

He sat back and gulped. It was one of those kinds of gulps people did in the movies. It would have been comical if her heart wasn't beating out of her chest. "I think I'm supposed to say congratulations?"

"Well—" she started.

"But, you're a lesbian," he interrupted.

Seriously?

"Or have you decided you're bi?"

"I'm not—" She was getting exasperated.

"Was it because we—"

"Maybe if you let me finish a sentence I can explain."

"How far along are you? You don't look pregnant."

She squinted her eyes at him. He should know exactly how far along she was.

"I'm sorry. I'm just so surprised."

A normal reaction at last. He was taking it better than she expected.

She laughed. "Yeah, well, me, too."

"Wow."

"I know."

"Do I know the guy?"

"What?" She was confused.

Mike put his hands on the table. "Is it a rude to ask? I haven't seen you date any guys. Unless you went to a sperm bank or something. Did you? I see the look on your face. I'm being nosey. I just haven't…it's…um, sorry. I need to shut up." He sat back in his chair.

She stared at him. Could he really be so clueless?

"Mike, I haven't been with any guys." She didn't want to say, "except you", and remind them both how pathetically embarrassing it had been between them. "And I haven't gone to a sperm bank."

"Well, I'm not an expert at how this works."

"You don't need to be."

He put out his hands. "It's cool. You don't need to go into detail."

Again, she stared at him. How was he not getting it?

"What? I'm sorry if I'm not responding right. I don't know what you want me to say. Wait. Were you expecting me to be jealous? I'm not. If that's what you're worried about. Just because we—" he waved his hands between them. "We both agreed it was a mistake and I—"

He stopped talking and his face went pale. He chewed the corner of his nail. He stared at her stomach.

She ducked her head to catch his eye.

He pulled his finger out of his mouth. "It's mine."

She nodded.

He made a choking sound, got up, and walked away.

18

"BAD NEWS. THE WOMAN YOU were flirting with seems to have another boyfriend. Or maybe she's dating them both." Betty whispered into Meg's ear as Meg handed her another paper cup with an order and a name scrolled on the side.

"What are you talking about? I wasn't flirting with anyone." She knew exactly what and who Betty was referring to, but she hadn't been flirting with Fiona, who was now sitting out on the patio. She didn't make a habit of flirting with women who were with other people. She wasn't rude. "I was being friendly. You should try it sometime," she teased.

Betty put the metal steaming pitcher under the wand and shot Meg a look over her shoulder. Meg laughed and took the next order. She enjoyed working with Betty. She hadn't been sure she would, but Betty was fun.

Meg hadn't been flirting, but she kept sneaking glances toward the patio. There was something about her. Yes, she was attractive. But there was something else. Maybe it was because she knew her from her uncle's coffee shop. It didn't matter. She seemed interesting. Meg wanted to know more about her.

"You're staring at her."

Meg handed Betty another order.

"I know her from somewhere."

"Your fantasies?"

"No. From The Artful Bean."

Betty stopped what she was doing. "Oh, I need to know more. Is "bean" a metaphor for something naughty?"

Meg shot her a look. "It's my Uncle's coffee house in Ithaca, you perv. I saw her there months ago."

Betty frowned. "That just became decidedly less interesting."

Meg watched Fiona hug the guy who had joined her on the patio. All the cute ones were straight. She sighed.

19

IN ALL OF FIONA'S IMAGININGS, she never expected he'd leave like that, without a word or a discussion. It was a relief actually, even though she knew they'd have to talk about it sometime. She took a sip of her coffee. The drink was cold now, and she considered going back in to get a refill. She looked over her shoulder into the shop, where the pretty barista was waiting on a customer. As much as Fiona wanted to talk to her again, she dreaded the chaos it caused within her. Instead, she opened her journal and began to read the last entry in the book.

Aunt Corny is right. Life goes on. Fuck my life.

She cringed. Trite barely described what she had written. What a load of crap! She closed the book and pushed it away from her. A jumble of thoughts filled her head, none coherent enough to follow for long. She put her chin down on her folded arms and shut her eyes. The light flickered through her eyelids as the leaves on the branches gently swayed above her. She tried to clear all thoughts from her mind.

With her eyes closed, the sounds around her became more distinct. She heard the door of the coffee shop open and close, and the ever-present background sounds of the city flowed around her. She listened to an inane conversation going on at a table several feet away. A car drove slowly by. The sounds were soothing.

She was finally starting to relax when a faint and unexpected sound caught her attention. She cocked her head toward the origin and listened intently, eyes closed. There it was again. The sound was high-pitched and familiar, and it was coming from the alley. It sounded like the mewling of very young kittens. Curious, Fiona opened her eyes. She listened again, then rose from her chair, leaving her coffee and journal on the table, and walked over to the mouth of the alley to investigate.

Street smart and typically leery of any alley, Fiona noted she was able to see quite clearly into the short, dead-end space. It sloped down slightly and ended at a shallow loading dock with doors on either end, one going to the coffee shop. Short flights of concrete steps with rusty handrails led up to the scratched and dented metal doors accessing the two businesses. Although it was a little musty and damp smelling, it was clean, as far as alleys went. With the exception of two ancient and rusted metal dumpsters covered with graffiti and a stack of flattened cardboard boxes next to the dumpster closest to her, the space was empty.

Fiona stepped into the shadowy space between the buildings, and the shrill cries grew louder. She moved toward the brick wall and peered behind the boxes on the ground. Sliding the top box a few inches to the side to let more light through, revealed a small group of tiny kittens lying in a mound on a piece of cardboard close to the dumpster. They were so young that their eyes were sealed closed.

Fiona looked around the alley, but the mother cat was nowhere in sight. She moved to the other side of the boxes and kneeled near the wall to get a closer look. From this angle she could see six of them all bunched up in a black and white heap. She had never seen kittens that young before. One kitten, all black and bigger than the others, pushed its siblings around, rooting for food.

Movement out of the corner of her eye caused Fiona to look up. A skinny black cat with white markings was crouched near the entrance to the alley, warily looking at her. A slack belly and distended nipples told Fiona she was looking at the feral mama cat. Fiona froze in place next to the wall. Her hamstrings soon began to protest the position, but she didn't dare move, lest she scare the cat away.

Mama cat inched closer, poised to flee at any movement. Fiona barely breathed as the cat approached. She lost sight of it as it crept closer to the other side of the cardboard pile, and she almost screamed in surprise when the cat leapt onto the boxes before moving quickly between Fiona and the kittens. The cat nudged the kittens together with its nose and the mewling of the kittens became frantic as they vied for position for the closest available nipple. The cat squatted protectively over her brood, never losing sight of Fiona, and slowly dropped down and allowed the kittens to nurse. In the comparative silence, the cat and Fiona gazed quietly at one another, and when the cat flicked its tail and blinked a few slow blinks, Fiona rested against the brick wall. The cat relaxed enough to lick her paws and groom her babies. Fiona lost track of time as she watched the simple, but magical, process of the cat tending to her young.

A door opening on the landing above them broke the quiet, followed by the loud crash of the door slamming closed, which echoed through the alley. Whoever it was couldn't see Fiona crouched on the other side of the dumpster. Before she could stand, the heavy lid of one of the dumpsters slammed open against the brick wall behind it. The noises frightened the mama cat, who sat up, suddenly alert. Fiona stood up, but not before another crash of something falling into the nearly empty dumpster rang out. The mama cat stood quickly, took a few steps away from her kittens, and then returned to stand over them in a protective crouch. She flicked her tail and twitched her ears in keen awareness. The crash was immediately followed by the sudden clatter of the lid falling shut. All the noise proved too much for the nervous cat, which leapt up in fright. In disbelief, Fiona watched as one of the kittens, latched onto a nipple, was dragged halfway across the top of the flattened boxes, before it lost its grip and fell off and the mother cat bolted from the alley. It all happened so quickly.

Fiona heard the door to the alley slam shut again. Whoever it was probably had no idea what they had caused. She moved toward the squirming black kitten, wondering what she should do, and then horror descended on her at the sound of screeching tires out on the street. Her heart leapt into her throat. In the ensuing silence, she knew it was the frightened cat.

Fiona ran to the street. The first thing she saw was the driver, a pale, middle-aged woman, stepping shakily from her car. Things weren't looking good. Fiona turned her gaze in the direction the woman was looking. The cat was lying against the curb near a bus stop across the street. It wasn't moving. Fiona ran over and crouched next to her, gently stroking the cat's side. The cat's eyes were open, but there was no response. Anxious, she jiggled the cat. There was no reaction, not even a twitch of her tail. The driver of the car approached, and Fiona looked up, unsure what to say. It wasn't the woman's fault. It wasn't anyone's fault. But Fiona was angry. The driver stared at the cat, with a hand cupped over her mouth, the other clenched to her chest, tears streaming down her face. Fiona's anger subsided, replaced with enormous sadness for the woman.

"Are you all right?" Fiona stood up.

"I couldn't stop in time." The woman looked a breath away from becoming hysterical. "I'm so sorry. Is it yours? Oh, my God. It's not moving. Oh, my God. Oh, my God."

"I heard car brakes. Is everyone okay?" Someone crouched next to the dead cat.

It was the barista from the coffee shop. Before Fiona could answer, the driver of the car started to sob.

"I tried to stop," she cried to nobody in particular. "Oh, poor kitty."

Fiona placed her hand on the woman's arm.

"It wasn't your fault." She tried to lead the woman back to her car, away from the cat. "It was an accident. The cat was startled and darted out of the alley. There was no way you could have avoided it. It was bad timing."

A car came to a stop a few feet away and a man called from the window.

"Is everything okay? Leona? Are you all right?" He put the idling car into park and got out of the car as he spoke. The woman rushed toward him and threw her arms around him.

"Honey! It was awful. I tried to stop…" The woman began to blabber as the man stroked her hair and looked around in confusion. Understanding seemed to dawn when he saw the cat.

Fiona realized she was staring. She turned to the barista, who remained crouched next to the lifeless form.

"This cat was nursing," the barista whispered. Her blue eyes registered sadness.

Fiona nodded, looking toward the alley. Quietly, so the woman couldn't hear, Fiona described what had happened. "Her kittens are in the alley. Someone slammed the dumpster lid and the cat bolted."

"I'm not sure we should tell her." The barista shifted from her crouch next to the cat and sat on the curb. She nodded toward the woman, crying into her husband's shoulder. Fiona was grateful the barista was there so she didn't have to deal with it by herself.

"You're right. She's already upset." They watched the man help his wife into the passenger seat of his car, which he had left idling in the middle of the street.

People continued to walk and drive by, squeezing past the two cars parked in the narrow street. Most paid no attention. A few stopped to ask what happened and Fiona explained as she waited to see what the couple would do.

After parking her car, the man checked on his wife and walked toward them.

"We're so sorry about this. We let my daughter use my wife's car and we were picking it up. I was a few minutes behind her. She hates driving in the city and this certainly won't help." He rubbed the back of his neck. "I don't know why I'm telling you all this."

Fiona glanced back at the cars. "Is your wife okay?"

"She's taking it hard. She loves animals. Did your cat get out or something? Is there anything we can do to make it up to you?" He looked between Fiona and the barista.

"Oh, the cat's not ours," Fiona explained.

"Sorry, I just assumed. Do you know the owner?"

"I think she's a stray." The barista stood up next to Fiona. "I've seen her around here before."

"Well, the least I can do is take it somewhere and bury it." The man shoved his hands in his pockets and rocked back on his heels as he studied the lifeless cat. "I'll go see what I have in my car." He walked back to his car, rooted around in the trunk, and returned with some mechanic's rags and a paper bag. They watched as he gingerly put the cat into the bag and placed it in his trunk. Before he left, he handed the barista a card with his information in case someone asked about the cat.

The street became peaceful again as the man's car turned at the end of the block. Fiona felt an uneasy sense of expectation and wondered what she should do about the kittens.

"Can you show me where the kittens are?" The barista rested her hand on Fiona's shoulder

Fiona hadn't forgotten the barista was there, but the touch startled her. She hadn't been touched by a beautiful woman in longer than she cared to remember. It was nice, even though it was only her shoulder and she barely knew her.

"They're over by the dumpsters." Fiona hoped her reaction hadn't been too obvious. As they walked toward the alley she glanced at the woman beside her. "You know my name. What's yours? Or should I just call you Dr. Coffee?"

"Meg." Meg paused to extend her hand to Fiona. They shook hands but it was weird—too formal—after all of the emotion of the scene they had witnessed.

"What's with Dr. Coffee?" They walked into the alley and she battled her normal shyness.

"It's my co-worker's idea of a joke. I'm a veterinarian."

"Veterinarian slash barista?" Fiona hoped the question wasn't rude.

"I recently passed my exams. I'm in transition. In the meantime, I'm helping a friend out by filling in at the coffee shop while they hire some new baristas."

"Congratulations on passing your exams. It seems fortuitous considering the current situation."

"Thanks. Although it didn't do anything for the mama cat."

"Poor thing." They were quiet for a moment and Fiona snuck another glance at Meg as they approached the dumpsters. She was struck again by a sense of having met her before. "You seem very familiar to me."

"I think you've been to my uncle's coffee shop in Ithaca a few times," Meg said. "The Artful Bean?"

Fiona knew exactly who she was when she made the connection. "Oh, yeah! I know the place. It's down the street from my Aunt Corny's house. I remember you. You worked the espresso machine there. Your hair was shorter." Fiona almost said she'd had a bit of a crush on her and had gone out of her way to get coffee several times just to see if she'd been working. She'd always been too shy to approach her, though.

Meg touched her hair. "I kept it short when I played soccer. I was going to say something when you came into Helga's a couple of weeks ago, but it was busy and you were with your boy… friend? Harpo?"

"Hah! Josh. Yeah, he's not my boyfriend."

Fiona pointed to the space at the base of the brick wall where the kittens were huddled and meowing louder than before. The gravity of the situation pressed in once again.

"There are six of them, I think," she said through a tight throat.

Fiona looked around for the black one, which had been on top of the pile of boxes when the mother had run away. She didn't see it at first, but to her relief, she soon found it unharmed under the edge of the boxes near the dumpster. She cupped it in her hands and said some quiet words to the weakly squirming kitten, amazed at how tiny it was in her hand. She moved closer to Meg to show her.

"These little guys are only a few days old," Meg said. She pet it with the tip of her finger. She was standing so close, Fiona could smell the herbal scent of her shampoo mixed with coffee. "I'd say four or five days at the most."

"Really?" Fiona lifted the kitten cradled in her hand to look more closely at the tiny little head with almost no ears and only puffy sealed slits for eyes. "I don't think I've ever seen a kitten this young before."

"They're going to need a lot of care." Meg went to look at the other kittens. "I'll call around to see if I can find a place to take them."

"The Humane Society?"

"The Humane Society would probably take them, but there are places specializing in kittens this young. We'll definitely look for a no-kill program though."

"No-kill?" Fiona didn't like the sound of the alternative.

"I wouldn't worry about kittens not finding a home," Meg said, sensing Fiona's concern. "But adult animals aren't always so lucky. We should find a place where the kittens won't be competition for the older animals."

"I can care for them." The tiny kitten in her hand already owned her heart.

"I'm not sure you realize what you'd be getting into." Meg gave her a smile which caused her skin to tingle.

"I can't imagine it could be too difficult." She had no idea why she was trying to convince Meg she could take care of the kittens, but it was suddenly important to her. "Keep them warm and clean. Feed them with a bottle a couple of times a day. Love and snuggles. How hard can it be?"

Meg pushed her hair behind her ear. "Difficult? No. Time consuming? Yes. They have to be fed every three to four hours. Day and night."

She hesitated at the news. It was possible over the weekend, but would be hard during the work week. "Yeah, it does seem like a lot of work." She wasn't ready to give up, though.

"In Seattle, we have a foster program for abandoned kittens." Meg pushed the boxes away from the wall and crouched near the kittens. "I'll check around here to see what programs exist. Once we know our options, we can talk about whether you want to keep them for now or not. I need to get back to work. Do you suppose you can watch them until I get off at six?" She checked her watch.

"Sure. I'll take them home in one of these." Fiona reassembled a medium-sized box, crossing the flaps to hold the bottom shut. "I live around the corner from here."

"Me too. We're neighbors." Meg smiled as she stood and walked over to the steps leading to the battered door of the café. "I'm going to tell Betty what's going on. I'll be right back."

Fiona gathered the kittens and put them into the box while Meg was inside. She checked each one of them and they looked perfect and healthy to her untrained eye.

Meg returned carrying a towel. "Here's something to put in the box with them. It's warm out, but they also like the comfort of being huddled up. It'll make them less stressed."

"Thanks," Fiona murmured as she arranged the towel in the bottom of the box, folding it over the kittens.

Meg handed her a folded piece of paper. "I wrote up a few things I thought might help." It was a neatly written list of instructions on how to care for the kittens. It was a relief—in the few minutes she'd been alone in the alley, she had begun to worry about what she'd gotten into.

"My number's at the bottom. You can call me for anything." Meg smiled and Fiona wondered what "anything" really meant, but she wasn't good at flirting. Not that it was the right time, anyway.

"It's convenient you're an expert at this sort of thing." She added the number to her contacts, folded the paper and put it in her phone case.

"Should I come by after my shift ends?" Meg asked as she backed toward the café door.

"That would be great. I'll text you my address." She watched Meg climb the short stairway.

"See you in a bit. Call if you need anything." Meg disappeared into the coffee shop and Fiona picked up the box. The kittens were meowing loudly.

Fiona grinned. It had been a long time since she had been excited about a new friend, and now she knew she was going to see her later. When she exited the alley, she spotted her coffee and journal sitting where she had left them. She'd forgotten all about them in all the excitement. Momentary relief washed over her. She threw away the cold coffee. A sigh escaped her. If anyone had taken the journal they would have been bored to death.

20

"SO, WHAT WAS ALL THE ruckus out there? One of the customers said there was a hurt animal?" Betty was making an espresso when Meg came back into the coffee shop. Leo, one of the part timers, was working the register. There was only one person in line.

"I came in to tell you earlier, but you were helping customers. A woman ran over a cat." Meg tightened the strings of her apron.

Betty's face fell. "Oh man. Is the cat dead?"

"Yeah."

Betty took the new order from Leo, but turned to look at Meg. "What did it look like? Please tell me it wasn't the black and white cat that hangs out in our alley. I leave food out next to the door for her. She's skittish but sometimes lets me scratch behind her ears."

Meg grimaced. "I think it may have been her."

Betty put the empty cup down on the counter. "Oh no. She was so sweet. I think she may have been pregnant, too. She's such a skinny little shit, but her belly has gotten pretty big. I haven't seen her in a few days. She's been eating the food I leave out, though. Did she look pregnant to you? Maybe it's a different cat."

Meg could tell Betty was barely holding back tears. She didn't want to see her cry, but she didn't want to lie to her, either. She signaled for Leo to make the drink and she led Betty to the back room.

"I'm pretty sure it was her. She was nursing."

Tears slid down Betty's face in the florescent lighting in the back room and she wiped them angrily away.

"I hope the driver feels bad for what she did. Why wasn't she watching what she was doing? Talking on her fucking phone? Did anyone actually see her murder the cat?"

"It wasn't her fault. There was a loud noise in the alley and the cat ran into the street. She didn't have a chance to stop. It wasn't anyone's fault. It was an accident."

Betty's face grew even paler than its usual shade. "A loud noise in the alley?"

"Yeah. Probably the shop next door throwing stuff into the dumpster," Meg suggested.

Betty's shoulders dropped. "It was me, Meg. I made the noise."

"What? No. You were on break. Remember? You were in the breakroom reading a comic book. I had to come get you to cover the front while I went and checked on the ruckus."

"It's a graphic novel," Betty corrected with a glare, but her face resumed its grief-stricken expression almost immediately. "But I had just sat back down. I took the old broken chair out to the dumpster. It's been in the breakroom for over two years, taking up space because no one could use it. But I had to choose today to throw the fucking thing out. Today. It was me. I made all the noise and scared the poor cat out of the alley to her death. It was me. It was my fault."

Meg put her arms around Betty and Betty surprised her by relaxing into the embrace. She sobbed into Meg's shoulder.

Meg smoothed her hair. "Hey, it wasn't your fault. It could have been any of us. How many times do you go out to the dumpster a day? Numerous times. There's no way you could have known."

Betty's head raised and she pushed away from Meg abruptly.

"We have to find the kittens!" Betty moved toward the back door.

Meg grabbed her wrist. "We found them. A woman took them back to her apartment to take care of them until we can find a foster home for them."

"The woman who ran over the cat?" Betty sounded disgusted.

"No. One of our customers. The woman who was out on the front patio."

"The one you were flirting with?"

Meg sighed. "I was not flirting."

Betty smiled through her tears and wiped her nose on a paper towel she pulled from the dispenser over the sink she was standing next to. "Is she nice? Will she do a good job? Should we check in on her?"

"I gave her some instructions and she has my phone number. I'll drop by after work," Meg explained.

"You work fast, Megster." Betty wiped carefully under her eyes to make sure her mascara didn't smear. Meg was glad to hear her normal hard-ass attitude return. The crying Betty was kind of scary.

"Shut up," she said with a smile and went back out front to help Leo.

21

FIONA UNLOCKED HER FRONT DOOR, deftly managing the box of kittens and her belongings as she wrestled with the sticky lock. By the time she got to her apartment, she was a swirl of emotions. So much had happened in such a brief period of time. She'd met Meg, told Mike she was pregnant, found the kittens, and the mama cat had died. She didn't know what to focus on and she wasn't sure she could pick only one.

To make things worse, snippets of her talk with Mike were beginning to creep into her thoughts. They needed to talk but she wasn't going to chase him down. He'd contact her when he was ready. It wasn't his problem anyway. Even if he wanted to be part of it, she wasn't sure if she wanted him to.

Then there was Meg. God! A crush should be the last thing on her mind. She had a pregnancy to contend with. Just thinking about it made her sick to her stomach. Or was that morning sickness? What a mess!

She kicked the door shut and made her way to the overstuffed sofa that took up half of the living room. Indirect sunlight from the high front window was the only thing illuminating the cozy room in her garden-level apartment. She gently placed the box at her feet as she sank down into the sofa's worn softness. The small room was just big enough to avoid feeling crowded. Other than the chair and sofa, a small pine coffee table sat in front of the sofa and two mismatched wooden bookshelves, crammed to overflowing, took up one wall. A lamp stood in the corner and a few framed photographs decorated the walls.

Trying not to think about Mike, Fiona placed her chin on her hand and peered into the box. The kittens were sleeping, a jumble of furry bodies huddled together in the corner. It was hard to tell where one ended and another began. Each of them was no longer than her index finger. Pink skin showed through their thin fur, especially on their little tummies. She watched the rise and fall of their round bellies. The occasional sleepy stretch, big yawn, and wiggly repositioning of limbs kept Fiona riveted. As she watched, a couple of the kittens woke up and became a little more active. Their little bodies trembled with the mechanics of movement as they bobbed their little heads and pushed with their tiny legs. One of them produced a weak meow, nuzzled its orphan siblings until comfort was found, and then went back to sleep. She wondered if the pushing was a quest for warmth or hunger. Part of her wished she could shrink herself and climb into the middle of their cuddled heap and nap among them. Her arms unconsciously wrapped around her middle as she sat and watched the little creatures.

Her phone buzzed and she reached over to retrieve it from the recliner. It was a text from Mike. She sat back on the sofa and sucked in a breath as she opened it up.

Sorry for taking off like that today. I think I was in shock. I guess I still am.

Fiona slowly let out the breath. How did he think *she* was managing?

I understand, she texted back. No need to make the situation worse with a shitty response, even if it was justified.

How long have you known?

About a week.

I never expected to be in this situation.

She didn't know how to respond. Did he think she ever expected it? It turned out she didn't have to respond.

I'll go with you to the clinic to have it taken care of.

How big of him, she thought.

I haven't thought it out that far, she texted back.

You're not thinking of keeping it, are you?

Like I said, I haven't thought it out that far.

There was a long pause.

Do I have to remind you that this doesn't only affect you?

Fiona was shocked. This didn't sound like the Mike she thought she knew. Fury and hurt flared within her and she was trying to figure out how to respond when he sent another text.

Sorry. I'm stressed. I need to stop texting. I might say something I regret later. Promise me you'll think about this logically before you make a final decision. Neither one of us is ready to be a parent. Give me a few days to think about things and we can talk then, okay?

She didn't even try to respond. How dare Mike think he could push her into a decision one way or another. It was her decision. No one else's. She rubbed her temples which were pounding now.

For someone who said he was in shock, Mike seemed to know exactly how this was supposed to unfold. She wished she had his level of clarity. So far, she hadn't even gotten past the fact she was pregnant.

She sat on the sofa and stared at the floor. A multitude of conflicting emotions swam through her. He hadn't even asked how she was doing. He was acting like this was all about him. And how could he be so casual about the expected next steps? Oddly, there was relief she didn't have to do all of this on her own. And then, she was scared about what this would do to her future. On top of it all, she was embarrassed. How had she let herself get into this mess? She couldn't think of a time when she had been more overwhelmed.

She dropped her head to her hands. Mike was right. This wasn't only about her. But, ultimately, it was her decision. She'd give Mike his time to think and hopefully she would have her decision made by then. She didn't have a whole lot of time. In the meantime, she had things to do. She found the piece of paper Meg had given her. Her eyes scanned the neat writing. At first she couldn't even see the words, her head was too full of scattered thoughts, but she forced herself to concentrate. The first thing on the list was something to keep the kittens warm. She went in search of a heating pad. When she placed it inside of the box under the towel, the kittens barely stirred. She set it to low and went online to find the closest pet store and to research flea remedies. The nearest pet store was a few blocks away. She hated leaving the kittens alone, but she knew they'd need food when they woke up. She jotted down a list of the things she'd need and headed back out. At least having something to do distracted her from her worries.

✾✾✾✾✾

"WELCOME TO PETOPIA."

Fiona smiled back at the clerk behind the register as the door whooshed shut behind her. She ventured into the well-stocked aisles. Several customers had pets with them and she stopped to pat a few as she looked for the cat section.

"Can I help you find anything?" a yellow-aproned woman asked.

Fiona consulted the list in her hand. "I need a natural flea remedy and some kitten formula." She told the clerk about how she had come to be nursing six very young kittens.

The clerk was very helpful and they gathered the items Fiona needed.

"That should do it." The clerk rang up the purchases and tore the receipt from the register, but before she handed it to Fiona, she turned it over and wrote a phone number on the back. "My personal number. Call me if you need any help. You have your hands full." The clerk winked at Fiona as she handed the paper to her.

Fiona grinned in disbelief as she left the store and tossed the receipt with the clerk's number into a garbage basket in front of the store. All it took was a box full of kittens to get women to hand over their phone numbers. Too bad the timing was so awful, she thought as she weaved through the foot traffic and turned onto her street.

A faint chorus of meows greeted Fiona as she unlocked the front door. Not a moment too soon, she thought, as she shut the door and stepped closer to look into the box she had left next to the couch. All of the kittens were wriggling around in their shaky, tenuous fashion, meowing louder than she thought possible. Her heart ached, knowing how they wanted their mother. She stooped over and reached into the box to pick one up, giving a sad smile when it pushed its bobbing head into her palm, looking for food.

"You're in luck, little one. I brought you something yummy." She rubbed her nose against its little pink one.

Fiona put the kitten back into the box and went into her miniscule kitchen to prepare the special kitten formula the way the woman at the store had explained. When it was ready, she settled down on the floor next to the box with the bottle, her back against the couch, and lifted all six of the kittens, placing them on a towel she had spread across her lap. They pushed around searching for food.

The feeding didn't go at all as she had expected. The kittens were obviously hungry and impatient to feed, but they didn't latch onto the nipple, or even try to suck. She had no idea how to guide them, other than to stick the bottle into their mouths. Fiona's frustration grew, as kitten after kitten attempted to feed, only to get more distressed as the formula dripped down their chins, but not into their mouths. The meowing became louder, the kittens' anxious rooting became more pronounced, and Fiona's frustration started to turn to a feeling of failure as tears welled in her eyes.

Fiona thought more than once about calling Meg, but the idea of failing at something so simple was overwhelming. She decided to give it one last shot. She lifted the black kitten, which was the largest and strongest, and the only one she hadn't attempted to feed yet. It was more aggressive than the rest, and it took the nipple much farther down its throat than the others had. Unbelievably, it began to gulp the formula down. The kitten drank heartily and only a little of the white fluid pooled around the corners of its mouth. She tried pushing the nipple further into the other kittens' mouths, and she almost wept with relief when they all did much better. After the last kitten was fed, she had a pile of sated kittens sleeping in the valley of her outstretched legs.

Relaxed, Fiona was content to sit and contemplate her tiny visitors. She placed her forefinger beneath the front paw of one of the kittens. Its fur was so thin the pink skin showed through along the leg. Five little toes with the barest hint of nail clutched her finger as she pushed gently at the soft, naked pad of the tiny foot. She rolled the kitten over and looked at its belly. It had a belly button and a round little tummy with almost no fur. She ran her finger along it and marveled at its softness. The kitten was too young for her to tell what gender it was. The little animal stretched and yawned, and Fiona watched as the little toothless mouth gaped open and the tiny head sprung up with the exertion before it flopped down again, all as the kitten continued to sleep. The feeling of satisfaction was more than Fiona could have ever imagined, and she sat for a long time contemplating their slumbering trust in her.

For the first time in over a week, hope rose within her.

✦✦✦✦✦

TWO HOURS LATER AND BRIMMING with confidence, Fiona's second attempt at nursing the kittens went far more smoothly. As she finished wiping away the few drops of formula around the mouth of the last kitten, she laughed at the limp critter in her hand. The kittens fell asleep as soon as they were full—whether the nipple was still in their mouth or not.

When Fiona placed the kitten into the box with its sleeping siblings, it roused itself enough to squirm into the tangled mass of bodies, before promptly falling back to sleep. Fiona hugged her knees to her chest in her spot next to the box in front of the couch and gazed at them, as she had all afternoon. She realized her day had sped away from her. On top of that, it occurred to her she hadn't thought about her own situation at all during the time she had been preoccupied with the kittens. Aside from the brief time with Meg, it was the first time in a week it hadn't eclipsed all other thoughts, and she was grateful for the reprieve. Unfortunately, as soon as she acknowledged them, the feelings of overwhelming uncertainty about what she should do next pushed themselves right back in. She immediately longed for the amnesia of sleep, but she knew that avoiding her problems would only make them worse in the end. The tune of her cell phone ringer saved her from the internal war playing out in her head.

Her heartrate sped up when she saw Meg's name on the display. Her dark thoughts slid away for the moment. "Hello?"

"Hi, Fiona, this is Meg. How are you and the kittens getting along?" Meg's voice was confident. Fiona imagined Meg's dancing blue eyes and smiled.

"We had a rough start, actually." Fiona sat back on the sofa.

"Oh?" Fiona heard concern in Meg's voice.

"I think we figured things out, though."

"That's good to hear. I'm about to leave the coffee shop. Are you still okay with me coming by?"

"I've been looking forward to it." Fiona cringed at her too eager reply.

"Me, too."

Meg's response soothed the twinge of embarrassment. Her feelings were swinging all over the place. "See you soon."

She tossed her phone back onto the recliner as she got up to clean the formula mess she'd left in the kitchen.

22

MEG HUNG UP THE PHONE, nervous about seeing Fiona again. There was no doubt she was attracted to her. But did it matter? She was leaving at the end of the summer. Even if Fiona had similar feelings, it wasn't going to do either of them any good to start something, only to have her move to the other side of the continent in a few short weeks. She told herself she was getting ahead of herself. She didn't even know if Fiona was interested in her. She was nice though, and so pretty. There was no reason they couldn't be friends. In the meantime, they had the kittens to deal with. It was a good excuse to find time to hang out with her.

She made sure the lids to the coffee cups she'd filled were tight and took off her work hat and untied her apron.

Betty sidled up to her. "Who's the coffee for?"

"You know the woman who took the kittens? I'm going by her place to see how they are and thought I'd bring her a cup."

Betty bit her lip. She'd been crying on an off all afternoon about being the cause of the mamma cat's death. Meg couldn't convince her otherwise. "Does she live close by? I see her here all the time."

"About a block away."

"So, you're making a house call?" Betty winked at her and raised an eyebrow.

Meg was way more comfortable with this side of Betty than the other.

"Is your mind always in the gutter?"

Betty flipped her hair back. "It spends a fair amount of time there, yes."

"Well, I'm only going to check on the kittens."

At the mention of the kittens Betty grew serious again and her eyes glistened with unspilled tears. "God knows I can barely keep a plant alive, but I can try to help with them. You know, if she needs a break or anything?"

Meg rested a hand on Betty's arm. "I'll let her know."

"It's the least I can do."

Meg's cell phone vibrated in her back pocket and she pulled it out. She stared at the name on the display and wondered if she wanted to answer it. Finally, curiosity won out. She signaled to Betty she needed to take it and headed for the back room.

"Hey, little brother," she said into the phone.

An amused snort sounded on the other end of the line. "Your impatient ass was ten minutes out of the womb before me and I'll never hear the end of it."

She laughed. "Nope. To what do I owe this rare phone call? Did they kick you out of Europe?"

"Not officially, no." CJ returned the laughter. "But, I *am* coming to town in a couple of weeks and I wanted to know if you were free to grab some food or something."

"I'll make time. When will you be here?"

"I haven't pinned it down yet, but I'll let you know."

"Where are you now?"

"London for a couple of days, then I head to Glasgow. Not sure after that," he said breezily, as if traveling aimlessly across Europe were an everyday thing for him. Maybe it was. She hadn't heard from him in a few months. Irritation rose in her. He didn't seem to care if anyone thought he was ignoring his responsibilities at home.

"Must be nice," she said not trying to hide her thoughts. Few people could take her from happy to irritated in such a short period of time.

He laughed again. "You had your chance. You chose to help out those two dy—"

"Hey!" she interrupted him before he used the derogatory term. Now she was angry. Classic CJ.

He laughed. "You are *so* easy to rile up."

She held her tongue. It did no good to argue with him. He did it on purpose and he enjoyed her emotional responses. She wondered what he'd do if she simply stopped speaking to him. He probably wouldn't care. Or he'd harass her until she did. Either option sucked.

"Anyway, I gotta run, but I wanted to let you know I'd be in town and see if we could make plans. I'll call you when I know the dates."

They hung up and Meg slid her phone back into her pocket.

Betty was waiting on a customer, so she said goodnight and headed over to Fiona's place. At least she wasn't nervous anymore.

23

TWENTY MINUTES AFTER THE LAST kitten was fed, the doorbell rang. When Fiona opened the door, Meg was standing outside, holding two steaming cups of coffee. She'd left the apron and the ball cap emblazoned with the Helga's logo on it at work and her hair was down. Fiona registered Meg's comfortably worn jeans and the form fitting black T-shirt, but mostly she was mesmerized by Meg's sparkling blue eyes. It was the first time Fiona had seen Meg's shoulder-length brown hair out of a ponytail and the hair framing her face made her already striking eyes stand out even more. A momentary sensation of being suspended in time seized Fiona, and she struggled to gather herself before Meg noticed. Fiona smiled, accepted the cup of coffee, and stepped aside.

As Meg moved past her, Fiona's stomach fluttered. She had to remind herself it wasn't a date and that her life was way too out of balance for her to even consider entertaining the attraction that pulled at her. Besides, she barely knew Meg. She was getting way ahead of herself and she needed to settle down.

"I took a chance you weren't coffeed out yet," Meg said, gesturing toward the cup. "My mom taught me to never come empty-handed and, well, this was all I could think of. This or a scone." She frowned. "I should have brought both."

Meg sounded a little flustered, and Fiona laughed. "It takes a lot of coffee for me to get coffeed out." Fiona smelled the steam coming from the lid. "Vanilla. This is perfect as long as it's decaf."

"It is," Meg verified. "I remembered."

"Thanks. You don't want to see me all hopped up on caffeine." She followed Meg into the small apartment. "What do the professionals drink?"

Meg raised her cup. "Chai latte for me. I *am* a little coffeed out so I had to switch it up. But normally it's a plain old drip for me." She made a cute face. "I know, boring."

Meg was delightfully expressive and anything but boring, but instead of telling her that, Fiona led her to the kittens. They were why she was there, after all.

"The little fur balls are over here. They don't have all that much fur, though, do they?"

"It fills in pretty fast." Meg bent over the box. "I love to nuzzle their fat, naked little bellies. How did it go this afternoon?"

"There was a lot of cuddling. Feeding was a bit of a fiasco at first, but once I got a little aggressive with it, they caught on and it resolved itself."

"Nice job. You must be a natural mama cat."

Fiona winced a little at the comment, but there was no way Meg would know how close to home she had accidentally hit. "I'm not sure if it's a problem or not, but none of them have gone to the bathroom yet. At least one of them would have gone by now, don't you think?"

They were standing nearly shoulder-to-shoulder, looking down at the heap of kittens. It wasn't quite seven in the evening and the streetlights wouldn't come on for another hour and a half, but dusk fell earlier between the buildings in the city. Fiona stepped away to switch on a lamp.

"Yeah…" Meg, drew out the word as she straightened up. She looked sideways at Fiona. "You have to help them."

"What do you mean, 'help them'?" Fiona didn't even want to imagine what that would entail.

"Well, part of the mother cat's job is to stimulate their bowels. It doesn't happen on their own."

"What happens if she doesn't?"

"Things build up and can cause very bad or fatal issues."

Fiona squinted at Meg. "And how does she do such a thing?"

"She licks their bum." Meg pulled her lips between her teeth. Fiona made a face and Meg laughed, putting up a hand. "You don't have to lick them. You use a wet cotton ball or a soft rag and rub it across their bottoms to make them go."

"Seriously?" Fiona grimaced, unconsciously covering her tummy. The mere thought of doing it made her want to be sick. "Yuck!"

"Are you squeamish?"

"Not usually. But I don't think I'm up for pooping them."

"It could be a problem if it bugs you." Meg lifted one of the sleeping kittens out of the box. She rubbed it against her cheek with a smile. "So freakin' cute! They smell good, too."

"Lavender oil. A dab on their backs near their tails helps with fleas. I read it on line."

"I've never heard of that. It's nice, though."

Fiona was pleased with herself. "You mean I taught *you* something?"

"You did." Meg smiled and Fiona's stomach did a little flippity-flop, which made her look away. "This is going to be a lot more work than I thought it would be. It'll probably get easier when I develop a routine and don't spend every possible minute watching them, I guess."

"That reminds me, I called around on my break earlier. I found a program a lot like the one in Seattle I told you about. They gave me the numbers of three people. The first woman I spoke to is already fostering two sets of kittens, but she said if we can't find someone else, she'd take these. I left messages for the other two and I'll let you know what they say when they call back. At least we know we have a place to take them. How long do you think you can handle caring for the kittens while we wait on the callbacks?"

"I guess it depends on the pooping thing." Fiona was both relieved and sad Meg had found someone to take the kittens. "I think I'm good with the feeding, though it might be rough doing it in the middle of the night. Lately, I've been sleeping like the dead. I hope I hear them when they wake up."

"The pooping thing actually isn't too bad." Meg pet the sleeping kitten in her palm. "I'll show you how to do it after they eat next time. When was the last time they ate?"

"About half an hour ago. They seem to need to eat every two hours or so, and they sleep in between."

"Do you want me to come back for their next feeding then?" Meg placed the kitten in the box and it squirmed into the heap of little bodies.

Fiona couldn't tell if Meg wanted to leave or if she was being polite. "I'm just hanging out. You can hang out here, if you want. Unless you have other plans."

Meg smiled. "I had plans to go to the laundromat tonight. I think I can put it off another night, though. Have you eaten? Do you want to order pizza or something?"

24

MEG WAS SECRETLY ELATED WHEN Fiona suggested they hang out. She hadn't been looking forward to doing laundry on a Friday night, either. She put the kitten she was holding back in the box and followed Fiona to the dining area where she was standing next to the table.

"Pizza is usually a winner for me," Fiona said, "but I had it last night." And the two nights before, but she didn't mention that. "Would you mind something different?"

"Not at all. You know the neighborhood better than me. Do you have a favorite place?" She'd only thrown pizza out there because it seemed like a safe suggestion. It actually wasn't one of her favorite foods.

"Do you like Thai food?"

"It happens to be my favorite." Meg was delighted and thought she could possibly fall in love with this woman—figuratively, of course, since they'd just met. But, so far, Fiona was almost too good to be true.

"The Lotus Garden is close by. It's one of the best in New York City."

"I'm surprised I haven't heard of it if it's near here. It's kind of my life's calling to find the best Pad Thai."

"Well, you'll probably have to go to Thailand to find the best, but The Lotus Garden is a really good second. It's a tiny little place a block off Broadway. You'll miss if it you walk past it unless you know to look for it."

Fiona went into the kitchen, fished a menu from a drawer, and brought it back to the table. Once they decided on what they wanted, Fiona called to place their order. Meg was amused that Fiona had the restaurant on speed dial and she was chatty with whoever answered the call.

"Delivery is two hours, but we can pick up in thirty-five minutes if you're up for a short walk?"

"A walk is fine." Meg went back to the kittens, scooped one up, and sat on the floor next to the box. "If you're a regular there, it says good things about the food."

"I eat there so often, Boonjira, the owner, calls me her daughter." Fiona knelt next to Meg and looked at the sleeping kittens. "I order from them at least twice a week, sometimes more."

"You weren't lying about liking it."

"Nope. I think Boonjira took me under her wing because I speak a little Thai. I get to keep in practice by talking to her."

"Very cool. You weren't talking in Thai to her now, though."

"I didn't want to sound pretentious." Fiona looked away and pushed her hair behind her ear self-consciously. The gesture intrigued Meg. Fiona seemed so self-confident at times, and then quite self-conscious at others. It was an interesting dichotomy.

"We've known each other for, what?" Meg looked at her watch. "Seven hours? That's like 47 hours in dog hours. You don't come off as pretentious at all." Meg bumped Fiona's arm to let her know she was joking.

"Most of which were spent apart." Fiona raised an eyebrow in a devious smirk. "But I guess my act is working."

"Totally." Meg laughed. Fiona made her laugh a lot. She liked that. "You went to Thailand? Have you traveled a lot?"

"It was my high school graduation gift to myself." Fiona sat back against the sofa.

"Wow. Quite a trip for a kid just out of high school."

"It really was. For a lot of reasons. I'm from a small mining town in Pennsylvania and before going to Thailand, I had never even been out of Pennsylvania aside from trips to Ithaca to see my Aunt Corny. Plus, I wanted to travel a little before I immersed myself in law school."

"What made you choose Thailand?"

"When I was a kid, I read a book about a woman who traveled all over Asia and Africa looking for her soul. It sounded mysterious and interesting. I couldn't stop thinking about it. Thailand called to me. It was an incredible trip—I'm glad I went."

"Did you go with friends?"

"I went by myself. None of my friends could afford it but I had been saving since I was a little kid."

"Did you find your soul?"

When Fiona's gaze dropped to her hands in her lap and she didn't answer right away, Meg could've kicked herself. She'd over-stepped a boundary. She had to remind herself they had only just met.

"I'm sorry. That's a very personal thing to ask," Meg said into the lengthening silence.

"Don't apologize. It was a great question. I was thinking." Fiona looked up at Meg with a smile. "I guess the answer is I'm still looking."

Relieved by Fiona's smile, Meg relaxed but shifted back to more casual conversation.

"Law school, huh? Do you have any big trips planned for when you finish?"

"I'm done. I got the results of the bar exam a couple of months ago. Now I'm an attorney at the law firm I was a research assistant for during my studies."

Fiona smiled and Meg could see the pride in her eyes. "Congratulations! My brother recently passed his bar exam and I know how tough it is. He had to take it twice."

"Ah. So, your brother is an attorney, too. One of my close friends didn't make it this time around. He was devastated. He never thought he'd be in the roughly twenty-five percent of people who fail on the first attempt. To be honest, I didn't either."

Meg remembered her brother's lack of concern when he failed the first time. Her mother and father, both attorneys themselves, had been completely surprised, but he'd been pretty blasé about it. It had been a weird time for the family. She didn't understand her brother sometimes. He had an attitude of privilege she couldn't fathom. Not wanting to get into the family drama with Fiona, she didn't share these particular thoughts. "We were all happy CJ, my brother, passed the second time. My father is looking forward to having him work at the family firm. Is the firm you work for the one you want to stay with for a while, or is it a stopping point along your career path?"

Fiona knit her brow. "I'm not sure right now. I used to think it was where I'd stay forever. Maybe it still is, but who knows?"

"Yeah. Forever is a long time," Meg agreed.

Fiona reached for her cup of coffee and took a sip. "You said you recently passed the veterinary boards?"

"I graduated from veterinary school last year and recently learned I passed the state licensing boards." Meg tried to suppress a proud smile. She wondered when the thrill of calling herself a doctor would fade.

Fiona lifted her coffee to cheer. "Congratulations, Dr. Coffee. How did you celebrate? I can imagine the exams are as grueling as medical boards."

Meg tapped her cup to Fiona's. "Thanks." She thought about the turmoil her decision to become a vet, and not a lawyer in the family tradition, had caused her family. They were proud of her for finishing school, but they weren't exuberant about it like they had been when CJ had finally passed the bar. But that's how it had always been. Meg knew it had more to do with their lower expectations for him than about her. In a way it was a validation of her consistent good work, but the lack of enthusiasm about her achievements was a bummer. It was classic sibling rivalry, and it was worse because they were twins. She kept her thoughts to herself. She didn't need to subject Fiona to all of that. After enduring years of her own twin brother teasing her about not having what it takes to be a real doctor, Meg was sensitive about it. Her brother had no room to talk, though, and she never let on how much it got to her—at least to him. She was surprised. Even after all this time, she continued to feel the need to defend her choice to become a veterinarian. "Grueling is a good way to put it. I found out I passed the day I moved here and haven't been in town long enough to make many friends. I'll probably celebrate when I move back home. As for comparing it to medical boards, we have to learn everything medical doctors do—maybe even more, since we deal with so many different species. So, yeah, it's pretty difficult."

"You have a lot to be proud of." Fiona reached over to pet the kitten in Meg's lap.

Meg's focus quickly shifted to the hand stroking the kitten lying on her thigh. All thoughts of sibling strife fled as she became intensely aware of the woman sitting so close to her.

"Well, we'll celebrate with good food tonight." Fiona seemed completely unaware of the affect she had on her houseguest. "I ordered a secret dessert from Boonjira. I hope you like fresh mango."

"Love it!" Meg shifted a little so the kitten was closer to her knees.

"Good! So, where did you go to school? You were in Ithaca. Was it Cornell? They have a veterinary school, don't they?"

"Good guess. My family is from Ithaca and Cornell is a family thing. We've lived there and gone to school there for generations. My grandparents and Uncle Arthur—he's the uncle who owns the coffee shop—still live there. My parents and one of my uncles moved out to Washington before I was born, but I was always expected to go back for school. When I did, I sometimes helped Uncle Arthur out at the coffee shop. As stereotypical as it may sound, the smell of roasting coffee reminds me of Seattle. I worked there more to cure homesickness than anything else. If I had to make a living at it, I'm not sure I would love it so much."

To Meg's relief, Fiona stopped petting the kitten in her lap. Her proximity was nice, but very distracting.

"Your passion for coffee must run very deep if you would rather work at Helga's than practice as a vet," Fiona said.

"It does, it seriously does." Meg laughed. "But it's a temporary thing. I actually have a practice in Washington waiting for me."

Meg was used to people either questioning why she didn't go into the family profession, or more recently, why she was working at a coffee shop when she could be working as a vet. For some reason, people assumed there was some sort of drama behind her decisions. In reality, she was only following her heart. But her decisions had caused drama in her family. As a result, she didn't usually go into detail, but Fiona was different. For some reason, she wanted Fiona to know more about her.

"I'll head back to Washington at the end of the summer to be my aunt's partner at her practice in central Washington. I was going to go right after graduation, but my mom convinced me to hang out and experience the city for the summer. She said I'd never have this opportunity again, once I started working at the practice." Meg checked Fiona's expression to make sure she wasn't boring her before she went on. "As far as Helga's goes, my friend Taylor owns it."

"Ah. I assumed Helga's was your uncle's, too, and it was named after his wife or something."

Meg almost choked on her coffee. Her Uncle Arthur was one of the gayest men she'd ever met. "It's named after Taylor's great aunt. I was helping her and her partner while they were in Europe, but then they extended their trip and had a few people out unexpectedly, so I decided to help for a few more weeks. I was going to be in town until the end of summer anyway."

"I'll bet they appreciate the help. Only a good friend would give up their summer like that."

Fiona's words made her feel happy. "They're good friends. Some of the kindest people I've ever met. I met them at my uncle's coffee shop when they came to Ithaca for a long weekend a couple years ago. We got to talking, I took them to some local places, and they told me to stop in if I ever made it down here. So, I did. We've been friends ever since."

"I know Taylor. Well, I know *of* her. It's hard not to notice floor-length dreadlocks."

"She's so beautiful in a gentle hippie sort of way. Karma is more delicate with her pale skin and almost white hair." Meg searched for the right word to describe Karma's ethereal beauty without making it obvious she had a huge crush on both of the beautiful women. They were very married though, and their devotion to one another was part of why she liked them so much. It didn't keep her from adoring them from afar, though.

"Ah, yeah. She always sits in the back corner of the shop with a laptop. I had no idea they were together, or gay even," Fiona said. "My gaydar is so broken."

Until that moment, Meg hadn't thought about Fiona being gay or not. She usually played things by ear if she was attracted to someone. And since she'd decided her pending move back home would prevent them from becoming much more than friends, she'd left it alone. But straight people didn't usually refer to their gaydar. Now, her interest in Fiona was piqued even further.

"Karma's a writer. She writes articles and books on organic gardening in the city and she's written a couple of cookbooks. Their trip was part work and part play. Karma's gathering information for another cookbook."

"No wonder the food at the café is so good. Does she make it?"

"No, but they use her recipes." Meg smiled at the memory of her first visit shortly after meeting them. "I went to dinner at their house once, and I went on and on about how delicious the food was. Karma has a great rooftop garden at their brownstone. We had vegetarian lasagna and an Italian soup so good I compared it to sex. Taylor asked if I was propositioning them. I barely knew them and I didn't realize they were messing with me. I stumbled over my own tongue trying to deny it. When they knew they had me, they both laughed and gave it away. Now we joke about it, but I very nearly died of embarrassment that night." Meg shook her head, absently petting the kitten in her lap, lost in the reverie. Suddenly, she wondered if she'd made Fiona uncomfortable.

Fiona laughed. "Sounds like I should be eating more food at the coffee shop."

Relieved, Meg laughed with her. "I recommend the cheese Danish. It's better than the soup."

"So noted."

Fiona pulled her legs underneath her. "So, you come from a long line of Cornell alumni. Very impressive."

"It's a family thing, like being an attorney. Both my grandfathers went there, as did my mom and dad, several of my uncles, and now my brother and I. Uncle Arthur went too, although he quit being an attorney to open the coffee shop. I guess he gave me the courage to go my own way, at least career-wise. I'm the only vet, besides my Aunt Claudia, but she married into the family." Meg didn't want to bore Fiona with the details of her family's expectations. Besides, it sounded like she was bitter, and she loved her family. She changed the subject. "I'm guessing you went to Columbia? It's close and it has a reputation for law."

Fiona nodded. "You should have been a detective."

"Is it a family thing for you, too?"

"I'm the first of my family to go to college. I'd always wanted to go to Columbia, though, even as a kid. It's in the city and I grew up in rural Pennsylvania, thinking the city was so glamorous. It was always my first choice and when they gave me a full scholarship it was a done deal."

"A full scholarship. Impressive."

Fiona dipped her head self-consciously, which Meg thought was charming. "I have to admit my focus was a bit intense, but it paid off. My aunt would have taken care of my tuition, but it was nice to earn my own way."

"Focus is usually a good thing. My parents probably would have liked a little more focus from me when it came to getting into college." Meg looked at her watch, surprised at how quickly time had gone by. "Do you think the food is ready? I'm starving."

Fiona grabbed Meg's wrist to look at her watch. "Yikes! It was ready half an hour ago. I'm surprised Boonjira hasn't called." They stood. "Hey, you said you had laundry to do. I have a washer and dryer here."

"I couldn't impose." Meg placed the kitten she had been holding into the box. She discreetly checked the temperature on the heating pad. It would have been awful if they inadvertently poached the little guys.

"Sure you can. You can buy me coffee the next time I go to Helga's, if it makes you feel better." Fiona picked up her keys and phone.

"An honest barter changes everything." Meg walked toward the door with

Fiona. "Clean laundry for the price of a cup of coffee. How could I refuse?"

Fiona shook her head. "I should have said coffee for a week."

"A week it is, then."

"You're worse than I am at bartering!"

"It's totally worth it. I've heard having an apartment with laundry hookups is a big deal in this city. You lucked out big time."

A waft of sweet chocolate decadence assailed them on Fiona's doorstep as they stepped outside. The bakery a few doors down was baking their famous chocolate croissants.

Meg took a deep breath. "The smell gets me every time. I've frequented the bakery more times than I should have since I moved to this neighborhood."

"Oh, the croissants are very good. Not as good as Mrs. Rickles' chocolate chip cookies, though."

"Who's Mrs. Rickles?"

"She's my next-door neighbor and my very own chocolate chip cookie connection."

"You have your own chocolate chip cookie connection?" Meg waited for Fiona to lock the door.

"Yup. She bakes me fresh chocolate chip cookies every Sunday."

Meg chuckled. "You're bragging now."

As she stood on the doorstep, Fiona's laugh ringing in her ear, Meg felt the perfect moment enfold her. In the magical moments before the streetlights snapped on and the ambient electric light replaced that of the setting sun, the warm July evening paused, caught in a fragile gauzy filter that evoked a sense of timeless belonging. The sounds of the neighborhood flowed gently around them. Smell and memory intertwined to bring Meg a sense of sublime happiness. The feeling was uniquely New York, and a tingle of excitement wiggled in her belly. This moment was why she'd stayed in New York for the summer. This was it.

Fiona seemed to sense the magic of the moment, because she closed her eyes and took a long breath. She looked so lovely in the golden light before dusk, and Meg stared at her. Fiona opened her eyes and Meg looked quickly away.

"Every Sunday. And they're usually still warm and chewy straight from the oven when she brings them over."

"I'm moving in, then!" Meg joked as they took the short stairway up to sidewalk level. "But seriously, you don't mind if I do my laundry at your place?"

"Not at all. I wouldn't have asked if I did."

Meg followed Fiona as she created a path through the light crowd, and relished the rare, non-humid, and comfortably warm summer night.

"Well, thanks. You don't know what a relief it is not to have to hunt up enough quarters since the change machine is always busted. Not to mention the hard, plastic chairs—if you're lucky to get one—which are often splattered with unknown, possibly biological, most definitely toxic, substances."

"Your relief may evaporate when you realize washing one load at a time takes a lot longer!" Fiona laughed.

"A small inconvenience if it means I don't have to keep a vigilant eye on three different machines, which are never even remotely close to one another." Meg didn't mention that extra time in Fiona's presence was hardly a drawback, either.

"I'm glad to offer you a reprieve from your normal laundry experience, then."

"Believe me, the pleasure is all mine." Meg held the door open to the restaurant.

When they walked in, a beautiful older woman dressed in traditional Thai clothing rushed over to give Fiona a hug. Fiona introduced Meg to Boonjira, and after a short conversation where Meg was impressed to hear Fiona's command of the Thai language, they collected their food and made their way to Meg's place to pick up her laundry.

The apartment was quiet when they entered, and Meg was relieved to find Aunt Vi wasn't home and, more importantly, entertaining one of her endless female companions. That would have been embarrassing. She hadn't thought about the possibility when she brought Fiona over, and a twinge of anxiety had hit her as they approached the door. She decided to make the laundry pick up quick just in case Aunt Vi came home while they were there.

Meg headed down the hall and noticed Fiona hesitate in the foyer. She motioned for her to follow. Because the spotlights of a billboard on the building across from hers provided more than enough illumination through the open curtains of her bedroom window, she'd gotten into the habit of not turning on her bedroom light at night unless she was painting or reading. She realized a couple of steps into her room that it might seem weird to be standing in a dark room with a woman she'd just met, so she turned to flip the switch. As she did so, she ran right into Fiona, who was only a step behind her. Her arm glanced across Fiona's chest, and the warm softness of Fiona's breasts beneath the T-shirt felt nice even as Meg jumped away, embarrassed.

"Sorry," she muttered and stepped to the side, reaching for the switch. She wondered if her face was as red as it felt.

"No harm, no foul." Fiona laughed.

"I'm usually not so clumsy."

"Oh, but I am," Fiona said. "I shouldn't have been walking so closely."

Shaking her head in amusement, Meg set the bag containing their food on the dresser and pulled out a change of clothes.

"Since we're here, I'm going to change out of my work clothes, if it's okay."

"Sure, no problem." Fiona stood in the middle of the room and looked around.

Meg took her clothes to the bathroom and changed quickly into a soft yellow T-shirt, shorts, and flip flops, then ran a brush through her hair. She considered brushing her teeth, but reminded herself this wasn't a date.

When she returned, she was unprepared to see Fiona looking at a canvas standing on an easel near the window.

"It's not finished." Meg stated the obvious in her unexpected nervousness over having Fiona appraise her work. "I'm thinking about painting over it."

"Oh, don't. It's lovely." Fiona studied the painting of a woman lying across an unmade bed.

Before she'd gone to work, Meg had worked on the sweeps of fabric tangled around the woman's nude body. She was pleased to see they looked real against the flesh of the woman's hip.

"Thanks." Heat rushed through Meg at the way Fiona looked at the painting.

"You're very talented."

"I'm not sure I would say that." Meg could always see the flaws in her paintings. They never turned out exactly as she envisioned them. It's why she didn't show them to anyone. Having Fiona see this one was excruciating.

"Well, I would. Do you use a live model?"

"Not since I took a class about a year ago, when I started drawing people. I used to only draw animals." Blushing, she nodded her head at the canvas. "She's a product of my imagination."

"It's gorgeous. I've always been drawn to people with artistic or musical talent. It's weird, but I sort of fall in love a little with them." Fiona laughed self-consciously. "You know, figuratively," she added quickly. "It's like you see a little bit of their souls. Or maybe it's jealousy, since I don't have a creative bone in my body."

Meg blushed at the comment. "I kind of get it. I feel the same way about musicians."

"I can't wait to see what she looks like when you finish her. You'll show me, won't you? Don't paint over her. She's too pretty."

"I can't quite see a face for her yet." Meg, feeling shy about her work, grabbed her laundry bag, stuffed the clothes she'd changed out of into it, and buckled up the flap. She pulled the canvas straps closed and the basket turned into a convenient backpack. Pushing her sketchbook into one of the outside pockets out of habit, Meg pulled the bag onto her back.

"Shall we?" she asked as she picked up the food.

25

THE KITTENS WERE STILL SLEEPING when they returned with the food and Fiona was ravenous. The vicious hunger of pregnancy demanded to be appeased. Meg placed the bag of takeout food on the tiny kitchen table and shrugged the laundry bag off her back.

"Do you want to start a load before we eat?" Fiona asked. "I'll show you where the machines are."

Turning toward the hallway, Fiona glanced at the flip flops Meg had left near the door and smiled.

"Oh. Sorry." Meg moved toward her shoes. "It's an old habit. No one in my family wears shoes unless they have to."

"I'd rather be barefoot, myself." Fiona kicked off her running shoes. "I like how comfortable it is to be around you."

Meg smiled and pushed her hair behind her ear. "Yeah. I feel the same."

Fiona enjoyed the way Meg's dazzling smile made her feel.

"The washer and dryer are in here." She opened the louvered folding doors next to the bathroom, which were halfway down the short hall leading to the only other room in the apartment, her bedroom. The apartment was small, but it was comfortable. The machines were full-sized, side-by-side, which was rare in New York City apartments, where space was always limited. If one was lucky enough to have their own washer and dryer, they were often apartment-sized stackable machines.

Meg dropped her bag on the floor in front of the washer. "This is going to be nice. After dormitory laundry rooms and city laundromats over the last few years, the thought of relaxing during the spin cycle is oddly satisfying."

"Oh yeah. I remember dormitory washers. I had many a load tossed on the floor by an impatient jerk when I left for a minute to go to the bathroom."

Meg sorted her clothing into piles. "I have three small loads, do you have any laundry needing to be done, or should I set the machines for smaller loads?"

The question took Fiona off-guard. She had never done laundry with someone else, not even when she lived in the dorms as an undergrad. The prospect seemed so intimate.

Meg seemed to sense Fiona's hesitation and she looked over her shoulder at her. "Are you one of those people who get weirded out by mingling laundry with someone else?" A smile played on Meg's lips.

"Who? Me? No. I'll bring it out." Fiona tried to be cool but kicked herself for being such a whack job.

She went to the bathroom to get her hamper. They silently separated their clothes into three piles before the machines—whites, darks, and something-in-betweens.

"I'll finish getting dinner ready," Fiona said, when Meg began the alchemy of adding soap and fabric softener to the rising water. Even with the twinge of unease Fiona felt, part of her actually liked the idea of Meg doing her laundry.

She pulled plates out of the cupboard and grabbed some silverware out of the drawer.

"You're using china?" Meg watched Fiona set the table.

"You didn't expect paper plates, did you? How gauche!" Fiona spoke in her haughtiest voice, not bothering to explain that Aunt Corny's china was her only dinnerware and she didn't do paper plates.

"Certainly not, Madame! Please forgive my barbarian ways." Meg performed a contrite bow.

Fiona held back a laugh. "Apology duly noted." She went back into the small kitchen and opened the refrigerator. "Can I get you a beer, wine, hard cider, water, milk, or orange juice? I have a small selection of liquor too, if that's your fancy."

"Beer sounds good. We can save the kamikazes for after dinner," Meg joked.

"I've got a stout, a pilsner, and a hefeweizen."

"You're like a regular liquor store," Meg laughed. "The hef sounds good."

"My friends leave one or two when they come over. I don't drink much and never by myself, so sometimes I have more beer in my refrigerator than I have food. I'm glad to get rid of some of it."

"Sounds like my roommate. Except it doesn't stay in her fridge very long."

Fiona wondered who Meg's roommate was, but since she didn't explain, Fiona didn't pry.

She gathered their drinks and brought them to the table, placing a frosted pint glass of beer before Meg and a glass of ice water near her own plate. They made small talk as they ate, discussing local restaurants and places Meg hadn't yet had a chance to visit.

"Tell me about the bar exam. Was it as hard as people make it out to be? Do you feel like a hardened lawyer now?" Meg asked.

Fiona chased a piece of mango around her plate with a fork, feeling nothing like a hardened lawyer. "Do I look like a hardened lawyer to you?"

"Actually, no. You lack the edge I associate with most lawyers."

Fiona cocked an eyebrow. "I'm not sure if that's good or bad."

"It's a good thing."

"Your parents are lawyers. Are they hardened?"

"Good question. Most of the time, they're just my mom and dad. But if you get them riled up, the lawyer comes out in full force, believe me."

Fiona winked at her. "Well, I guess you haven't seen me riled up yet."

Meg nodded. "True. So, tell me about the exam."

Fiona hadn't thought of the exam in easy/hard terms. She simply prepared for it and took it. She put her fork down, leaned back in her chair and crossed her arms as she considered the question.

"See, now you look like a lawyer." Meg pointed at her folded arms.

Fiona laughed and uncrossed her arms. "I can only go by my own experience," she said finally. "The exam was a lot of work to prepare for, but it wasn't hard. Either you know it, or you don't. I think—no, I know—some people I went to school with underestimated the work and got psyched out about it, which made it harder for them." An image of Mike played through her mind. "Your family is full of lawyers. What do they say about it?"

"My parents used to describe it like you did. But then my brother failed the bar. After that, they made it sound almost impossible. I'm sure it was to make him feel better. From what most people say it sounds a lot like the veterinary boards. If you study hard enough, you should do okay."

"Yeah, I suppose so, although I don't think I'd ever pass anatomy." Fiona grimaced.

"And I'd never pass law history."

"I had a study group I worked with for three months, and I took a six-week clinic to prepare me for the bar."

"My brother did the study group thing the second time and it worked for him. He didn't tell us until he passed, though. I just recently heard about it from my mom. We thought he was wandering around Europe, where he ran off to after failing the first test. I guess he didn't want to tell us if he took it and failed again. Let me guess. You passed the bar the first time you took it, right?"

Fiona sensed some tension in Meg when she spoke about her brother, but she didn't feel comfortable asking about it. "Well, the firm I work for gave me lots of study time, and the group helped. So, yes. I passed it the first time. There's about a seventy-five percent success rate for first-time takers, maybe a little more. It also depends on the time of year you take it. July takers have a higher success rate for some reason. I took it in February though."

"It sounds like you worked hard to succeed. CJ failed the July test, but passed in February."

"We had a few second-time takers in our study group. They helped us understand what the real test would be like—well, at least most of them. One guy, Charlie, seemed to get off on trying to scare us," Fiona said.

"Sounds like something my brother CJ would do." Meg sat back in her chair. "He likes to mess with people."

Fiona gathered their plates. When Meg moved to help, Fiona stopped her. "I've got this. Finish your beer." She stacked their plates and took them into the kitchen. The mere thought of Charlie made her angry. His arrogance and shitty attitude were irritating, but the way he treated Mike was cruel. "I'm sure your brother is nothing like this guy. He was a piece of work. He seemed like a nice guy most of the time, but he had a mean streak. Good-natured kidding would have been cool. You know, to ease some of the tension. But this guy went out of his way to mess with people's heads. Especially my friend Mike's. I'm sure that was one of the many factors that played into Mike failing the exam." Fiona put the leftovers into the refrigerator and started to rinse the dishes. She thought about how he'd wrapped Mike around his finger. She hoped Meg hadn't noticed the bitter tone in her voice. Then the night with Mike came back to her and the familiar embarrassment flooded her. If Charlie hadn't made Mike so upset by bringing that woman to the party… The steel door in her mind tried to slide shut against the memory, but trying to forget didn't make her any less pregnant.

"He sounds like a real winner." Meg moved to the counter separating the kitchen from the dining area as she sipped her beer.

"Thank goodness, I'll probably never see him again. I heard he's moving back home to some cushy job in his family's law firm."

She turned off the water, left the dishes in the sink, and went back to the table. Meg followed her and sat down, too.

"Hey, don't knock the family gig, lady. Having to work with family carries its own challenges."

She remembered Meg was going home to work at her Aunt's veterinary clinic. "Sorry! I didn't mean you. I meant *he* doesn't deserve his good luck. I usually don't wish ill will on people, but he's just such a jerk."

Meg laughed. "No worries."

Fiona dropped her head on the table and then looked back up. "Ugh! Dramatic change of subject. Is CJ your only sibling?" Fiona asked.

"Yep. We're twins. I call him The Little Prince. He hates it."

"You're twins? Do you look alike? Are you very close?" Being an only child, she often wondered what it would be like to have a sibling, let alone a twin.

"Most people say he's a blond version of me—which he also hates. We used to be a lot closer. When we were little, we did everything together. But we started drifting apart in middle school. I was into sports and he had finally given up on them. In high school, I played on various teams and he got into partying. We moved in completely different circles. I think the sports thing was too much for him. He's never said, but I guess it's hard for a boy to be upstaged by his sister." Meg's eyes were distant as she talked about it. "It put a wedge between us. He started calling me dyke and lesbo when I'd leave for practice. It was before I even… anyway, he was cruel. It hurt, but I never said anything to anyone, because I knew it was because he was embarrassed about his lack of athleticism. When we got older and other kids said the same things to me, well, then he became my big defender. He couldn't hit a ball with a bat to save his life, but he was vicious in a fistfight. No one better fuck—" Meg stopped herself. "Sorry. But, no one could mess with his sister."

"That's for fucking sure." Fiona laughed and winked at Meg in response to the blush creeping up her neck at the accidental slip.

Meg laughed, too. "Things were a little better then. Even though he continued to call me names, no one else did." Then her smile faded. "Until I told him I was going into veterinary school instead of law. I actually thought he'd be happy. No comparisons, you know? But he freaked. He was so focused on us doing the law school thing together. I think he intended to sort of coast along with me, like I would help get him through school or something. It was a bad time for us." By the expression on her face, the memories looked painful. "He was such a jerk. Not just a jerk. He was mean. He's still an asshole, but we get along better now. Probably because we don't see much of each other anymore."

"It must have been hard for you." Fiona wanted to hug her, but they hardly knew each other.

Meg tapped the table. "Sorry. I didn't mean to get so dark. It's in the past. We're grown-ups now."

"No need to apologize. It's probably not a very good memory for you."

"Well, they say time heals all wounds, right?" Meg sat up and smiled. Fiona suspected it was her attempt to make the moment less awkward.

"So I've heard." Fiona thought she should try to remember that herself.

"How about you? Any brothers or sisters?"

"No. Just me. My parents wanted a bunch of kids, but my mom had complications when I was born. I was lucky she was able to carry me full-term."

"I'll bet they dote on you, then."

"They did. They weren't rich, but they tried to give me everything I needed and most of what I wanted. They stopped short of spoiling me, I guess. They were awesome."

"You use the past tense. Are they no longer around?"

"They died in a car accident." Fiona waited for the inevitable pity response. She hated it, but knew it was normal.

"I'm so sorry. We seem to be hitting on some painful memories. I think I started it."

"It's okay," Fiona said with a small smile. "How could you know?"

"I'm sorry anyway. When did it happen? If you don't mind me asking."

"I was eighteen." Fiona leaned back in her chair. "A drunk driver—one of my classmates, actually—sideswiped them and they went over an embankment on their way home from my graduation ceremony. Their car ended up in the river."

Meg looked distraught. "How horrible! I couldn't imagine losing either of my parents, let alone both. I don't know what to say except I'm so sorry."

As usual, Fiona felt removed from the story of her parents' deaths. The hardest part in telling it was the whole exchange of sympathy part of it and people feeling sorry for her. Especially Meg, it turned out. But even so, for some reason, Fiona wanted Meg to know. "It was hard for a while, but I buried myself in school, which helped. I also saw a therapist to support me through it."

"Have you been on your own since then?"

"Kind of. I was getting ready to leave for college, so my life was on the brink of change anyway. It sort of kept me from dwelling on the loss. I spent most of the summer in Thailand, then college started shortly after I got back. As an undergrad, I stayed with my Aunt Cornelia for the summers and most of the holidays. Aunt Corny was my mom's aunt. I had always been close to her. She didn't have any of her own grandchildren and I had always stayed with her a part of every summer as a kid. She tried her best to make me feel as if her home was my home."

"You talk in the past tense about her, too."

"She died last year, right before I graduated from law school. She had a massive stroke. No warning. She had always been so healthy and vibrant. I thought she'd live forever." Fiona's voice trailed off and she cleared her throat. "I've only recently gotten to the point where I don't cry when I think about her. I took her death harder than I did my parents'. Makes me feel guilty."

"Why? You feel what you feel, right?"

Fiona shrugged. "A therapist said I was channeling the loss of my parents into the death of Aunt Corny. She said expressing pain and feeling pain are different things and I might have felt safer expressing Aunt Corny's death because I wasn't as close to her as I was to my parents. You know—all that psychobabble stuff. I get it, but I hate talking about it. I don't know why I'm telling you all this. You're probably thinking it's time to run for it." Fiona tried to laugh, but it came out a little forced.

"Not even remotely. If it makes you feel any better, I've seen my share of therapists."

"Have you lost someone?" She realized she was prying. "You don't have to answer."

Meg waved her hand as if to dismiss the thought. "I don't mind. I'm grateful I haven't lost anyone close to me. I saw a therapist to help go through the whole coming out process. I think you've probably figured out by now that I'm gay. I hope it doesn't bother you."

"Not at all. Why would it bother me? I'm gay too. I thought you might have guessed."

Meg looked amused. "It crossed my mind, but I never assume."

"I'm told it's a guessing game with me." Fiona relaxed into her chair. She felt a stronger connection with Meg at the new information. With it came an underlying sadness, though. Under different circumstances this might have been the start of something more for them, but there was too much at stake for her to act on the attraction she was feeling. She sensed Meg was feeling it, too. "I have no gaydar whatsoever. It would be cool if we had a secret signal, don't you think?"

"It would certainly help." She made a show of looking Fiona up and down. "But, I usually have impeccable gaydar."

Fiona snorted. "Like I said, most people can't call me at first. Plus, with all the pregnancy horm…" She slapped her hand over her mouth and sat up. Her dinner suddenly sat heavily in her stomach. She bolted out of the room and barely made it to the bathroom in time.

As she hung her head over the bowl and cursed her weak stomach, she wiped her mouth with a hand towel. She glanced at the door, which was wide open. Great. She stood weakly and quietly closed the door. Had she really blurted out her secret to Meg and then treated her to the disgusting sound of her puking her guts out?

26

MEG STOOD PLANTED BESIDE THE table in the dining area, unsure of what to do. She wanted to help, had even jumped to her feet when Fiona darted away, but she was paralyzed in place by uncertainty and stunned by what Fiona had said. Pregnant? Meg started across the living room and hesitated outside of the closed bathroom door. She heard the water running and waited a moment before saying anything. She knew some people hated it when others tried to help them. Was Fiona like that? They had a connection, but Meg was very aware she hardly knew her. She decided to do what felt right.

"Do you need anything?" She asked through the door.

"I'm fine. Be out in a sec," Fiona called out. Meg suspected the brightness in Fiona's voice was forced since she'd just heard her throw up. She was hovering outside the bathroom but she didn't know what else to do. She was wondering if she should leave when Fiona opened the door, looking everywhere but at her.

She backed up a step to let her pass.

"Are you okay?" She berated herself for the stupid question as she trailed Fiona back to the living room.

"I'll be fine in a minute." Fiona gave her a weak smile, as she folded herself into the corner of the sofa and hugged a throw pillow to her chest. Fiona's glassy gaze was such a contrast from her smiling eyes of just a few moments ago.

Had she heard right? It wasn't unheard of for lesbians to get pregnant, but given the obvious biological limitations, it was usually a well-thought out plan and Fiona didn't look like she was particularly happy about it.

Not knowing what else to do, she fetched Fiona a glass of water.

"So… you're pregnant?" She handed her the glass and moved over to the other end of the sofa to sit sideways, facing Fiona. It seemed rude to ignore the elephant in the room.

Fiona didn't answer at first. Meg could almost see the thoughts tumbling through her mind, trying to decide what to say and what not to say.

"I found out last Friday," Fiona said at last.

A crush of thoughts careened through Meg's mind. The first and loudest, she was ashamed to admit, was a caution to distance herself from the situation. After all, she would be leaving for Seattle soon. Fiona needed stability and Meg had nothing to offer in the way of help. As her mind tried to sort through the excuses, Meg's heart could only see Fiona, looking small and lost.

"How far along are you?"

"Exactly eight weeks."

Meg took note of Fiona's certainty regarding the date of conception. And was that rancor in her voice? Meg wasn't about to ask her if the baby was planned or if she was happy about it. Something told her the answer was no to both. Or maybe she had planned it and her partner had somehow fallen out of the picture leaving Fiona in a bad position. Regardless, she wasn't going to ask.

"How are you feeling?"

"Physically or emotionally?"

Meg was glad to see her color was getting better. "I meant physically, but both, I guess."

"Tired. Hungry. Embarrassed." Fiona pulled the pillow tighter to her, covering half of her face.

"Embarrassed?"

Fiona sighed deeply. She looked at Meg for the first time. "Look, I didn't mean to blurt that out. I probably seem like a psycho-emotional shitstorm right now, but I haven't even thought this through yet. I'm not sure I'm prepared to bring you, or anybody else, into… my issues. We barely know each other, for Christ's sake. You don't need this." Fiona's voice grew soft as she turned away. "I don't even know how to talk about it."

Meg paused a moment before she replied. It sounded like some of her suspicions were on target.

"I understand. You're right. We just met. I like you, though. And I'm kind of trapped here right now, what with my laundry in the middle of a rinse cycle and all." Meg smiled and shrugged toward the hall where they could hear the muffled sound of the first load spinning in the washer. The sound abruptly stopped and they looked at each other. Meg was happy to see a small smile play around the corners of Fiona's mouth. "We can talk about other things until the laundry is done. Or we can sit quietly. Whatever we do sure beats sitting among the discontents at the laundromat."

They fell silent for several moments. It was an easy silence, as the pressure of expectation had been eliminated. Fiona seemed to relax a bit.

A small meow floated into the quiet room and they both moved forward to peer into the box. A bond had been forged between them over the kittens, and Fiona's situation didn't seem to factor into it, at least for the time being.

Fiona stood up. She seemed mostly composed now.

"I'll get the kittens fed. Why don't you transfer the laundry? Then you can teach me that pooping thing." Fiona threw the pillow she had been hugging at Meg, who caught it with a laugh.

27

FIONA PREPARED THE BOTTLES AND took them back to the living room to feed the kittens. Meg was transferring the laundry, and to Fiona's relief, she was starting a second load. Fiona thought she might have made a run for it as soon as the puke show commenced, but their new friendship was a bright spot in the midst of a dark time and, selfishly, she wanted to preserve it. At least she wouldn't have to figure out a way to tell Meg about being pregnant now. It would establish the distance she needed to keep and they could hang out a little. That is, if Meg didn't run away after she processed the info, which was still a possibility. Fiona was thinking about the possibility when Meg sat on the floor next to her and watched her nurse the first kitten.

"You look like you're a pro at feeding now."

Fiona enjoyed the compliment, especially since Meg was the real pro. "It took a bit to get the hang of it."

"The kittens are enjoying it."

"Really? They don't purr or anything, and I can't tell if they're getting enough. I keep feeding them until they pull away—or fall asleep, which is more often the case. Like this little guy." Fiona laughed when the head of the kitten she was holding simply dropped away from the tiny nipple.

"You're doing fine. They're purring, you just can't hear it yet. Give them a little while, then it'll sound like a broken toy engine until they smooth it out."

"It's so weird to me. I always imagined newborn kittens to be more… advanced. Like they are in the pet store."

"Pet store kittens are between six to twelve weeks old. These ones will be doing all the advanced stuff soon enough."

A monster yawn hit Fiona but her hands were full, so she yawned into her shoulder. She laughed. "Sorry. It's not your company. I promise. Snuggling with the kittens makes me tired. Actually, I'm tired all the time. I hear it's natural for a woman in my condition."

"Oh, speaking of which. One of the no-nos for a woman in your condition is litter boxes." Meg used her fingers for air quotes. "I guess you're off the hook about pooping the kittens."

Fiona hoped her relief wasn't too obvious. She placed the last kitten back in the box. "To be honest with you, I wasn't sure I was going to be able to do it anyway. I have a healthy gag reflex."

"It isn't very gross. I'm going to do it in the bathroom where it will be easier to clean up. You can watch from a distance if you want." Meg unplugged the heating pad so she could take the box into the bathroom.

"If it's okay with you, I think I'll stay out here." She felt a little guilty about letting Meg do it. "Is it rude to pawn it off on you?"

"It's fine. I'm used to this kind of thing. All I need are cotton balls and a clean towel."

Fiona fetched the things Meg needed and left them on the counter by the bathroom sink.

"You kids have fun in here. Give me a shout if you need anything." Fiona backed out of the room. She hoped Meg didn't take her up on it. Just the thought of it made her want to gag.

28

"POTTY TIME WENT WELL. NOW it's time for night-ni…" Meg's voice trailed off. Fiona was curled up against the arm of the sofa, fast asleep. She put the box down and covered her with a throw blanket from the back of the recliner. Fiona didn't stir—not even when Meg gently lifted her head and pulled the magazine out from under her cheek. With great care, she lowered Fiona's head, pausing a minute to push back a strand of hair and watch her sleep.

She considered the situation. The kittens would probably wake up in two to three hours for another feeding. Fiona was obviously exhausted. There were a couple more loads of laundry to do. She decided to stick around and see how the next feeding went. If Fiona was up for it, she would leave. If Fiona seemed like she needed help, she'd be there to lend a hand.

She slipped her sketch pad out of her laundry bag and settled into the nearby recliner. There were worse things she could be doing on a Friday night than hanging out with a new friend and a box of cute kittens.

29

A RIBBON OF EARLY MORNING sunlight slipped between the drawn curtains and sliced across the otherwise dark living room. As the sun rose, the beam slowly slid across the room, until it rested directly across Fiona's sleeping form. Fiona threw an arm over her face to block the light and turned her head away. Always quick to wake, the tickle of light was all it took to bring Fiona out of the mists of sleep. She stretched and opened her eyes. Wincing from a crick in her neck, she was surprised she was on the sofa. She didn't remember lying down or getting a blanket the night before. Carefully pushing herself upright and rubbing the tight tendons of her neck and shoulders, she looked around the shadowy room. A form lay in the recliner across from her. The steady sound of breathing told her Meg was sleeping.

She rose quietly and crossed the small living room, glancing into the box where the kittens slept. They were cuddled in a furry pile. She stood for a moment and watched Meg sleep, enjoying the opportunity to study her openly for the first time. Fiona noted Meg's long, dark lashes resting on her cheek, and how her shoulder-length hair parted slightly to the left. A pulse beat slowly at the base of Meg's throat, and Fiona's gaze lingered there, before it traveled down to Meg's hands. Her fingers were long and graceful. One held a pencil between relaxed fingers, resting atop an open sketchbook in her lap. Fiona could see part of a drawing. It was of her, sleeping on the couch. Fiona wanted to lift Meg's hand to get a better look but she didn't want to wake her. She studied her sleeping guest for several minutes before her full bladder forced her to back away.

In her room a few minutes later, Fiona smiled to see neat piles of clean laundry, folded and stacked upon her bed. A momentary twinge of guilt passed through her when she realized Meg had not only finished her laundry after she nodded off, but she must have taken care of the kittens during the night too. Despite the crick in her neck, she was more rested than she had been in a long time.

Fiona completed her morning routine, before emerging from her room in fresh jeans and a T-shirt, invigorated, happy, and more than a little ravenous. It was strange to have an overnight guest and she wondered what to do. Would it be rude to eat breakfast without her? Hunger pangs gave her no choice. She walked stealthily past Meg who was still sleeping soundly, and considered their options for breakfast. A quick survey of her cupboards inspired nothing, and a lonely slice of dried out pizza sat orphaned among the left-over Thai food, expired eggs, beer, and useless condiments in the otherwise bare refrigerator. She was a pathetic host, and didn't think she could wait long enough to cook anything, anyway. Pregnancy had definitely unleashed a demon hunger within her. She decided to run out and grab some food while Meg slept. Gathering her keys, she quietly slipped out through the door, and made her way to Helga's in the early morning sunshine.

The café was moderately busy for a Saturday morning and Fiona took her place in line. She recognized the cashier as the barista who had made the coffee the day before. Fiona had been served by her many times, but she'd always been a little intimidated by her. She gave off a street smart aura that went beyond the style of her clothes or makeup, which Fiona could never aspire to. Today the woman was sporting a hipster look of black dyed hair in schoolgirl ponytails, and whiter-than-white skin showcasing large, generously lined eyes with false lashes. They'd exchanged coffee orders and an occasional smile, but they'd never engaged in small talk, so when the barista spoke to her after taking her order, Fiona was surprised.

"You're the woman who took the kittens yesterday." The barista selected the muffins Fiona pointed to in the case, along with two large portions of spinach quiche from a tray. Without having to look at the handwritten nametag, adorned with several safety pins featuring skull and crossbones pendants, Fiona knew her name was Betty.

Fiona nodded and fished her card out of her wallet.

"It's so cool you're taking care of them." Betty looked up through thick, evenly cut bangs. "I wish I could take one—when they're older, of course. Meg said you guys were looking for a more permanent place to take them.

Good thing she's a vet, huh? God, she's incredible. Beautiful and smart. It's so weird she wants to work here. I don't mind, though. I don't mind at all."

Fiona smiled and wondered if she and Meg had something going on. Fiona couldn't picture them together, but under the thick makeup, visible tattoos, and multiple piercings, Betty was a beautiful woman, if a little on the young side. The twinge of jealousy Fiona felt surprised her.

"Yeah. Meg's great and the kittens seem to be doing well." Fiona tried to ignore the green-eyed monster she had no right to feel. "I figured out how to feed them, but I think I'm going to have to turn them over to someone who knows what they're doing."

"Yeah. It's a lot of work." Betty said from over her shoulder, as she poured coffee from the industrial sized brewing vats behind the counter. "One of my cats had kittens when I was a kid. They meowed all night."

"They were mostly quiet last night." Fiona was careful not to say anything about Meg spending the night.

"Well, the food's on the house." Betty refused the card Fiona held out to her. "And if you need any help with the kittens, let me know. I already told Meg, but you can count on me if you need anything."

"Thanks. That's really nice of you." Touched by the gesture and the offer of help, Fiona took the bag and coffee tray Betty held out to her.

30

AFTER FEEDING AND POOPING THE kittens, Meg washed and dried her hands in Fiona's bathroom. The apartment was quiet in the early morning. She studied her reflection in the mirror. She looked tired but her hair wasn't a mess. She was wondering if she should go back to Vi's apartment, when she heard someone at the front door. They sounded like they had a key, and Meg wondered if her presence in the apartment would be a surprise to whoever it was.

After Fiona had fallen asleep on the couch the night before, Meg had debated whether she should go home. They hadn't discussed her staying the night, but she hadn't wanted to leave the job of managing the kittens to Fiona without talking about it first. She was glad she'd stayed. The kittens had woken for feedings several times during the night and Fiona hadn't stirred once. When Meg woke to the kittens' meows this last time, Fiona wasn't on the couch, and when Meg went to the bathroom she noticed Fiona's bedroom door was closed. She wondered if she should knock on Fiona's bedroom door to tell her someone was there.

Whoever was at the door was having a difficult time with the lock. Meg figured hiding in the bathroom would look more suspicious than anything else, so she went to help. She turned the knob but the lock was sticking because the doorframe was so swollen from the humidity. Meg forced the lock and pulled the door open. Fiona stood on the door step with her hands full and a surprised look on her face. Her keys fell to the ground with a clatter against the metal threshold.

"Let me help." Meg's voice was husky from sleep. Fiona stepped to the side to let her pick up the keys. She recognized the bag the food was in. "I smell quiche!"

"I didn't have anything here besides the leftover Thai food. Did I wake you?" Fiona carried the food over to the table. She looked fresh and well-rested even in the dim light of the closed-up apartment. She opened the blinds and the room was filled with golden sunshine. The room was transformed, cheerier in the morning light. Colorful accents brought the place to life.

"I fed the kittens." Meg peeked into the bag. "I didn't know you left. I thought you were in your bedroom. I was relieved to see it was you when I opened the door. I wasn't sure if I was going to be greeted by a jealous girlfriend or something."

Fiona handed her a cup of coffee. "Jealous girlfriend?"

"If you were in your bedroom, and the person at the door had keys…" Meg lifted her shoulders.

"Oh, yeah, I get it. There's no girlfriend."

"Boyfriend?" Meg looked pointedly at Fiona's belly.

"Definitely no boyfriend." Fiona sipped her coffee. "I thought we covered all this last night."

Meg didn't think a refresher on how babies were made was necessary. She was relieved there was no significant other, but she'd be lying if the mystery of Fiona's pregnancy didn't pique her curiosity. She wasn't about to pry, though.

"Yeah, we did. This quiche is the bomb." Meg changed the subject and Fiona removed the food from the bag.

"I met Betty. She didn't let me pay for it."

"She feels like crap about the cat."

"Why?" Fiona went to the kitchen and returned with forks.

"She was the one who slammed the lid. She cried about it through the rest of our shift yesterday."

"Oh, poor thing." Fiona stopped mid-forkful. "She didn't say anything. I'll admit I was super pissed at whoever did it at first. But honestly, how were they to know?"

"Exactly what I told her. It didn't help, though."

"Well, I guess I can understand." Fiona took her first bite of the quiche. She rolled her eyes in ecstasy. "This is *so* good!"

"Thanks!" Meg laughed at Fiona's puzzled look. "It's Karma's recipe, but I mixed it up last night before I left. Betty cooked it this morning."

"Excellent team effort, then!" Fiona dug in with gusto. "Oh, by the way, thanks for taking care of the kittens during the night. And for doing my laundry. I didn't mean to fall asleep on you."

"It was my pleasure. The kittens are easy and I'll do your laundry anytime in trade for breakfast delivery."

"You're on!" Fiona laughed.

"So, what are your plans for the day? I have to be at the coffee shop at eight, but I can stop by during my lunch break and I'm free after four, so I can watch the kittens if you have stuff you need to do." Meg didn't want to overstay her welcome, but the kittens were a lot of work, some of it which Fiona couldn't do.

"Thanks, but I have nothing happening until Tuesday when I have to go back to work. I was planning on going to a co-worker's Independence Day party, but the kittens are a good excuse to miss it. From experience, I'd be the only single person there."

Meg would have volunteered to go with her, but since she hadn't asked her, she didn't.

"Well, I'll get out of your hair then. How 'bout I come by after work and poop the kittens? They should be good until then."

"Sounds fantastic. You're not in my hair, by the way. I like hanging out with you. How about I make you dinner tonight? You know—to reward you for doing the dirty work."

Meg was glad to have plans to see her again. "Sounds like I'm getting the better end of the bargain is what it sounds like! I'll see you around five then."

Meg finished off the rest of her coffee, picked up her bag of clean laundry, and walked across the street to her apartment.

31

FIONA PEEKED THROUGH THE BLINDS and watched Meg cross the street. She watched the sidewalk for several minutes after Meg disappeared from view. The sudden emptiness of her apartment was a gaping void behind her, so she continued to stand there quietly, staring out of the window. It didn't take long before she became oblivious to the passersby, but she couldn't have said what was on her mind as she stared into the distance. Sometime later she was happy to be rescued from her mindless trance by the sight of Meg standing on the cement stairs leading to her door. Meg returned her gaze with a strange half-smile. Fiona smiled back, and went to meet Meg at the front door.

"Hey you! You were totally zoned-out there."

"Yeah. I can be a hard-core space case. Did you forget something?"

"My phone." Meg picked it up from the table next to the couch and cleared her throat. "Do you do it often?"

"Do what?"

"The zoning out."

The unexpected scrutiny made Fiona uneasy. "Not really. Only when I don't want to think about the more dreary aspects of my life." Fiona tried to dispel her unease by making fun of her situation. Her joke fell flat, even to her.

Meg stared at the phone in her hand, looking like she wanted to say something but feeling uncomfortable about it. And why wouldn't she? Fiona was aware she'd been being painfully vague and it put Meg in a weird position.

Meg seemed to gather herself. "Fiona, you haven't told me much about the situation you're in, but from what I do know, you have some serious things you need to figure out." She paused for a few seconds before continuing. "Tell me to shut up if you want to, but I like you, and I think it's important you face things now before you run out of choices." She said it gently and Fiona knew she was concerned. She realized at that moment that she trusted Meg. She wouldn't judge her if she told her more about the situation. Well, she *probably* wouldn't.

Meg looked like she was surprised at her own frankness. Fiona wanted to tell her it was okay, but at the same time, she wanted to ignore it. It was her way of dealing with hard things—pretending like they didn't exist. Old habits die hard. She took a deep breath instead.

"I know," she said softly. "I'll tell you all about it if you want. But first, I have to do some facing of things like you suggested. Don't worry. A couple of minutes of staring into the abyss this morning doesn't mean I'm going to avoid it all together."

"Um, Fiona, unless you left and came back, you were in the same spot for over twenty minutes. I watched you from the step for at least five minutes before you even realized I was there. It was a little freaky, like you'd left your body or something."

Fiona found it hard to believe. Twenty minutes? It was weird even for her. She tried to relax. "I must have zoned out hard, then."

"I'd say so. I was beginning to think you were asleep standing up." Meg laughed uneasily. "You were staring right through me."

Fiona wanted to say there was no way she wouldn't notice Meg, but obviously she had. She sighed. "As tired as I've been lately, sometimes I'd love the ability to sleep with my eyes open. Especially at work." Her second attempt at lightening the mood went down like a lead balloon.

Meg gave her a half-smile but it didn't erase the concern in her eyes. "Well, I've got my phone. I'll get out of your hair. I hope the kittens let you take a nap or something."

Fiona sensed an uncertainty in Meg. "You're not in my hair." She reached out and ran her hand up and down Meg's arm. "I enjoy spending time with you."

The smile Meg gave her reached her eyes. "Me, too." She picked up the sketchbook. "Do you mind if I leave this here? I don't have time to swing by my place before work and I don't have anywhere to store it there. Betty's sort of nosey."

Fiona grinned. "Sure, but I can't promise not to snoop, myself."

"You can snoop all you want, but Betty, well, Betty is Betty. Anyway, I'm not sure how good any of it is." Meg's eyes landed on her empty cup. "Is that my coffee cup? I'll take it with me. You know, recycle, reuse, reduce—save the planet, and all!"

Fiona, who was closer to the table, handed the cup to Meg, who was standing at the door. "Have a great day at work, dear. Dinner will be ready at five." Fiona surprised both of them by giving Meg a quick peck on the cheek as she handed her the cup.

"Yep. Gotta bring home the bacon!" said Meg, not skipping a beat. She even managed an imaginary tip of her hat as she shut the door.

32

IT HAD ONLY BEEN A brief kiss, but Meg's skin tingled where Fiona's lips had touched her. She couldn't remember how she'd responded, it had been such a shock. She hoped it wasn't anything stupid, but it probably was. She waved at Betty, who had been there since six a.m. for the opening shift and was taking a customer's order. It was unusual for Betty to open, but the schedule was all out of whack with people being sick or on holiday. Meg rounded the counter and grabbed her apron off the hook in the breakroom.

"Your girlfriend came into the shop this morning."

Meg took her spot at the espresso machine and pulled her apron over her head. Betty held out a cup with an order written on it. Meg ignored the cup, put her hands on her hips, and smiled at her.

"Good morning. I'm fine, thanks for asking. And you?"

Betty rolled her eyes. "I'm up before noon. How do you think I am? I'm curious about your girlfriend, though."

Meg took the cup and placed it next to the espresso machine. She tied her apron and started making the coffee. "I don't have a girlfriend."

Beth pursed her lips. "So, it wasn't you she was buying breakfast for? I was all sorts of impressed with your Casanova moves yesterday, but now I'm disappointed."

Meg leaned over and whispered: "Your customers will be disappointed if you don't start taking their orders."

"You suck," Betty whispered back, before turning her attention to the short line.

"How are the kittens?" Betty handed the next order to Meg.

"They're doing well, with healthy appetites."

"I couldn't sleep last night thinking about the mother cat. I feel so bad."

"Betty, it wasn't your fault."

"I keep telling myself that, but it doesn't change anything."

They kept working for several minutes, Betty taking orders and Meg making the drinks, until there was a short break in customers. Saturday mornings were always busy, even on holiday weekends. Meg wiped down the machine and Betty straightened the merchandise by the register before she picked up a pen, spinning it through her fingers.

"So, she's not your girlfriend?"

Meg emptied the knock box into an empty coffee bean bag. Taylor sent the used grinds to local urban gardens. "I just met her."

Betty flipped the pen in the air and caught it, spinning it through her fingers. "My last three serious relationships started as one night stands."

"One night stands may be your M.O. but they aren't mine."

Betty dropped the pen. "Come on. You never had a one night stand?"

"Sure I have, but I don't sleep with people I like right away."

"Oh! So, you admit you like her?"

She did. At first, she'd been attracted to her because she was pretty. Her smile and laughter were contagious. But then she'd discovered how smart and compassionate she was. The way she'd handled the woman who hit the cat was amazing. So far, Fiona was absolutely intriguing. The pregnancy thing was a shocker. If she wasn't planning on moving in a few weeks, would she want to date her? It didn't matter. She *was* leaving.

"I do. But she's got some stuff going on and I'm leaving in a few weeks."

Betty made a face and waved her hand. "So you have some fun for a few weeks. What does she have going on? Those guys we saw her with yesterday? Is she seeing one or both of them?"

"She's not seeing anyone."

"She doesn't date women?"

"She's a lesbian."

Betty cocked an eyebrow. "I don't see a problem then."

A customer came in and Betty took their order. Meg thought about what dating a pregnant woman would be like. Would Fiona even consider it? What about the kiss? It had been brief and only on the cheek, but Fiona *had* kissed her. Some full on lip locks hadn't affected her as much as that peck on the cheek. There was definitely some sort of chemistry going on between them, but did she really want to go there?

"Can I tell you something in confidence?" Meg asked when there was another break in customers.

Betty's head whipped around. "You slept with her, didn't you? I knew it!"

"I did not sleep with her." Meg turned back to the machine. "Never mind."

Betty grabbed her wrist. "No! No! You can totally trust me. I have kept secrets that would put people in prison if I told anyone. I am a lock box, the place where secrets remain. Come on. Tell me."

"I don't know…" Meg pulled her arm away.

Betty shook her hair back. "Hey, it's cool. You don't need to spill your guts to me. I joke around a lot, but I'm actually a good listener. If you want to talk about something, I'm here for you."

Meg hesitated. She did want to talk about it and she liked Betty. "Well, I don't know if she wants anyone to know. So, please keep this between you and me?"

"Absolutely." Betty turned an invisible key in front of her mouth.

"She's pregnant."

"Oh, wow." Betty fell back against the counter. "I didn't see that coming."

"Me either."

"And you said she isn't seeing anyone?"

"Yep."

"Are you sure she's a lesbian?" Betty crossed her arms.

Meg nodded. "She told me."

"So, how did she get…?" Betty cradled her hands in front of her belly.

"I don't know. She hasn't told me."

"Interesting. There *is* technology."

Meg stuck her hands in her apron and lifted her shoulders. "None of my business. The thing is, I'm not sure how I feel about dating a pregnant woman."

Betty pointed at her. "It *would* be your business if you started dating. You *do* want to date her, right?"

"If the pregnancy thing hadn't come up, I might have asked her out, yes. Except I'm leaving. There's that, too."

Betty nodded. "Well, maybe you can hang out and see what happens. You leaving sort of limits how far things can go anyway."

"True. Maybe we can enjoy each other's company. No expectations."

"I personally like no expectations." Betty smiled.

33

FIONA LOCKED THE DOOR AFTER Meg left and dropped onto the sofa. She pulled her legs up under her and thought about the quick kiss she'd given Meg. Her lips tingled and the smell of Meg's unique fragrance lingered in her memory. She sighed and opened the sketchbook. The painting she's seen in Meg's room had already demonstrated her talent, but she was amazed at what she saw on the pages of the book she held in her hands. Most of the drawings were of people, although there were a few objects and even a couple of abstracts. Fiona knew very little about art, but she did know the sketches were good. All of them, even the barest of outlines, conveyed feeling, and Fiona knew that what she was looking at was, in a sense, Meg's journal. She probably didn't intend it as such, but the stories told in some of the pictures were personal, and Fiona was honored Meg trusted her with them.

Fiona pored over the book and noticed that, like the painting, none of the women in the sketches had faces—they were either undrawn or purposefully obscured. Initially she assumed it was because Meg didn't like to draw faces, until she got to the last one. The sketch of her. Meg had drawn her sleeping with her head resting on the arm of the sofa. The expression on her face in the sketch conveyed tenderness and vulnerability. Fiona wondered what Meg had been feeling when she drew it.

When the kittens started to stir, Fiona finally put the sketchbook aside to tend to them.

Once the feeding was complete, she decided she would put her contemplative mood to good use. She fetched her journal from her room and went back to the sofa. After wasting several minutes staring at the leather-bound book in her lap, she opened it to the next blank page. Placing pen to paper, the familiar resistance to think about her situation returned. Frustrated, she almost tossed the journal to the side, but instead she mentally braced herself and consciously held the door open in her mind.

Overwhelmed, a myriad of feelings swept through her and she found it difficult to focus on a single, coherent thought. In an effort to stop her head from spinning, Fiona turned to the last entry in her journal. It was the entry from the night of the pregnancy tests.

I took a test and I failed it.

The understatement of the words embarrassed her.

She remembered the first moment she suspected she was pregnant. She'd been getting ready for work and felt a little off. Attributing it to not having eaten breakfast yet, she'd powered through, blow-drying her hair, when, out of nowhere, sudden nausea brought her to her knees in front of the toilet. In that moment, she went from thinking the chances of her being pregnant were impossible, to maybe-possible, to a couple weeks later and seven tests later, holy-shit-I-guess-it's-time-to-face-the-facts-I'm-fucking-pregnant-possible.

She thought about the night she took the pregnancy tests.

Aside from the sudden nausea, she'd been sleeping more than usual, but it never seemed enough. She was ravenous all the time, even though the smell of most food made her want to hurl. Other times, she couldn't eat enough, especially pizza. Oh, and her nipples. Her unbelievably sensitive nipples. She'd become overwhelmingly aware of them. And finally, as much as she hated the term, there was no better description for it—she was horny. Surprisingly, before the hair-drying incident, even with so many indications, it hadn't crossed her mind she may be pregnant. Even when she missed her period, the idea was so farfetched that pregnancy didn't even dawn on her.

The thing was, what had happened between her and Mike—the absurd, awkward, very unsexy groping they'd done—had hardly been sex. They'd both been drunk. She wasn't even sure he'd even reached the target, truth be told. She shuddered in embarrassment. Or was it horror?

Either way, when the sudden nausea hit her, the suspicion took hold.

She was running low on deodorant anyway, so she stopped by the CVS on her way home from work and picked some up, along with a 5-pack of store brand pregnancy tests that were promptly deposited next to the bathroom sink and left untouched for a week. Then, last Friday, she'd needed the deodorant and saw the box she'd been ignoring. Expecting a relieved laugh, she took out one of the tests.

She hadn't even finished washing her hands after taking it when the results window started to display a big fat *YES*, though it was supposed to take up to five minutes. Thinking the test had to be defective, she took another one and received the same result. The same with the remaining tests—*YES, YES*, and *YES*. But with each positive result, her disbelief grew stronger. Convinced it was a defective batch, she went back down to the CVS and bought the most expensive test they had. She had her pants half-off before she even got to the bathroom. The little pink '+' in the results window on the two tests she took from the brand name kit confirmed what she'd seen from the first five. She was pregnant. Disbelief turned to shock, and shock turned to fear. What the fuck was she going to do?

The night of the seven tests, Fiona went into her dark living room, sat on her couch, and checked out. She tried to write in her journal, but when it didn't go as well as she'd hoped, she zoned out all weekend long. She didn't change out of her pajamas. She didn't shower. She barely ate—even when hunger pangs caused her stomach to ache. She slept or sat in her living room—sometimes on the couch, sometimes in the recliner—and spaced out. On Monday, she almost made up a contagious illness, but instead she went into work and kept herself busy. It was a good way to not think about her situation.

Now, a week later, with what felt like her whole life behind her and an abyss ahead of her, she sat in her living room. But this time, she did think about her situation.

It took her a while to realize it, but while she was actually *thinking* about everything, she didn't *feel* anything. If she had to describe it, she'd say she was blank and detached.

She picked up her pen and opened her journal. She sat with pen poised. Several minutes passed before she wrote anything down.

What should I feel?

She stared at the words she'd written, trying to find the emotions she thought she should feel. Nothing would come. Finally, she took a guess and wrote something down.

Anger?

She didn't feel it, but it was something at least.

She was surprised to hear the kittens stir again. Hadn't she just fed them?

A look at the clock said it was almost half-past four. Somehow the afternoon had slipped by without her realizing it. Shit. She had promised Meg dinner, but she had to feed the kittens. There was no way she could get something started in time. Resigned, Fiona prepared the formula and sat down next to the box to feed the kittens.

By the time Fiona had finished with the kittens and had opened the pantry door to look for something to make for dinner, there was a knock at the door.

34

MEG WAS NERVOUS. GOING TO Fiona's house wasn't a date, but it sort of felt like one. And she was enough of a dork to have picked up some flowers on her way over. As soon as she did she doubted herself, almost throwing them away twice before she found herself at Fiona's front door. If she hadn't already rung the bell she would have considered throwing them away a third time, but instead, she hid them behind her back.

When the door opened, Fiona's smile was as sweet as she remembered and she timidly produced the small multi-colored bouquet of Gerbera daisies from behind her back.

"A little something for staying at home and taking care of the kids all day."

"My favorites!" Fiona smiled and took them. "Thank you!"

Meg was glad she'd kept them. "I figured you probably had a rough day, plus it's the least I can do since you're making dinner."

"Well, I suck. I haven't even started dinner yet." Fiona backed up to let Meg pass.

"Is there any of the Thai food left?" Meg didn't care so much about dinner—it was hanging out with Fiona she was looking forward to.

"Oh, yeah, plenty. Enough for a couple of nights, actually." Fiona looked relieved. "Are you sure, though? I can whip something up…"

"I love leftover Thai food almost as much as I love leftover lasagna—which is a lot." It was the absolute truth.

Fiona bounced on the balls of her feet, making her look like a little kid. "You're the awesomest. Flowers, poop expert, graceful acceptance of an inept host. I don't deserve you."

"True." Meg smiled to let her know she was joking.

Fiona laughed. "Let me find a vase for these. You're so sweet!" She took the flowers into the kitchen. "How was your day?"

Meg followed her into the kitchen. "It was good. Busy. Betty gave me crap all afternoon, though."

"About what?" Fiona placed the flowers in a vase full of water in the center of the dining room table, before walking back into the kitchen to get the food ready.

"The coffee cup. She noticed your name written on it from this morning… and, well, let's just say she doesn't believe I slept on the recliner last night." A blush crept up her neck.

Fiona grimaced. "Is it going to be a problem for you?"

"No. Why would it be?"

Fiona pursed her lips in a way Meg found quite cute. "Betty has a crush on you."

"She's a kid." Meg took dishes out of the cupboard while Fiona prepared the food.

"A very attractive kid, whom I imagine is at least eighteen." Fiona put a plate of food to heat in the microwave. She rested her elbows on the counter and cocked an eyebrow at Meg.

Meg laughed. "She's twenty-one. A very mature twenty-one, I'll admit, but she's a kid."

"Don't forget attractive," Fiona reminded her.

"She's attractive, yes." Meg wondered what Fiona was getting at. Was she worried she and Betty were an item? Or, worse, was she actually interested in Betty? Meg didn't like the idea at all. "Do you want me to put in a good word for you with her?"

Fiona looked surprised. "What? No! I was wondering if maybe you would be into her if you knew she was into you."

"Even if she was, and I'm not convinced she is, I'm definitely not interested. I think she puts off a flirty vibe to lots of people. It's part of her thing. But she's young. She needs to play the field, try things on, see what's out there. She doesn't need to hitch herself to a twenty-six year old who will probably cramp her style. Otherwise, she'll never know what she wants when she's twenty-six herself."

Fiona's expression relaxed and she nodded, appearing to agree with Meg. Meg got the feeling Fiona had more to say, but she turned her attention to the food instead.

"So, a little of everything?" Fiona asked, as she started scooping food onto the other plate.

35

FIONA AND MEG SETTLED DOWN at the dining room table to enjoy their leftovers. A comfortable quiet had descended upon them moments earlier as they performed a graceful dance while they prepared their plates in the small kitchen. Fiona had never been so comfortable in another person's presence outside of family, which had ended with Aunt Corny's death. The unique connection was unfamiliar and scary. Bringing it up with Meg was also scary. It was too soon to feel, let alone voice, such a thing, especially with the dark cloud of uncertainty hovering over her future. That alone told her she had no business acting on her burgeoning feelings. Despair threatened to overwhelm her, but she tamped it down and asked Meg more about her day. Meg didn't seem to sense the tumult within her, for which Fiona was grateful.

Fiona pointed to the colorful daisies in the middle of the table. "I love Zoom Zoom Bloom."

"How did you know where they were from? I discovered the shop today. The steel buckets of colorful daisies on the stoop drew me in."

"The wire wrap on the stems." Fiona used her fork to point out the thin wire twisted up the long stem to keep the heavy heads from drooping. "They're the only shop I know who takes the trouble to match the wire color to the flower. Quality is in the details. "

Fiona watched Meg regard her for a moment.

"What?" Self-consciousness washed over her. She wiped her mouth. "Do I have something on my face?"

"Actually, you've got something right here." Meg pointed to the corner of her own mouth.

Fiona wiped her mouth. "Did I get it?"

"Other side."

"Ugh!" Fiona was embarrassed, wiping a bit of noodle from her lip. "You can't take me anywhere."

Meg laughed. "Before the unfortunate noodle interruption, I was about to tell you, you're a woman of startling contrasts."

"What do you mean?" Fiona was amused.

"Well, my experience is that most lawyers don't…" But Meg didn't finish.

Fiona tried to prompt her. "Most lawyers don't what?"

"What I mean to say is, lawyers usually lack, um, they don't usually…" Fiona was amused to see Meg put her fork down and pull her hands down her face in frustration before she tried one more time. "Attorneys are awesome people, but they can be a little stiff sometimes. And you aren't. That's all that I meant."

"Because I'm a messy eater? I promise I can behave myself in a restaurant." Fiona enjoyed seeing Meg flustered.

Meg chuckled. "You're funny. It's other stuff. You notice details like wire colors on flowers and kitten belly buttons. Basically, what I should have said was, I've been around lawyers my whole life. Most of them are stuffy and rigid, but you're not."

Fiona put down her fork. "Interesting. I've never been a very introspective person, but lately I've worried I was getting a little set in my ways—going through life with blinders on, you know? I don't want to be that person." She waved her hands in front of her belly. "I guess my situation has inspired me to re-evaluate stuff. It's a little daunting, I have to admit."

"I think it would be weird if you didn't get a little introspective, you know, in light of things."

"I'm playing everything by ear right now. I have no idea how things will go." She wasn't ready to talk about it yet. Hell, she could barely think about it. She picked up her fork. "But enough about me. Tell me why you decided to become a vet and not a lawyer in the tradition of your family. Was it the stiff thing you mentioned? You're definitely not a stiff lawyerly person! Or was it simply you didn't want to go into the same profession as your brother?"

Fiona was grateful Meg followed her redirect. "It's simple. I love animals. Only people who honestly love animals choose to go to school for as long as we do, foregoing most of the perks of a medical doctor."

"Perks?"

"You know, little things like prestige and much higher pay. Vets definitely aren't into it for the money, that's for sure. Especially small town vets."

Fiona was intrigued by Meg's answer. "It sounds like vets are in it for the right reasons. I can honestly say it isn't the case with all lawyers. Sometimes we hate our clients, but we're in it for the money, most of us."

Meg shook her head. "I couldn't do it. I love animals. All of them. Well, maybe not arachnids. Spiders creep me out, but don't tell anyone." She winked and it gave Fiona a little flutter in her stomach. "When I was a kid, I rescued stray animals. But when I was in junior high, Uncle Samuel, my dad's brother, married Aunt Claudia, and it changed my life. It shocked the family when he left the family law firm in Seattle to practice law in Okanogan, where my aunt has her clinic. Like you, he defies the lawyer stereotype. He's super laid back. You remind me of him a little."

Fiona liked the comparison. "Most people would describe me as anything but laid back."

"Maybe relaxed is more like it."

She smiled. "It's probably the company."

Meg shook her head. "Maybe. Anyway, the first time we went to visit my aunt and uncle, I fell in love with the clinic. After the first trip, my mom let me go out to Uncle Samuel's and Aunt Claudia's for part of every summer. And now I'm going to be my aunt's partner."

"Where is it again? Oka-something? When do you leave?" Fiona hoped her expression didn't show her disappointment. She didn't want her new friend to leave. She'd just found her and Washington was on the other side of the country!

"Okanogan. It's a small town in the central part of Washington near the northern border. Way out in the boonies. I'll probably head back sometime in September."

Fiona pushed the last of the food around on her plate. "From New York to the boonies. Quite the contrast."

"Yeah. New York is great—Seattle is better—but I like small town life. I'll get my city fix when I work at the Seattle vet hospital twice a month. I don't think I can go cold turkey."

"I can sort of relate, although it's the opposite for me. I grew up in a small town. I want to live in the city and visit the country." Fiona voiced the story she'd believed for years, but the truth was, she wasn't sure what she wanted now. She was at a crossroads and her feet felt like they were nailed to the middle of the intersection. "I've heard Washington's pretty."

Meg's eyes sparkled. "It's beyond pretty. It's beautiful." They gathered their empty plates and took them into the kitchen. "Back to you. Tell me about your job."

"Threadlocke and Guernsey hired me three years ago as a paid intern while I was finishing up law school, which turned into a clerk position. They mentored me until I passed the bar and gave me a job as an attorney. I sort of feel tied to them because they've invested so much in me."

Meg started rinsing dishes. "Where would you go if you weren't with them?"

"I'm not sure. T&G is a great firm. Exceptionally good to their staff. They don't handle the types of cases I want to handle, though. They're focused on corporate, which is mostly administration. I want something more high-powered." Fiona reached around and turned off the water. "Out. I'll do dishes later."

"Yes, ma'am!" Meg smiled and dried her hands on the hem of Fiona's T-shirt as Fiona dragged her out of the kitchen and made her sit down.

She settled back into her seat laughing, pulling on the edge of her now damp shirt. "You got me all wet."

Meg cocked an eyebrow. "I do have that effect on women."

She blushed. "You know what I mean!"

Meg shook her head. "Sorry. It just came out. So, you want to go to court and badger the witnesses and trick the defendant into confessing?"

"Well, when you say it like that, it sounds kind of dorky, like I want to be a superhero or something." She winked. "Which I do."

"Don't we all, in our own ways?" Meg leaned forward and rested her chin on her hands.

Fiona thought about it. She'd been joking, but Meg had a point. "True. So, yes, it's exactly what I want to do. I want to strategize, build cases, and provide powerful representation for my clients, whether it's working for the defense or the prosecution. I didn't go to law school to file incorporation paperwork and initiate legal name changes."

Meg's eyebrows rose. "Ah, so you desire the excitement and drama. Do you like criminal law?"

Fiona considered it. "Not criminal law exclusively, but some. I want to work at a firm representing high-profile cases. T&G represents wealthy corporate clients who want high-quality legal services, but they don't get many high-profile cases."

"So, in the meantime you're filing name changes and filling out incorporation paperwork waiting for the sexier work?"

"Yep. I do anything they give me. I take all the cases the other lawyers don't want to take. I figure it's how I'll hone my skills and ingratiate myself to the partners."

Fiona moved over to the sofa where it was a little more comfortable. Meg followed. They each took a side, sat down, and pulled their legs up so they faced each other with their backs against the overstuffed arms. Fiona hugged her knees to her chest and put her chin on her knees while Meg sat cross-legged, with one arm lying across the back of the couch. Fiona imagined they looked like long-time best friends settling in for a good talk.

Meg pushed her hair behind her ear. "It sounds like you have a solid plan laid out. How does the baby factor in?"

Fiona blew out a loud breath and dropped her forehead to her knees. Her mood went from relaxed to anxious in a heartbeat. She wondered if Meg knew how close to the bone her question was. She was scared, especially since she didn't have all the answers yet. But everything she knew about Meg was safe, and Fiona was so tired of keeping everything inside. Having Meg near was a comfort, but she didn't want to scare her away with her issues.

"Hey." Meg touched her leg. "You don't have to get into all this if you don't want to. We can switch channels if you want."

"I'm that obvious, huh?" Fiona peeked up with a nervous laugh. "I haven't talked to anyone about it yet. I'm not sure if I'm ready."

Meg rubbed Fiona's leg once and removed her hand. "I'm a good listener when you're ready."

Fiona lifted her head to see only acceptance in Meg's amazing blue eyes. It gave her the confidence she needed. "I did some of the thinking we talked about this morning." She hugged her legs more tightly to her chest. "Am I coming off as much of an emotional wreck to you as I do to myself?"

Meg tilted her head. "You're fine. It just seems like you have a lot going on."

"You're probably thinking about running for the hills." Fiona joked but she had a hard time meeting Meg's eyes.

"I'm not planning on running anywhere, Fiona. Would it help if I promise to tell you if you make me uncomfortable?" Meg rested her hand on Fiona's knee.

Fiona took a bit of courage from the hand on her knee. She put her hand over it so Meg wouldn't take it away. "Sure. Sounds like a plan."

"How about you tell me why you chose to be a lawyer."

Fiona laughed. "It's kind of a funny story."

"I like funny stories."

"Well, believe it or not, I wanted to be a high-priced hooker before I decided to become a lawyer." Fiona watched Meg's face.

"A what?" Meg sputtered, shaking her head, looking like she was unsure of what she had heard.

"I know, I know." Fiona laughed.

"You certainly know how to start a story." Meg shook her head.

"Books are to blame."

"You'll have to explain."

Fiona smiled. She'd never told anyone this story before. Not even Aunt Corny. "I was twelve years old. I grew up in Pottstown, Pennsylvania and we lived out in the country, close to the mine where my dad worked as foreman. I was an only child and there weren't any kids nearby, so I read a lot. And when I say a lot, I mean a *lot*. By the time I was twelve, I had read all the books the librarian would let me check out. I read so much, I had started to reread some of my favorites. So, you can imagine my delight when I found three storage boxes full of books in the attic of our house one day. I think they were left there by a previous owner. They weren't the kind of books my parents read, but when I asked my mom if I could read them, she shuffled through them and gave her approval. I'm not sure what she was thinking, though. Some of them were definitely a little too adult for a twelve year old. All summer I gorged myself on books by Stephen King, Jackie Collins, Michael Crichton, and many other authors who don't skimp on adult-themed detail. Besides acquiring a lifelong terror of vampires and possessed animals, I found myself drawn to life as a call girl after reading a book called *Sharkey's Machine*. I hardly remember what the book was about, but there was one character in it—"

"Let me guess. A high-priced hooker?" Meg suggested.

Fiona tapped the tip of her nose and laughed. "Bingo! She lived what, to my countrified mind, was 'The Life'. She was rich, glamorous, had a great high-rise apartment in the city. There was some mobster guy in the picture, but it seemed like she called the shots. Sure, she was a hooker, but she wasn't sleazy. She wasn't out on a street corner trading sex for drugs. She got to choose the guys she slept with. To my twelve-year-old, hormone-addled mind, sex was awesome. Everyone talked about it. Everyone wanted to do it. Why not do it for a living? So it became my plan, until—"

"Wait." Meg sounded incredulous. "Let me get this straight, you read a book and you decided to become a hooker? At twelve years old?"

"A *high-priced* hooker," Fiona corrected her. "But, then, I met Tammy and she opened my eyes. She took my nose out of a book and showed me what real life could feel like."

"She must have been some kid."

"She was." Fiona returned to a distant memory. "It was the beginning of summer vacation and my mom dropped me off at the library one day while she ran her errands. Usually I was the only kid there, but that day, sitting in the chair I normally sat in, was this tiny wisp of a girl I had never seen before. She knocked my socks off. She was so wonderfully cool and different. She didn't dress like the kids in my town. She had this long, wild blond hair and the greenest eyes I'd ever seen. Not boring like mine. A beautiful, brilliant green. The color of tree frogs. And they sparkled when she talked."

"Your eyes are anything but boring," Meg said.

Fiona smiled, pleased by the compliment. "Thank you. Anyway, I was captivated. When she asked me what I was staring at, I realized I had been standing there with my mouth literally hanging open. I almost died from embarrassment. I stammered something and then went to hide between the closest bookshelves. She followed me, though, and introduced herself. Somehow, I found my voice. She turned out to be nice and I found out she had moved there at the beginning of the summer. We discovered her dad worked with my dad and she was going to go to my school in the fall. Since she was new, I filled her in on the town, the school, who was cool as far as teachers and kids went, and who to avoid. We talked so much, the librarian told us to be quiet or leave. So, we left and walked around the block.

"The second time around the building, Tammy grabbed my hand and pulled me behind the library sign. The bushes hid us, and we sat on the cement foundation of the brick sign and talked. It didn't occur to me to wonder why we were there. I was just happy to be there with her. Who knows now what we talked about, but when Tammy asked if I had ever kissed anyone, my stomach fluttered. I considered lying. But the question was too important, so I told her the truth."

"And?" Meg sat up, rapt.

"I hadn't." Fiona shook her head. "But I told her I was sure I would be good when I did. I'd read lots of books about it."

"What did she say?"

"She asked me to prove it."

Meg licked her lips. "Did you?"

Fiona nodded. "Not a quick peck, either. I went all out on it. Open mouth. Tongue. Everything. And she kissed me back. Her arms slipped around me, and one of her hands even inched under the bottom of my shirt. It was incredible. It was like I had learned to fly. When she pushed me away, calling me a pervert, and ran away, I was in a daze. It had all happened so fast."

Meg slapped her own knee. "What? But she started it!"

"Yeah. I know. I didn't know how to feel."

"Pissed off. It's how *I* would have felt."

"I think I was more embarrassed than anything. Eventually, the hurt and anger set in. But that first kiss made me feel like nothing else ever had." Her skin tingled thinking about it.

Meg sighed. "Wow."

For a second or two Fiona was there, in the hidden spot behind the sign. "Later that summer, lying low while I figured out what my new feelings were about, I read *The Firm*. That's when I tossed the hooker dream and started thinking about becoming a high-powered lawyer."

"I'm glad you didn't read *Scarface*," Meg teased.

Fiona laughed. "I was so impressionable. At least the ethics of *The Firm* didn't rub off on me, right? I know now the new dream was a way to keep my confused mind off of things. I dove right in by charting out a career plan, complete with a spreadsheet pinned to my bedroom wall charting potential schools, curriculum, extracurricular activity, community service, etcetera. My mom got into it, too. She helped me find out more about law school."

"What happened with Tammy?" The look on Meg's face made Fiona laugh.

"I begged my mom to take me to the library almost every day the rest of the summer, but Tammy never came back. I did see her at school in the fall, though. I caught her looking at me sometimes, but otherwise she avoided me like the plague."

"Harsh."

Fiona shrugged. "It could have been worse. As far as I know, she never told anyone. I crushed on her hard all the way through middle school and high school, but nothing else happened—with her or any other girl—until the end of my senior year. Besides a lot of bad poetry." Fiona laughed self-consciously. Meg nodded her head, like she knew the feeling well, too. "I even dated a few guys, but never seriously. I was totally in the closet. Pennsylvania rural communities are pretty conservative today, so imagine a few years back."

"I was lucky to live in Seattle. It's hyper-liberal. It wasn't a cake walk, but I never needed to hide who I was," Meg said.

"I didn't know anyone like me, so I was afraid."

"What about Tammy?"

"She wasn't out. She always had boyfriends. For all I knew our kiss was her only experience with a girl."

"You never talked to her again?"

"Not until a few days before graduation. Tammy and I were both on the graduation dance committee and somehow we ended up outside the gym, hanging streamers. I figured we'd continue to ignore each other. It was a habit by then. But she surprised me and started making small talk. It was surreal after all those years. She asked me about my scholarship to Columbia, which had been announced at the senior awards assembly earlier in the day. Every time she looked at me, her green eyes would stop me cold. I could barely keep track of our conversation. Then, I looked up from whatever I was doing and she was staring at me. I got scared. She asked if I remembered the kiss. I shrugged. Even though I had relived our kiss just about every night since it happened, I didn't admit it to her. She asked if I was going up to the lake after graduation. Every year, the graduating class rented all of the cabins at the lake to celebrate. I told her I was planning to meet my friends up there, and she said she was, too. Then she asked if I wanted to drive up with her. I didn't know what to think. I actually thought about *Carrie*. Like she was planning something mean. I think I told her I already had a ride or something, but when we were putting away the ladders in the custodian's closet she kissed me again. I was shocked."

"I'll bet." Meg looked enthralled by the story. "What happened next?"

"Graduation was the next evening, and I couldn't wait for it to be over. Tammy's kiss had started a fire and I couldn't wait to be alone with her. I was terrified it was a trick, but deep down, I knew it wasn't. We talked on the phone all night, until early in the morning. I finally told her I would ride up with her. During the ceremony the next night, Tammy, who was two rows in front of me, kept turning around to look at me, which drew some attention, but I didn't care. My folks left the ceremony ahead of me and I told them I would get a ride and see them at home after the dance before I went up to the lake. After the dance, walking through the student parking lot with Tammy, I was as nervous as hell. We had talked so easily over the phone the night before and had been mostly friendly at the dance in front of all the other students, but when we were alone and I was getting into her car, I couldn't form a coherent sentence."

Meg pulled her knees to her chest. "Were you planning on sleeping with her?"

"I'm not sure what I was planning, actually. I was meeting my friends and she was meeting hers. We were all sharing the cabins. But I was hoping *something* would happen. The road to the lake ran by my house and we were going to stop and pick up my stuff on the way. She had her bag in the trunk. I remember her reaching over to hold my hand and being so aware of the heat between our palms. We were almost to my house when traffic stopped. It was dark outside, so she and I made out a little as we waited for traffic to break up. It was just as tingly as I remembered. At some point, when traffic hadn't moved and someone had set up some emergency floodlights ahead, I opened the door to see if I could see what was happening. A car was upside down in the river. I had no idea it was my parents'. Cars look different upside down and it was dark. We went over to watch what was happening. They had already pulled two people out and they were on the rocks by the river covered with blankets. I knew they weren't alive. It wasn't until they started winching the car out of the water and I saw the bumper stickers on the back bumper. One was an honor student sticker from my middle school and the other was a Phillies sticker. My dad was a huge Philly's fan. He didn't miss listening to a game." A lump lodged in her throat. It had been years but she hadn't told the story to many people.

Meg took Fiona's hand. "My god. What did you do?"

"I don't remember a whole lot. I know I ran down the bank to the river. I must have fallen at least once because I had gashes on my knees and hands the next day. A man tried to stop me, but I pushed past him. I went to my parents. I moved the blanket. Their eyes were open, but they were gone." Fiona wiped her eyes, which had welled up with tears.

"Oh, wow. I can't even imagine how horrendous that must have been for you."

Meg searched her face, but Fiona couldn't look at her. "I was hysterical at first. They sedated me in the ambulance. Afterward, I didn't cry at all until the funeral, where I cried until I collapsed." Fiona wiped away more tears. "I don't know why I'm crying now. I haven't cried about it in years. That week is such a blur to me now."

Meg squeezed her hand. "Sometimes things need to come out."

"Yeah." Fiona finally looked at Meg and physically shook herself. "I almost cancelled my trip to Thailand but I'm glad I didn't. I had moments where my grief overwhelmed me, but most of the time there was so much to see and do, I didn't have time to think about it. I stayed longer than I expected, and by the time I got home, my Aunt had already taken care of selling the house and storing all of their belongings. I came back in time to leave again for school. The first few years of college, I stayed with Aunt Corny in Ithaca during the summer, but when I started law school, I moved into this apartment. I went up to visit when I could, which was a lot since she was the only family I had left. It was on one of those visits that I first saw you in your uncle's coffee shop."

"I wish I had talked to you back then." Meg rested her chin on her knees.

"What stopped you?" Fiona knew her own reason was shyness. She didn't think Meg was very shy.

"We were always so busy. One time, though, I followed you out of the shop. But when I caught up to you, you turned around so abruptly, I lost my nerve." Meg laughed. "I walked right by, pretending to dig something out of my apron. I was working, so I walked around the block and went right back into the shop."

"Oh, my God!" Fiona covered her face with her hands. "I remember! I said hello as you walked by, but you didn't respond."

Meg looked surprised. "You did? I guess I was too embarrassed to hear you."

"How hilarious!" Fiona laughed. "I noticed you too, you know."

Meg cocked her head to the side. "It's weird how we ended up meeting here, huh?"

"Definitely." Fiona glanced at the box where the kittens slept.

"So, after Thailand…?"

Fiona had almost forgotten she was telling a story. She shrugged. "Nothing much, really. I went to college and passed the bar. I submerged myself in schoolwork—maybe more than I should have, because I didn't have much of a social life. I focused on getting an internship at a good firm when I got to law school, and I did. I wasn't a complete hermit, though. I had a few friends I hung out with sometimes. It's funny, my social life picked up during the months after law school when I was studying for the bar. It was probably the most grueling time academically, yet I saw more of my friends because we had study groups. I was working part time during the day at the firm and spending hours and hours with people from group at coffee shops, the library, and even bars, pouring over books and studying my ass off. Our group took the exam course together to prep for the February bar exam. It took until May to get our results. The wait was brutal. It was such a huge shock to go from studying non-stop, so hard, and for so long, to just… waiting. The Friday when the results posted, the study group website was absolute chaos with e-mails, posts, updates, and instant messages from everyone in our group. All but one of us passed. We all went to The Limerick Lounge to celebrate. It was such a huge high to have all those years of law school finally behind us. We were ready for the big time."

"Did you celebrate more than you should have?" Meg teased.

Fiona grimaced. "That's an understatement."

Meg groaned. "I still can't look at tequila without feeling a little queasy after I finished my undergrad degree."

Fiona groaned. "I can totally relate."

"Must have been your last hurrah, huh? I mean, since…" Meg looked at her middle.

She nodded and bit her lip. "Depends on what you mean, but I got pregnant that night."

Meg wasn't sure what to say. "I don't want to pry, but… um… how… I mean…"

She sighed. "I was so stupid." Fiona told Meg the rest of the story, how she'd been stupid and drunk, and how she'd felt sorry for Mike, agreeing to have sex with him. God! The clumsy groping, the uncomfortable pairing. She described how she'd immediately regretted it, the night of the seven pregnancy tests, and the difficulty of facing Mike again.

Meg listened without interruption, and when Fiona finished, she cleared her throat. "You haven't told him yet?"

"I did. Yesterday at the coffee shop."

"How did he take it?"

"He got up and walked away." Fiona ran her hand through her hair. It was a relief to tell someone about it, but now she worried that Meg thought she was messed up. And maybe she was.

Meg rested her forehead on her knees. "I feel like a schmuck for so blithely telling you how you needed to face your issues earlier today. Who am I to talk? It was presumptuous of me. I'm sorry."

"You were fine." Fiona stroked Meg's head. Her hair was so soft.

Meg looked up. "Look at you. Comforting me when it's your life we're talking about. Do you have any idea what you're going to do?"

Fiona hesitated. She worried Meg would get tired of hearing about her situation. "It helps talking to you. I haven't talked to anyone about it. It's nice to get it out." Fiona had to look away. She felt safe and cared for—something she missed more than she knew. She met Meg's amazing eyes after a moment. "The scariest thing is figuring out what's next. I can't seem to make myself go there."

"Sometimes it helps to list your options."

"I haven't even begun to think about options yet." Fiona sighed and ran her hand through her hair again. "I don't even know how I feel about it."

"What do you mean?"

Fiona stared at the ceiling, trying to find words to explain. "I feel blank inside. I don't know how to feel about any of it. If I don't know how I feel, how can I figure out what to do?" Even as she said it, her eyes welled up and an overwhelming sense of despair swept through her. She was afraid. She was angry. She was full of regret. More than anything, she was confused. Confused about what she should do. That wasn't blank. It was overwhelming. Her life plans had never featured a baby.

She was mortified when a sob escaped her throat and she buried her head in her hands, but she was powerless to stop crying once it started. Meg slid down to her side of the couch and pulled her into a hug. She sank into the warmth as she let despair consume her.

36

MEG'S HEART ACHED AS SHE held Fiona. She cradled her, one hand smoothing Fiona's hair, the other holding her tightly to her chest. Fiona pressed her face into her neck until her sobs faded and she relaxed in her arms. Meg continued to hold her until her breathing became steady and deep. The muscles in her arms began to complain, but she didn't let go; she settled back on the sofa to let Fiona lie more comfortably against her. Meg memorized her features as she slept peacefully in her arms. She pressed her lips to Fiona's forehead where she kept them until she started to nod off herself. At that point, Meg slowly stood with the sleeping woman cradled in her arms, and took her to the bedroom. As Meg lowered her onto the soft down comforter covering the bed, Fiona unconsciously tightened her hold around Meg's neck. Meg didn't have the heart to wake her, so she stretched out beside Fiona and continued to hold her.

Meg had almost drifted off when she heard the feeble cries of the kittens in the living room. It had been a few hours since they had last fed and she knew the kittens needed to eat, so she reluctantly extricated herself from Fiona's embrace. Meg moved quietly into the hall, leaving the bedroom door open a crack, and made her way into the kitchen to prepare the formula. When she approached the cardboard box, warm bottle in hand, six tiny heads bobbed to attention even though they couldn't see her. Their stubby little tails shook with anticipation as their little mouths opened and closed with their fervent cries for food.

After the kittens finished eating and she completed the glamorous job of pooping them, she went back to Fiona's room to check on her. Though she hadn't planned on it earlier, she decided to camp out on the sofa so she could tend to the kittens for the rest of the night. Fiona wasn't in any state to deal with them, and Meg wanted to be there if Fiona needed her.

She pushed the bedroom door open, and when the light from the bathroom across the hall spilt across the bed, Meg was surprised to see Fiona rise onto a bent elbow. She had gotten under the covers, and in the dim light, Meg watched the comforter slide down to expose a bare shoulder. Her heart skipped a beat before she noticed the strap to Fiona's tank top had slipped down. Fiona had changed into her pajamas.

"You okay in here?" Meg asked from the doorway.

Fiona squinted and put a hand up to block the light that was shining in from the doorway. Or was it to hide her tear-ravaged face? "I thought you left, and then I heard you humming to the kittens." Her voice was sleepy.

"Was I humming?" Meg rested her shoulder against the doorframe.

Fiona stifled a yawn. "I couldn't tell what it was, but it seemed familiar."

"Did it sound like this?" Meg walked to the foot of the bed while humming a verse of something she remembered from childhood. She rested her hands on the footboard of Fiona's sleigh bed as she finished the verse.

"Ah, *Molly Malone*. That's it." Fiona sang a bit to herself. "*In Dublin's fair city where girls are so pretty, I first set my eyes on sweet Molly Malone. As she wheeled her wheelbarrow, through streets broad and narrow, crying "Cockles and mussels! Alive, Alive Oh!"*

Fiona's voice was clear and sweet, just a touch off-key, and Meg's attraction to her doubled. She knew then; she was already in deeper than she thought.

"Aunt Corny used to sing it to me when I stayed the night at her house when I was a little girl. Did your mom used to sing it to you?"

Meg laughed at the thought of her mother singing. "My mom isn't much of a singer. She's on the very lawyerly side of the spectrum we spoke about last night. I honestly don't know where I picked it up. It's what comes out when I hum for comfort. I don't even know the words."

The women were quiet for a few moments. Meg continued to stand at the foot of the bed, looking down at her hands on the footboard, and Fiona dropped her head onto the pillow.

"Meg… would it be weird if I asked you to stay the night?"

It was just a question. There was nothing timid or needy in the sound of it. If there had been, Meg might have felt a little uncomfortable, but she understood Fiona's desire for company and she had already decided to stay anyway.

"Not at all. I had planned on camping out on the sofa to take care of the kittens anyway."

"Would you mind staying in here with me? I don't want to be alone."

Again, it was just a question.

"Sure." Meg rested her forearms on the footboard, the fingers of her hands laced loosely before her. Her casual posture belied her pounding heart. She didn't expect anything to happen between them, not with Fiona in the emotional space she was in, but it didn't minimize her growing attraction to her.

"I hope I'm not too much of a pain in the ass." Fiona drew the comforter up under her chin. "I usually prefer to be alone to deal with my problems, but there's something comforting about you."

"You're not being a pain at all." Meg didn't share that she usually retreated a little when people were in crisis, uncomfortable with her own ability to offer any comfort. Animals were easy. Humans were hard. But something about Fiona triggered a very different response and she wanted to help. "How are you feeling now? Do you need anything?"

Fiona draped an arm over her forehead. "I feel like I was hit by a truck, to be honest. But the nap helped."

"You're beautiful when you cry, you know." Meg didn't know why she said it, but it was true.

"Oh, come on." Fiona pulled the comforter over her head.

"Really. It broke my heart, but you are definitely beautiful when you cry. My fingers itched to draw you."

"I'm not sure I could look at a picture like that." Fiona pulled the covers back down. If the light had been on, Meg was sure she'd see Fiona blushing.

She backed out of the room. "I'll be right back with water and tissues."

"Thanks. You're my hero."

When Meg returned, she also brought ibuprofen and a wet, warm washcloth.

Fiona draped it over her eyes and lay back. "I'll pretend I'm at the spa and try to forget I smeared snot all over the front of your shirt earlier."

Meg was encouraged by Fiona's humor. "This T-shirt's seen worse. I'm going to shut off the lights and bring the kittens in here. I'll be back in a couple of minutes."

When Meg came back and put the box of sleeping kittens at the foot of the bed, Fiona was lying on her back with the warm washcloth over her eyes. Not knowing if Fiona was asleep or not, she stripped down to her tank top and panties and carefully climbed into bed.

As she settled in, Fiona rested a hand on her arm.

"This warm compress feels wonderful. Thanks for taking care of me."

Meg settled her hand over Fiona's, and loosely intertwined their fingers. Soon she heard the even sound of Fiona's breathing. She quietly got up and removed the washcloth from her closed eyes. She slipped back under the covers, but had a feeling that sleep would be a while coming as she tried to relax into the pillows.

Minutes later, she was breathing as deeply as Fiona.

37

FIONA WOKE TO THE SOUND of her phone vibrating on the night stand and the warm comfort of Meg spooning her from behind. Meg's arm draped around her waist was a bliss Fiona couldn't describe. The last thing Fiona wanted to do was move from the warm embrace, so she let the call go to voicemail and enjoyed the feel of Meg's soft breasts against her back.

Unfortunately, her full bladder didn't allow her to enjoy the cuddle for very long, and with a sigh, she eased out of Meg's embrace and got out of bed. She picked up her phone on the way to the bathroom to check the time. It was past two a.m. The call had been from Mike and he'd left a message.

When she was finished in the bathroom, Fiona hesitated outside the doorway to her room. Her finger hovered for a moment over the play button of the message before she pressed it. She held her breath as she walked to the living room and sat on the couch in the dark to listen.

"Hi, Fi. It's me. Mike. Um. Of course, you know it's me." He paused. "I'm sorry about the way I came off the last time we texted. I was a little freaked out about the news. Okay, a lot freaked out. I acted like a jerk and I handled it badly. I know I said I needed some time to think about it, but I think I want to talk to you about it now. I'll be cool this time. Promise. Give me a call when you get this? That's it, I guess. Thanks… Bye."

She wasn't sure she wanted to talk to him about it anymore. It was selfish, but she deserved to be a little self-involved about this. Mike was, well, Mike was Mike, and she didn't have the energy to support him through whatever feelings he had to process. And, honestly, she didn't think he had any say in the matter. It wasn't like they planned to get pregnant when they'd made their drunken decision to… god, she didn't even want to think about it. But now her body was host to their mistake and she didn't want any interference around any decision she made, if she could ever bring herself to think about it.

She was startled when the phone buzzed in her hand. It was Mike again. She considered letting it go to voicemail, but she knew she had to deal with it sooner or later and she decided to get it over with.

She blew out a breath and answered. "Hey."

"I'm so glad you answered." Mike sounded surprised.

"What's on your mind, Mike?"

"I know it's late. Or early, depending on whether you've gone to bed yet. Were you sleeping?"

"As a matter of fact, I was."

He didn't seem to hear her.

"I think you should have the baby."

"What?" She was confused. "Two days ago you were… never mind." She sighed. It didn't matter. It was her decision to make and she wasn't going to argue with him.

"I know. I've gone back and forth about it, but I strongly encourage you to have it."

She sat back on the couch. "I haven't made up my mind."

"Then you should have it. If you can't make up your mind, it means you should have it." He sounded wired up for two in the morning.

She rubbed her temple. "Mike, I don't want to have this discussion with you now."

"Why not? It's my kid, too." He sounded belligerent, not like the Mike she knew.

If he was going to be like this, she didn't want to have this conversation with him ever. Maybe if he were more reasonable, maybe more empathetic, it would be different. But he was making it all about himself. Which was exactly what got her into this mess in the first place. Was this how their relationship had always been? She was always helping Mike out with his issues. When had they ever had a discussion where he wasn't the primary topic of the conversation? It hadn't bothered her really. Until now. And, right now, she needed someone to take care of her. Meg was doing that. Not Mike.

She tried to hide her irritation with him. "Mike, I promise I'll tell you what I decide."

"Don't you want to talk about it?"

"Truthfully? No."

He made a frustrated sound. "I think this should be a joint decision, don't you? Shouldn't I be allowed to have some input on this?"

She wanted to tell him she probably would have talked it out with him if he weren't being so self-centered about it, but then it occurred to her—was she being the same way? It wasn't the same, though, was it?

She sighed. "What do you want to say about it that you haven't already?"

"Uh…"

She waited for him to continue.

He made an impatient snort. "Nothing. Only that I want us to have the baby."

"Us? And what would your role be in it?"

"I'd be the dad," he said, as if it were obvious.

"And how do you see your role playing out?"

He paused. "I'm not sure."

"Hmmm…" Exactly what she thought he'd say.

"How do you see it playing out?" he asked.

Her response was immediate. "You see, I don't. Ever since I was a little girl I had my life planned out before me. I was going to be a lawyer. I was going to live in the city, have a cool apartment, and never once did a kid factor into this."

"Plans change, Fi."

She could see it was something he understood. After all, his dream of being an attorney had taken a brief pause while he prepped for the next exam. Maybe he was trying to take control of something. Too bad she wasn't going to let him. "Yeah. I get it, Mike. But this is a big change. One I'm not sure I want to make."

His tone changed. He must have thought she was entertaining the idea. "Well, maybe you should think about it."

She sat forward and rested her elbows on her knees. She was done with this conversation. "I've been doing nothing but thinking about it, Mike."

"Well, try to think about what it might be like if you went with your plans, but there was a baby involved."

She sighed. "Again, how do you see it playing out? I mean between you and me? Are you expecting us to become a family or something?"

He paused. "Kind of."

What? "Seriously? You think we're gonna get married and forget who we are?"

"God, no!"

She sighed with relief. "Then what do you see?"

"Maybe some sort of shared thing."

"Fifty-fifty? Like you have it for a week and I have it for a week?"

"I don't know, exactly."

"Or maybe you want to be a weekend daddy?"

"I'm not sure."

"Figure it out, Mike. How do you see this going?"

"I don't know!" He sounded exasperated. "All I know is I want to have some sort of role in the baby's life. I want to be a dad. I don't know how good I'll be, but I want to try."

"I see. But you want me to take care of it mostly, right?"

"Well, I don't know anything about babies. You'd probably be better at it than me. Maybe when it's a little more self-sufficient I can take it more often."

She fought the urge to hang up. So, she'd be doing all the work. "I think we're getting ahead of ourselves here. I haven't decided to keep it yet."

"Just promise me you'll talk to me first." He pleaded. "Please, Fi. Promise me."

"I have to go now." She hung up the call without waiting for him to say goodbye and dropped her head into her hands. She hadn't heard Meg come into the room, but she felt her sit next to her. A warm hand rubbed her back. The comforting warmth made her want to cry.

"I heard you talking. Do you need anything?"

She wiped her nose. "I'm okay."

Meg took her hand. "Was that him on the phone? The father?"

"Yeah."

"It sounds like you haven't worked things out yet."

"Not even close."

"Well, come back to bed. It's the middle of the night."

Fiona let Meg lead her back to the bedroom where they crawled back into bed and assumed the position they had been in before Fiona had gotten up to go to the bathroom. Fiona once again thought about how easy it was to be around Meg. She was mulling it over when she fell back asleep.

38

MEG WOKE TO THE SOUND of cardboard brushing against fabric. When she opened her eyes, Fiona was holding the box of kittens, trying to back quietly out of the bedroom. She looked gorgeous in the light streaming through the cracks between the sheer curtains of the high bedroom window.

"Sorry. I tried to be quiet," Fiona whispered.

"No worries." Meg yawned and stretched herself awake. The tank top she'd worn to bed had pushed up to below her breasts, and she noticed Fiona breathe deeply and look away. Meg smiled and languidly completed her stretch before she pulled the shirt back down. "I think I was about to wake up on my own anyway. What time is it?"

Fiona rested the box on her hip. "Seven-thirty. Breakfast is almost done. Do you like biscuits and gravy?"

"Love it." Meg sat up. "I like the gravy on the side, though. Otherwise, the mushy bread kind of grosses me out."

"I'm glad you told me." Fiona grinned. "I have a feeling you would have politely gagged down mushy biscuits."

"Probably."

"I'm worried about the kittens." Fiona nodded at the box. "When did they eat last, do you remember?"

"About five this morning." Meg guessed, since she'd blearily stumbled through the last feeding without checking the time. She was glad to do it, but the kittens had woken up several times in the night. "They should be fine. Besides, they're healthy. You can let them tell you when they need to eat."

"How many times did you feed them last night?"

"Let's see." Meg held up her hand to count on her fingers. "I fed them at nine-thirty, again around midnight, then at one, three, and five."

Fiona put her hand on her forehead. "I slept through all of that? God, I'm such a shit!"

"You have plenty of justification for sleeping through it. Besides you need your sleep." Meg swung her legs over the side of the bed and stretched again. Fiona looked away again and she remembered she was wearing only white bikini panties for bottoms. She reached for her shorts.

Fiona focused on the kittens in the box. "It doesn't seem quite fair. You lost a lot of sleep, you know, between my drama and the kittens."

"I'm okay with it. Really." Meg stood and pulled on the shorts. "The kittens should usually go longer between feedings at night, but they're probably responding to the energy."

"You must be wiped out, though."

Meg walked over and took the box from her. "I'm fine. I don't have to work today, so I can nap if I need to."

"That makes me feel a little better." Fiona led them into the living room. "How about I feed the little monsters while you eat?"

"Deal!" Meg's stomach growled as the scent of peppery sausage gravy and fresh baked biscuits assailed her senses.

39

"THIS IS AWESOME!" MEG TOOK another bite of her biscuit. She was sitting at the table and Fiona was on the sofa, tucked against the overstuffed arm, feeding the kittens. They could see each other over the back of the sofa.

"Thanks." Fiona smiled. "They were my dad's favorite. I remember wearing a dishtowel as an apron, standing on a chair, helping my mom. She'd roll the dough out and I'd press out the biscuits with the biscuit cutter."

"What a great memory." Meg took another bite. "Your mom and dad sound like they were good people."

"They were." Fiona's eyes suddenly stung with tears. Her feelings were always so close to the surface these days.

Her phone vibrated on the table next to her. A glance at it said it was a text from Mike. Irritation replaced the previous bout of sadness.

Hey, Fi. Seriously. Don't make any decisions without me. K? I deserve to be part of this.

Seriously?

She frowned and turned the phone over without responding.

"You doing okay this morning?"

Fiona looked up from her phone. Meg was watching her.

"Um, what?" She shook her head. "I mean, yeah. I'm good." What had they been talking about? She couldn't remember.

"You suddenly look pissed off."

God. She so did not want to talk about Mike right now. She'd woken up in such a good mood. She'd slept really well and waking up next to Meg had been beyond nice.

Her phone vibrated again. She wasn't going to look at it. Screw Mike. He didn't get to tell her what to do.

"There it is again. You're frowning." Meg continued to eat her biscuits, but she looked worried.

She didn't want Meg to be concerned about her, to feel responsible for her. She waved at her phone. "Mike texted. I don't feel like talking to him right now."

Meg nodded. "You have a lot on your mind. Do you want to talk about it?"

She normally wouldn't want to talk about it, even with someone as safe as Meg—not about such a personal decision. But she'd woken about an hour before Meg, thinking about the phone call, and for once, her thoughts hadn't been all over the place. She'd gotten up and taken her journal out to the living room to write down what she remembered of the conversation, along with some of the emotions and questions it had elicited. When she'd finished writing, she had names for many of the feelings that had eluded her for so long. The emotional release of the night before had washed away the fear of being overwhelmed, and a huge sense of relief started to fill her.

She opened up.

And it felt so good.

She told Meg about the phone call, the night she'd gotten pregnant, and Mike's reaction when she told him about the pregnancy.

All of it.

When she finished, she fell into an uneasy silence, having never opened up so completely to herself, let alone another person. She was exhausted and exhilarated at the same time.

She pushed her hair back self-consciously. "As ridiculous as it sounds, I have never once re-evaluated my life plan since the day I decided to become a lawyer at fourteen years old. Seriously. Never once. I'm following a plan made by a fourteen year old. Regardless of whether I keep the baby, I guess I should spend some time figuring out if I need to re-evaluate that plan."

She'd finished feeding the kittens while she talked and got up to wash her hands in the kitchen. Meg followed, taking her dishes after eating every last bit of the biscuits. They went back to the living room and plopped down on the couch.

Fiona rubbed her eyes. "Sorry for the emotional and verbal vomit. I'm not used to spilling my guts to people."

"You're exhausted. It's not surprising. You've had quite an emotional roller coaster the last few days. Part of me wants to keep you company today so you don't feel like you're alone, but another part wonders if you need some time to yourself." Meg sighed. "You're probably sick of me by now, anyway."

She put her hand on Meg's leg. "Weirdly enough, I am not even close to being sick of you. It's probably the other way around."

"Not at all. I enjoy hanging out with you."

"As much as I want to ask you to stay and hang out with me today, you're right. I need to figure out what my next steps should be." She watched the kittens sleep. "Can I call you later?"

"You better." Meg stood up. "Thanks for breakfast. It was delicious. I'm going to the park for a run and I'll probably do some painting when I get back. My roommate said something about going to the river to watch the fireworks when it gets dark. But call me whenever you want to. I'll have my cell."

"I forgot today is the 4th. My days are all out of whack." She walked Meg to the door. "I don't want to interfere with your plans."

"You wouldn't be interfering. I'd love it if you came with us."

Fiona didn't want Meg to leave, even though she did need to do some more thinking. And probably take another nap. "I'll let you know later, okay?"

Meg stepped out onto the doorstep. "Sure. Give me a call if you need anything."

"You've been so good to me."

As Meg turned to go, something overtook Fiona and she grabbed her hand. Meg stopped with a bemused look on her face. Fiona didn't know how to express the swirl of emotions roiling inside of her. Instead, she threw her arms around Meg and held on like she was drowning. Meg seemed to sense what she needed and held her tight.

Reluctantly, Fiona let go after a few minutes, but she could have stayed like that all day.

Meg smiled. "Call if you want to go with us tonight. I'd love it if you did." Then she took the steps up to the street two at a time.

40

MEG SQUINTED INTO THE SUNLIGHT, buzzing from the hug. Her body hummed everywhere their bodies had touched, especially her hands, which had rested on the bare skin of her back. Her smooth, soft skin. It had taken everything inside her to resist letting them wander.

Thank goodness for the lighter than usual holiday traffic, because her distraction could have been dangerous as she jaywalked across the street to her building. It wasn't even nine o'clock and the thin fabric of her T-shirt was sticking to her back by the time she entered the air-conditioned building. With all the energy coursing through her body, she decided to get a run in before the heat and humidity of the day had a chance to fully descend upon the city. She couldn't imagine hanging out in the solitude of her room right now.

Thankfully, the apartment was silent when she entered, and she went directly to her room. Regardless of Aunt Vi's "don't ask, don't tell" relationship with Sherri, their relationship had become increasingly volatile as Sherri grew less tolerant of Aunt Vi's wandering eye. Meg was in too good a mood to deal with it this morning. All she could think about was holding Fiona.

It only took a few minutes for Meg to get ready and head back downstairs. She stopped on the steps outside the building to stretch before she began a slow jog toward Morningside Park, a few blocks away. One benefit of the heat was how quickly her muscles loosened. She soon fell into a comfortable gait. The route she took was a favorite. Nice and shady in the morning, it ran along Morningside Drive, through Morningside Park, down to 110th, where she crossed over to Central Park.

When she first considered staying in the city for the summer, Meg had dreaded running along what she imagined would be gray city streets. She had been happily surprised to find the location of Vi's apartment made for pleasant runs, through parks and paths along the Hudson River, which were only a few blocks in the other direction.

Usually hyper-vigilant when she ran in the city, the light traffic and easy pace lulled her into a daydream. Her mind drifted toward the night before, when she'd slept beside Fiona. She'd intended it to be a purely protective gesture, but the soft warmth of Fiona's body had resulted in a decidedly different effect. Realizing she was going down a mental path she shouldn't, Meg took a minor detour through a sprinkler to cool herself down. Back on the sidewalk, and dripping wet, Meg laughed at herself and picked up her pace.

By the time she arrived at Central Park, Meg had achieved a pace she could sustain for the duration of her run and she was feeling good. Easily navigating the curbs and barriers at the northwest entrance to Central Park, she disappeared into the shady paths taking her to the reservoir and back. Fueled by the possibility of seeing Fiona later and running in the shade of the foliage in the park provided her with seemingly endless energy. The contrast of city and nature was profound in her thoughtful state. She looked forward to going back to the open landscapes and brilliant greens of Seattle at the end of the summer, but she was going to miss the surprise of nature in the middle of a concrete landscape.

Dripping with sweat, and on an endorphin high from her run, Meg shut her bedroom door and plopped down on the edge of her bed to kick off her shoes. Her cell phone rang. Hoping it was Fiona, she was slightly disappointed when it was her mother calling. She considered letting it go to voicemail but answered it instead. She fell back across her bed.

"Hello, my mother. How are you doing this bright and sunny Sunday morning?" She smiled into the phone.

"Hello, daughter. I'm glad you're enjoying the sunshine. It's gray and overcast here. The forecast predicts rain today. No fireworks this year."

"Believe it or not, I miss the Seattle rain. What has you up at…" She consulted her watch/pedometer on her wrist, "…not quite nine a.m. Pacific Time? I thought Sunday was your basking day. You shouldn't be up for another hour, at least."

Her mother sighed. "Unfortunately, as I get older, I find it harder and harder to sleep in. I can't stay asleep past eight anymore. I do miss the basking."

She heard the rustling of a newspaper in the background. She imagined her mother sitting on her usual stool at the enormous granite kitchen island, reading the paper and drinking French Roast from her favorite over-sized coffee mug. A pang of homesickness squeezed her heart.

"I must have gotten my early rising from Dad. I've never liked to sleep in." Meg barely held back the "unless I have company" qualifier dangling from the tip of her tongue. Her mother was fine with her being gay, and they were close, but their relationship had never been one in which they exchanged that flavor of personal information.

"I know. How you used to torture me, interrupting my Sunday basking with your youthful energy!" Her mother said "youthful energy" as if she were saying "dirty socks", but she knew her mother was kidding. She had loved it as much as they had when she and CJ had bounded into the room on Sunday mornings after cartoons and cereal, and after their father had left to play golf. She and her brother would snuggle against their mother and the three of them would talk about everything and anything. She missed those days.

"So, what's up, my mother? What is the nature of this unexpected call? Is everything okay?" She usually made her weekly call on a weekday, since weekends on both coasts were always so hectic. Meg had already talked to her mother on Wednesday, so the Sunday call was unusual.

"Everything's fine, honey. I had to wait until your father went golfing. I know you know his sixtieth is coming up in three weeks. Do you think you can come out for a surprise party?"

"Mom…" Meg issued an exasperated sigh, "Dad hates surprise parties. He made you promise never again after the last one."

"I know!" She had a tone of mischievous glee in her voice. Most people would never suspect her mother of her devious humor, but it was one thing Meg truly loved about her. "Exactly why he will never suspect this one."

Meg dropped her arm over her eyes. This was not going to go well. "You promised, though."

"Technically, it's CJ's idea, so I'm off the hook."

She knew the surprise party would happen whether or not she approved. "He's going to hate it." She groaned. "Of course I'll be there."

"Excellent!"

Her mother was probably clapping her hands in the kitchen three thousand miles away.

They spoke for a few more minutes and then hung up after giving each other hints about what they planned to give her Dad for his birthday. Grinning and tossing the phone aside, she finished undressing and put on her robe to take a shower. As Meg stepped into the hallway, Vi's bedroom door opened and she stepped out in her pajamas, holding two empty coffee cups in one hand. Vi smiled a greeting at Meg as she shut the door behind her, but not before Meg got a glimpse of a woman lying across the bed reading the Sunday Times. The woman was not Sherri. Vi smiled sheepishly then disappeared into the kitchen. Meg didn't want to be around if they decided to have morning sex, so she hurried through her shower.

41

THE DISHES WERE DONE, THE bed was made, and the kittens were asleep. Sunshine filtered hazily into the front room through the gauzy fabric Fiona kept drawn over her window so the riff-raff of the city couldn't see directly into her living room. She would have preferred to let the light shine in unobstructed, but a sidewalk-level apartment provided too much visibility into a single woman's apartment. Content with the light she did get, Fiona curled up against the arm of the sofa, prepared to think some deep thoughts.

The prospect of her uncertain future couldn't compete with the memory of the hug she'd given Meg, though. An erotic shock surged through her when she thought of Meg's hands on her back, lightly touching the exposed skin above her tank top between her shoulder blades and the body memory took her thoughts to when she had awoken next to her.

The soft light of dawn had trickled in through the edges of the bedroom blinds, and she'd been given another rare opportunity to observe Meg candidly. She lost herself in the soft beauty of her face, relaxed in sleep, a slight smile playing across her exquisite mouth. Fiona had wondered what dream was featuring behind her delicate eyelids.

Her gaze had moved to Meg's toned arms, and she had remembered how easy it had been to fall into them the night before. She craved to be there again, but in the early morning shadows, she was too bashful to simply slide over and pull Meg's arms around her. She remained on her side of the bed, staring at Meg's athletic body lying so near, sprawled out on her stomach with the covers kicked off. Her hungry eyes traced a path along the wide swath of bare flesh between the bottom of Meg's tank top and the lace band of her bikini briefs. She had imagined her bare belly pressed to Meg's, and her skin had tingled with intense longing filling her chest. Her eyes moved back to Meg's barely parted lips, and she had imagined how their lips would feel together. How Meg's mouth would taste.

She'd forced herself to roll over and go back to sleep before her eager hands began to wander on their own.

On her couch, lost in the memory, desire seared through her once again.

Unbidden, a sense of shame stole into her reverie. She thought about her clinginess and crying, along with her needy request for Meg stay with her. Mercifully, her shame evaporated when she remembered Meg's tender ministrations and warm embrace. A smile flickered across her face and she was tempted to linger on the memory, but a feeling of uncertainty swept through her.

A question had lurked in the recesses of her mind as she sobbed the night before, and had waited impatiently near the surface as she slept. The question was a tough one: should she keep the baby?

Never had she even remotely considered she would find herself faced with this particular decision. She was a lesbian, for Christ's sake. Lesbians had to go out of their way to get pregnant—it was never an accident.

For Fiona, the idea of pregnancy was even more remote than for most. Her plan had never contained a partner, let alone a child—though neither option had been intentionally discarded. Her plan was simple and clean: career first, everything else came after. All the details of her carefully planned life had focused on her career. She'd never spent any time on what the "after" would look like. Having never been in a relationship, she sometimes thought it would be easier to skip the partner and kids thing all together.

There had been times when a wisp of desire swept through her, unexpected—when the ghost of a dream had lingered, or the casual gesture made by an attractive stranger had caught her eye. In those rare instances she had considered love and desire, but it had been easy enough to file the detail away for "after". Most of the time, though, relationships and desire weren't on her mind, and it was easy to think she'd get along fine without it.

Now she was facing something she hadn't planned, and it was time to figure out what to do.

Fiona picked up her journal and listed her options:

1. Adoption
2. Abortion
3. Keep it

It was a short list, but the hardest she had ever had to consider. She forced herself to think.

Adoption meant carrying the baby to term, and a pregnancy would limit her career plans—at least temporarily. It was the emotional impact of giving up the child once she had it that she struggled with. Having no family left, she knew having a child out there somewhere would be difficult for her. In addition, she wasn't sure she could distance herself enough to hand her baby over after feeling it move inside her. Adoption might be too hard.

An abortion was easier for her to envision. A benefit of having avoided introspection was the distance she felt from the presence in her womb. In contrast to the dedication and vigor with which she had pursued her career over the last several years, it was almost no contest when weighing the options. She would get her life back. No looking back. Right? Right…

But, the more she thought about it, the more difficult it became. Would she always wonder, "what if?" Would she always carry the sadness of could-have-beens?

Keeping it was another option. Even if it was the hardest of the three for her to imagine. The simple thought of carrying a child was scary enough, but building a life with a child? A child didn't factor into the kind of life she envisioned for herself. Eighty-hour workweeks. Travel. High stress. But maybe with some practical planning… she could practice law for most of her pregnancy, take six to eight weeks maternity leave, hire a nanny, get a bigger apartment. She had the money for it, thanks to the inheritances from her parents and Aunt Corny. So, a quick diversion, and then right back to the original plan. No problem, right?

There were lots of problems with it, actually. But, it could work.

One problem with keeping it was that Fiona knew she could never raise a child in the city. Sure, plenty of people did it, but she didn't want to be one of them—especially if she was going to be a working mother. Letting a nanny raise a baby was bad enough, but children should play outdoors. A child should roam freely, unafraid of predators, unsullied by the ugliness lurking in the cracks and shadows of a city existence. She knew pressures existed no matter where one chose to live, but she knew more of them existed where more people lived, and she wanted to provide the best environment for a kid to grow up healthy, happy, and safe. She thought any child—but especially her child—should have memories of walking barefoot through streams and ponds, hunting toads, climbing trees, lying on their back on cool green grass, and counting the stars on a clear night.

So where did it leave her?

Abortion?

Adoption?

Keep it?

Fiona had done well up until that point, but her mind couldn't grasp the finality of a decision.

Her phone vibrated. Mike again. She kicked it off the table.

Anger filled her. Rage churned a hole in her gut. Fuck Mike for his privileged angst! Fuck him for making her feel sorry for him! Fuck him for causing her to rely on her right to choose! She threw her journal across the room and buried her head in her hands. Fuck! Fuck! Fuck!

She lurched up and retrieved her phone. Six messages in addition to the one she'd already read. All telling her—not asking her—telling her to include him in any decision. To wait until they talked it out. Mike had never been pushy. This change was too much. It was her choice goddamn it! Her choice. Hadn't she done enough for him?

Grateful for the freedom to make the choice, she cursed the man who forced her into the necessity of making it. Soon, though, her rage swung around to herself. She'd been a willing participant. What the fuck had she been thinking? It was too much to think about. Fiona curled into a ball on the couch. Her head throbbed, her heart hurt, and her mind spun with the one question she couldn't answer. She was tired, and she didn't want to think. She sought the dark, cool comfort of sleep.

Before the mists of sleep had a chance to claim her completely, however, a plaintive meow broke the silence. Fiona slowly uncurled and looked at the box next to the couch. More kittens' voices joined the first, and the ensuing chorus was both a welcome relief and a frustrating interruption. She forced herself from the couch.

Fiona peered over the edge of the box and laughed at the unexpected sight of a perfectly positioned row of kittens, all with their noses pressed to the side of the box, pointy little tails shaking with the effort of their demand for nourishment. Six pairs of milky blue eyes squinted up at her.

Their little eyes were open! Fiona reached over, and grabbed her cell phone from the recliner. She had to take a picture to show Meg.

42

MEG WAS PAINTING WHEN HER phone flashed. The music in her headphones was on loud enough to drown out the sex and drama she'd been subjected to all morning. She would have left after her shower, but it was too hot to wander around the city, so she'd cranked her music and got lost in her painting, instead.

She picked up the phone to find a text from Fiona. A tingle of excitement unfurled in her stomach. Maybe she'd decided to go watch fireworks with her. She opened the message and was tickled to see a picture of the kittens with their eyes open. She replied.

So cute!

A moment later, Fiona texted back.

The big one is standing on all fours now. He can't walk without falling, but he's holding himself up.

Another picture came through.

OMG! He's really standing. Thanks for sending the picture!

I couldn't let you miss the milestones. What are you up to?

Painting. I went for a run, but it's too hot to wander around outside now. What about you?

Oh, you know. Pondering the mysteries of the universe and trying to figure out what I want to be when I grow up.

Well, I'm a phone call away if you need it.

Thanks. I'll call you later and let you know if I'm up for fireworks.

She dropped her phone on the bed, a little disappointed Fiona hadn't gotten bored hanging out by herself. She totally understood, though. She faced her painting again. The creative flow she'd found earlier wasn't filling her fingertips anymore. She pushed one of the headphones away from her ear and immediately heard the rhythmic thumping of Aunt Vi's headboard. God. Again?

She couldn't handle it. She covered her paints and brushes, picked up her phone, and left the apartment. She'd rather hang out at the coffee shop than be in a room next to the Energizer Bunny.

43

HALF AN HOUR LATER, FIONA sat on the sofa with a pile of sleeping kittens in her lap, the white one in her hand. She studied its perfect little body, sprawled out, sleeping soundly in her palm. She could tell they had grown a little in the two short days she'd been caring for them. She ran her finger over the kitten's back and picked up the tail, letting it drop. Stubby little whiskers poked from beside the kitten's soft nose in neat little rows. The tiny pink nose was like cool velvet, as she rubbed it lightly against her own. The little puffs of kitten breath didn't have a smell. It would change, she knew. She remembered her childhood tabby, Groucho. His breath had always smelled a little like rotten fish.

Fiona picked up her phone to take a close-up picture of the kitten and nearly dropped it when it rang in her hand.

"Hello?" She spoke quietly and nuzzled the kitten.

"Hi, it's Meg. How are you doing?"

"I'm taking a sanity break with the kittens right now." Fiona was happy to hear Meg's voice. It was a nice break from her own dark thoughts.

"Oh, are you feeding them? Do you need me to call back later?"

"We're finished. I have them piled in my lap, giving them some snuggle time, while I selfishly soak up a little of my own."

"Sounds comfy." The smile in Meg's voice was nice. "I'm sorry to intrude on your thinking time."

She held back a scoff. "I could use the break."

"Well, I got a call-back from one of the foster people, Teri. She said she can take the kittens on Tuesday."

What? Fiona felt like she'd been punched in the gut.

"Fiona? Are you still there?" Meg sounded concerned.

"Yes. Sorry." She tried to hide the sadness trying to squeeze her chest.

"You're upset, aren't you?" Meg asked quietly.

"Yeah. Stupid, I know." She tucked the phone against her shoulder and rubbed the tears springing to her eyes.

"No. It's not stupid. I'm gonna miss the little guys myself."

"I'll bet you're not crying about it." Fiona produced a weak laugh and a sniffle at the same time.

"I guess not, but you have lots of reasons to blame it on. If it makes you feel any better, I'm sad, too."

Meg always seemed to say the right thing. "You're so sweet. I'm fine. Just thinking things over. Hearing your voice helps."

"Will you call me later?"

"Yes." She wanted to ask her to come over right then. She'd spent enough time thinking. She wanted to not think for a while.

"Then, later, 'gator. Call me if you need me in the meantime."

"I will. After a while crocodile."

Fiona impatiently wiped a tear from her cheek as she dropped the phone on the cushion beside her and studied the tiny white kitten in her hand. What was wrong with her? She couldn't keep them all. Hell, she didn't even know what to do with the baby. But, how was she going to let someone take these precious little things away? It made her heart ache to know she would have no idea what would become of them after they left.

Her phone vibrated on the cushion beside her. Expecting a text from Meg, she let out an impatient puff of air when she saw Mike's name on the display.

Fi. Please. I'm sorry for being so insistent. I don't know what else to do. Can we talk?

This message sounded more like the Mike she knew and her heart softened a little for him.

We can talk. But give me a little time to think. So later, okay? She texted back.

That's all I ask. Thank you.

Fiona dropped the phone again and gave the white kitten another kiss and placed it in the box where it continued to sleep, oblivious to the world around it. Then she did the same with the kittens in her lap. When she lifted the last one, the black kitten, the one she secretly called Cardboard, she felt more than heard a tiny rumble. She put it closer to her ear. An uneven and faint purring was coming from the little guy! She listened for a few minutes before she put Cardboard in the box.

Fiona went into the restroom to wash her hands and to splash water on her tear-stained face. Looking at her face dripping with water in the mirror, she froze. She wiped her face and looked deeply into her own eyes. They were the same hazel eyes she'd seen in the mirror the last twenty-six years, yet they seemed new to her. It wasn't the shape, or the color, or even the faint laugh lines. The difference was, there was a certainty in them she had never seen before.

She knew what it meant.

She was going to keep the baby.

And it had nothing to do with Mike. It was about her entire life. Her life plan was officially set back to square one, yet suddenly she was filled with relief and a sense of lightness she hadn't had since she was a kid. It was like when she had kissed Tammy behind the Pottstown public library sign— when she had known for certain she liked girls. She knew for certain about the baby now. It was fucking scary, but she was keeping it.

All of the confusion left her as she stared into the mirror. Having the baby was the beginning of her new life plan. Strike that. No more life plans. Having the baby was going to be the beginning of whatever came next.

✱✱✱✱✱

FRESH FROM THE SHOWER AND sitting on the edge of her bed as she towel-dried her hair, Fiona wallowed in her new-found peace. She hadn't figured out her next steps, but for the first time in her life, she didn't care. She had plenty of time to figure it all out, but right now she finally understood what it meant to live in the moment.

With a surge of happiness, she threw the towel she held into the air and batted it playfully to the floor. Whipping her damp hair back, she fell backward onto her bed with a huge smile. She burst out in giddy laughter and hugged herself. Finally, she kicked herself up into a standing position, repositioned her towel, and walked purposefully out to the living room to find her cell phone. She didn't want to waste her good mood by herself.

She keyed in a number, and while the call connected, she walked over to the kittens and watched their round little bellies rise and fall with the steady rhythm of sleep. She smiled when Meg answered.

"What are you up to?"

"I'm at the coffee shop watching Betty abuse the customers."

Disappointment descended over her and she became very aware she was standing in a towel in her living room, talking to Meg. "I thought you didn't have to work today."

"I'm not working. It's a long story. I'll tell you about it next time I see you. You sound like you're in a good mood?"

Was she? She was! "I am!"

"Awesome!"

Meg's enthusiasm made her feel even better. "About your invitation to go see fireworks, I'm not sure I should leave the kittens alone for so long, but if you don't have plans after, do you want to come over and hangout or something?"

Meg made a sound on the other end of the line. "Yeah… those plans sort of fell through. I'll tell you about it later."

She was curious about the story Meg kept alluding to but she was happy at her own good luck. More time with Meg! "Does that mean you can come over earlier?"

"I can be there in two minutes. I'm already leaving the shop."

Butterflies tickled Fiona's stomach. "See you in a few, then."

Fiona tossed her phone onto the recliner and sprang to her feet. Two minutes to get dressed wasn't much time. She stopped by the bathroom on the way to her room to brush out her damp hair, and was about to pull a shirt out of her closet when she heard a knock on her door. Sighing, she walked into the living room in her towel.

44

"THAT WAS QUICK." FIONA GRABBED Meg by the wrist and pulled her in through the door, slamming it before Meg knew what happened.

"Sorry, but I didn't want to give anyone a free show." Meg realized Fiona was in nothing but a towel. Her mouth went dry. She was staring, but the situation seemed to warrant it.

"Is this your usual, lounging-around-the-house attire?" Meg looked down at her own shorts and T-shirt. "I feel overdressed. Where do you keep the towels?" Meg grabbed the hem of her T-shirt, as if she were going to pull it off, and Fiona slapped at her hands.

"I guess I should have gotten dressed and then called you. I wasn't thinking." Fiona backed down the hall. "Be right back."

Fiona seemed different. There was something lighter about her, happier. It seemed to exude from her and Meg liked it. Fiona had always been pretty to her, but she was breathtaking right now. Maybe it was because she was wearing only a towel. Whatever it was, wow. Just wow.

Aware she was still standing by the front door, Meg tossed her phone and keys next to Fiona's on the recliner, and wandered over to the kittens. Sound asleep as usual. She knelt to pick one up, and absently rubbed the kitten across her cheek. The kitten was adorable, but it was the thought of Fiona in the towel raising the goose bumps along her skin.

A few minutes later, Meg heard Fiona's bedroom door open, and she gently placed the kitten back inside the box. She watched it burrow into the pile of siblings as Fiona entered the room behind her and put a hand on her back. Meg wondered if Fiona knew she was driving her to distraction with the towel and now the feel of her hand on her back was doing interesting things to other areas of her body.

"Sorry about the towel situation."

She cleared her throat. "It was definitely my pleasure." Meg stood up and stepped back. She needed a little space from Fiona—she didn't trust herself with her. "They're starting to open their eyes. Did you know…" Meg stopped in midsentence as she completed her turn and got a good look at Fiona, who was standing there in her bare feet and damp hair. She was doing up the last button on her jeans. Maybe she was in hurry to get dressed, but Fiona had only fastened a couple of buttons on her shirt. Either way, several buttons of the diaphanous shirt were undone, and the shirt hung open, revealing a good portion of the top of Fiona's breasts and most of her smooth, flat stomach. Meg lost her train of thought, as she took in the sight. Fiona could have easily been an Abercrombie & Fitch advertisement.

"Did I know what?" Fiona was looking down, focused on the buttons of her shirt.

Meg closed her mouth and turned back to the kittens, trying to remember what she had been about to say, thankful Fiona hadn't caught her gaping like a hormone addled teenager.

"Oh, um, did you know short-haired kittens open their eyes earlier than long-haired kittens?" God, did she sound as distracted as she felt?

"I didn't. Why are they different?" Fiona finished buttoning and peered down into the box, a casual hand rested on Meg's lower back again, apparently unaware of what she was doing to her. If she were aware, would she keep doing it?

Meg paused. Again, she struggled to pick up the thread of the conversation. Playing for time, she cleared her throat. With no clue as to what to do with her hands, she bent and retrieved a kitten from the box. The milky blue eyes reminded her of Fiona's question.

"Uh, I'm not sure, but it's true for every breed. Even in a mixed litter with both long and short-haired, the long-haired kittens will open their eyes several days after their short-haired siblings." Meg was glad to have her expertise to fall back on to steady herself and grateful her voice didn't give away her sudden case of nerves.

"Interesting. You should have seen them this morning. Wait… I have a picture." Fiona went over to the recliner to get her phone. She pulled up the picture and walked back to show Meg. "Look at all of them in a little row. Their stubby little tails crack me up."

Meg tried to concentrate on the picture, but it was almost impossible with Fiona standing so close, their arms touching from shoulder to elbow, and the soft fabric of Fiona's shirt caressing Meg's skin. Her heart skipped a beat. Fiona had left the top half of her shirt unbuttoned. The glimpse of skin and a lacy pink bra had her attention, as did the subtle fragrance of bath oil wafting from Fiona's scrubbed skin and wet hair. The tantalizing scent and view filled Meg's senses, and she took it all in, captured in an aural web.

"Cute," she managed to get out when Fiona shifted a little, breaking physical contact.

Fiona tossed her phone back onto the recliner and seemed to realize her shirt was unbuttoned past the bottom of her bra. "Sorry. Didn't realize I was flashing you." Pink crept across her cheeks as she buttoned up.

"I… I hadn't noticed." God she was a terrible liar. Did Fiona have any idea how sexy she was? She put the kitten in the box and stroked the others as Fiona went into the kitchen to get a glass of water.

"You said you had a story to tell me." Fiona looked at Meg with an expectant expression.

"I did?" What story? Meg struggled to respond as she tried not to stare down the path of skin and lace suddenly appearing before her as Fiona leaned towards her. What was she? Twelve? One glance at a woman in a towel and now her libido was going gangbusters! Her eyes moved around the room, landing on anything but Fiona's cleavage.

"Yeah, when I asked why you were at the coffee shop on your day off." Fiona, seeming to notice Meg's distraction, looked down at her shirt, blushed, and buttoned another button. But not without a small smile.

"Oh, yeah," Meg said, distracted. What were they talking about? Day off. Oh, yeah. Did she really want to go into it? She hated to be a gossip, but she had to tell someone about the stress at the apartment—besides, it helped tether her wandering eyes. "Things got a little out of hand at the apartment today."

Fiona looked interested. "How so?"

"I told you I had a roommate, right?"

Fiona nodded.

"Well, she has a lover and…"

Fiona's eyes grew big. "Did you walk in on them having…?"

Meg groaned. "Oh, God, no! Well… not with her and her lover. Not this time."

Fiona gasped. "So, you have before and with someone else? Intriguing."

Meg sighed. She was going to have to give the back-story now. "Vi had company this morning when I got home—and it wasn't Sherri, her lover. So, I holed myself up in my room and started painting. After a while, I heard angry voices and a lot of noise. When I opened my door to see what was going on, Sherri was tossing clothes out into the hall. Then Vi's overnight guest made a dash for the door, half-dressed."

"Yikes! Uncomfortable!"

"A total understatement. I wanted to close my door and give them privacy, but I had to make sure no physical violence happened."

"What was Vi doing?"

"She started to follow her guest, but only made it a few steps before she came back. It was so weird. One minute, Sherri was screaming and throwing stuff, and the next, Vi grabbed her and they started to make-out like teenagers. I honestly think they would have gone at it, right there in the open doorway, if the guy across the hall hadn't opened his door. I think the other woman was gone by then, otherwise he would have had an eyeful. Then, they disappeared into Vi's room. And the walls between Vi's room and mine aren't exactly soundproof." Meg ducked her head and groaned.

"You poor thing!" Fiona tried to cover a laugh. "I'm sorry. I don't mean to laugh, but it's like a bad movie!"

"I'm afraid to go home." Meg looked up through her eyelashes, only half-joking. "But now you see why the fireworks are off. At least the traditional ones."

"Good one! I don't blame you, though."

Meg mirrored Fiona's stance, and they stood there thinking their own thoughts for a moment.

"Suffice to say, that's why I was at the coffee shop on my day off," Meg said after a minute.

"Well, you can use the excuse of the kittens to stay the night again, if you want."

"A very tempting offer." Meg pretended to think it over. Excitement threaded down her spine, even though she'd be spending the night on the couch.

"Awesome!" Fiona pushed away from the counter and clapped her hands. "Slumber party! Besides, I'm lousy at night feedings."

"Ah. I see how it is." Meg joked. She'd feed and poop a million kittens to spend more time with her.

"I'll bribe you with food. Pizza? And popcorn for hors d'oeuvres?"

Meg pretended to think it over. "I could go for some pizza and popcorn."

"Grab something to drink from the fridge and I'll place the order and pop the corn."

"Sounds like a perfect plan." Meg went into the kitchen and opened the refrigerator.

45

"SO… THE WHOLE THING ABOUT your roommates. How they went from fighting to… whatever. It's so weird to me." Fiona balanced her plate in one hand, tucking her legs under her. They were on the couch with their pizza and drinks—beer for Meg and water for Fiona—facing one another from either end, in what was starting to become their usual position. The music she'd put on played quietly in the background. So, this was what hanging out with a friend was like. In the past, hanging out for Fiona almost always included studying or watching her friends get drunk because they didn't have to study. This was nice. Relaxing. Except she was more than a little turned on by Meg's story. She shouldn't be. It was kind of dysfunctional, what with the cheating and all, but it was a story about sex. Between two women. She couldn't help herself.

Meg swallowed a bite of pizza. "It was pretty intense. Some couples need that, I guess."

Fiona mulled it over. "I don't get it."

Meg grinned and raised an eyebrow. "Three words. Make. Up. Sex."

Fiona blushed. "Seriously?"

"It's the only thread keeping some couples together—Sherri and Vi, for example. I'll bet they would've split up long ago if not for it."

Fiona would never admit to her excitement. She blamed it on her whacked out hormones.

"But shouldn't there have been an apology or something in-between?"

Meg lowered the slice of pizza she was about to bite into. "Come on. Haven't you ever gone from fighting to fucking before?"

Heat crept up her neck. "I… well… um… no," she stammered. Mischief flashed in Meg's eyes. Fiona liked it and was afraid of it at the same time.

"Aw, come on. Everyone has." Meg seemed to enjoy teasing her.

"Not everyone." Fiona concentrated on her pizza. Her tone, more than the actual response, was probably a killjoy, but she suddenly felt exposed. She usually didn't care what others thought. Meg was different, though.

"Did I get too personal?" Meg looked concerned.

Damn! It had been so chill and now she'd made it weird. Typical. "No. Not at all." Fiona wanted to go back to a few minutes ago when they'd been laughing. "I'm sorry. You didn't say anything wrong." Fiona blew out a long breath and put down her pizza.

Meg looked like she was searching for a way to take the conversation back to neutral ground. "What they did wasn't your run of the mill make up sex though. It was kind of rough. I'm not into it, which is why I ran away as soon as I could, but I don't judge them if it's their thing." Meg tilted her head back, thinking. "I guess I do judge. But to each their own if they get off on it, it's safe, and more than anything else, consensual. I have my thing and you probably have your thing. It's all cool as long as everyone's a willing participant, right?"

Meg was so cute trying to tie it all up in a nice little bow. But now Fiona was frustrated. Meg was making certain assumptions. Should she tell her?

She blew out a breath. Well, it was now or never. "The truth is—make-up sex, rough sex, bread-and-butter sex, whatever sex—I wouldn't know, because I've never had it. And, honestly, I usually don't care. I don't even think about it. But lately—and I know it's the hormones—I have been thinking about it. A lot." She didn't mean to sound angry, but it came out that way. She sighed. "And well… I got embarrassed about it. So, I'm the one who should be sorry."

Meg looked completely taken by surprise. "You shouldn't be embarrassed." Disbelief clouded her expression. "Never?"

"Never. Not counting…" Fiona waved one of her hands to dismiss the thought. "But that definitely did not count."

She ate some more of her pizza and tried not to look at Meg because she didn't want to see pity or whatever sad reaction she might have. Besides, it was just sex for Christ's sake. Why'd everyone want to make it into such a big deal?

When Meg didn't respond, she snuck a peek. She was surprised to see anger.

"So—Mike? He talked you into your first time?"

She waved her hand. It wasn't Mike's fault. "It was consensual."

Meg's brow knitted even more. "But it was your first time."

Fiona laughed self-consciously. "You make it sound like he stole my virginity or something. Virginity is a state of mind, not some prized possession or something."

Meg's eyes darted back and forth like she was trying to figure out a good way to say her next words. "I didn't say 'virginity'. You're right. But your first time with someone—your first time with anyone—is a special thing. It can be a romp in the hay, a way to blow off steam, or it can even be mind-boggling sex, but it should be the way you want it. Not a thing you do to get someone to stop begging you for it." Meg's hands were curled into fists.

Fiona hadn't wanted to get into it. Her experience with Mike had been embarrassing, and if she had the choice to do it again, she wouldn't do it. But, in a way, it had been as much a test for her as it had been for him. She pulled one of Meg's hands into her lap and gently uncurled her fingers.

"Part of the reason I slept with him was to see if I could actually feel it." Confusion clouded Meg's face. "Not physically feel it, emotionally feel it." Meg still looked confused. "After my parents died, I shut down. I channeled everything into school. My therapist said it was guilt about wanting to be with Tammy the night of the accident. I don't know. But after than night I never felt that kind of excitement again." Until now, she almost said, but bit it back. "So, when Mike asked me to have sex with him, I saw it as a way to see if I could turn it back on."

"But you're a lesbian. He's a… man."

She laughed. "Well, it wasn't a perfect plan. I sort of figured my body might respond even if—." She shook her head. "Anyway, not a perfect plan."

Meg coughed. "You didn't enjoy it?"

Fiona snorted. "Not even close. He tried. We both tried. Neither of us were into it. I'm surprised he even… well, you know." Embarrassing.

Meg squeezed her hand. "Sorry I brought it up. It wasn't any of my business." She shook her head.

"You were just tripping on my sullied maidenhood," Fiona joked. She'd spilled her secret to Meg and was relieved that she didn't feel stupid anymore. It almost sounded more logical than she'd given herself credit for. She'd been so focused on having fallen pregnant, she hadn't thought much about whether her experiment had worked. At a minimum, it proved she actually wasn't into guys. Mike was hot, as well as sweet and considerate—to a point, anyway. And while her body hadn't responded, it was definitely responding now. It had when she woke up beside Meg, and again when Meg told her the story of Vi and Sherri. She wasn't dead inside.

"I find it very hard to believe a woman as beautiful and as sexy as you has never…" Meg's incredulity showed on her face. "God, I'm being an asshole. It's just, well… you know what I mean, right?"

Sexy and beautiful? A flock of birds took flight in her stomach, but she shrugged her shoulders. "Like I said, I shut down."

"Surely you've dated?"

Fiona shook her head. "Not much. I wasn't into it."

"Even if you weren't into it, other people must have asked you out." Meg tried again. "How did you keep them away?"

Fiona was flattered at Meg's disbelief.

"Contrary to what you may think, I haven't been swarmed by interested parties. And the few who did ask, I wasn't interested in." Fiona shrugged.

"I can't believe I'm going to even ask this." Meg rolled her eyes and paused as if she wondered if she should continue. "But, if you haven't been attracted to any women, and besides those mostly innocent occasions with Tammy… are you sure you're a lesbian?" Meg quickly rushed on. "I know my question is unevolved and offensive. And judging by the look on your face, you do too. But I find it so completely beyond any kind of reasonable understanding that someone as remarkable, beautiful, sexy, and smart as you hasn't had a parade of people knocking at her door. At least one woman should have made it through!"

Meg looked so adorable in her earnestness, and she'd called her sexy again. A surge of excitement flared through her entire body. "I'm absolutely, one hundred percent sure I'm a lesbian. And while I find it flattering you think women would flock to me, they don't."

"Wow. They are so missing out." Meg looked astonished, which was flattering.

Fiona pushed Meg's shoulder. "Now you're projecting."

Meg looked amused. "What do you mean?"

"Well, you've probably been with scads of people." Meg's eyebrows rose.

Shit. That sounded bad. "Yikes! Let me try again. You're such a wonderful, smart, beautiful, sexy, outgoing, beautiful… did I say beautiful already? It doesn't matter… but, you're everything I said, and so much more. I know you have your pick of women, and I am positive several of those women—but not too many," she added, holding out her hands, "must have been successful in talking you into their beds."

Meg blushed. "Not really. I went a bit wild when I first started college. At least for me, but not like most of my friends."

"I'm surprised." Fiona was enthralled, even as a small wisp of jealousy snuck in.

"The lesbian dating pool was relatively small in college. Larger than my high school, but a little too incestuous for me. It didn't take long for everyone to have dated someone I knew. I had a few relationships, but I didn't get around as much as some of my friends." Meg hesitated before she added, "I think once I got the sex-for-sex's-sake thing out of my system, I decided it should be about love, or at least on the road to potential love. At least for me."

Fiona wondered what it would be like to make love to Meg and her entire body responded, some places more than others. "How many times have you been in love?"

Meg blew out some air, but she was smiling. "This conversation has run the gamut on deepness, hasn't it?"

"You don't have to answer if you don't want to." She hoped she would, though.

Meg tilted her head. "I thought I was a couple of times, but realized it was wishful thinking. I'm still waiting."

A faint meow interrupted the conversation, followed by another.

"I'll feed them, if you poop them." Fiona offered.

"Is it just me, or have we skipped the whole romance thing and jumped right into the taking-care-of-a-house-full-of-kids part?" Meg asked as they got up.

Fiona didn't skip a beat. "I have to admit, pooping kittens never factored into any fantasies I've ever had about finally getting a beautiful woman into my bed," she said with a gentle pat on Meg's back, and then walked into the kitchen to get the formula ready.

46

MEG STOOD WHERE SHE WAS for a moment. Her stomach did a flip, before a flutter rose up in her chest. Had Fiona said she fantasized about her? She forced her legs to move toward the bathroom.

"Hey, can you grab a fresh towel for me while I heat this up?" Fiona called from the kitchen, popping her head out from behind the refrigerator door. "They're in the bathroom closet."

"Sure thing, boss lady." She was surprised her voice sounded normal.

The bathroom was large for such a small apartment, and the linen closet took up half of one wall. There were several doors and drawers for storage, and with her mind on everything they'd just talked about, Meg simply opened the nearest door. It didn't contain the towels, but it did contain some interesting bottles and jars. Absentmindedly, as she went over their discussion in her head, she lifted a bottle of lotion and squirted some onto her palm. The scent of sage and lavender filled the air. It smelled deliciously like Fiona. In an uncharacteristic display of nosiness, she continued her voyeuristic exploration of the cabinet. A stacked row of decorative tins took up one of the shelves. Curious, she picked one up. The first contained hair clips and bands. Another contained a few cosmetics and nail polish. Yet another had an assortment of loose buttons. The contents were less intriguing than the actual collection of tins, and far less intriguing than their owner. She grabbed the last tin from the stack she'd been snooping in and opened it, glancing toward the empty doorway. In the bottom, nestled on a silk cloth, was a vibrator. A simple, nothing fancy, twist-to-operate, battery-powered vibrator—but it was Fiona's. Her center tightened as erotic images of Fiona flashed through her mind. She quietly returned the tin to the bottom of the stack in the cabinet and shut the door. Feeling a bit guilty, she was happy to have fodder for fantasies for days now.

Distracted by her thoughts, Meg sidestepped to the cabinet door closest to the shower, where she found a neat stack of towels. She grabbed one and turned to leave, but the entire stack of towels tumbled to the floor. The towel-valanche wasn't enough to divert Meg's wandering thoughts from a certain tin, and she was thinking about its contents and the woman in the next room when she knelt down to refold the half-dozen towels scattered at her feet. She nearly jumped out of her skin when Fiona spoke to her from only inches away.

"I wondered what was taking you so long." Fiona knelt next to Meg and helped her with the towels. "I was going to tease you about snooping."

"Snoop? Me?" She hoped she didn't sound guilty.

Fiona grinned. "I know—you aren't as devious as me."

She snorted self-consciously. Had Fiona seen her? She hadn't kept a very good eye on the door.

"If we were at your house, I'd snoop." Fiona winked at her, stuffing the stack of towels back into the cupboard.

"I don't believe you."

"I'm a total voyeur. You can tell so much about a person from the contents of their medicine cabinet. So, feel free to snoop away if you want. I'll warn you, though. I'm boring. There's not much to get worked up about. No exotic pills or unguents. Maybe some hemorrhoid cream, but that's for the dark circles under my eyes—I swear!"

"I'm not sure I believe you." Meg teased.

"It's sad but true. Unless you count my vibrator in a box on the other shelf. Boring stuff."

Meg nearly dropped the towel. "So boring." Was her voice a little higher than usual? She refolded the towel.

Fiona put her hands on her hips. "Don't judge. I have some erotica in my nightstand. You might find some links to some spicy websites on my browser history, too… Although it's been so long, I'm sure I've cleared that history by now." Fiona dropped her hands and sighed. "Okay, I admit it, I'm not a very interesting snoopee."

If Meg hadn't had a towel tucked under her chin folding it, her jaw would have dropped to the floor.

She cleared her throat. "Thanks for the full disclosure." God, she was turned on. Boring, her ass! She turned to make sure the cupboard was closed in an effort to restore her composure. "Feel free to browse my drawers anytime."

They searched each other's eyes and then burst out in laughter. The double entendre hadn't even been funny, but it helped to break a little of the tension building between them. Taking a deep breath, Meg walked unsteadily back to the living room.

47

KITTEN DUTY HAD BECOME A well-mapped out routine. While Fiona got the bottles ready, Meg took the kittens out of the box and got them arranged on her lap where she played with them as Fiona fed them one by one. Meg would clean each of their little mouths off after they'd finished eating and place them back in the box to sleep through their food coma. Once all the kittens had fed, Fiona took the bottles back to the kitchen, while Meg took the kittens into the bathroom to poop them. Finally, Fiona turned off the lights in the living room while Meg tidied up from poop duty.

They hadn't discussed the night's sleeping arrangements, and Fiona didn't want to assume anything just because Meg had slept in her bed the night before. After a moment of indecision, Fiona headed for the bedroom, hoping Meg would come find her. Nervousness danced in the pit of her stomach as she changed into a tank top and boxers.

She sat on the edge of the bed in the muted light of the bedside lamp and rubbed lotion onto her arms. When she looked up, Meg stood outside the door, the box of kittens in her arms.

"Ready for bed, stalker lady?" Fiona's heart thudded like a jackhammer. She didn't have any expectations, but she knew what she wanted, even if it wasn't a good idea.

Meg shifted the box in her arms. "I was just coming to say goodnight."

"Why are you doing it from out there? Come in here." She put the lotion bottle back on the nightstand. "I'm not going to demote you to the sofa simply because I'm no longer a basket case. What kind of host do you think I am?"

Meg laughed, but looked undecided, so Fiona got up and took the box from her, putting it on the floor at the foot of the bed. She went back to where she'd been sitting and put some lotion on her legs. Meg walked around the bed to the other side. When Fiona looked over her shoulder, Meg had stripped down to her tank top and panties.

"Do you want some jammies?" she asked.

Meg slid into bed beneath the feather comforter. "I'm good. Unless you'd prefer I wear something else."

Fiona turned off the light. "I want you to be comfortable."

"This is fine." Meg sighed as she settled in under the covers. "Your bed is so comfortable. It makes the bed at Aunt Vi's feel like a slab of concrete."

A boom went off outside and Fiona wondered what it was until a flash of red followed by blue outlined the blinds in her bedroom window. Fireworks! She'd almost forgotten.

"They set them off over the Hudson," Fiona said. The pops and booms sounded like they were right outside her window.

It had taken all of her will to keep her eyes open while she fed the kittens, but now she wasn't sure she was ready to sleep. She crawled into bed and rolled over to face Meg. As the comforter settled over them, she could smell Meg's scent, a mix of something herbal and sandalwood.

"I've decided to keep the baby." It just came out, although she hadn't planned on saying anything yet, wanting to wait to see if the decision stuck. Apparently it had.

Meg rolled onto her side and studied her. "I knew something major had happened. You have a happy, glimmery thing going on."

Fiona couldn't hide her smile. "I do?"

Meg nodded with a smile and reached out with both arms. When Fiona settled in her arms, her head lying in the curve of Meg's arm and chest, Meg rested her cheek against her forehead and stroked her hair. It was a delicious feeling—both the relief of telling Meg she was keeping the baby and being held so affectionately. She couldn't remember a better feeling.

"Congratulations, Fiona. You're going to make a great mother," Meg whispered.

Fiona didn't think she had any expectations, but she realized she had been worried about Meg's reaction. A wave of relief flowed through her and she began to cry, but her tears held no trace of the fear or sadness she'd been struggling with the past several days. She had decided to embrace the unexpected and to jump into the unknown with eyes, arms, and heart wide open. And jumping without a net to catch her was the most liberating feeling she had ever experienced. When Meg squeezed her tight, she couldn't imagine sharing the moment with anyone else.

<h1 style="text-align:center">48</h1>

THE WARM SOFTNESS OF FIONA in her arms was intoxicating. Meg didn't know how she found the courage to do it when she opened her arms to her. Only seconds before, she'd been tight as a drumskin, with sleep a million miles away, wondering how she was going to get close to Fiona without being weird about it. The night before had been natural. Fiona had been upset and she'd comforted her. Tonight was different. The day of thinking had obviously been good for her; this was the most relaxed Meg had ever seen her. She'd had a softness about her all evening, like she was lit from within. And that was a problem.

She liked Fiona. Like, really liked her. It was bad. So many things stood in the way of anything happening between them, but Meg was feeling things she shouldn't feel.

When Meg stood outside the bedroom watching her, she thought she was going to ignite. Dressed in nothing but the tank top and boxers, Fiona was a goddess. Knowing her feelings were wrong, Meg had every intention of bunking it on the couch, but Fiona had been firm about her sleeping in the bed with her. How could she say no? She knew she was justifying things, and it was wrong to want someone who was having such a hard time, but Meg couldn't help it. She'd probably never do anything about it, what with everything stacked against them, but it didn't mean they couldn't be friends, right? Friends who maybe cuddled sometimes.

Now, she was holding her and Fiona seemed lighter and happier than she'd ever seen her. For a minute, when Fiona had started to cry, Meg had worried the lightness had faded, but it turned out to be relief, and Meg couldn't blame her. Her life was going to take a whole new trajectory now, but it was her decision. Meg couldn't help but feel happy for Fiona. She wished she could be around to see how it all played out for her.

Fiona snuggled in closer, wrapping her arm around her, draping her leg over hers. The closeness was glorious but she wanted to be closer. An ache pulsed through her. What were they becoming to one another? She didn't know, but her fingers itched to touch her, to feel her. She stroked Fiona's thick hair and held her, kissing her head, breathing deeply. Fiona's body relaxed, her breathing growing slower and deeper. Was it possible she was asleep?

Meg adjusted slightly against Fiona and sighed. She could lie there and hold her forever. It was the last thing Meg remembered thinking before she drifted off, too.

49

SOFT MORNING LIGHT ILLUMINATED THE bedroom and Fiona tightened her embrace around the form pressed against her, nestling into the softness. Breathing in the scent of Meg, she drifted contentedly between sleep and awake, erotic warmth swirling around the edges of her consciousness. She pressed her hips closer, seeking pressure against the gentle pulse trembling between her legs. The space between awake and asleep held her captive. A smile played across her lips as she nuzzled into Meg, before she dipped back into the drowsier end of the sea of sleep in which she floated.

When Fiona reluctantly began to surface from her sleepy cocoon, it took several minutes for her to realize she wasn't next to Meg at all, but rather the pillow Meg had slept upon. Her disappointment was acute. Trying to keep the fantasy alive, she kept her head buried in the Meg-scented pillow and extended a tentative arm, seeking the warmth of the woman who shared her bed and dreams.

Not so much as a warm body-shaped indent met her seeking fingers. She propped herself up on one arm and looked blurrily around the empty bedroom. Her disappointment wrecked her, and Fiona buried herself in the pillow and tried to conjure back her rapidly fading dream. It was no good. The details were little more than vapor, but the sensations surging through her body were real and urgent. Unable to quell her feelings, Fiona groaned and rolled out of bed.

She expected to find Meg sitting on the floor feeding the kittens when she entered the living room, but Meg wasn't there. And after a brief search of her tiny apartment, Fiona realized Meg was nowhere to be found. The letdown was brutal. She had never yearned for the touch of another person as she had in those moments upon first waking. Loneliness enveloped Fiona like a cold cloak, yet her body still throbbed with desire. She considered going back to bed to attend to the almost painful ache, but she knew that wouldn't satisfy her longing.

She wanted Meg.

The note left on the table was some consolation, although it did little to dispel her loneliness and frustration. No one liked to wake up without a good-bye from their overnight guest—even if nothing had happened. Meg's neatly printed message said she wanted to get a run in before work, but that she'd be off work at five and that Fiona should call her. Fiona had the day off and wondered what she was going to do with it.

The minutes slid by at glacial speed. Fiona passed the time tending to the kittens, ignoring more texts from Mike, and shuffling half-heartedly through her caseload. It didn't take long before she found herself second-guessing whether she should call Meg, even though Meg had specifically asked her to. Was she being nice? Did she want to see her? Or was it just a check-in? She wasn't anyone's responsibility.

Once the idea entered her mind, she couldn't stop wondering. Did Meg think of her as a responsibility? She replayed the last few days in her mind, cringing to remember her displays of embarrassing emotional instability. Fiona decided not to call. Meg would call her if she wanted to see her.

At a little after one, she was washing her plate and silverware from lunch, when a knock on her door filled her stomach with butterflies. Hoping it was Meg, she put the plate in the drying rack and quickly dried her hands. She was about to open the door when hesitation made her look through the peephole. Mike stood on the other side of the door biting the skin around his thumb. She pressed against the wall. No. No. No. She wasn't ready to talk to him. He finally left when she didn't answer the door.

At least after Mike's appearance, she had something to think about other than whether or not she should call Meg. When five o'clock finally rolled around, Fiona's resolve started to soften. She picked up her phone repeatedly, only to put it down without dialing. Finally she had to walk away from the phone completely. She made it all the way down the hall before its draw became too powerful. She picked it up again, but another knock at the door made her jump. Was it Mike again?

A quick look through the peephole filled her with elation and she forgot about her earlier worry. It was Meg. She couldn't have hidden her smile if she tried. She opened the door and bounced on her tippy toes.

"I was just thinking about calling you." As if she hadn't been obsessing over it all day.

"I'm glad," Meg replied with a smile. Was that shyness in her eyes? "I almost went home instead of coming over. I've been greedy with your time lately."

"I was thinking I was the greedy one," she admitted. "It's what kept me from going down to the coffee shop to see you today."

Meg laughed. "I was hoping you would, actually. Betty teased me about watching the door all day."

She was relieved she wasn't the only one wondering about things all day. She followed Meg into the living room.

"Have you gone out at all today," Meg asked.

She tilted her head. "I haven't been out of my apartment since I went to the coffee shop to pick up breakfast a couple days ago.

"You need to get out, then. How do you feel about picking up some dinner and taking it to Morningside Park? We could take a blanket and sit on the grass."

The almost painful longing Fiona had woken up with, the longing to touch Meg—kiss her and so much more—had not faded throughout the day, and she thought maybe it would be a good idea for them to get away from the apartment. "A picnic sounds divine. I can go after I feed the kittens."

"Why don't I run and grab some food while you do that?"

Thirty minutes later, the kittens were fed and Meg had returned with a brown paper bag from McNeely's Deli. Fiona carried a blanket under her arm as they walked the two blocks to the park. She was nearly skipping with happiness about being with Meg. The sun was still high in the sky and the day was moderately warm, but the humidity was low and a nice breeze carrying the scent of water from the nearby Hudson River made the evening perfect for a picnic.

A block from their destination, they heard faint strains of music, which to their delight led them to an unexpected gathering of musicians and onlookers congregated in an open area inside the park. Music filled the air. Fiona spread the blanket out in a shady spot and Meg opened up the bag containing their dinner. They were on the outskirts of the crowd, and the turkey sandwiches, potato salad, and kosher dill pickles Meg had picked up were wonderful. Meg even had a surprise for her—a jumbo double chocolate caramel brownie, which they shared while watching the eclectic audience enjoy the music.

Fiona had gone to school or lived in the area for over seven years and had never known about the casual group of musicians who performed regularly in the park. It was a happy surprise to enjoy it for the first time with Meg. She was amazed at how the musicians improvised. Sometimes one or two performed together, while at other times the entire group came together, creating a symphony of sound that somehow weaved itself together perfectly. It was amazing and Fiona was possessed by the magic of the evening.

"The people watching is almost as fun as the music," Meg said, bobbing her head along with the music.

"Look at the joy. The woman over there is sparkling with it." Fiona discreetly motioned toward a woman several yards away, dancing with an unreserved passion, her long skirt swirling around her, her bare feet keeping time with the music in the thick green grass. There were quite a few people dancing, including one curly-headed little girl of two or three, who was swaying with innocent intensity. She screamed with glee when the song was over, jumping and clapping her chubby little hands.

Fiona basked in the euphoria that had enveloped the crowd. "I'll bet people float away from here on streams of bliss, no matter how rough their days may have been."

"They'd have to be dead inside not to," Meg agreed.

The musicians played until the sun began to set; the drums the last to perform, beating a slow tempo, seeming to invite night to fall. As people began to disperse, Meg and Fiona walked slowly back to Fiona's apartment, enjoying the peace that had descended when the last drum stopped playing. The streetlights flickered on as the evening light made way for darkness—or what acted as darkness in the ever present ambient light of New York City.

Fiona inhaled the night air and sighed. A sense of being in the exact right place, at the exact right time, with the exact right person, filled her. "I love it when I can smell the Hudson in the evening like this. Something about it reminds me of the river back home where my dad took me fishing when I was a kid. It would be just me and my dad sitting on the muddy river bank, holding our poles, watching the water bugs skim across the surface near the edge of the river."

"What a great memory," Meg said quietly. "I can honestly say that being in the city has not once reminded me of home."

"Is that good or bad?" Fiona glanced at her.

"Neither." Meg shrugged. "I love Seattle. I also like New York. Ithaca was nice, but the winters are harsh."

"A little cold for you?" Fiona laughed.

Meg made a ticking noise. "Cold is an understatement. Feet of snow. Biting winds. Frozen fingers and toes."

"I don't think I could live somewhere where it doesn't snow."

"It snows once in a while in Seattle, but even when it does, it doesn't stick. Hearing my mom complain, though, you'd think it was Siberia."

"I didn't know it snowed there. I picture it as always green."

Meg nodded. "The city shuts down when it does. But inland is different. In Okanogan, where my aunt's clinic is, they get around ten inches a month on average during the winter months—not too much, not too little. Perfect for snowshoeing and cross country skiing."

"Besides a layover in LAX, I've never been to the west coast, let alone the Pacific Northwest," she said. "I'd like to visit some time."

"You should." They descended the steps to Fiona's front door.

Fiona keyed the lock, but the key wouldn't turn all the way. "It's the humidity." She handed the blanket to Meg and wrestled with the tricky deadbolt, tugging and trying to turn the key as she whispered an inspired curse. "I hate this door sometimes!"

"A little graphite sprayed in the deadbolt would probably make it easier to open," Meg said, as Fiona found the perfect tug/key-turn combination and the bolt finally slid open.

She took the blanket from Meg. "I think my landlord gave me some for the keyhole on my storage space."

Meg inspected the deadbolt. "I can see if it helps."

"Sure. Hold on." She pushed the door open and went to find it.

A few seconds later, she came back with a small spray tube. Meg squirted some inside of the strike hole in the doorjamb and then a little onto the bolt and tested it. It worked beautifully. The bolt slid in and out with ease.

"That should do it!" Meg looked pleased with herself.

"Feeling handy, are you?" Fiona teased.

Meg gave her a roguish grin. "As much as I don't give a damn about gender roles, it's a bit of a rush when I get to unleash a little of my inner butch."

Fiona snorted and covered her mouth. "Be careful what you wish for. I'll be calling you more often to display your handywoman skills."

She laughed aloud when Meg hooked her thumbs in her pockets and strutted into the living room. She didn't look the part in her REI hiking shorts, black tank top, and Rainbow flip flops. "Is there any wood you need chopped, Ma'am?"

"Dang! I chopped all the wood this morning." Fiona flopped onto the couch after she gave Meg's arm a little shove. Meg laughed and flopped down beside her.

"Well, you know who to call now."

"Seriously, though. You don't know how much of a pain it's been—especially when I'm loaded down with grocery bags. Where'd you learn that trick?"

Meg shrugged. "I'm not sure. I've always just been good with my hands."

"Now I know who to call. You know. When I need a good pair of hands." Fiona knew how it sounded and tried to suppress a smile. She almost succeeded, but when Meg looked at her, they both burst out laughing.

Fiona wiped a tear from her eye and got up to put the tube of graphite away. As she rose, she slid her hand along Meg's neck. "You sure get red when you blush."

Meg stopped laughing and when she locked eyes with Fiona she suddenly found it hard to breathe. Fiona slowly pulled her hand back, and nearly brought it to her lips. She cleared her throat. "What are we going to do with the rest of our night?"

50

A THOUSAND RESPONSES WENT THROUGH Meg's mind, but the one thing she really wanted to do was probably not what Fiona had in mind, even though her eyes and her touch—god, her touch!—seemed to indicate otherwise. The skin on her neck was hot where Fiona's fingertips had swept across it and if Fiona thought she was blushing before, the heat rising to her cheeks was like a brush fire now. It was all she could do to stay on the couch and try to breathe normally.

"What's wrong?" Fiona asked. "You were all swagger a minute ago. Now you're just staring at me."

Meg blinked a few times to clear her head. Fiona must think she was having some sort of episode or something. "I… I was trying to think of something to do."

"We could watch a movie or something. Were you planning on staying over again?"

She had been hoping to stay over. The situation with Vi and all her drama was sure to continue at her place, but more than anything, she enjoyed sharing the bed with Fiona. As much as her attraction had continued to grow for her beautiful new friend, and as much as she would have expected her frustration about not being able to do anything about it to keep her from sleeping all night, she was surprised to find it was the opposite. She'd slept extremely well with Fiona by her side. But, was Fiona hoping to have her bed to herself tonight?

She sat forward. "Do you want me to leave? Are you tired? Because, I can leave if you need—"

"I'm not tired. I like having you here and a movie sounds good, actually." Fiona popped the lid to the graphite on and off the tube. Was she nervous?

"Are you sure? Because it's not a big deal. I can poop the kittens and take off, if you want."

Fiona scrunched her forehead. "Well, to be honest, I feel bad relying on you to wake up in the middle of the night every night. It's not fair for me to get to sleep, while you do all the work."

In Meg's eyes, Fiona had been doing almost all of the work—getting the formula, feeding them all day, staying with them all the time. "You're with them all day, though. And you need your sleep."

Fiona's shoulders relaxed. "I've been feeling so much better with all the sleep I've gotten the last few days. And for some reason, I seem to sleep better when you're here. It won't be so hard to get up and go to work in the morning. By the way, are you sure you're okay taking them tomorrow?"

Meg smiled and tipped her head to the side. "I have the day off and nothing better to do. So I guess it's settled. I'm staying over."

Fiona smiled back. "Good. It's settled."

As if to support their decision, the kittens woke up and started to meow.

Meg got up from the couch and looked into the box. Six little heads looked up at her expectantly and the volume of their pleas increased threefold. "Perfect timing, kids."

Fiona headed toward the kitchen. "I'll get the formula ready if you get the wee beasties ready. You know where the clean towels are."

"Aye aye, Captain." Meg headed to the bathroom. As usual, the specter of what was hidden in the tin in Fiona's cupboard titillated Meg's imagination. She tried and failed to push it from her mind as she attended to the kittens.

From start to finish, it took them about thirty minutes to get the kittens fed and pooped. Soon all six were sleeping soundly in Meg and Fiona's laps, while Fiona scrolled through the movie selection on her streaming feed. "I haven't been to the movies in so long, anything will be new to me. You pick."

Meg stroked the belly of one of the kittens in her lap, amazed at how much they'd grown in the last few days. "How about a comedy?"

"Are you into romantic comedies?"

"It's one of my very favorite genres."

"Mine, too!"

In the end they settled on an old Meg Ryan film and recited most of the lines together. About halfway through the film, Meg looked over and caught Fiona staring at the kittens in her lap with the saddest look on her face.

"What's wrong?"

Fiona looked up and her eyes were glittering with tears. "Once they go to the foster home tomorrow, I'll never see them again."

Fiona's sadness pulled at Meg's heart and she used the remote to pause the movie. "They'll go to good homes. I promise."

"But, I'll miss them." Tears rolled down Fiona's cheeks. Meg didn't know what else to do. She pulled her into a hug. With kittens in both of their laps, the position wasn't incredibly comfortable, but Fiona held onto her. Eventually, Fiona pulled away and wiped her nose on the hem of her shirt. "God, you must be sick of me bawling all over the place."

"If anyone has the right to cry, it's you."

Fiona rolled her eyes. "Because I'm such a sad sack these days? I wish we met when I wasn't such a wreck."

Meg ran her hand along Fiona's arm. "You're not a wreck."

"Believe me, I am." Fiona wiped her nose again. "And now, I'm a snotty wreck. I have to change my shirt. Actually, I think I'll go to bed. You can finish the movie if you want. There are only a few minutes left."

Meg put the kittens in their box. "I've seen it enough times. I'm tired, too."

They got ready for bed, and once again, Meg declined Fiona's offer of pajamas, wearing her T-shirt and underwear to bed.

As soon as they crawled under the covers, Fiona moved to Meg's side and snuggled in. The physical response Meg had was stronger than the night before, and she wondered what it would be like to explore the beautiful body within the circle of her embrace. She dozed off with a hungry ache and less than innocent thoughts of the woman who fell almost immediately asleep in her arms.

51

THE CLOCK SAID SHE HAD a few minutes before the alarm would go off, but Fiona was wide awake and didn't want to get out of bed. She blamed it on the woman who had her arm draped around her, gently cupping her breast, but she wasn't complaining. She snuggled further into the soft body pressed along the length of her back and tried not to groan when electric bolts of desire pulsed through her body and converged between her legs. This time, the body next to her was very real.

In the predawn shadows, she lay on her side and floated in the erotic comfort of Meg's warmth. She could barely stand it. Breasts against her back. Bare legs tangled among hers. Strong arms wrapped tightly around her. She ached with desire. Shifting further into the warmth, her core pulsed and Meg tightened the embrace in her sleep. Fiona couldn't hold back a shudder when Meg's lips brushed across her exposed shoulder. Gooseflesh rose all over her as warm breath tickled across her skin. Arousal coursed through her. Meg's leg, so close to her core, tempted Fiona in ways she'd never felt before. As much as Fiona didn't want to move, she needed to get up before she did something embarrassing.

Once again, she had slept like a log. She hadn't heard the kittens at all during the night. Meg must have attended to them, so it was only fair to let her sleep. She slid from the cocoon of warmth and sat on the edge of the bed. A sound of displeasure made her turn in time to see Meg reach out in her sleep. Fiona almost crept back into bed at the sight, but instead she turned off the alarm and watched Meg sleep for a few more seconds before she stood.

A short while later, Fiona was showered and ready for work. She had some time to spare before she set out on her short walk to the office. Most days, Fiona went into the office early, but with Meg in her bed, she found it hard to leave the apartment. A shiver ran through her at the thought of the possibilities lying under the feather comforter. She stood at the front door contemplating the short distance spanning the real world and the fulfillment of her desire. It was pure terror that helped her decide to leave for Helga's, instead. With nothing in the house for breakfast, she'd get coffee and muffins for Meg.

The trip to the café was refreshing, and Fiona bathed in the beauty of the morning. The tension she'd woken with began to fade to a pleasant ache. When she made it back to the apartment, Fiona grinned when she didn't have to wrestle the door to get it unlocked.

She tiptoed into the bedroom and silently placed the coffee and muffins on the bedside table. She realized Meg had moved over and was lying on the side of the bed she had recently vacated. A quiver ran through her when she imagined Meg seeking her out in her sleep. She pushed a strand of Meg's hair from her face, leaving her finger to rest along her cheek. A small smile made its way to Meg's full lips, and Fiona almost traced it with her finger. Instead, she withdrew her hand and backed out of the room. God! She was acting like a weird stalker!

She left a key with a note in plain view on the kitchen table and gave each of the kittens a kiss goodbye. Unsuccessfully fighting back tears, she lifted Cardboard last and cradled him against her cheek. He pushed his little front paws against her face, nuzzling her, and her heart broke. She'd miss him so much! Finally she put him back, took a deep breath, and left the apartment. The warm sunshine barely registered this time. She hadn't expected to fall in love with the kittens. She walked slowly so her tears would dry before she arrived at the office.

Once at work, Fiona hoped her caseload—most of which was still the work of a research assistant because of the transition—would be a good distraction, but she found it difficult to stay focused. It was repetitious and mind-numbing, not nearly challenging enough to keep her mind engaged. Irritation at the partners for not hiring a research assistant to backfill her old position welled within her. She knew her anger was derived from sadness about the kittens, but it didn't make it go away.

The whir of the printer was hypnotizing as she watched the last few pages drop into the tray. A bird glided by the large window behind her desk and her mind wandered down the path of her unknown future. Her thoughts came to a vision of her playing outside with a little girl. In her daydream, the toddler was raising her arms for a lift into a tire swing, like the one Fiona's father had put up in her front yard when she was a young child. Wispy, blonde curls haloed a cherubic face, and Fiona saw herself lifting the smiling toddler up into the swing. She gave the little girl a kiss before giving her a gentle push. Fiona smiled at the picture in her mind, and imagined getting an enthusiastic hug around her neck from chubby little arms.

What was going on? Her imagination was running rampant today!

Trying to focus on her work, Fiona's eyes shifted to the stack of papers lying in the printer tray, but as she went to pick them up, her eyes drifted back to the amazing cityscape sprawling before her. It was then she realized she was going to need to leave the city to raise her child. It was all there was to it. She loved being a lawyer, and she had never envisioned practicing anywhere else but in the city, but now she knew she had to think of her child, which meant moving away. Where would she go, though?

The first places she thought of were rural Pennsylvania and Ithaca. Aside from New York City, they were the only places she knew, but she didn't want to go back to either of those. She needed somewhere new. A new place to start a new life. In an interesting twist, for once in her life, she didn't feel like she had to figure it out right then. The details would work themselves out when she needed them to. She laughed at herself. What a strange turn around for a woman who had only recently had her entire life planned out.

*****

FIONA OPENED HER FRONT DOOR after work and automatically looked for the kittens. The box was gone. She knew it would be, but it didn't stop her from looking. The empty space near the recliner unleashed the sadness she'd fought all day. A sob stuck in her throat as she tossed her cell phone and keys onto the recliner. The apartment seemed empty and too quiet. It had only been a few days, but it felt like the kittens had always been there. And now they were gone. She stopped trying to fight back the tears. She dropped her bag onto the kitchen table and collapsed onto a chair as her grief poured from her.

After several minutes, she spotted the note written on the back of the one she had left for Meg.

Fiona smiled through her tears. It was just like Meg to try to allay her sadness. Knowing she could see the kittens again made her feel a little better. She went to her room to change into some warm up pants and a T-shirt. She stopped in the doorway. She looked at the bed and it occurred to her that there was no reason for Meg to stay the night with her now that the kittens were gone. It made her feel their absence even more.

52

BY NOW, MEG COULD TELL time by the ebb and flow of the customers at Helga's. It was almost five and the shop was mostly deserted, with only two customers in the back who had been heads down over computers at separate tables for the last two hours. It would soon pick up when the caffeine addicts checked out of their day jobs. Meg was wiping down the espresso machine while Betty, who had the closing shift, sat casually on the back counter, swinging her legs in time with the music playing over the shop stereo, topping off the creamer and sweetener dispensers. Betty had picked the music that day, and it was an all-girl rock band Meg had never heard. She listened with half an ear to Betty describe opening for the band in the Village over the weekend.

"The bassist was wildly hot. Thor. Wicked name, huh? Her girlfriend did not appreciate me talking to her. How was I to know she was attached?" Betty chuckled. "Thor didn't seem to mind, though."

"Mmmhmm." Meg wondered how Fiona was doing.

"But I draw the line at married chicks, you know?"

"Yeah." Meg remembered how good Fiona felt in her arms last night.

"I should have paid more attention to the lead singer, though. Redd got cozy with her and I'm sure the bulge in the jeans under her leather chaps was not a roll of socks. Girlfriend was packing. I'd bet my tips for the month on it. I'll have to get the deets from Redd tonight at rehearsal."

"Interesting." Remembered threads of the erotic dreams she'd had of making love to Fiona floated through her mind. Her body responded much like it had in her dreams. She hoped she hadn't let her hands wander too much in her sleep. Fiona had brought her breakfast, so she probably wasn't upset if they had. Had they?

A minute or two went by and Meg realized it was quiet. She looked over her shoulder. Betty was sitting there, hands dangling between her knees, staring at her with a contemplative look.

"What?" she asked.

"You haven't heard a word I've been saying, have you?"

Meg turned and leaned her butt against the cabinet. "Bassist. Thor. Hot. Lead singer. Bulging leather pants. I was listening."

"Uh huh." Betty nodded with a smirk.

Meg heard the jingle of keys hitting the granite surface behind her and turned to see Fiona standing there.

"How long have you been here?"

"Let's just say I can't wait to hear more about the bulging leather pants of which you speak."

Betty snorted behind her.

"Shut up." Meg threw the cleaning rag at her. "I'm sure Betty'd give you every horny detail if you give her the chance."

Betty hopped down. "You watch the register and me and Fi—"

Meg blocked Betty's exit. "You stay here, hot stuff."

All interest in singers who packed was forgotten as Meg went around to join Fiona.

Fiona's smile brightened considerably when she approached. It made Meg quiver.

"Hey gorgeous," Meg said and then tried not to grimace. Had she really called her gorgeous out loud? She blamed Betty. "How was your day?"

Fiona pushed her hair behind her ear. "My day was okay, but it's better now."

She didn't seem to mind the gorgeous comment. Meg was captivated by Fiona's sparkling eyes.

Betty, who was again sitting on the rear counter, put her finger in her mouth and pretended to gag before she slid off her perch. Meg rolled her eyes and Fiona turned to look.

"Why don't you two love birds go sit down or get a room or something?" Betty twirled the rag Meg had tossed to her.

"Love birds? You're high." Meg snorted, but her face grew hot.

"Whatever." Betty threw the rag at Meg. "Take your googly eyes somewhere else. I'm getting nauseated."

Meg caught the rag. "I have an hour left on my shift."

"I got it. Get out of here." Betty motioned with her hand to the nearly empty coffee shop. "Somehow, I'll manage the hoards on my own."

"Fine. You won't have me to kick around anymore." Meg teased, taking off her apron.

When she and Fiona were outside, Meg automatically turned in the direction of their street, but Fiona grabbed her arm and pulled her in the opposite direction.

"I'm taking you to my favorite hole in the wall pizza joint. I've been craving it all day. Plus, the apartment is depressing."

Meg stopped and Fiona turned around. The sad look on Fiona's face made her heart ache. She missed the kittens, too. "Come here." She opened her arms and Fiona walked into them, molding against Meg, as if she'd craved the touch for a long time.

"I'm not gonna get snot all over you again." Fiona laughed and stepped back after a couple of minutes. She wiped her eyes and sniffed.

"I'm a vet. Believe me, I've had worse."

Fiona held up a hand. "I won't ask. I'm starving and I refuse to ruin my dinner."

"What's the name of this hole in the wall pizza joint, anyway? And what if I already ate?"

"Hole in the Wall Pizza Joint," Fiona said, walking again. She didn't say "duh", but it was implied in the tone of her voice. "You can watch me eat then. I'm starving."

"It was a hypothetical question. I haven't eaten." Meg grinned.

A block and a half later, they stood before what, from the outside, seriously did look to be a hole in the wall. Nestled between two buildings was one of the narrowest restaurants Meg had ever seen. When they entered, it barely accommodated a single row of small tables down one wall, with just enough room to walk along the other to get to the back bar to order. What the restaurant lacked in width, it made up for in length, and Meg wondered how they passed fire inspection. They walked single file past the mostly occupied tables and walls filled with framed black and white headshots of celebrities who had eaten there, all the way to the back counter where they placed their order of one large pepperoni, mushroom, and black olive pizza with extra cheese.

A table freed up as their order was ready and they snagged it.

"This smells amazing." Meg placed the pie on the table.

"I think this looks good." Fiona placed Meg's beer next to the pizza as she took a sip of her own lemonade.

Meg sighed after taking a long drink. She didn't want to rub it in, but the beer—actually a porter—was delicious. "I'll buy you several after… you know." She nodded at Fiona's middle.

Fiona frowned, but shrugged. "So. The kittens are in foster care." Her shoulders sagged as she took a bite of pizza.

"Yes." The first bite of pizza filled Meg's mouth with heavenly flavor. She may have moaned. "I want to curse, this is so good!"

"I know, right? I should own stock I come here so often." Fiona bit into her pizza. Meg wanted Fiona to look at her like she looked at that slice.

"Huh?" Meg watched Fiona wipe her mouth. What had she said?

"I asked about Teri, the kitten foster lady. How was she?"

"She seemed very nice. I could tell she knew her way around a kitten."

"Did you see her hold them? Did she love on them?" Fiona rubbed her eyes. "Listen to me. I'm crying again and acting like it was an interview, or something."

Meg took Fiona's hand. "I get it. She was confident with them and she treated them as if they were precious."

"That's how you treat them. The first time I saw you with them, I thought the same thing about you."

Meg glowed with pleasure at the compliment, and was about to tell Fiona how much it meant to her, when a voice cut into their conversation.

"Fi? Is that you? I knew it!" A woman approached the table.

"Maureen!" Fiona jumped up and hugged the woman. "It's been ages!"

"Due to no fault of my own, Ms. Never Returns Phone Calls." The tall redhead peered over Fiona's shoulder, looking Meg up and down. "Who's your friend?"

Meg wasn't sure she appreciated the scrutiny. Who was this woman? She put down her pizza and stood. "I'm Meg."

Fiona laughed and let go of her friend. "I suck. Maureen Mallory, my dear friend from law school, meet Meg Jordan…" Fiona searched Meg's face, and Meg wondered what was going through her mind. Who was she to her? "Meg is my dear friend from the coffee shop."

"Dear friend" was good, right? She could live with "dear friend". Couldn't she?

So, this was one of Fiona's friends from school. Aside from Mike, the baby daddy, Fiona hadn't said a whole lot about her friends but everything she'd said had been good.

"Coffee shop friends, huh?" Maureen looked amused.

Meg wondered why Maureen was amused. It seemed a bit condescending toward Fiona. She seemed nice enough, though. Nevertheless, a protective urge welled up within her. "Helga's. It's down the street from Fiona's apartment."

Maureen chuckled. "I know where it is. But I wasn't aware Fi had been making new friends there."

Fiona seemed to think it was funny. "Meg, don't hate my rude friend, she's only sizing you up to make sure you aren't a serial killer or something."

"I'm definitely not a serial killer. Nice to meet you." Meg held out her hand. She wasn't sure what she expected, or if she even had any expectations, but the stunning redhead before her was a surprise. She had nothing on Fiona, and she wasn't her type at all, but Meg could see why half the heads in the restaurant were turned in their direction.

Maureen took her hand. "You look awfully familiar."

"Probably from Helga's," Fiona suggested. "Meg's helping out while the owner is away."

"That's probably it." Maureen studied Meg before she turned back to Fiona. "You look more beautiful than ever, Fi. Being out from under all those books seems to agree with you. I feel like we haven't seen each other in weeks!"

Fiona looked away. The good cheer she'd exuded at seeing Maureen dimmed. Meg knew then that Fiona hadn't told her about the baby. "Sorry. I've been tied up with things."

"I'll bet." Maureen gave Meg another appraising look like she was looking at a prize squash at a county fair. "We need to catch up. I want to hear more about what," she raised an eyebrow, "or who, has you tied up."

Fiona blushed and Meg wanted to laugh. Maureen's inference was clever, even if it was off-base. "Do you want to join us?" Fiona asked.

"I can't. Josh is waiting for me back at the apartment."

"Don't you mean Robert?" Fiona asked.

Maureen grimaced. It was her turn to look away. "Yeah, um. No. I meant Josh."

Fiona frowned and tilted her head. Meg watched the interaction with interest. She knew Josh from the coffee shop, if Maureen was talking about the same Josh who'd been there with Fiona and liked to call himself Harpo.

From the look on Fiona's face something pretty major was being discussed.

"Is Robert out of town?"

Who was Robert?

Maureen studied her fingernails. "I've been meaning to call you. Like you, I've been a little tied up." She looked up. "With Josh."

Fiona looked confused. "What about Robert?"

Maureen shook her hair back. "Robert moved out."

Fiona's eyebrows shot up and grabbed Maureen's arm. "Wait. What? I'm sorry about Robert, but you and Josh? I knew he had a thing for you, but… whoa."

Meg told herself to get the details later. This was good.

Maureen bit her bottom lip and wrinkled her nose. "Yeah. We've been seeing each other since right before we got our results back, actually." She obviously worried about Fiona's reaction.

Fiona mimicked Maureen's expression. "But Robert…"

"We're not proud of it. It just sort of happened, and you know Robert and I weren't happy. If I had to do it again, I'd have broken it off with him first."

"I see."

Maureen pinched her eyebrow and studied Fiona like Fiona's opinion would define everything going forward. "I suck. I know."

Fiona ran her hand up and down Maureen's arm. "I'm not judging you, Maureen. We could all see how unhappy you were." She bounced. "Oh, my gosh! I can't wait to tease Josh. This is great. I mean, I'm happy for both of you." Fiona hugged Maureen.

Maureen laughed. "God! I've been wanting to call you, Fi. But, I didn't know how to tell you and, well, we hardly get out of bed. The sex is phenomenal and—"

Fiona put her hand over Maureen's mouth and made a gagging sound. "Okay! Okay! I get it." Meg found the exchange juvenilely adorable. Maureen laughed.

"Pie for Mallory!"

Maureen looked toward the voice. "There's my order. I'm so glad I bumped into you. Nice to meet you Meg." Maureen backed toward her waiting pizza and blew a kiss at Fiona. "I'll call you soon, promise!"

Meg watched Fiona watch Maureen walk away and they both sat down. It felt like a tornado had whipped through the tiny restaurant, and it was time to regroup.

"No wonder she hasn't been stalking me lately." Fiona sounded like she was still shocked.

"Stalking you?" Meg took a bite of her pizza and was surprised it was still warm. So much had been exchanged in the span of a few minutes.

"It just occurred to me that she would have never let me barricade myself in my apartment if she hadn't been preoccupied with something. Now it makes sense… Oh!" Fiona stared into the space over Meg's shoulder.

"What?" Meg looked behind her, expecting Maureen to be there, but there was no one.

"Josh was trying to tell me about them the first day I saw you at Helga's. God, I'm a lousy friend." Fiona smacked her forehead.

"You know him from school, too, right?" Meg asked.

"We all went to law school together. Mike, too. They're probably my best friends. Josh and Maureen are good people. I'm glad they're together." Fiona ate some of her pizza and closed her eyes. "God, this is so good."

"Do they know about…?" Meg gestured toward Fiona's belly.

Fiona grimaced and shook her head, but didn't stop eating. "No. I haven't had the courage to tell them yet. It's awkward, what with Mike… you know? And I didn't know if I was going to keep it."

"Are they going to freak out?"

"Probably." Fiona looked like she was considering it. "I need to tell them. You saw how dramatic Maureen can be."

Meg nodded her head. It was best not to comment, she figured. They both ate their pizza.

After a moment, Fiona spoke. "It's pathetic that I haven't told my best friends, huh?"

Meg understood. "You needed time to process it on your own first. They should understand."

Fiona reached over the small table and grabbed Meg's hand. "Where would I be without you?" Her eyes gleamed with emotion. "Thanks for being here for me. I feel like we've known each other much longer than we have."

Meg smiled and squeezed her hand.

✶✶✶✶✶

THE LAST OF THE DAY'S light had faded from the sky, and the streetlights were on when they left the pizza place to go home. They talked about the neighborhood, architecture, work, and several other topics. A few blocks from the restaurant, they heard the low strains of a cello coming from the open window of one of the apartments. The sound floated down over them and they paused to listen next to the stairs leading up to the building.

"You know… I've never wanted to spend so much time with someone." Fiona sounded a little vulnerable and Meg wanted to reassure her. She moved closer, but didn't touch her.

"I've been thinking the same thing." The music, the night air, the surroundings—they all culminated in a perfect moment and being closer to Fiona seemed so right.

She watched Fiona trace the lines along the stone column next to the stoop.

"I've always been so focused on my future. Or maybe I've just never met anyone like you before, but I like this. I like being here. I like being with you."

Meg's heart melted. "I'm glad, because I like being here with you, too. Aunt Vi isn't always the most eloquent of people, but she said something to me a few days ago. She said, if you constantly live for tomorrow, you miss out on your todays." She laid her hand next to Fiona's on the column. "You definitely help me remember to appreciate my todays."

"I haven't always been like this, you know." Fiona searched her eyes.

"I know. That's why there's still hope for you." Meg teased.

They walked on in silence for a moment. The sound of a lone tree frog echoed through the night.

"It never ceases to amaze me when I hear country sounds in this big city," Meg said.

"Did you get to play outside a lot as a kid? I imagine you outside in all the green they have in Washington."

Meg snorted. "Are you kidding? We were outside from dawn to dusk. We have this creek running along our property. One time I caught a bunch of pollywogs. I filled the bathtub with water, figuring I would raise them there, but my mom found them and pulled the plug. Down they went. I cried for hours." Fiona took Meg's hand and squeezed. She didn't let go of it after, and Meg interlaced their fingers. "When my dad came home he asked what was wrong. When I told him, he said they had gone to the ocean and would be happier in the wild. It made me feel better. Of course, I know better now."

"I had a similar experience with some baby birds. They fell out of a nest in a tree near our house when I was a kid. I put them in a shoebox with some old rags and tried to take care of them. One day they were gone. My mom said they'd grown their feathers overnight and flew away. Looking back, I know that wasn't the case. They were too young. They probably died, but my mom gave me hope."

"You have a knack for saving baby animals, huh?"

Fiona laughed but it sounded sad. Meg was sorry she brought them up.

"I hope the kittens fare better than the baby birds," Fiona said.

Meg squeezed her hand, enjoying the warmth of it against her palm. "I have no doubt they will."

Too soon, they arrived at Fiona's front door. Meg didn't want the evening to end, but she suspected Fiona didn't either. She missed the kittens a little more for not giving her an excuse to spend the night again, and immediately felt selfish for it.

"Well, I guess this is goodnight." Meg looked down at their intertwined fingers.

"I wish I didn't have to work in the morning." Fiona looked into Meg's eyes as if she were trying to read her thoughts.

"Me too."

"Give us a hug, then." Fiona held out her arms.

Meg laughed at the pathetic Irish accent, but stepped into Fiona's arms. Memories of holding Fiona while she slept the night before swept through her mind. She wracked her brain for an excuse to see her the next day. When Fiona released her, she had to force herself to let go, too. The surprising sensation of warm lips against her own was a surprise, igniting a rush of electricity through her body. She melted into Fiona, returning the kiss with a moan. Fiona's lips were an epiphany, softer and warmer than Meg had dared to imagine. Fiona opened her lips to explore Meg's mouth, and the first soft brush of Fiona's tongue against hers sent a wave of heat rocketing between them, making them both tremble. No longer just a kiss, it was a promise of things to come. Backing Fiona against the front door, her hands moved up to hold Fiona's head as she pressed the length of her body against her. Lost, Meg gave herself over to the woman in her arms. She knew she wasn't going to be leaving as a fire of need engulfed her.

53

LOST IN THEIR KISSES, FIONA had no memory of entering the apartment, nor did she remember the walk to her bedroom, but suddenly there they were, and the edge of the bed was pressed against the back of her thighs. All she knew was the heat of the kiss, driving pleasure into the furthest edges of her body. She sank into the sensation of Meg's mouth exploring hers with a passion that was more intense than anything she had ever felt before. God. Her kisses. Her hands. Her body.

She trembled with desire as Meg lowered her onto the bed. Together, they moved to the center of the bed. Meg hovered above her, kissing her, touching her. She was already past the point of no return. She wanted Meg more than she'd ever wanted anything.

Meg pulled away. Not far, but Fiona tried to pull her back. "Are you sure about this?" Meg's voice was low and out of breath. Fiona's skin tingled to know she was the cause of it. She reached up and kissed her again.

Fiona groaned as the lips she couldn't get enough of pulled away again. Her eyes flew open. Meg's incredible eyes searched Fiona's, the question reflected in their depth. She took Meg's face between her hands. Her eyes traced a path that her thumbs gently followed, and they grazed the dark lips she craved to kiss again. "Oh, God, yes. I'm sure." She pulled Meg's head down, kissing her with deliberate intent to show her how ready she was.

Meg smiled into the kiss and Fiona started a trail of kisses down her chin, across her jaw, and down the curve of her neck. The journey was a discovery. She inhaled Meg's scent as she learned the landscape of her graceful throat, feeling the rapid beat of Meg's heart beneath her lips. She paused to nip and lick the tender flesh, eliciting another deep groan. Meg claimed her mouth once again and the weight of her body spread over Fiona.

A long moan escaped from deep within her throat when Meg's thigh pressed against her center. Meg rocked gently, teasing more moans from her. Fiona's sex pulsed. Her hips moved, seeking more pressure. Their kiss became fervent, and Fiona sucked and explored Meg's lips, driving both of them into a higher frenzy.

She was a supernova, dense with desire, on the verge of either imploding or igniting. There was no room for anything else, yet the feelings mounting within her continued to grow. Fiona slid her hands under the edge of Meg's shirt and ran them along her bare skin. The feel of Meg's skin was silk against her palms and when Meg arched into her, Fiona wanted to scream from the powerful sensations coursing through her body. It was a revelation on a scale she'd never known possible, and her body, mind, and soul burned.

Fiona sensed Meg was riding the same intensity of sensation. She could feel it in her kisses, sense it in her touch, see it in her eyes. Fiona had never wanted anyone the way she wanted Meg. It took every ounce of her will not to shove her hand down the front of Meg's pants to seek out the wet heat she knew awaited her. She was on fire.

Meg wiggled out of her shirt and sports bra, causing Fiona's need to expand. She took in the body before her and let her hands wander, exploring her abdomen, her rib cage, her hips, rising to brush along the sides of her breasts. Meg guided her hands to cup her breasts and she leaned into her, her eyes dark with desire. Fiona had never seen anything so beautiful. Her own nipples strained against the thin material of her bra as she circled Meg's nipples and finally took one into her mouth, relishing the texture, reveling in Meg's response to her tongue. A deep and imploring moan trembled from Meg's throat, echoing between them.

"I've never wanted anyone the way I want you, Fiona." Meg whispered, before taking a gasping breath.

"God, you feel incredible, Meg. I've never felt so… so… much." Fiona was overcome with the soft warmth of Meg's breasts cupped in her palms, her nipple playing against her lip. "I want to touch you everywhere."

"I want you so badly." Meg's voice was thick with emotion as Fiona's tongue and lips continued to explore her breasts. Fiona wrapped an arm around Meg's waist, and pulled her close as she held a breast in one hand and kissed and sucked the other. The pleasure Fiona received from the taste and feel of Meg's tender skin was something she had never imagined. Her passion surged, threatening to break her open.

Meg's breathing grew more and more jagged with every movement of Fiona's lips and tongue. A throb pulsed in Fiona's lower belly as Meg rocked against her, her thigh pressed into the warmth between her legs. She craved to feel Meg's bare skin pressed against her. Meg began to unbutton her shirt.

"I'm about a millisecond from coming." Meg pulled back, disengaging Fiona's exploring lips from her breast.

"Then let me keep doing it." Fiona tried to pull her back, but Meg laughed and rolled to her side. The movement took the pressure from Fiona's center and she tried to follow it.

"I'd like my first time with you to take a little longer." Meg pushed Fiona back against the mattress and continued to unbutton her shirt. With each button opened, Meg stroked the revealed skin, causing goosebumps to rise across Fiona's torso. With tantalizing slowness, Meg finished unbuttoning her shirt and pulled it off. And with a flick of her fingers, Fiona's bra was unclasped and sliding off her shoulders.

Fiona barely breathed while Meg's eyes traveled across her body, their path leaving a trail of heat on her exposed skin. When Meg pulled her close, Fiona purred, experiencing the feel of their soft, warm breasts pressed together for the first time. She wrapped her arms around Meg, relishing the silken skin gliding against her. Her desire for more leapt to an aching imperative.

"Nothing I ever imagined…" Fiona was unable to finish her thought. She needed to kiss Meg. The sensations swirling through her body, mind, and heart were too complex to express any other way. A thrumming electric charge pulsed between them. It was an all-consuming need to touch and be touched.

"I want to feel all of you against me," Fiona whispered against Meg's mouth. She arched into the press of their bodies. A deep throb beat within her, a precursor to what she knew was coming.

"I'm struggling not to rip the rest of your clothes off." Meg sounded out of breath. "You're making me crazy."

"We'll have time for slow later. I want to feel you inside of me, Meg. I can almost feel you now." She could barely believe the words coming from her mouth. This was new territory, but she was safe and felt secure enough to ask for what she wanted. She impatiently reached between them to get to the buttons of Meg's shorts and slid them down her sculpted thighs, along with her underwear. Meg seemed just as impatient. She moved her hands into the waist of Fiona's warm ups and pushed them down. Fiona rolled away to kick them from her feet.

"God, you're beautiful, Fiona."

Meg's hands wandered across her abdomen and chest, causing her muscles to contract and her need to heighten even further. She couldn't speak, she could only feel. She pulled Meg on top of her. With her legs spread, Meg's bare thigh came to rest on her center and she gasped. The pressure sent a tremor through her body, and she instinctively moved her hips to chase relief. Meg's center found her thigh and she rocked with her. It made her crazy, the wet heat against her thigh. Nothing prepared her for this. They kissed and Meg slid her hand between their bodies, pressing her fingers against the slippery peak of Fiona's clit. Powerful waves of exquisite sensation flowed through her and Fiona cried out. Her rocking became more insistent, and her eminent release built within her. It was impossible to control herself, so she gave up, throwing her head back, arching against Meg, who kissed her exposed neck and drew circles around Fiona's clit with her fingers.

"Oh, my God, oh my God." Her words were a chant and a rhythmic pulse surged within her, becoming more and more powerful. Her cries became incoherent when she experienced the exquisite press of Meg's fingers as they slid deep inside.

A rush of warm wetness flowed out of her, and she felt a similar wetness leave Meg, slicking over her taut thigh where Meg straddled her. Meg thrust into Fiona with long firm stokes and kept cadence with her hips.

Fiona opened her eyes and caught Meg watching her. It was as if her own physical feelings were being reflected in Meg's expressions, driving her excitement even higher. Her indescribable pleasure expanded beyond measure. It filled her body and her heart.

"Oh God… Meg!" Fiona cried out in a hoarse voice, as she lifted her hips and shuddered. Her hands grabbed the sheets and her heels dug into the mattress, but her eyes never left Meg's as the powerful storm rushed through her. Meg's eyes held her riveted by the electric power of her stare, and she could almost see the incandescent heat flowing between them.

The waves of her passion begin to slow, as did Meg's thrusts, and she relaxed back down onto the mattress, letting the sheets slip from her fingers. Her breath came raggedly as her heart battered against her chest. She finally closed her eyes. She needed to catch her breath and the look in Meg's eyes threatened to send her back into ecstasy. Her muscles involuntarily tightened around Meg's fingers, still deep within her, and she squeezed her legs together. Unexpectedly, her need surged again, sweeping away the exhaustion that had begun to descend upon her after coming harder than she ever had before. Meg seemed attuned to her body and her eyes registered the flare of renewed energy in Fiona's depths. She slowly moved her fingers inside Fiona's heat, coaxing her with pleasure. Fiona's body, trembling from the shattering storm, surprised her, and the power of a fresh tsunami brought her right back to the brink.

"Oh God, it feels so good. I can feel you everywhere." Fiona rocked gently with the small motions deep within her. "Please don't stop. I'm… going to come again."

And, as if saying it made it happen, Fiona arched dramatically as an orgasm almost as powerful as the last one quaked through her.

Meg kissed Fiona's neck and moved slowly down Fiona's body, kissing a trail through the valley of her breasts, across her stomach, around her navel, finally to find home in the warm wet folds between Fiona's thighs. Fiona basked in the attention from Meg's lips, but she wasn't sure she could handle any more sensation, although she relished the feeling of Meg's fingers filling her. She sighed deeply, closing her eyes as Meg's lips softly caressed her center.

Fiona caught her breath and lifted her head, pulling her arms up so she could rest on her elbows. "That was incredible." Her voice was breathless. Meg opened her eyes but didn't move from her position. Her tongue slid over Fiona's open center, forcing a surprised moan from Fiona's throat and a new wave of arousal to course through her. "I can't."

Meg's eyes shone with amusement and she took Fiona's clit between her lips and gently sucked, stroking it with her tongue. Fiona was startled by the immediacy and power of the earth shattering orgasm lifting her from the bed. Her head dropped back and her entire body shook. She had absolutely no control as wave after wave of incandescent pleasure flowed through her. This time, she didn't even try to acknowledge or name her pleasure. It simply was, and she was swept away.

"Come up here. Please," she gasped, weakly, pulling at Meg. "I want to hold you while I catch my breath so I can…" She kissed Meg, who moved to her side. "So I can do to you what you've done to me.

54

LOW MUSIC GENTLY PULLED MEG from a deep and comfortable sleep. She sighed contentedly to find herself lying in the warmth of Fiona's arms, her head resting on the pillow of Fiona's shoulder. She opened her eyes—one of the splendid breasts she had been delighting in all night long was mere inches from her lips. She wet them in anticipation of wrapping them around the dark peak just as a hand stroked her back. The gentle touch on her bare skin made Meg stretch like a sated cat, and she pressed against the length of Fiona's body. Well-used muscles declared themselves, and she sighed with pleasure at the memory of how those muscles had been used. She tilted her head up and found herself looking up into the hazel eyes of the most incredible woman she had ever known.

"Good morning." She slid up to Fiona's ear and kissed the sensitive skin below it. Fiona turned her head to provide unencumbered access. Meg rolled closer, her body partly atop Fiona's. A surge of desire she didn't think possible, considering the exploits of the night before, made her heartbeat quicken. It was as if she hadn't already come half a dozen times or fallen asleep exhausted in the middle of a long kiss.

Fiona tensed beneath her and moved her leg, tangling it with Meg's. Meg brought her lips to Fiona's mouth, smelling herself on Fiona's skin. Just like that, they were again lost in each other.

55

SEVERAL MINUTES LATER, WHILE THEY lay splayed amidst the disarray of sheets and pillows, Fiona took in the low sounds of the radio playing. She sighed.

"Work. There's no way…" She rolled over and took one of Meg's nipples between her teeth before she could complete her thought.

"Oh, God. I'm begging you. Don't go." Meg moaned as wetness spilled from her swollen center.

Fiona released the nipple from between her teeth to answer, and Meg swiftly pushed her onto her back, draping her body over her.

"Not fair." Fiona spread her legs so Meg could settle her hips between them. She recognized the evil glint in Meg's eyes. The memory of Meg looking up at her from between her legs made her shiver.

"You haven't seen how unfair I can be when I want something." Meg began a trail of lingering kisses, starting at Fiona's mouth, ending right below her belly button. Fiona watched, her heart racing faster the lower Meg traveled. She lifted her hips, biting her lower lip as Meg's eyes looked toward the treasure she sought. Fiona dropped her head and let the sensation carry her away.

56

MEG TRAILED HER FINGER ALONG Fiona's spine as Fiona talked on the phone.

"Thanks, Twyla. I'll see you tomorrow." Fiona ended the call and put her cell phone on the bedside table. "Well, that's taken care of."

Meg smiled and pulled Fiona closer to her. "I am surprised at you, counselor." She watched her own hand dance across the bare skin of Fiona's hip.

They were lying on their sides, facing each other. Meg had never seen a woman look as beautiful as Fiona, with her hair tousled, lips swollen from kisses, her eyes soft from their lovemaking.

She was wondering how they were ever going to get out of bed with the constant craving she had for the beautiful woman before her.

"Surprised at me for what?" Fiona captured Meg's wrist, bringing the hand up to her mouth to kiss the palm and then each finger. She smelled herself on Fiona's fingers. A pulse raged through her at the thought of what those hands had done to her.

"I had the impression you were so responsible, but here you are, playing hooky." Meg's voice cracked on the last word when Fiona caught one of Meg's fingers between her lips. Fiona's tongue flicked the tip of her finger and the muscles between Meg's legs contracted as if Fiona's tongue was playing on her clit. They stared at each other intently, while the blinding desire they had for one another rose to a crescendo. Finally, Fiona blinked and seemed to shake herself from the trance she had fallen into, releasing Meg from her hypnotizing stare.

"I was coerced." Fiona finally said.

"Coerced?" Meg forgot what they'd been talking about.

"Coerced into playing hooky. I can prove it."

"How's so?"

"By the unique marks I can describe on intimate parts of your body. Like the cute little freckle right next to your nipple, right here..." Fiona kissed the freckle in question. "And then there's the tiny little mole on the inside of your left thigh, right here where your leg meets—"

"You... may have a point," Meg whispered, as she shut her eyes and allowed Fiona to demonstrate where the mole was.

57

FIONA DIDN'T REALIZE SHE HAD fallen asleep until she awoke to gentle kisses trailing down her back, and the soft feather-light tickle of Meg's hair trailing behind. She was lying on her stomach, her arms splayed above her head. She smiled but didn't open her eyes.

"Mmmm… feels nice." She turned her head so Meg could kiss her ear but didn't open her eyes.

"Wakey. Wakey."

"I'm awake, but barely." Fiona moaned.

"I need food or I might resort to cannibalism." To underscore her point, Meg gently bit Fiona's shoulder, which made Fiona's sex clench. Meg's touch did wonderful things to her.

"Cannibalism is illegal," Fiona laughed.

Meg kissed the shoulder she'd bitten. "I'd leave no traces to implicate myself. I'm that hungry."

Fiona enjoyed the weight of Meg's body on top of her.

"Um… Meg?"

"Yes, Fiona?"

"You need to get off of me so I can… you know… get up."

"Ah, makes sense." Meg sighed.

Fiona laughed as Meg rolled off of her, and Fiona bounded up to get dressed. She stood for a few seconds looking at Meg, who lay on her back across the bed. Totally naked. Totally ravishable.

"You know, food is overrated." Fiona stopped pulling on her shorts. She couldn't tear her eyes away from the naked goddess in her bed. She dropped her shorts and began to crawl right back into bed, but at that moment her stomach chose to issue a loud protest. They both laughed as Meg's stomach responded in turn.

"Sounds like we're outnumbered." Fiona stood back up and pulled on her shorts.

58

MEG SAT ACROSS FROM FIONA in a patched and faded Naugahyde booth
at The Budget Diner. When they had finally taken their eyes off one another
for a minute to check the time, it had surprised her how much of the day
they'd spent in bed. Not quite five p.m., it was a little early for the dinner
rush and they pretty much had the entire place to themselves. But, even if
the restaurant had been crammed full of people, Meg wouldn't have noticed
anyone but Fiona. They seem to have unleashed a crazy obsession with one
another. She couldn't keep her hands to herself, and Fiona seemed to be
having a hard time, herself.

"I don't think I've ever had better pancakes," she said. The triple-stack
of buttermilk pancakes she'd ordered was almost gone and she was thinking
about ordering another one.

"I think you're just hungry. I've had them before and they're your run of
the mill flapjacks." Fiona pointed to her own sandwich. "Now, this grilled
cheese. It is the absolute bomb."

Meg was relieved when the business of eating provided a break from
their trance-like fixation on one another, but it also let the significance of
having become Fiona's lover sink in. What did it mean? All of the reasons
she'd once listed to herself about why it was probably a bad idea—the pregnancy, the fact she was leaving at the end of the summer—tried to distract
her from the elation of having had some of the best sex of her life. However,
it was the feelings she was having that were first and foremost on her mind.
Not the physical feelings, but the emotional ones. Being with Fiona the way
they had been last night—and most of the day—had been an expression
of something bigger than mere intense physical release. Every touch had
been a promise. Of what, she wasn't sure, but she craved the connection the

unnamed promises inferred. While she ate her pancakes, she thought about the newness of her feelings, along with the gravity of some the circumstances they faced.

"I'm stuffed." Fiona fell back against the booth and held her stomach.

"I was wondering if I should order another pancake." Meg smiled as she took her last bite.

Fiona looked amused. "Seriously? That was quite a stack."

"I think the amount of… exercise we've had in the last twenty hours depleted my reserves." Meg winked at her and picked up the dessert menu. She laughed when Fiona's cheeks reddened.

"Well then. Eat up, because I think I need more exercise."

Meg's center tightened. "In that case, we should order some food to go and I'll have a slice of cheesecake, too."

Fiona fixed Meg in her gaze. "Do you always feel this way after sleeping with someone?"

Meg grinned. She was transfixed when Fiona looked at her. "Hungry?"

"No."

"Then, what do you mean by 'this way'?" Meg questioned, but she guessed what Fiona was asking. If it was what she thought it was, it came dangerously close to the thoughts she had been having herself. Her stomach filled with butterflies.

Fiona looked deeply into her eyes. What she saw in Fiona's gaze made her pulse jump.

"I mean, impatient to touch you again." Fiona's eyes dropped lower. "My mouth waters when I remember how you taste. Fluttery pulses in my lower belly." Fiona's eyes rose and held her gaze again. "The fact that when I squeeze my legs together I can feel you inside of me, and I want to…"

Meg didn't know how, but suddenly she was on the other side of the booth, kissing Fiona in a way she normally wouldn't kiss someone in public. She wanted to tell her how she felt the same way, and there were things going on inside of her she had no words for.

A rattling of plates on the other side of the restaurant broke through the avalanche of desire Fiona's words had swept up in her, and Meg realized she was very close to doing something very inappropriate in public. When their lips parted, she withdrew her hand from beneath the hem of Fiona's T-shirt and tried to catch her breath. Laughing self-consciously, she moved back to her side of the booth, stealing a careful look over her shoulder to make sure they hadn't made a scene. The scattering of diners hadn't seemed to notice, aside from a skinny young man sitting at the end of the counter. He'd pinged her gaydar when they walked in. He winked at her and she smiled back.

"Are you sure this is your first time? I feel like I'm the newbie now." She laughed self-consciously. "No. I've never felt this way before. And yes, that's exactly how I feel right now. I'd add something about my heart, but I think you'd say it so much better than me." Meg played with her spoon, suddenly nervous she had revealed too much, too soon.

"I'm scared." Fiona seemed to sense Meg's worry. "But I don't care. Being with you is worth any risk."

She couldn't speak for a moment. With those simple words, Meg knew what she was feeling was love.

59

THE REST OF THE WEEK went by like a car with a tricky transmission—too quickly when Fiona was with Meg, and much too slowly when they were apart. Fiona managed to make it into work the remainder of the week, but getting out of bed was torture. When she was in the office, she did little but daydream about Meg. Her body was alive with feelings and cravings she had never imagined, and when they were together, she couldn't keep her hands to herself. Between the daydreaming and lack of sleep, she was grateful for the mundane nature of her work. If it had required much more brainpower, guilt would have incapacitated her for not providing her client with the counsel they deserved. When Friday rolled around, she looked forward to sleeping in with Meg the next day. Maybe they wouldn't get out of bed at all! On the way home, she had a bounce in her step in anticipation.

Her excitement about spending the weekend with Meg increased the closer she got to her apartment. Yet she was almost home when an unexpected bout of insecurity came over her. They hadn't discussed seeing each other that night. She had assumed they would, like they had every other day since they'd met. But an unfamiliar and unwelcome voice in the back of her mind whispered words of doubt, and Fiona began to worry. Because they had spent every free moment together for the past week didn't mean Meg wanted to continue doing so.

Fiona's buoyant mood had nearly evaporated by the time she slid her key into the lock on her front door. She never imagined uncertainty of this kind and was a little embarrassed about how quickly she had let herself become so used to seeing Meg every day.

Fiona changed into shorts and dropped heavily onto her living room sofa. She'd planned to go down to the coffee shop to wait for Meg to get off work, but now she was worried she was being too clingy. Six o'clock approached, Meg's quitting time, and yet Fiona sat in her too quiet apartment, trying not to think about what Meg was doing. Was Meg thinking about her, too? Fiona knew Meg cared deeply for her. A single touch from her conveyed as much. So why the sudden insecurity? She never imagined love to feel like this.

Wait.

Fiona sat up.

Her heart beat quickly in her chest.

Love?

No. It wasn't possible to fall in love so quickly. Was it? Maybe she was mistaking lust for love. Meg was the first woman she'd ever slept with. She didn't get attached. Her life had always been too busy, too complicated. And now, it was more complicated than ever. Was she mixing up the novelty of physical desire with emotional attachment? She didn't even need to think about it. She knew the answer. It was love. If she took the physical out of the equation, she would feel exactly the same way. The revelation filled Fiona with elation and fear, but the elation won out. Her entire body tingled with happiness, and she hugged herself in barely suppressed joy. More than anything in the world, she wanted to see the woman who held her heart, and she chastised herself for wasting time on insecurity. If Meg told her she had things to do, Fiona would be happy to give her space to do them, but in the meantime, she was going to go see the woman she loved.

✿✿✿✿✿

SHE WAS ON HER WAY out the door when her phone rang. Without thinking, she answered.

"I didn't expect you to answer."

Shit. She stepped back into her apartment, shut the door, and rested against it. "Uh, hey."

Mike's voice sounded small, unsure. Her irritation at him for blowing up her phone with texts and calls over the last few days eased a little when she realized, like her, he was probably having feelings he'd never expected to have before. But, when Mike didn't respond immediately, she didn't know what to say to break the silence. Was it up to her, anyway? He'd been the one to call. So, she waited.

His nervous laugh eventually filled the silence. "I didn't expect you to answer. Now, I don't know what to say."

"Maybe you can start with what you were planning to leave in the message," she suggested.

"I forgot what I was going to say." He sighed. "Wait. I lied. I was sort of mad about you not talking to me, so I was going to—" He stopped. "Forget it. You answered. So, it doesn't matter. God, Fi, I'm so glad to hear your voice."

He sounded like the old Mike. She missed him, but she still didn't know what to say.

"Are you there?"

"Yeah. I'm here. I'm having a hard time trying to figure out what to say without talking about the thing I don't want to talk about with you." There. She'd said it without mentioning it and letting him know she still wasn't ready to talk to him about it.

"Can I get you to promise me you won't make any decisions without talking to me first?"

"Mike…"

"I don't think it's too much to ask. Do you?" He sounded earnest, not angry.

She wanted to tell him he didn't have any say in the matter, but it wasn't true. Ultimately, she got to call the shots, but he did deserve to be heard. He wasn't an asshole. He wasn't her enemy. He was her friend who provided half the DNA of the hitchhiker currently residing in her womb.

"It's not too much to ask. I just need some time."

"So, you'll talk to me before you make any decisions?"

Should she tell him she'd already decided to keep it? No. He'd probably want to discuss how they'd share custody and she didn't want to think about it. It was too much to think about. She didn't want someone else telling her how to take care—. No. She wasn't ready to discuss it.

She blew out a breath. "Yes. I promise to talk to you. Not now, though. I'm not ready to—"

"It's cool." He sounded relieved. "I get it. I know how I feel about all of this. A gazillion different emotions all jumbled up together. I can imagine how you feel about it, what you're going through."

That was unexpected. She didn't think he gave a shit about what she was going through. This was the old Mike she missed.

"Thanks Mike."

"Can I check back in in a week?"

She wasn't sure she'd have much more to say to him, but it sounded fair. "Sure. Give me a call next week."

"You're the best." He sounded so relieved. She was glad she could provide him with a little peace. Now if she could just find some for herself.

60

MEG RAISED HER HAND AT Fiona's door, but before she could knock, the door opened and there was Fiona, keys in hand standing on the doorstep. It was comical, really. Meg stood with her hand raised in a loose fist, ready to knock on a door no longer there, and a slow smile transformed her face.

"Hi beautiful!"

Fiona looked startled, but she smiled. Meg's heartrate skyrocketed and she kissed her hello. Her stomach fluttered when their lips parted. "I hope you aren't sick of seeing me."

"Not at all. I was actually on my way down to see you. I would have been there earlier, but I'm running slower than usual tonight." Fiona gave her another kiss. "Someone's been keeping me awake later than I'm used to."

Meg pretended to frown. "Anyone I know?"

Fiona held her hand up next to Meg's head. "I don't know. She's about five foot seven or eight..."

"Seven-and-a-half."

"...five foot seven-and-a-half; shining brown hair smelling of the forest rain; amazing blue, blue eyes capable of melting you with a glance; soft, full, talented lips; and magic fingers that burn me with their touch... any of this ringing a bell?"

"Hmmm..." Meg pretended to think it over. "Sounds familiar. She's been keeping you up all night, you say?"

"Yep. I'm exhausted."

"If you need time to rest, I can leave." She tried to hide her disappointment. She didn't want to leave. She'd be happy to watch her take a nap, but she couldn't read Fiona's expression. If anything, she looked a little guarded.

"What do you want to do?" Fiona asked.

Did insecurity drift across her face?

When in doubt, she always went with honesty, even if it terrified her. "I'd rather sit and watch you sleep than be away from you." She shook her head. Gross. Didn't sound creepy at all. "Let me try again without sounding like a stalker. If you want to chill, I'm happy to be near you. But if you need some alone time, I can skedaddle too."

The guarded look on Fiona's face disappeared, but she paused and Meg was prepared to go spend time at Vi's.

"Quite the opposite." Fiona played with her earring but she looked relieved. "I feel the same way. To be honest. I was running slow tonight because I was wondering if I was suffocating you."

"What? I'm not ready to come up for air yet. Not even close." Meg took Fiona's hand and walked her into the apartment, out of sight of the passersby. When the door closed, she wrapped her in her arms and thoroughly kissed her. She pulled away only to catch her breath. "I love every minute with you. I don't see it changing any time soon."

Fiona's response was hardly more than a whisper. "Me too."

This time, when their lips met, the heat of their kiss was off the charts. Meg held Fiona's face in her hands and tried to catch her breath. "All I can think about is taking you into the bedroom and devouring you." Fiona played with the hair on the back of her neck, causing tingles to travel down her spine.

Fiona traced her lips with her tongue. "I wouldn't object. I'm kind of obsessed."

Meg's breathing hitched. She was so ready. But they needed dinner and probably a little fresh air. "I like how you think. How about this: why don't we get some dinner first? You and the baby need more nourishment than this obsession with each other is allowing. So… what if we grab some dinner to go, and head over to the park and watch some soccer?"

Fiona kissed each corner of her mouth. "And the devouring would come after?"

Meg's resolve to spend some time together outside of bed was starting to crumble with each new kiss. "Yes. We watch some soccer and then come back for the devouring."

"Okay." Fiona's tone said it wasn't exactly what she had in mind, but she kissed Meg one more time and slipped out of her arms. "We better leave now, then. Before I change my mind." The look she gave her was smoldering and Meg almost suggested they order in.

Meg cleared her throat. "Right. Time for soccer."

Fiona opened the door. "I played in college. Did you play?"

"I used to—until I blew my knee out. Now I watch."

Fiona grimaced. "Ouch! So that's the story behind the scar on your knee?"

"Yeah, I was a forward and one day I pivoted on a long drive and that's all she wrote. Mid-season during senior year at college. Surgery fixed it, but fear of reinjuring it made me give it up. The day my knee blew—" She winced at the memory. "I remember the way it popped. The pain was excruciating, but the sick feeling I got when I found my kneecap floating where it shouldn't have been…" She puffed out her cheeks. "Just thinking about it makes me nauseous. What about you? What position did you play?"

"I was a defensive mid-fielder. I stopped playing during undergrad. It was too much to keep up with all the practice and studying."

When they neared the park, Fiona smelled pizza, so they decided to grab a slice from the food truck for dinner. When they took a seat on the metal bleachers, the teams were warming up on the field in their brightly colored jerseys.

Fiona took a bite of her slice. "It's salads for me from now on. Pizza three times in one week is a little ridiculous. Don't get me wrong... I love it. But I'm going to gain a ton of weight if I keep eating junk food at this rate. Hold on. You have a little grease right…" She bit her lip and wiped Meg's chin with her napkin.

Meg grinned at the grease-wiping gesture. "Thanks."

A whistle from the referee signaled warm-ups were over, and the teams took their positions. Right from the kick-off, it was apparent the teams were mismatched. A few of the women on the less-talented team had good control of the ball, but most of them had lousy footwork and almost no strategy. Nevertheless, it was still fun to watch fit women compete for the ball, and Meg and Fiona kept up a steady conversation as they watched the game.

"Tell me about Cornell," Fiona said, during a timeout. "I'll bet you had the grades and test scores to get in on your own, but did it help coming from a long line of alumni?"

Meg sighed. "It's a long story. The grades helped and a soccer scholarship didn't hurt, but the alumni thing is probably the only reason I actually got in."

Fiona gave her a soft shoulder bump. "Sounds like there's a story I need to hear."

Meg snorted. "It's boring."

Fiona gave her the smoldering look again, making Meg's stomach flutter. "I find nothing about you even remotely boring."

Meg laughed. "Remember, you asked. Let's see. To sum it up, I subconsciously attempted to sabotage my acceptance by forgetting to submit my application on time." She shrugged.

"Explain 'subconscious sabotage.'"

She should have known Fiona would want details. "I think I told you before, it was a forgone conclusion CJ and I would go to Cornell Law?"

Fiona nodded. "Like your parents and grandparents."

"Well, somewhere along the line, I decided I had a voice in the matter. I decided I'd go to the University of Washington."

"University of Washington over Cornell?" She narrowed her eyes. "Was it a girl?"

Meg held up a finger. "Bingo. A few of my friends were headed there, too. But, mostly it was because of Hannah Wertz. She was so pretty, and an amazing soccer player. I was crushing hard. Plus, the more my family pushed toward Cornell, the more I pushed back. Classic teen rebellion. My mom made me fill out the paperwork for both schools while I complained about the unfairness of it all." Meg laughed to remember her angsty teenaged attitude. "It was pathetic. I hadn't told my mom I was gay yet, so I couldn't tell her about Hannah. The reasons I was giving her were weak. It caused a lot of stress. I threatened to run away."

"Would you have done it?"

"I was just being dramatic, but my parents freaked out. That's when I started seeing a therapist and she encouraged me to come out."

"Your teen angst was in full bloom, huh?"

"And then some," Meg said with a smile.

"I can't imagine you being so emotional."

"Trust me, I have a hard time believing it, too. It threw my folks for a loop, for sure." She could laugh about it now, but she imagined how frustrated her parents must have been in the war zone she'd created back then. "The thing is, I always knew I would end up going to Cornell. I don't know why I pushed back so hard. My crush on Hannah faded, yet I continued to push back. It came to a head when my mom found both packages, stamped and ready to go, but sitting on my dresser a few days after the submission deadline. Mom never snooped—at least not in my room. Despite my bad attitude, I was a good kid. My brother, on the other hand…" She waved a hand. CJ was a piece of work. "Well, he was a different story. I don't remember why my mom went into my room, but I've never seen her so angry. She was li-vid. Normally, the angrier my mom gets, the calmer she acts. She's a lawyer, after all. You should have seen her, though. She was furious, actually spitting as she yelled at me. I had no excuse, either. I had simply forgotten." She shook her head at the memory.

"How'd they fix it? Application deadlines are strict," Fiona asked.

"My parents enlisted anyone they had ever known who had any pull with the admissions office. Something worked, because the board of admissions, which never, ever, ever made exceptions, finally relented. Then we had to wait for the formal acceptance letter. By then, I'd gotten over my rebellion. I was never so relieved as when the letter came."

"I take it your brother had no problems with his application?"

"My mom filled out most of the application for him and supervised the essay parts. She even took it to the post office for him, and then followed up with calls to key decision makers. I'm sure CJ's acceptance was almost exclusively based on the family alumni thing. His grades barely met the minimum acceptance criteria."

"Your parents are tenacious."

"You're telling me." Meg snorted. "All of the hard-sell efforts they did for CJ made the additional calls they had to make for me that much harder."

"I'll bet," Fiona said.

She wrinkled her nose, unsure what she hated more; coming off as an entitled rich kid to Fiona, or her actions as a child, which made her sound like she'd always been an entitled rich kid. Basically, both. She sighed. "I'm grateful for everything they did. I know most people don't have the resources and ties my family does. I'm embarrassed about my behavior, though. I acted like an entitled brat."

Fiona squeezed her shoulder and Meg leaned into it. "Don't be so hard on yourself. You had some issues to work out."

"True. A couple of years of therapy taught me that my efforts to undermine my acceptance into college were an attempt to break free from my family's expectations." Oh, God. Was she coming off as some new-age hippie? She needed to stop over-thinking things.

Fiona's brow knit. "Oh yeah? In what way? Their expectations of you being straight?"

"They were actually cool about that part. Everyone except CJ, but that's a whole different story." She swept her hands to the side, probably a little too vigorously, but it wasn't something she wanted to get into right then. "The main thing was being a vet and breaking tradition, but I already told you about that."

Fiona tilted her head. "It seems kind of old school the whole following in the family footsteps thing."

Meg sighed and shrugged. "It was expected. We knew we had to work to get into Cornell, but we also knew we had a leg up on the other applicants. CJ always wanted to be a lawyer, but he seemed to think it was going to be handed to him. My parents were always pushing him because of his iffy grades, using me as an example. It became this thing I was supposed to do, and I went along with it. Until I didn't. And then, bang. Rebellion time."

"You definitely don't seem the type to purposely shake things up, but it's nice to know you haven't always been so perfect." Fiona lightly punched her in the arm.

Meg couldn't help the incredulous look on her face. "I'm far from perfect, as you'll eventually find out. So, there's my story. Were you out to your parents when you were a teenager? How did they react when you came out?"

The game started back up and their attention was caught by the activity on the field. When Fiona didn't answer her question after a few minutes, Meg wondered if she'd stumbled onto something she didn't want to talk about.

The ball ended up near the weaker team's goal almost immediately and the stronger team scored another goal. It was almost painful to watch.

"My parents died before I ever had to tell them. And because I rarely dated, it didn't come up with Aunt Corny before she died, either." Fiona sounded sad.

"How do you think they would have reacted?" Meg asked. Fiona's sadness was understandable. It would be so hard not to have a family to talk to about this kind of thing.

Fiona's brow furrowed. "I honestly don't know how my parents would have reacted. The subject never came up. They weren't religious and didn't talk about politics, unless it was union stuff." She lifted her shoulders. "I want to say they'd have been cool with it. But, I think I would've gladly dealt with any reaction they might have had, just to have them back. You know, given the choice." She stared into the distance for a moment and then shook herself. Did she feel all alone in the world? Meg wanted to tell her she wasn't. Not with her around. "As for Aunt Corny, I'm sure she at least suspected. She had this way of using gender-neutral pronouns when she talked about dating. 'A beautiful woman like you must have people lined up at the door for dates,'" Fiona mimicked.

Meg laughed. "You should always talk like an old woman. It's hot." More seriously, she added; "I wish I could have met your aunt. She sounds like an amazing woman."

"I wish you could have, too. And my parents. They were all amazing." She sat up to stretch and Meg admired the swath of skin revealed around Fiona's waist. She forced her eyes away before she gave in to her desire to touch it. They watched a little more of the game. The routing continued.

"Was your family accepting when you told them?" Fiona intertwined her fingers with Meg's and scooted closer to her on the bench.

"It was almost disappointing, the lack of furor it caused, considering the drama queen I was back then." Meg stroked Fiona's fingers. "I don't think they were overjoyed at the news, but they took my little announcement in stride. Kind of like they expected it. My dad gave me the whole 'we love you no matter what' speech, and my mom took me aside for an embarrassing mother-daughter moment. She wanted to know if my announcement was due to becoming sexually active—which, aside from one awkward kiss with Hannah, it wasn't. That came later, at summer soccer camp. They were probably relieved I wasn't gonna wind up pregnant." Meg laughed before she realized what she said. Then she felt like a jerk.

Fiona took it in stride. "Hey, I'm gay, and it didn't keep me from getting knocked up!" Fiona saved Meg from a stammering attempt at an apology. Instead, they both laughed and watched some more soccer.

The weak team finally scored a goal. Meg was sure the other team let them since the score was so lopsided. It was rec ball, after all. She gave coolness points to the team captain.

"Every once in a while, my mother lets me know it isn't impossible for lesbians to produce grandchildren, but mostly, they don't make an issue about it. They're generally supportive and curious about my love life."

"How about your brother? Has he outgrown his troublemaker phase yet?" Fiona asked.

Meg paused. That was a good question. "I don't know. I haven't talked to him much in the last several months. We had a little blow up a while back. My parents don't even give me updates anymore, and I don't ask. He must have told them not to. It's like him to be petty and shitty. They did tell me he passed the bar the second time around though."

"You sound surprised?"

"I kind of am. Last I knew, he was partying somewhere in Europe. When I called him to say congratulations, it was the first time we'd talked in over ten months. He was at a pub celebrating with some of his classmates, and he was sweet like he used to be. It made me miss him."

"What happened to cause the blow up? If you don't mind me asking."

"It was after he failed the bar. He laughed about it. Like it was no big deal. My parents made a big announcement about him joining my dad's firm and when he failed and acted like it was no big deal, well, it was so… so privileged. I called him an immature asshole and he called me a self-righteous bitch."

"Yikes!" Fiona's eyes widened.

"I know. I shouldn't have said anything. It wasn't my business."

"I think I would have done the same thing. Is he working in Seattle with your parents, now that he's passed the bar?"

Fiona's validation was nice, even though she continued to feel guilty about causing the whole thing. "It's probably the only thing I do know about him right now. After the way he acted, my parents won't hire him at either one of their firms. Nor will they recommend him to any of their friends or colleagues—not until he can demonstrate he's grown up a little."

Fiona's eyes, which were on the game, suddenly went wide. She grabbed Meg's forearm. "Oh, my God! Did you see the foul? The ref must be blind."

"I missed it, oh wait, yeah, she definitely cleated her. Look. She's limping. I've gotten red-carded for less!" Meg had to admit she was struggling to follow the game. Even Fiona's casual touches sent heat radiating through her.

"This is soccer, not hockey! We came to watch hot chicks, not a brawl." Fiona shouted as she waved a fist in the air. But her smile belied her words and Meg couldn't help but laugh.

"I could stay home and get my fill of hot chicks."

A blush crept up Fiona's checks. "How'd you turn out so perfect?" The smolder from earlier was back.

"Down girl!" Fiona's hand kneaded her thigh, causing a stirring up higher.

Fiona laughed. "I mean it. You're amazing. But how is it your brother turned out the way he is and you the way you are? You had the same childhood, right?"

"He's irresponsible and selfish. Maybe my parents could have done a few things differently—like not helping him with his application to Cornell or fixing his mistakes all the time. CJ's so secretive and they never tell me when he gets into scrapes, but I suspect he's gotten at least one of his girlfriends pregnant. Mom and Dad think I don't know. Maybe he'll outgrow it, or even has by now. Who knows? But, despite his immaturity, he's a very sweet guy. He'd do anything for a friend, and his heart is usually in the right place. He just needs to settle down."

"If he's anything like his sister, he can't be all bad. Is it crass for me to ask how he supports himself if he's not working or living at home with your parents?"

Fiona rested her head on Meg's shoulder and she loved it. She didn't like talking about her family's money, though. She didn't feel attached to it and all it did was make people act weird. She planned to build an animal sanctuary with hers when she settled down some day. "I'd wonder the same thing. I suppose he's living off the trust we each received when we turned twenty-one. He never has to work if he manages it right. I think having access to money is part of his problem."

Fiona seemed to think about it. "What does he live for, if he doesn't have a dream?"

"Exactly. I think being a lawyer is his dream. I'm not sure, though. My mom said she had to hound him long distance to go to his study group sessions."

"Study group definitely helped me. Not everyone passed though, even with it. Mostly I think it was just that Mike was preoccupied with Charlie. He'd have passed if he'd been focused."

A knot settled in Meg's stomach at the mention of the baby's father, even though she didn't know him except for the stress he was putting Fiona under. "Aren't you glad school and tests are all behind you now?"

Fiona nodded and the game was over. The score was a blowout, but the teams were talking and treating each other warmly, even the cleater and cleatee. Meg wished people could take the example and act civilly on and off the field.

61

"I NEED A GARGOYLE," MEG announced, as she speared a piece of lettuce and lifted it to her mouth. Fiona liked the way she ate, politely, but with enthusiasm and without self-consciousness. But, then again, Fiona liked everything about Meg.

It was Saturday afternoon and they were sitting beneath a tree in Morningside Park watching a group of teenage boys toss a frisbee. Fiona hadn't spent much time outdoors since she'd moved to the city, and she was happy about spending more time in the park since she'd met Meg. Also, Karma and Taylor had come back from their vacation and Meg no longer needed to fill in at the coffee shop, so they had the weekend to themselves. After the pizza conversation at the soccer game, Fiona insisted on making their meals healthy ones. Meg had teased her about how they surely had to be burning off any excess calories in bed over the two weeks they'd been sleeping together, but Fiona just smiled and continued to break apart the lettuce for their lunch.

"How random. A gargoyle?" Fiona said.

Meg smiled and nodded her head. "You heard me right. A gargoyle."

"For what?"

"My dad." Meg's tone implied how obvious the answer was.

She was still confused. "Okay…" Fiona drew out the word in an invitation for Meg to expand on her answer.

Meg laughed. "My dad's birthday is on the twenty-fourth and I need to get him a present." She seemed to be enjoying the bizarre conversation.

"So, you want to get him a gargoyle," Fiona said.

"Yes, a gargoyle."

Fiona tried not to roll her eyes. "What ever happened to getting your dad a nice tie or a gift card to the Olive Garden?"

Meg laughed.

"My brother and I have a standing tradition of getting our father unique gifts for his birthday. Over the years, we've found it harder and harder to figure out a good gift for him. He wants for nothing, and when he does want something, he goes out and gets it. It's so frustrating. He's impossible to shop for."

"What about hobbies?"

"The only hobby he has is golf, and he already has every gadget for golf ever made. One year, CJ and I began getting him gifts he had to display in his office, and thus, the tradition was born. So far, CJ has the distinction of having given him the most outrageous gift—a merman sculpture."

"Why is it so outrageous? I know the typical sculpture would probably be a mermaid, but with all the comic book movies out these days, it doesn't seem too out there."

"It's a full-sized merman. Seven feet tall from head to tail. Super-hunky, too. But, dad has it on display in his office. It's quite the conversation piece, he says."

Fiona chuckled. "I can see how that would be hard to top!"

"I try to keep my gifts from being too gaudy, so I'll probably never be able to top the merman. Unusual gifts of quality are my focus—things to make a visitor to his office raise an eyebrow, but not necessarily comment on them. That's why I need to find the perfect gargoyle."

Fiona knew the place to take her. "Well, I've got you covered. We'll go this afternoon."

Meg looked surprised as she chased a walnut through the dregs of her salad dressing. As if she didn't believe her. The best thing was, the gargoyle was probably the least interesting thing she'd be introducing her to that afternoon.

62

AN HOUR LATER, MEG AND Fiona decabbed in front of an industrial
looking building near the Village. Fiona took Meg's hand, walked her to a
graffiti inscribed metal door, and pushed the buzzer. An automated lock
clicked almost immediately, and Meg looked for a camera before she noticed
Fiona looking up and waving. Meg followed Fiona's gaze, but couldn't see
whoever might have been leaning out through one of the many multi-paned
windows propped open above them. Fiona pulled the door open and they
moved into a shallow, dimly lit lobby. The only features in the stark-white
room were an elevator, a dozen or so mailboxes, and a door with a sign
reading 'Stairway' above it. The smell of pine cleaner and musty architecture
tickled Meg's nose. Fiona approached a set of steel doors with a lever handle
and yanked the lever to the side to open the heavy doors. Meg gaped when
an old-fashioned elevator was revealed.

Meg studied the contraption. She wasn't an expert, but the lift looked
at least a century old, if not older. Steel mesh enclosed the upper walls. She
could see all the way up the shaft. "Whoa. I've only seen this kind of elevator
in the movies. This is cool."

"I know, right? I always get a kick out of using it."

Fiona tugged the accordion gate open and stepped aside to let Meg in.
Meg watched with interest as they rose through the skeleton frame of the
eight-story building and Fiona wrestled with the lever to stop the elevator
with a lurch.

"It looks easier when Tammy does it." Fiona let out an apologetic laugh
when Meg flung her arms out to keep from falling down at the abrupt stop.
The deck of the elevator was about two feet lower than the eighth-floor
landing. "Let me ease this puppy up a skoosh."

After a few bumps and jumps trying to line the elevator up with the landing, Fiona finally gave up and opened the gate. They both laughed as they stepped up the six inches or so of gap.

"You must have failed Bellhop 101 in undergraduate school." Meg pretended to struggle with the step up.

"Yeah. I looked especially good in the little cap and white gloves, too," Fiona responded when Meg had both feet safely on the hallway floor. As Fiona stepped across the hall and pushed the buzzer next to the enormous metal door, she looked over her shoulder at Meg with a mischievous grin. "I kept the uniform. I can put it on and we can play Mistress and the Bellhop, if you want."

Meg suppressed a gasp. Fiona was a fast learner. She liked it. She liked it a lot.

A series of clanks and scrapes sounded from the other side of the massive metal door. When it finally swung open, a petite woman with arresting green eyes and blond dreadlocks stood barefoot in the doorway. Meg hardly had time to take in the dirty white cargo shorts, ancient Ani DiFranco concert tee, and tie-dyed bandana the woman wore, before she flung herself into Fiona's arms. Laugher filled Fiona's eyes as she returned the woman's hug and looked over at Meg.

"Fi! Great goddesses, woman! It's been forever! Go on in, let me just get the gate." The woman pulled herself away from Fiona, pushed both Fiona and Meg into her loft, and trotted over to the elevator to shut the gate. "The gate has to be shut to call the elevator. I've been the victim of my insensitive rat-fuck neighbors on more than a few occasions." She screamed the 'rat-fuck neighbors' part down the elevator shaft as she said it. "Eight flights of stairs are a bitch to haul groceries up, let alone a three-hundred-and-forty-five-pound chunk of fucking granite."

"I heard that, Tammy, you putrid cunt!" A woman's voice came floating up from the elevator shaft behind her.

Tammy laughed and shook her head.

"Sophia. She's a brilliant artist, but she's got a filthy mouth on her. She'll probably come up in a little bit, the nosey whore. Pardon the mess, but it's my life!" Tammy shooed them further into the loft and closed the door.

Meg looked at Fiona with a questioning look. "Tammy from the library, Tammy?" she mouthed at her. Fiona smiled and nodded back. "Whoa!" mouthed Meg, and Fiona put a hand over her mouth to keep from laughing.

Tammy finished securing the heavy door and joined them. The three women stood in a small circle in the center of a huge loft, and Meg realized when Tammy said "pardon the mess", she wasn't kidding. The place looked like a war zone with a thick coat of dust covering everything. Huge chunks of rock sat on battered handmade tables among rubble and grit. Spaced among them stood several canvas-enshrouded objects on similarly constructed low pedestals. The far-left side of the room had a roughed in area with bare drywall covering the outside. Meg assumed it was Tammy's living area.

"Meg, this is Tammy. Tammy, this is Meg." Fiona introduced the two women and put her arm around Meg's waist.

"It's nice to meet you, Meg." Tammy offered her a thickly calloused hand, which she shook. "So, you're the woman who finally won Fi's elusive heart, huh?"

"I'm hoping so," Meg responded with a smile, looking at Fiona and then back at Tammy. "It's nice to meet you, too, Tammy."

In a hundred years, she would have never pictured the Tammy of Fiona's past as the bohemian woman before her.

Tammy had an engaging smile. Meg couldn't help smiling back. "You seem like a nice person." Tammy's voice was warm before she lost the smile and an edge crept out with her next words. "But you'd better treat her right. It's the only warning you'll get." Tammy kept hold of her hand and she pulled her close. An edge of menace laced her gaze. Tammy may have been almost a head shorter than her, but the fierce look and impressively toned arms, presumably from hauling granite around, made Meg think Tammy could probably kick her ass. "Artists are an unstable lot, so I could easily plead insanity. With good behavior and a little dose of Jesus I'd be out in two years, probably less. A small inconvenience for my best friend."

Meg believed every word.

"Oh, come on Tammy! Don't scare her away!" Fiona laughed.

Meg realized she'd been holding her breath when Tammy laughed. She released it in a shaky puff.

"I'm just messing with her, Fi! Well, mostly," she added, with a raised eyebrow in Meg's direction. "I love this woman and I am a little protective. But I can already see she's happier than I've ever seen her. You must be doing something right. She's absolutely glowing!"

Fiona dipped her head but didn't say anything and Meg tightened her arm around Fiona's waist.

"So, you're looking for a gargoyle, Fiona tells me." Tammy fixed her brilliant green eyes on Meg.

Meg swallowed. "Yep."

"Well, you came to the right place. Follow me."

Meg and Fiona followed Tammy to a row of industrial metal shelves in the far back area of the loft. As they approached the dark area, Tammy pulled a chain hanging down and several bare bulbs hanging from the open ceiling lit up the space. Crowded on the racks were hundreds of sculptures.

"The gargoyles are over here." Tammy walked them toward one of the shelves in the center of one of the rows.

Meg glanced at the sculptures on some of the shelves they passed and found Tammy's subjects ranged widely. She didn't have a chance to study any, but she could sense a unique quality in each piece they passed. The work was detailed and beautiful.

"You've sculpted all of these?" she asked.

"These are mostly castings of the originals. It looks like a lot, but most of it is the mass-produced shit I make a living from. I'll barf if I have to make another garden gnome, woodland fairy, or fucking angel. Here we are."

Meg looked around at multiple racks filled with cast metal gargoyles.

"I went through a gothic phase a few years ago and this is the labor of that dark time."

Meg scanned the section and was thoroughly impressed with Tammy's work. When she'd decided on a gargoyle, she hadn't had a specific thing in mind other than she wanted an ugly statue to give to her dad. Something hideous he'd have to display in his office. Looking at Tammy's work, she realized she'd minimized the artistic potential of the gift. The effect of giving him one of these wouldn't be exactly what she'd planned. But then her eyes fell on a statue on one of the bottom shelves and knew she had found exactly what she was looking for. It was a weathered bronze monkey gargoyle, about a foot tall, holding the scales of justice from its mouth. The wings were battered and folded against its back, and it held an open book in its hands. The detail in it was impressive and it was so ugly it was beautiful. The best thing about it was, it was perfect in its artistic portrayal of evolution and the law.

"This one is perfect!" Meg crouched before the sculpture. There were four copies behind the one she indicated, so she wouldn't feel bad for taking the only one.

"You found one of my personal favorites." Tammy squatted beside her and nodded her approval.

When Meg looked at her and began to pick it up, Tammy motioned for her to leave it and to follow her to another set of racks where the granite original perched upon the shelf.

"Is this the original?"

"Yep." Tammy grabbed a card with a string attached to it from a stack at the end of the shelf and handed it to Meg, along with a pen. "I'll have it shipped to you. Jot down the address you want it to go to on this."

"Do you usually sell the originals?" Meg printed her parents' address on the card and wondered how she was going to get her mom not to peek at it before she got there. She wasn't worried about her dad. He never picked up the mail, but she didn't want her mom to see it before anyone else did and take away half the fun.

"Not usually. And definitely not to Fi's girlfriend."

Meg looked up from her writing, confused.

Tammy laughed at the look on her face. "It's a gift. From me to you."

"Really?" Meg and Fiona asked in unison.

Tammy thumped Meg on the back. "Yes, really."

Once Tammy tied the tag to the sculpture and Meg repeated her thanks enough to be embarrassed by her own stammering, Tammy showed Meg and Fiona around her studio. All of her work was amazing, even her despised mass production pieces. And her current work was much larger than the shelf-sized pieces she'd shown them. Tammy was an amazing artist and her personality poured out of everything she created.

They were peeking under another tarp when the huge metal front door banged open, and a woman who looked to be in her eighties charged in, dressed in coveralls with the top rolled down over her waist, displaying a sparkling white tank top. Her flip flops slapped her heels as she approached. She held a large glass pitcher and a stack of red plastic cups. The pitcher was filled with red liquid, ice cubes tinkling merrily against its sides.

"Sangria, anyone? It's hotter than a whore's snatch in here!" It was the voice from the elevator shaft. Meg wasn't usually surprised by colorful language, but she blushed at the woman's words.

"Sophia! Fuck me! I forgot to lock the door to keep your putrescent ass out of here!" Tammy raced toward the old woman and liberated the pitcher and cups from her hands. "Sophia, meet Meg and Fiona!"

"I hope you both drink, or you're going to have a soused old bitch on your hands!" Sophia said cheerfully, and did a hop-step over to the table where Tammy set the pitcher.

"Her sangria is fucking awesome." Tammy filled up four glasses. "But she's an obnoxious drunk, so take your share or I'll have an unwanted guest sleeping on my couch."

63

"THAT WAS FUN." MEG RAISED an arm to call a cab as they exited Tammy's building into the muted light of early evening. She hadn't even lowered her arm before a yellow car pulled to a stop at the curb before them.

Fiona steadied Meg as the sudden stopping of the car before them caused her to stumble. "Whoopsie! I have you!"

"Came in faster than I expected. Plus, I might be a little drunk." Meg giggled. It was the cutest thing Fiona had ever heard. In a sly game of trading cups, she and Fiona had successfully managed to make Tammy and Sophia think Fiona was enjoying the sangria, while Meg did most of the consuming.

"Maybe a lot drunk." She helped Meg open the cab door and watched her climb across the seat.

Meg winked at her when she got situated in her seat. "I cannot tell a lie. I'm a lot more than a little drunk." She giggled again but quickly changed her expression to something a little more serious. "So, she's Tammy, huh?"

"The one and only." Fiona laughed as she got into the car. She told the driver to head to Morningside Heights.

Meg wrapped her arms around Fiona and snuggled against her. Her body was pliant and heavy. Fiona delighted in the feel of the embrace as the cab made its way to her apartment.

"She wasn't at all what I imagined her to be."

Fiona smoothed Meg's hair. "She's always been a little different."

"You didn't say if you ever saw her again after your thwarted graduation getaway." Meg's words were a little slurred. "I sort of thought she was out of the picture." She popped her head up. "Did I sound jealous? I'm not. Well, maybe a little." Fiona squeezed her. Meg had absolutely nothing to worry about. She loved Tammy. She was the one constant in her life and she knew she could count on her forever. But on a day to day basis, Tammy would drive her crazy, she knew that as certainly as she knew she would drive Tammy nuts. It's what made them such great friends.

"We've managed to stay in touch, although through no fault of my own," Fiona said. "I was a mess after my mom and dad died. Tammy stayed by my side almost non-stop until after the funeral and she was the one who took me to the airport when I left for Thailand. She was amazing. When I got back, though, she had already left for her college, and I was off to mine. Once Aunt Corny sold the house, there was no reason for me to go back to Pottstown, so I didn't. But we manage to see each other at least once a year."

Meg snuggled back into Fiona. "I like her."

"Me too." Fiona rested her chin on Meg's head, breathing in the smell of Meg's hair.

"I have a question." Meg sounded like she might fall asleep.

"I don't want to sleep with her." Fiona stroked the back of Meg's head. "If I had, we would have done it by now. We're past that."

"Good to know, but it wasn't my question."

"Oh?" Fiona lifted her chin and gazed down at her.

Meg sat up. "Will you come out to Seattle with me for my dad's birthday?"

A flutter of excitement tickled Fiona's stomach. She didn't even have to think about it. "I'd love to."

"I thought I'd have to talk you into it!" Meg studied her like she didn't quite believe it.

"I was already starting to miss you and it isn't for another two weeks."

"Week and a half, actually. I plan to go out a little early so I can talk to my aunt about the clinic and look for a place to live. Can you take a few days off? I know it's sort of last minute. I should have asked sooner."

She'd have to clear it with work, but she'd make it happen. "Sure, or I can work remotely while I'm out there."

"Great!" Meg hugged her. When she sat back, she had a big smile on her face and Fiona thought she was cute as hell. "My mom's going to be excited."

"Why will she be excited?"

"I've never brought a girlfriend home."

"What have I agreed to?" Fiona covered her face with her hands. "This is going to be a big deal isn't it?"

"Don't worry. My mom's cool." Meg pulled Fiona's hands from her face.

She was laughing, so that was a good sign.

"Is the rest of your family cool?"

"Totally. I don't expect CJ to be there. He's the only one who might be a dick. But not specifically to you. He's a dick in general."

"How did I get myself into this?" She playfully hit Meg in the stomach. She was still nervous, but mostly excited.

64

FIONA SPLAYED HER HANDS AGAINST the shower wall, her head directly under the stream of warm water, her body continuing to respond to the orgasm that had rocked through her. Meg held her from behind and kissed the side of her neck. Their bodies were pressed together, slick and warm. Would she ever get enough of this beautiful woman?

"I'm not sure I trust my legs right now." Fiona turned her head to give Meg more access to explore her neck.

Meg didn't even try to suppress her smile. "Exactly what I was going for."

"Mission accomplished." Fiona turned off the water.

Meg reached out of the shower, grabbed a towel from the cabinet, and wrapped it around Fiona, pulling her close and trapping her against her body. Meg stared deeply into the beautiful eyes that had enthralled her from the first moment she had seen them. The gaze meeting hers seemed to wrap around her, and her heart skipped a beat. Something huge welled up inside of her, filling her with a sense of blissful expectation and excitement. She watched as Fiona's pupils dilated until the ring of color was a thin band around the dark point, seeming to pierce her soul. They stood there, staring at each other. I love you, whispered Meg's heart. I love you. I love you. And she heard the answer of Fiona's heart too, though neither of them uttered a word.

Time stood still, their bodies pressed together and their eyes locked. It could have been hours or minutes or days. The sudden sound of the doorbell barely roused them from their trance. Neither of them moved.

✳ ✳ ✳ ✳ ✳

"YOOHOO!" A MUFFLED VOICE CALLED through the front door. The doorbell rang again. "Yoohoo!" The voice called out again. "Fiona, dear. It's me. I have yummies for you!"

Fiona tore her eyes from Meg's. She'd seen something in Meg's gaze that both scared and filled her with elation. She was frozen where she was, wrapped in Meg's arms, feeling new and mysterious things. She smiled apologetically. "It's Mrs. Rickles. I know she heard the shower running. These walls are paper-thin."

Meg grinned. "The theme from The Golden Girls is permanently imprinted in my brain."

The doorbell rang again.

Fiona pushed the shower curtain open and Meg grabbed her wrist. "I'm not done with you. Let her go."

The look in Meg's eyes made Fiona shiver, but she had to answer the door. "I promise. She won't leave and I'm sure she'll use the key I gave her, thinking I must have slipped in the shower." Fiona squeezed Meg tightly, unwilling to leave her arms. Normally she didn't mind, but normally she didn't have a gorgeous woman's naked body wrapped around her.

She kissed Meg, stepped from the open shower, shrugged into her robe, and pulled her wet hair up into towel as she walked quickly to the front door.

The doorbell sounded yet again. "Yoohoo!" Mrs. Rickles' muffled, yet cheery voice called through the door.

Fiona opened the door as her diminutive neighbor was about to slide her spare key into the lock. The surprise on Mrs. Rickles' face was almost comical as she stood on the stoop in a house dress and sturdy heeled shoes, holding up a large plate of chocolate chip cookies. A leather purse looked huge dangling from the crook of her elbow. As always, Mrs. Rickles' violet hair was perfectly coifed, and, as usual, her bright red lipstick was a little smeared, the result of her own unsteady hand. The old woman's surprise morphed into a bright smile. It was impossible to be irritated at her effervescence, though.

"Is that a turban you're wearing, Fiona dear?" Mrs. Rickles squinted up at her.

"I have a towel on my head, Mrs. Rickles!" She spoke loudly as Mrs. Rickles was a little hard of hearing.

"Oh, yes, yes, yes! Silly, me. I seem to have misplaced my glasses again. I heard the shower. It was on so long, I thought maybe you might have fallen. I'm very pleased to be wrong." Mrs. Rickles chuckled and shrugged her shoulders in amusement. "I have warm, gooey cookies for you, my dear."

Mrs. Rickles held the plate out to Fiona, trying to look around her and into the apartment.

"Come in, Mrs. Rickles. Thank you for the cookies." She took the plate with one hand and hugged the woman with her free arm. When she pulled away, she hooked her finger under a beaded chain tucked into the light sweater Mrs. Rickles wore over her house dress. "I think we found your missing glasses."

Mrs. Rickles tugged the chain out from beneath her sweater and looked at them with amazement before she slid them onto her face. "So, we have!" she exclaimed.

Fiona stepped aside as the little old woman walked slowly through the front door.

"I'll make us some tea. I have someone here I'd like you to meet." Fiona glanced down the hallway as she passed. "Meg? Come meet Mrs. Rickles."

Meg poked her head out of the bedroom. She was clutching the towel around herself. Why wasn't she dressed yet?

Mrs. Rickles held up a T-shirt she'd found on the couch. Oh! Their clothes were still in a pile on the couch from when things got hot and heavy in the living room before they'd moved to the shower.

"I caught you in the middle of doing laundry, I see." Mrs. Rickles began to fold the T-shirt.

Fiona gently took the shirt and picked up the little pile. "I'll just put these away."

Meg was in the bedroom when she took the clothes back and they both burst out laughing.

"Can I borrow some shorts?" Meg whispered. She gave her a clean pair of shorts and a T-shirt. Meg kissed her. "I'll be out in a sec."

When Fiona went back to the living room, Mrs. Rickles was sitting at the kitchen table in the chair she usually chose when she came over for tea.

"Do I finally get to meet the young lady you've been spending so much time with?" Mrs. Rickles asked.

"Meg will be right out."

Mrs. Rickles held a finger to her chin. "Meg, is it? Short for Margaret?"

Fiona was about to answer, but Meg appeared beside her and beat her to it. "Yes, ma'am, it sure is. Most people guess Megan. It's nice to meet you."

Mrs. Rickles waved her over. "Come sit next to me."

"I'll get the tea ready," Fiona said.

Meg sat in the chair next to Mrs. Rickles. Fiona smiled when Mrs. Rickles placed her hand over Meg's. "My name is Margaret, too. I always longed for others to call me Meg," she said wistfully. "Meg is so much more glamorous. But my mother always called me Maggie, so Maggie it was, and Maggie it remains."

"My brother used to call me Maggie. Now he calls me Megs."

"You do not strike me as a Maggie," Fiona called to them as she put the pot on the stove.

Meg laughed. "Me, either."

"Tea or coffee, Meg?"

"Milk please," Meg said. "There's nothing better than milk with fresh baked chocolate chip cookies!"

"Not if you're lactose intolerant, dear," Mrs. Rickles said, waving her hand in front of her nose like she smelled something foul. "I'm afraid I'd be a very unwanted guest if I indulged in so much as a tablespoon of milk." Her eyes grew dreamy. "And, oh, how I love milk. I miss it so much. More than my dearly departed Walter, I dare say."

Meg snorted and then tried to hide it with a cough. Fiona watched her reaction with amusement. Mrs. Rickles was definitely a character. Some of the things she'd heard the four-and-half-foot woman say had more than surprised her. She looked so innocent in her bifocals and pink cheeks lined with a roadmap of wrinkles.

"The water will be ready in a few minutes," Fiona said. She stood behind Mrs. Rickles, patting her arm. She winked at Meg, who looked like she was still trying to hide laughter. She didn't blame her. Mrs. Rickles was a riot without trying.

Mrs. Rickles reached up and put her timeworn hand over Fiona's. "I do so adore having tea with you, Fiona, dear."

"I do, too, Mrs. Rickles."

"And now we also have Meg. It's a proper tea party!" Mrs. Rickles tittered. "Now, tell me how you know each other. I notice you visit quite a bit, dear. Our Fiona seems happy for it. How did you two meet?"

Fiona explained the situation with the kittens. Mrs. Rickles spent most of her days watching the neighborhood from the comfort of the recliner in her living room so she wasn't surprised by her observations.

The old woman clucked her tongue. "Such a sad beginning to a wonderful friendship. But, they say relationships forged in fire make for stronger ties. So, there's that. And you work at the coffee shop on the corner, Meg? I can't say I've visited Helga's. Tea is… well, it's more my cup of tea." She laughed at her own joke.

Meg laughed politely, which pleased Fiona. "We have some excellent teas to offer. One of the owners actually grows many of the herbs and flowers they use. You may like them."

Mrs. Rickles looked like she had some doubts, but she smiled at the information. "Well, if I can get my ancient stumps to carry me down there one day, I will sample their teas on your recommendation, Meg. But it won't happen until the fall, I dare say. This heat will melt the teats off a swine!"

Fiona laughed. "I'll take you down when it's cooler, Mrs. Rickles. I haven't tried their teas yet either. Speaking of which…" She went into the kitchen and retrieved a silver tray displaying the tea service she had inherited from Aunt Corny. She'd already filled the silver cream and sugar containers, added a container of honey, and had placed dainty china cups, saucers, and biscuit plates on it. Bags of Mrs. Rickles' favorite tea, Twining's English Afternoon, were in two of the cups, and milk was in another. She took the tray to the table and placed a saucer and cup at each seat. She then placed a tiny silver spoon on the edge of each saucer.

"I should have known you'd have a fancy tea set," Meg said.

She lifted her chin and stifled a laugh. "A proper lady would never consider having high tea in coffee mugs."

"I think it's absolutely delightful." Mrs. Rickles clapped her hands. "My mother always had tea in the afternoon. Nothing as elegant as this, but she always had shortbread biscuits on hand for drop-in guests. Pity the child who put a grubby paw on her Lorna Doones!"

She'd heard the story several times, but the nostalgia gleaming in the older woman's eyes made Fiona smile.

"I have Lorna Doones in the cupboard if you'd like some, Mrs. Rickles." Mrs. Rickles usually abstained from the sweets she brought over, but on the occasion when she treated herself, Fiona had the cookies on hand, just in case.

Mrs. Rickles patted Fiona's arm. "I'm tempted, dear child, but tea is fine for me today. Doctor's orders."

The teakettle began to whistle and Fiona popped back into the kitchen to transfer the hot water into the china teapot, before she brought it back to the dining room table where she poured it for Mrs. Rickles' and herself.

"I hope you like chocolate chip cookies." Mrs. Rickles pushed the plate toward Meg.

"I've heard about your famous cookies. I don't know the last time I had a homemade chocolate chip cookie." Meg selected a cookie.

Fiona smiled at the anticipation on her face.

Mrs. Rickles took a sip of her tea, closed her eyes, and sighed. "The tea is delicious, as usual, Fiona dear." She turned to Meg. "When did you get out of the service, Meg?"

Meg tilted her head. "The service?"

Mrs. Rickles looked confused. "Fiona mentioned you were a veteran."

Meg's eyes fill with understanding. "I'm a vet, but not that kind of vet. I'm a veterinarian, an animal doctor."

Mrs. Rickles laughed and the corners of her eyes crinkled up. "Oh! Silly me. I just assumed the military. If you're a veterinarian, why are you working at a coffee shop?"

Fiona smiled into her cup. Mrs. Rickles was being direct, as usual.

Meg didn't seem to mind. "I was helping the owners while they were out of town. They're friends."

"Your being a veterinarian explains the help with the kittens. I was wondering why Fiona would require help from a veteran," Mrs. Rickles said before taking a sip of her tea. She looked amused. "I was thinking it was an unusual way to get into a woman's pants."

Fiona almost spit out the tea. The expression on Meg's face was priceless. She had no response, so she picked up a cookie and took a bite. "Delicious cookies."

65

THAT WAS INTERESTING. MEG CLEARED the table while Fiona walked Mrs. Rickles back to her apartment. Her face burned again at the comment about getting into Fiona's pants but she laughed. What a character!

Meg's cell phone vibrated in her pocket and Gilda Radner's Let's Talk Dirty to the Animals started to play. Aunt Claudia. She'd been meaning to call her to talk about extending her time in New York and going to work at the clinic later in the fall or maybe the first of the year. Everything was so new with Fiona, she didn't know how to plan. She placed the dishes next to the sink and answered.

"Aunt Claudia! How are you?" She relaxed against the counter.

"Megsie! So glad you picked up. I half-expected you to be out exploring the city. The last time your uncle and I were in New York, we barely slept. Sightseeing every minute, eating everything in sight! We probably…" Meg listened for a couple of minutes as her aunt described her trip to NYC. Aunt Claudia always started conversations in the middle. Eventually, she took a breath. "Oh, listen to me! You asked how I'm doing. I'm doing well."

"And Uncle Samuel?"

"Also doing well. Are you in the middle of anything, honey?" The rattle of pots and pans punctuated Aunt Claudia's response. Uncle Samuel must be making breakfast, because everyone in the family knew Aunt Claudia couldn't cook to save her life and Uncle Samuel rocked at French toast. "I wanted to know if you've settled on a date to be back in Washington. No pressure, or anything, I'm just trying to get my schedule figured out."

"Oh." Meg's smile faded. Her time with Fiona suddenly had a limit. "I haven't actually settled on a date."

"Do you think we could pin down a date in the next few days?" She didn't blame her for pressing it. They had a business to run. "I don't want to pressure you, sweetie, and I would have waited to talk about it when you're out for your dad's birthday but, well… you're the first of the family to know. I'm pregnant!"

It was great news! She was elated for her aunt and uncle. They'd been trying for another kid for years, but Claudia kept on having miscarriages during the first few months. "What? How awesome! Congratulations. You've been trying for so long. When are you due?"

"In January. We waited to get past the first trimester to tell anyone because we wanted to make sure nothing happened. The thing is, we also just discovered we're having triplets."

"Whoa! Triplets?"

Aunt Claudia blew a breath out. She sounded both nervous and excited. "It's a long story, but in-vitro has a higher chance of multiples. That means I probably won't work until I pop like I did with your cousin, seeing as I'm carrying a litter. Triplets also rarely go to term." Aunt Claudia laughed. "I'd like to get you all set up and comfortable at the clinic before it happens. Do you think the first of September will work for you? It would give us at least two months to get you up to speed."

Her chest constricted. Aunt Claudia had been so supportive of her plans to stay in the city for the entire summer. It was the least she could do for her. "The first it is."

"Excellent! I knew I could count on you. Thanks, Megsie." Her aunt sounded so relieved. "We'll see you for your dad's party in the meantime, right? It's been so long since everyone has been together in one place. I can't wait to see what you get him for his birthday."

Meg spoke with her aunt for a few more minutes without revealing anything about the gargoyle and hung up. She tried to ignore the battle in her heart between working with her aunt at the clinic and spending more time with Fiona. Who would have thought she'd have such a hard time choosing between her life's dream and a relationship that might not even have a future?

66

"MIKE. SERIOUSLY. YOU NEED TO stop." Fiona stood in the hot sun and grasped the wrought iron fencing in front of her apartment. She should never have answered the phone when it rang after seeing Mrs. Rickles to her door. He'd been cool the last time, though, so she thought he would be this time, too. She was wrong.

"Fi, this isn't just about you. It affects me, too. And our baby. It isn't fair for you to pull this power play."

Had he really said "our baby"? "You're getting way ahead of yourself. This isn't some sort of power play." She wanted to hang up. Who the hell did he think he was? "This affects my entire fucking life. I need some time to figure out what I'm going to do and I don't need you breathing down my neck about it every day."

She heard him take a deep breath.

"You asked for space. I've been giving you space. I call once in a while to check in. All I'm saying is you need to factor me into what you decide. I want this baby."

A swarm of responses flew through her mind, none of them very nice. She counted to ten. "I'll let you know what—"

"When? When will you let me know?"

She almost hung up, but instead, she took a deep breath. "I'll let you know what I decide in a few weeks."

"What's a few? I need a date." He was sounding like a lawyer now.

"You'll know when I call you." She hung up.

It was hot and she was angry. She took a few deep breaths and went back to her apartment. Meg would make her feel better.

When her eyes adjusted to the lower light in the apartment, Meg was standing in the dining area staring at her phone.

"Hey you. Waiting for your phone to ring?" The sight of Meg made her feel better. She wasn't going to bore her with the details of yet another crappy call with Mike. She could use a hug, though, so she walked over to her and stood a few inches away.

"I just got off the phone with Aunt Claudia."

"The one with the veterinarian office in Ooka—I give up." She laughed. Meg smiled. "Okanogan."

"Is everything okay? You look… pensive?"

"She wants me to start working on September first."

All the wind was sucked from Fiona's lungs. "September first?"

"Yes." Meg looked down at her phone.

Fiona blew out a long breath. They'd never talked about a date, only the end of the summer. September was technically summer, right? She wanted to negotiate, but she knew it wasn't the time. "That gives us all of August, I guess." She stepped toward Meg, who wrapped her in her arms.

"Yeah, I guess it does." Meg rested her forehead on her shoulder.

First Mike and now this. Fiona's chest tightened up. But Meg looked as upset about it as she was. Meg was always taking care of her. It was her turn to step up. She squeezed her tight. "I don't want to worry about tomorrow and ruin the time we have." She pulled her head back to gaze into Meg's eyes. As usual, she fell deeply into the blue, blue depths.

"I like the way you think." Meg smiled and she lifted one of Fiona's hands to rub across her cheek. Her hand was warm and soft.

"Someone I know told me that."

"That someone is very wise."

"Yep. One of the wisest people I've ever known. Too bad she's moving back to Washington."

"Yeah…" Meg let the word trail off and they stood there quietly for a moment, each lost in their own thoughts.

67

FIONA SAT AT HER DESK, looking around her miniscule office at Threadlocke and Guernsey. It seemed like a lifetime ago when her sole purpose in life was to move down the hall and into one of the corner partner offices. Now she laughed at her old blindered focus. Such a trivial thing to fixate on, when the rest of her life was in free-fall.

Aside from the picture sitting on her desk, the one of her parents taken a few weeks before their accident, her office was bare. There were no pictures on the walls, no plants on the credenza in front of the window, no knick-knacks placed around the space. She hadn't even brought in any of her own personal law books. Aside from the picture, there wasn't a single thing displayed in the office reflecting her personality. Nothing. The irony of her nearly sterile workspace hit her like a gentle punch. Sterile office; sterile life. She hadn't made any friends at the office, aside from Twyla. She never went out to lunch with anyone, preferring to work through lunch. In fact, she rarely left her office except to visit the firm's extensive law library. At least leaving the firm would be painless, she thought to herself, as she opened a drawer in her desk and pulled out the stack of boring cases she was more than halfway through. Her goal was to be finished with them by the time she left on vacation with Meg. There would be more when she got back. There always would be. But, hopefully, when she got back she'd know what to do with her life. She was done with planning it down to the minutest detail, she just needed some sort of direction.

Sighing, she flipped open the top file, powered up her laptop, and tucked into her work.

The case happened to be for a company based in Seattle. She smiled at the synchronicity and thought how she would be there in a few short days. She looked up the company's website to get more information for her research and she noticed an ad in the browser featuring Seattle jobs. On a lark she clicked on it.

✿✿✿✿✿

SEVERAL HOURS LATER, FIONA HADN'T completed a single case and she was deep into Columbia's career development website. She hadn't limited her search to Washington; in fact she found more opportunities on the east coast. Her research had also opened her eyes to career paths she had never even considered, including opening her own firm. She didn't think she'd have an opportunity to check into any of the Washington prospects when she was in Seattle with Meg, nor did she seriously consider them as real possibilities—after all, who picked up and left everything they knew for a relationship a few weeks old?—but the exercise gave her a much needed feeling of possibility, especially with Meg leaving in a few short weeks. And possibility felt good.

68

THE CLOUDS WERE LOW OVERHEAD but the late afternoon rain had stopped, at least temporarily, which was a good thing for the Wednesday after work traffic. Meg drove the rental car down interstate 5 on their way from the airport to Meg's family home in the Highlands area of northern Seattle. Meg had the window partway down, and though it was a bit chilly, even in late July, it settled her soul. She breathed in the damp and salty air, tinged with pungent dankness. She was home, and she couldn't think of a better feeling than to be here with Fiona. Her heart was full.

She realized she'd been talking non-stop since they'd left the airport. Part of it was how much she wanted Fiona to love her family. The other part was how nervous she knew Fiona was to meet them. She stopped her running commentary and hoped the surrounding landscape, in its breathtaking, rain-rinsed clarity along the Puget Sound would give Fiona some peace. She imagined Fiona's eyes taking in the handful of watercraft out on the water. Was she imagining walking along the water's edge in heavy boots and a warm jacket, hands wrapped tightly around a steaming cup of coffee?

Fiona laid her head against the headrest in the rented vehicle. "I finally understand the tone of longing in your voice when you speak of Washington."

Some of the tension between Meg's shoulder blades melted away.

"I can't imagine living anywhere else. The clinic is more inland, but it's beautiful there, too."

Fiona took her hand. "The closer we get to your parents' house, the more I want to throw up."

Meg took her hand and glanced over at her. Fiona looked cute for someone who was about to be sick. "Are you sure it isn't morning sickness?"

"Aside from the fact it's late afternoon and I haven't experienced much morning sickness so far, I think I can safely say it's probably the thought of meeting my girlfriend's family for the first time that's making the salad I had for lunch want to decorate the inside of the windshield."

Meg looked over at her. "Am I officially your girlfriend?"

Fiona blinked a couple of times. Meg wondered if she was about to take it back, but then she smiled. "I'd say you're my girlfriend. I don't let just anyone into my pants, to use Mrs. Rickles' phrase."

Meg squeezed her hand. "I like that."

"The girlfriend part? Or the getting into my pants thing?"

Meg kissed her palm while watching the road. "Oh, I definitely like getting into your pants, but I think you already knew that. I was talking about the girlfriend part."

"Good. It's settled, then. We're girlfriends." Fiona giggled, making Meg laugh. "Can I call exclusive rights to you now?"

She held Fiona's hand to her chest. "Honey, you've had exclusive rights to me since the day I saw you with those guys at Helga's."

"What guys? Oh, wait. You mean Josh?"

"Yeah, and the other guy you had coffee with on the patio."

Fiona seemed to search her mind and frowned. "Oh, yeah. Mike."

Meg wasn't sure why she hadn't put two and two together. "The blond guy was Mike?"

"The one and only." Fiona paused. "Speaking of which, I'd kind of like it if you didn't bring up the baby to your parents this weekend, if it's okay."

Meg tried to think if she'd already said something to them in their weekly calls, but she didn't think she had. Her mom had been so focused on making sure her dad didn't find out about the surprise party, she'd rushed off the phone each time, so she hadn't had a chance to talk about much.

"No problem. I figure it's your business to bring up, if you want to."

"I suppose we might want to tell them some time." She laughed nervously. "Actually, you and I should talk about it first, don't you think?"

Meg swallowed hard. "About the baby?"

Fiona shifted in her seat and faced her. "We agreed we're girlfriends. But what does that mean? I'm having a baby. I haven't even said that out loud more than a handful of times. I have no idea what it means for the future, including our future."

"And I'm moving back to Washington in September." The turnoff to her

parents' house came up. She sighed. "We're here." She pulled up to the gate at
the end of the driveway and stopped the car.

Fiona grimaced. "I hate thinking about you leaving. I shouldn't have
brought it up, especially now, when I already feel queasy."

Meg took her hand again. "It's stuff we need to talk about. But you're
right. Now's not the time." She pointed at a camera mounted on the wall near
the gate. "They know we're here."

Fiona looked around. "You didn't tell me you live in a fortress."

It was Meg's turn to grimace. It hadn't even crossed her mind to tell
Fiona about her family's wealth. Unlike other girlfriends, some who had
been attracted to her for the money, it had never seemed like a thing she
needed to discuss. Besides, it was her parents' money. Not hers. At least not
for a long time, she hoped. "I should have told you, but—"

Fiona caressed her hand. "It never came up. Why should it?"

Relief washed over Meg. "I guess we have some things to talk about. But
maybe, just for this weekend, we relax and let you get to know my family?
We can figure all the other stuff out later. Deal?"

Fiona smiled. "Deal."

She punched a code into the discreetly hidden keypad inside of a
manicured bush and the gate rolled open.

Fiona peered down the driveway. "Other than the dress I brought for the
party, all I packed was jeans and shorts."

Meg laughed and squeezed her hand. "They're going to love you, Fiona.
Jeans and shorts are fine."

She pulled the car into the portico near the front door of her parents'
enormous Tudor-style home. No sooner had Meg shut off the ignition, than
the front door opened and Rebecca, the family's housekeeper who'd been
with them since before Meg had been born, raced out. The handsome, older
women swept over and had Meg in a tight embrace as soon as Meg's feet hit
the clay-tiled ground.

"Meg, Meg, Meg! I am so happy to see you. It feels like Christmas to
have you here!" Rebecca released Meg and held her at arm's length to look
at her adoringly. "Your mother showed me the pictures of your graduation.
I was so upset I couldn't make it, but you won't get me on a plane. No, sir!
Maybe when I was younger. But now I'm older than the hills. I have to worry
about blood clots and the flu." She waved a finger at her. "I hope you took
precautions. Airplanes are virtual disease factories." She glanced at the other

side of the car when Fiona's head appeared over the roof. "Are you going to introduce me to your special friend?"

Rebecca clasped her hands before her with barely contained emotion. Her sparkling eyes moved from Meg to Fiona and back again, waiting for an introduction.

"Sorry, Rebecca," Meg said, knowing full well she hadn't had a chance to get a word in edgewise yet. "Rebecca, this is my girlfriend, Fiona." It gave her a thrill to call Fiona her girlfriend, and the smile on Fiona's face indicated she liked it, too.

Fiona came around the car and extended her hand. "It's nice to meet you, Rebecca. Meg has told me so much about you."

"Give an old woman a hug." Rebecca opened her arms wide and wiggled her fingers impatiently until Fiona gave her a hug. "I like you already, Fiona! Welcome to Chez Jordan!"

"Are Mom and Dad home from work?" Meg asked.

They stepped into the bright, high-ceilinged foyer. Soft lighting from subtle wall lamps helped brighten the gray day seen through the many windows.

Rebecca closed the front door. "Your mom stayed home today, and we expect your dad shortly. I'm surprised your mom isn't down yet."

The words were no sooner out of Rebecca's mouth, than a woman's voice called out from above them. "Meg!"

Meg took Fiona's hand and squeezed. All eyes followed the graceful arc of the stairs, which rose along the wall to the right. A slightly older version of Meg appeared on the upper landing and paused briefly while a bright smile overtook her face. The resemblance was remarkable. Same smile, same build, same hair color, same stance. Meg watched Fiona look from her mother to her, probably amazed at their likeness. She'd been hearing it all her life and she was proud of it. Her mother was a stunning woman.

Her mom raced down the wood stairs wearing a pair of black yoga pants and a flowing white-cotton shirt, enveloping her in a fierce embrace. "You're here! You're both here." Her mother released her and gave Fiona the same warm hug. "Welcome to Seattle, Fiona."

"Fiona, meet my mom, Reese."

"Thanks for having me, Mrs. Jordan. So far, Seattle has been beautiful, as is your home." Fiona no longer looked nervous. Meg knew she'd relax as soon as she'd met her parents. She was especially happy her mom wasn't wearing her work clothes. Lawyerly Reese Jordan was a force to be reckoned with. Mom around the house Reese Jordan was way more easy going.

Her mom waved at the windows. "You should see it when the sun comes out. Oh, and please call me Reese."

"I was telling her the same on the way from the airport," Meg said. "It's when people come crawling out of their caves in search of some vitamin D."

"I hope we see some sunshine, then," Fiona said.

Meg's mother led them further into the house and Rebecca excused herself to check on something in the kitchen. "I'm glad to finally meet the woman who has caught our little butterfly! I'm happy you could come."

Meg laughed when Fiona's cheeks turned pink and she took her hand. Fiona squeezed her fingers. "I wouldn't have missed meeting you and seeing where Meg grew up."

"I hope you brought hiking boots. Our Meg grew up in the trees, streams, and forest behind this house." Meg's mother laughed. "Come into the kitchen. You both must be starved. Let me whip up a snack while I interrogate you."

Fiona looked over at Meg, who smiled and rolled her eyes. They followed Reese into the enormous kitchen.

Her mother's idea of a snack was rarely something simple—at least for normal people. Meg wasn't surprised when an array of ingredients were retrieved and assembled into bruschetta in less time than it took her to make a cup of coffee. While her mother expertly sliced bread, she asked Fiona about work and if she liked living in New York City. While the bread grilled, and the tomatoes, garlic, mozzarella, and basil were chopped and grated, her mom asked Fiona about her childhood and school. By the time the snack was pulled from the broiler, her mother was asking about her future plans, which Fiona kept relatively vague.

Meg had been right about the interrogation, even if it had been gently administered. Fiona didn't look too phased by it, though, and Meg was happy her mother seemed to like her—not that she'd had any doubt.

"How are the surprise party plans coming along, Mom?" Meg asked as she took down some small plates.

"As far as your father knows, you two are here to join him in a private family celebration for his birthday and the club." Her mother was nearly trembling with the excitement. She had taken off her apron and stood with a glass of white wine as she watched Meg and Fiona devour the bruschetta.

"The rest of the family will trickle in over the next two days and will be staying in town so he doesn't suspect anything. Even CJ will be here. He called yesterday."

Meg tried to hide her disappointment. The last time she'd asked, he wasn't coming.

Her mother looked a little worried and Meg shifted in her seat as her mother studied her. She didn't want to make the situation any more uncomfortable than it already was. "I'm glad he's coming. Dad will be pleased." And she was happy about that.

Her mother's expression reflected her excitement again. "He said he couldn't make it at first, so your dad isn't expecting it. It'll be another little surprise. He's flying in late Friday night with a friend. You should be back from your trip to Okanogan before they get here."

Oh, jeez. He was bringing "a friend". She'd seen the women CJ hooked up with at school. He had a thing for overly made up women with big hair and super tight clothing. He'd never brought one home, though. Maybe it would keep him from being too much of a jerk.

"Does he have a girlfriend?"

Her mom waved her hand. "Oh, I have no idea. He never tells me anything. It's not a girlfriend, though. He's a classmate, from what I can tell. He hasn't even told me his name. They'll get here after Dad goes to bed. And then your dad will be out golfing with his buddies before CJ wakes up, so it won't be hard to keep him under wraps until the party." She clapped her hands. "This is so fun!"

"What's so fun?" Meg's father walked into the kitchen and they all turned to look. Meg snuck a glance at her mom, who looked calm. Her mom had a view of the doorway, so there was no way he could have heard their conversation.

"Why, having your daughter here with her girlfriend, dear."

He stopped next to Fiona's chair. "Of course! So glad you could come and visit. Fiona, is it?"

Fiona stood and shook his hand. She seemed to study him and Meg wondered if her nerves were back. She hoped not. Her dad might look imposing in his suit and tie, but he was one of the most laid-back people she actually knew. "It's nice to meet you, Mr. Jordan."

Meg hugged her dad to show Fiona he wasn't as intimidating as he looked in his tailored suit and power tie.

Her dad was a handsome man—tall and athletic, with strong features and a smidge of gray at the temples of his perfectly groomed, dark brown hair. In his work clothes, his warm and expressive eyes were what saved him from appearing cold or intimidating, and the hug he gave Meg was as warm as Reese's. When he let go, Meg took Fiona's hand and squeezed.

After a few polite words, he excused himself. "It's a delight to meet you, young lady. I'm going to run upstairs and get out of this monkey suit. I'll be right back."

When they heard him ascending the stairs, Meg's mother leaned over. "That was close."

They chatted for a few minutes before Meg's father reappeared, a different man in a pair of well-worn hiking shorts and a faded T-shirt from a 5K he and Meg had run more than a decade earlier.

✱✱✱✱✱

AFTER DINNER, THEY MOVED INTO the living room. The gas fireplace was already casting a soft, flickering light as Fiona and Meg followed Reese and Mickey into the cozy room. Meg looked at Fiona to check in, and Fiona squeezed Meg's hand with a smile.

Her dad poured wine for himself and her mom after she and Fiona said they didn't want any. Meg did want some, but she didn't want to call attention to Fiona, since they didn't know about the baby.

Her dad handed a glass to her mother and ignored the furniture, sitting on the rug in front of the fireplace with his back against the hearth. Her mom flopped down beside him, and Meg chose a spot across from them, leaning her back against the loveseat. Fiona looked amused at the seating arrangement, shook her head, and sat next to her on the floor.

"We're floor dwellers in this family," Mickey said, taking a sip of his wine.

"Tell me how Vi's doing," her mother said.

Meg filled her mom in on the latest drama between Sherri and Vi, a story which had been unfolding in their weekly phone calls. Sherri had finally put her foot down about the other women, and Vi had given up her extracurricular love life. Living in the apartment had become peaceful, even though Meg spent more time at Fiona's house than at Vi's.

Soon, the conversation turned to Fiona and her work, specifically about the firm she worked at, her caseload, and her plans for the future. Meg was surprised when Fiona told them she was currently at a crossroads with her career and was looking around. Aside from saying she'd prefer a more high-powered position, Fiona hadn't mentioned anything about looking for another firm.

Her mom cradled her wine glass between her knees, and winked. "Well, Mickey and I have a little pull with at least one or two of the law firms in the area."

Her mother was as subtle as a Seahawks fan during a playoff game. Ugh! "Mom, you're terrible!" She looked at Fiona, who, thankfully, looked amused. "Don't let them pressure you into anything."

Fiona stroked her hand but responded to her parents. "I'm keeping my options open."

Despite her chastisement of her mother, excitement flared in Meg's stomach. Could some of those options be in Washington? She tried not to get her hopes up, but it was difficult. Wouldn't Fiona have told her already if she was open to moving across country?

"I'm not going to lie and say it wouldn't make me happy if our Meg found a reason to practice in Seattle rather than all the way over in Okanogan," her mother said.

Meg groaned and gently kicked her mother's outstretched leg. "You know I have to work in Okanogan. I've promised Aunt Claudia."

Her mother tilted her head, looking resigned. "I suppose two hundred miles is a lot closer than two thousand."

The conversation drifted onto other topics, but Meg couldn't wait to ask Fiona about the options she'd been considering.

69

THE NEXT MORNING WAS CHILLY and clear. Meg and Fiona were on the road to Okanogan before the sun even started to peek over the Cascade Mountains. They were only going to be gone one night, so they'd packed a simple overnight bag and left after quick showers before anyone else got up.

Fiona sat with her feet propped up on the car's dashboard, a travel mug of coffee cradled in her hands. She gazed blearily out through the passenger side window at the wet countryside rolling alongside them. She was amazed at the contrast in landscape as they moved further from the coast. She'd never seen so much open landscape in her life.

The night before, Meg had shown her the route they would take, which was a big loop out through the south and back via the north. It would give Fiona a good look at the Washington countryside. Fiona was engrossed in the views and deep in thought. One of the law firms she had seen in her recent career search happened to be along the route they were taking on the way back the next day, in a little town called Winthrop. She had no intention of visiting the attorney selling his practice, but she was eager to at least get a look at the area as they drove through.

She still hadn't told Meg she was considering moving out of the city, let alone away from the east coast; it wasn't a done deal and she didn't want to burden Meg with her indecision. When Meg had asked about it when they'd gone to bed last night, she'd told her she hadn't made any plans—which was true, but the more she thought about it, the more alluring a job in Washington sounded. However, Meg hadn't talked much about what would happen after September came around, and she didn't want to make any assumptions. In fact, Reese's thinly disguised suggestions the night before had been the closest they had ever come to discussing their future together.

As the landscape flew by, she knew she should bring up the topic of their future together, but the thought overwhelmed her, so she tucked it away for a little while longer.

They made good time and arrived in Okanogan just before lunchtime. The rain had disappeared on the east side of the Cascades, and the sun was bright in a cloudless sky. As the countryside fell away to clusters of farmhouses, and then to small-town streets lined with homes and businesses, Fiona fell in love with the rural feel of the town and the countryside surrounding Okanogan. It was much smaller than she expected, and she looked on in wonder at the small businesses and homes as they drove down Main Street. A river followed the road along one side, and Fiona loved it immediately.

They headed down a residential street where homes and businesses stood interspersed until they pulled to stop before a converted one-story brick house with a large front porch. Brightly colored flowers lined the cement path leading up to the front door. Manicured bushes stood along the front porch and along either side of a large, neatly trimmed front lawn. With the exception of the simple wooden sign hanging in the front yard next to the walkway, the clinic looked like a well-kept private residence from the outside, and it blended in nicely with the homes on either side.

Fiona climbed out of the car and stretched before following Meg into the building. She was surprised to find that the inside looked as clinically professional as the outside looked homey. The waiting area held a few patients and their owners.

A short woman in red and yellow scrubs covered with dog bones stood behind the counter sorting patient files. When she looked up at them, she tossed the folders aside and screeched. "Meg! I didn't know you were in town!" She hurried around the counter and gave Meg a big hug.

Meg returned the hug with a huge smile. "Gail! You look wonderful, as usual! Claudia didn't tell you I was coming?"

"I wanted it to be a surprise." Fiona turned to the deep and melodious voice. The woman emerging from the back office was one of the most beautiful women she'd ever seen. Aside from being pregnant, the woman looked like she could have stepped off of the cover of an issue of Vogue, if they featured medical scrubs. She was tall, statuesque, and her coffee colored skin was flawless. Her hair was swept up under a scrub cap, but Fiona guessed it was perfectly coiffed under the fabric hat. She moved with a fluid grace, but as she rounded the front desk to give Meg a hug, she knocked some of the patient files onto the floor. Before Gail could get there to help, Claudia conked her head on the edge of the counter as she bent to pick them up.

Meg grabbed her by the arms and pulled her into a laughing hug. "Same old clumsy Aunt Claudia! It's great to see you!"

Claudia patted her belly. "Pregnancy makes me even clumsier, I'm afraid. Thank goodness it's not evident in the procedure room!"

Meg smiled and put her hand on her aunt's stomach. "It probably doesn't help that you're expecting a litter! You don't look pregnant enough to be carrying three of them in there, though."

"Believe me, it feels like three, maybe four!"

Warm eyes the color and depth of amber turned to rest on Fiona, who stood next to the front door captivated by the reunion. Suddenly shy, all she could manage was a smile.

Claudia stepped toward her. "This must be Fiona!"

Meg hurried to Fiona's side. "Fiona, I'd like you to meet my Aunt Claudia."

"It's so nice to finally meet you." Fiona offered her hand.

Claudia ignored Fiona's outstretched hand and gave her a hug "Posh! Handshakes are for strangers. I am so honored to meet the woman who has finally captured my beloved niece's heart."

"Thank you. I don't know what to say. Meg's family has been so welcoming and kind. I'm so happy to finally meet you!" Fiona was surprised at the sting of tears when she thought of the warm welcome she'd received from everyone. Maybe it was hormones, but she knew it probably had more to do with having no family of her own.

"Why don't we go down to Reggie's for lunch? Renee, our vet tech, can handle the lab work for the folks in the waiting room." Claudia didn't wait for a response before she asked Gail to hold down the fort and headed for the door. She took off the cap and pushed it into her rear pocket as they walked out the door. As Fiona had guessed, not a hair was out of place on the elegant twist.

They walked two streets down to a diner directly out of the fifties. Claudia greeted every person they passed and Fiona enjoyed the bright sunshine on her skin as Meg and Claudia caught up.

At the restaurant they slid into the vinyl seats, Claudia sitting across from Meg and Fiona. A server, who Claudia knew by name, handed them worn menus and took their drink orders, before Claudia asked Fiona about living on the east coast. Fiona answered the questions, but privately mused over the interest Meg's family showed about the city. It didn't hold a candle to the paradise in which they lived.

Eventually the conversation drifted toward clinic talk, and Fiona sat back quietly, enjoying the lively discussion between Meg and Claudia.

When they finished eating, Meg and Claudia still had lots to talk about, so Fiona suggested they go back to the clinic while she drove around the little town and did some sightseeing. Meg was reluctant at first; she said she didn't want Fiona to feel abandoned, but Fiona finally convinced her she was happy to wander about on her own. That settled it, and Fiona said she would meet Meg back at the clinic at five.

✸✸✸✸✸

FOUR HOURS TO KILL UNTIL she had to get back to the clinic gave Fiona an unexpected opportunity to drive to Winthrop. When she'd first seen the law firm for sale online it had caught her eye because it was so close to Okanogan, but she hadn't seriously considered it. She hadn't made up her mind about anything to do with her career, let alone following Meg back home, since they'd never discussed what would happen after August. Even now she wasn't prepared to do any real investigating, but at least she could get a good look at the town.

The highway between Okanogan and Winthrop was forty miles of beautiful, open landscape, broken by thick copses of trees near the rivers and lakes dotting the area. She drove with her window open for most of the way to take in the fresh scents of the open country. Driving slowly through the small towns she passed, Fiona saw a side of life she had never experienced. She thought she knew about small towns having grown up in Pottstown, but that was a bustling metropolis compared to the hamlets she passed along her route. As Fiona approached her destination, a little less than an hour after she left Okanogan, she had fallen even more in love with the Washington countryside. She parked on the street in front of the general store, got out of the car, and took a look around.

The town was little more than a single main street, and much of the architecture was old western-style wood-frame buildings. She almost expected to see cowboys walking down the wooden sidewalks. No sooner did the thought cross her mind, than two men in cowboy hats walked out of a diner touting The World's Best Wild Berry Pie. The small-town cliché struck her as hilarious and she actually laughed out loud. She could admit to being a little disappointed when the cowboys jumped into a big red Ford truck instead of mounting horses.

She shook her head and used her phone to pull up the information she had stored about the law practice she had seen for sale. She highlighted the phone number and hit send, although she had no idea what she would say once she had someone on the phone.

"Winthrop Feed. What can we do you for?" a friendly female voice answered.

"I'm sorry," Fiona replied, about to hang up. "I was trying to contact Daniel Thomas. I must have the wrong number."

A sweet giggle filled her ear. "No, sweetie. You got the right number. Hold on a sec."

Fiona laughed quietly when she heard the woman's muffled voice call out for Danny. Fiona envisioned fingers held over the receiver. Fiona looked around the street to see if she could see the feed store, and found she was practically across the street from it. The building was one of the only freshly painted buildings along the street, most of them featuring either faded white paint or splintery stained wood finishes. The store name painted in white over red on the tall façade stood out brightly: Daniel's Feed Store. To Fiona's delight, there was a real wooden sidewalk along the front of the building, along with what looked to be a watering trough with an antique hand pump next to it. It could have come from the 1800s.

"This is Danny, what can I do you for?", a gravelly male voice asked through the phone.

"Hello, Mr. Thomas. My name is Fiona MacGregor and I'm calling about a listing you posted on a website offering your practice for sale."

"Now, that's interesting." Daniel Thomas suddenly sounded more like an attorney than a feedstore owner. "My practice is for sale, but I never listed it on a website… oh… wait a sec…" he said, and Fiona heard the woman who had answered the phone saying something in the background.

"You did?" Fiona heard Daniel Thomas ask, his voice muffled slightly. "I would never have thought… You kids and your computers… I reckon that's where she saw it then. Thanks, Katie!"

Fiona felt like a voyeur listening in on the easy exchange. The man's voice was back in her ear.

"Ms. MacGregor? Sorry about that. It looks like my assistant Katie posted it. How can I help you?"

"I'm in the area and I was hoping I could drop in and talk to you for a few minutes," Fiona said, although she had no idea what she would say. The easygoing attitude of both voices on the other end of the line eased her discomfort in asking.

"Sure. When did you have in mind?"

"Well, to be honest, I'm parked across the street. Would right now be an inconvenience?"

"Not at all. Come on over, but I have to warn you, today is delivery day and I'm in my work clothes."

Fiona heard a woman's chuckle in the background.

"I'll be there in a minute."

Fiona closed her car door and looked down to make sure she wasn't too rumpled. She was thankful it was delivery day at the feed store—she had forgotten she was in jeans. The rainy chill of the morning had made her decision for her when she got dressed. At least they were her best jeans and she had on a white button-up shirt, rather than the shorts and T-shirt she had planned to wear.

Crossing the street toward the feed store, behind which stood an open-sided barn where two flatbed trucks were parked, she watched several men tossing heavy bales of hay as if they were made of Styrofoam, stacking them high under the barn overhang. Equipment arranged neatly in the open space near the barn indicated the store also rented farm apparatus.

Fiona stepped onto the wooden planks of the sidewalk, and within a few strides, she was through the open doors of the feed store. Darkness pressed in around her in contrast to the bright sunshine of outside. Tinny country music played through speakers hung in the rafters of the store, and the smell of dry grain and something earthy tickled her sinuses as she stood inside the doorway and waited for her eyes to adjust. She looked up at the dirt streaked windows near the rafters of the tall open-ceilinged building, where dust motes drifted lazily in the bands of sunshine piercing the inside gloom. Rows of unlit industrial-style lights hung alongside a handful of gently rotating ceiling fans. Fiona swatted at a black housefly buzzing near her ear. Pallets piled with sacks were neatly displayed in long rows radiating from the narrow aisle cutting through the store before her. In the back of the store under an open loft, florescent lights illuminated an area where dry goods were displayed. To her right, a large door suddenly slid open, allowing the bright sunshine to pour in. A battered pickup truck backed up to the curb and a young man, dressed much like the cowboys she had seen leaving the general store, maneuvered a pallet jack under a stack of seed and deftly raised it up and moved it into the bed of the truck. The truck settled under the weight with a creaking groan.

"You must be Ms. MacGregor," the gravelly voice from the phone called from the rows of feed beside her. Fiona turned her attention from the truck to see a tall figure moving toward her. When he drew close, Fiona was surprised to see an older man, perhaps in his early seventies, though his walk suggested a much younger man. His voice on the phone didn't even hint at his advanced age. He was dressed in what Fiona started to identify as the town's uniform; cowboy hat, boots, jeans, blue work shirt, complete with bandana knotted at the neck. His shirt had a liberal dusting of straw dust on the shoulders. Fiona guessed he had been out back with the trucks when she called.

"Yes, but please call me Fiona." She smiled as she offered him her hand. His hand was huge and calloused, but his grasp was gentle when he took hers.

"Call me Danny. Hell, half the town calls me worse!" he joked. "Can I offer you a cup of coffee? We have an espresso machine."

She liked the old cowboy immediately. "Water would be great, if it isn't too much trouble. I don't want to keep you too long if you're busy. I was passing through town and thought I'd see if you were available, otherwise I would have made an appointment."

"Water's no trouble at all, and, for the record, I am always available for interruption when it's delivery day," Danny said with a wink. "I have two pairs of strong hands working here at the store for the heavy lifting and they can do it by themselves. Not to mention the two young bucks who drive the rigs. But the macho man in me won't shut up until I get in there with them. My old-timer's back thanks you for your good timing!" He laughed as he walked them toward the back of the building. Fiona was again surprised at Danny's ease of movement. He may have joked about being an old-timer, but Fiona had no trouble imagining him hoisting the bales of hay.

Following Danny past the dry goods section toward the office, Fiona saw a woman, who looked to be in her early forties, sitting on a stool behind an ancient cash register. Like Danny, she wore a blue work shirt, jeans, boots, and a cowboy hat. The woman absently turned the pages of a magazine, but her eyes followed Danny and Fiona. She tucked her curly red hair behind her ear as she watched them walk into the office. Before he shut the door, Danny poked his head out.

"Fiona and I have some business to discuss, Katie. Can you hold down the fort for a little bit?"

Katie looked up from her magazine. "Sure thing, Danny. Let me know if you need anything."

Danny chuckled and shook his head as he shut the door. "I'm sure you'll know before I do."

"Excuse me?" Fiona wasn't sure if Danny was talking to her.

"I'll bet you a shiny new quarter Katie's got her ear to the door already. We don't get visitors often."

Fiona laughed and looked around the large office as Danny grabbed a clean coffee cup from a row hanging next to a water cooler. She had expected a more utilitarian office, but a beautiful antique desk dominated the spotless wood-floored room. There were no windows, but a pair of Tiffany-style lamps on either corner of the desk provided soft lighting, as did a standing lamp in the corner of the office. An antique cast iron stove stood quietly along one wall, and Fiona guessed it was used for heat during the winter. Two comfortable looking stuffed chairs sat upon an expensive looking rug facing the desk, and a couple of antique wooden filing cabinets flanked the door. A handful of beautiful landscape paintings adorned the walls. The office was exactly what she would have expected of an established lawyer in a much larger city—not Daniel Thomas of Winthrop, Washington.

Danny handed her the water and propped himself against the desk. He took off his hat and set it down on the gleaming wood surface, running a hand over the top of his thick, salt and pepper head of hair, before crossing his feet at the ankles and stuffing his fingers into the front pockets of his jeans. He was the epitome of a modern cowboy getting ready to chat with his buddies down at the corner store. He hadn't asked her to sit, so Fiona stood where she was, sipping her water.

"You say you saw the listing Katie posted for me, huh?" Danny tilted his head.

Fiona nodded. "I did." She had a thousand questions she wanted to ask, but she was happy to let him take the lead in the conversation.

He rubbed a hand down his face. "One of the reasons I'm retiring is I'm just too old to keep up with all that computer stuff. I go online to check my e-mail and stocks, read the news, and to do a little shopping, but not much else. Katie takes care of all of the work-related stuff. My clients deserve someone who is a bit more current with technology."

"I can understand," Fiona said. "Most of my current caseload requires hours of online research."

Danny nodded. "I'm sure you're a wiz with the Internet. Young people today seem to be born with technical skills. No offense intended about the young people remark. In fact, I'm amazed at how easily young people pick it all up."

Fiona liked Danny the more they chatted. She smiled. "My aunt used to say the same thing."

"I take it you're not from around here."

"No. I happened to be in the area, so I thought I'd chance meeting you. I work at a firm in New York City, but I'm thinking of making a change. I'm just exploring my options."

"You're a long way from New York," Danny observed with an easy grin.

"It almost feels like a different world."

"I can imagine, though I've never been east of the Mississippi." Danny moved the chairs in front of the desk so they faced each other. "Why don't we take a load off? My feet are killing me. What kinds of questions can I answer for you?"

Fiona settled into one of the chairs. "I hadn't thought past driving by for a look, to be honest. I guess the main thing on my mind, and I hope this isn't too personal, but how do you support yourself with what I imagine is a limited client base?"

She was relieved to ask the one question she had been mulling over since she started thinking about leaving the city for a smaller town.

Danny didn't appear bothered by her direct question and answered her easily as he sat down behind the big desk. She finally saw a glimpse of his age in the way he eased himself down onto the chair.

"My main source of income comes from contracts with three large ranches and the township which retains me. We also have fairly big contracts with the City of Seattle, Winthrop, and another with Okanogan. Then there's local folks with sporadic divorce filings, drawing up of wills, and other legal work requiring an attorney, which combine to make a tidy living. Then there's the feed store, which does pretty well. I'm sure it doesn't compare to a big city attorney's salary, but out here, where the cost of living is next to nothing, it's more than enough to live on comfortably."

"Would all of the contracts and clients come with the sale of the practice?" Fiona asked.

"The contracts would transfer directly, but you would have to renegotiate them when their terms come up. If I remember correctly, they each have a year or more to go. As far as the ranches go, you would have to reach out to them yourself, but I've talked to each of them and they're willing to give a new attorney a chance. I'm not sure about Roy out at Long Mesa Ranch. He's a great client, but he's definitely a good old boy, and he may have an issue with a woman representing him. We've never talked about it, but he's mentioned poker nights and hunting trips with the new lawyer. Between that and his sense of humor… well, we can discuss it later if you decide you're interested. If so, I would give you the contact information for each of my clients, old and new. The feed store comes with the price of the practice."

Fiona's mind was racing with the information they discussed, inspiring more questions. She was trying to figure out what they should skim over now so she could think about it and go into more detail later if it came down to it. Then there was the feed store… wait….

"Did I hear you correctly? The store comes with the practice?"

"Yep." Danny nodded.

She didn't know anything about running a store. "Is it a deal breaker?"

Danny crossed his arms. "Think about the feed store as your marketing tool. Most everyone in the area comes here for tack and feed for their animals. Even the ones who don't have farm animals usually have a dog or cat, and everyone needs jeans. We're the only retail store for forty miles around. They come in for dog chow and they leave with an appointment to have a will drawn up." Danny winked at her. "Besides, I'm too old for running this store and no one around here wants to buy it, or if they do, they don't have the money. The town relies on this store and a small handful of others for economic stability. I can't just close it down. Ergo, the store goes with the practice."

She told him she understood his logic and he opened her eyes to many factors she had never considered before. They chatted for a little while longer before she headed back to Okanogan, telling him that she would definitely be in touch. As she opened the office door to leave, she wasn't surprised to hear a rustle on the other side and to see Katie scurrying to her seat.

✸✸✸✸✸

"CLAUDIA THINKS WE CAN BUY some land outside of town to open a large animal clinic. She hasn't been able to pursue the idea because she's so busy on her own. Once I come on staff, we can get a couple more vet techs and expand." Meg pulled the comforter down on the bed and climbed in.

Fiona was happy to see Meg so excited about everything she and Claudia had discussed while she'd been visiting Winthrop. Her mind was going over her own visit with Danny, while she and Meg got ready for bed in the guest room at Claudia and Samuel's house. She tried hard to actively listen, but she was grateful Meg was too preoccupied to notice her distraction.

She and Meg hadn't had a moment alone since Fiona had returned from her drive to Winthrop. The evening had been busy with meeting the other two Jordans—Meg's Uncle Samuel and her eleven-year-old nephew, Raphael. Dinner had been followed by games, and before she knew it, it had been time for bed. All of the activity had helped Fiona push aside thoughts about the vast new set of options opening up for her, but now, with the day winding down, her mind was filled with questions and possibilities. Some were exciting, some were scary, and all of them seemed to require way too much energy to concentrate on right then, but her mind wouldn't let go. Part of her wanted to talk to Meg about it, but she had reservations about laying all of it on her when she was busy contemplating changes of her own. It was completely unfair to expect Meg to deal with a baby and a new girlfriend on top of everything else. Fiona decided to think some more and get things figured out before she brought anything up with Meg.

Fiona situated herself in bed, her mind churning over the excitement filling her since she'd gotten back from the visit with Danny. She liked him. She liked Winthrop. She liked Washington. Everything just seemed right. And she couldn't help but feel something guiding her here. The feeling was so intense, in fact, she had to consciously force herself not to discuss a possible offer with Danny before she left. The desire to take the leap right then had surprised her. But the strength of the urge had scared her, too. She wasn't impulsive like that. She was a thinker. A planner. Yet, as she had driven out of Winthrop, she had looked in her rearview mirror, knowing she was going to be back.

317

Meg switched the light off and Fiona lay in the semi-dark, the only illumination coming from the moonlight from the open windows. Meg looked so beautiful in the silver light. All thoughts of the day fled Fiona's mind as an intense feeling of love unfurled within her chest. She'd gotten used to the powerful rush of emotion, but she hadn't had the courage to tell her yet. Fear and excitement welled within her as the words filled her throat.

Meg reached over and pulled her close. Her lips were warm against her mouth.

"Are you doing okay?" Meg trailed kisses along her jaw. "You've seemed kind of quiet this evening."

"I'm just taking things in, but I am so much better than okay." Fiona brushed her fingers along Meg's warm neck. The familiar touch of Meg's skin made everything all right. It always did.

"Good, because I want one-hundred-percent of your attention for the next several minutes."

Fiona's stomach tightened and her core pulsed as Meg began the slow process of removing her pajamas.

70

THEY TOOK THEIR TIME DRIVING back to Seattle after having lunch with Aunt Claudia again. Meg stopped at many of the scenic overlooks along the way, and took a few short side trips so Fiona could take in the scenery. She wasn't sure if it was the company or the scenery flowing by, but Meg was filled with a sense of almost overwhelming well-being. Everything was as it should be and the future was a vast and exciting realm of opportunity and possibility. She had no idea what the future held, exactly, but she knew she wanted it to include Fiona.

By the time they got into Seattle, the damp steady rain they had left had been replaced by deep blue skies, and a gorgeous sunset was descending over the Puget Sound. This was the Seattle she wanted Fiona to see, off the highway, resplendent in green, with beautiful skies.

Nearly home, Meg pulled over to wait for the sun to go down over the water. The overlook she selected was deserted and far enough away from the highway. From their view, they had the whole world to themselves.

They got out of the car and faced the colorful horizon. Meg pulled Fiona to her so Fiona had her back against her chest, and they watched the dark red sun start to slide behind the islands across the indigo ocean. The cool air off the sound gently blowing into their faces carried a slight chill, and Meg caressed the tiny goosebumps on Fiona's arms. She ran her hands up and down Fiona's chilled skin, nuzzling Fiona's neck. A small shiver ran through Fiona, who leaned into the gesture.

"Are you cold?" Meg asked quietly, her lips near Fiona's ear.

"Not in your arms, I'm not." Fiona pulled her head back and looked into Meg's eyes. What Meg saw in Fiona's gaze made the rest of the world recede. The soft light of the setting sun reflected in her eyes, and her face was bathed in the fading light, making it appear as if it were lit from within. "God, you are so beautiful, Fiona. You take my breath away." Her heart ached with enormous emotion, filling her chest and body to the very edges. So powerful was the feeling, the hairs on the back of her neck and scalp stood on end. She began to tremble.

"Are you cold?" Fiona pressed closer into the circle of Meg's arms.

"Not in your arms, I'm not." Meg whispered through the lump in her throat, gazing deeply into Fiona's shimmering eyes.

The emotion holding them was too powerful for words and she fell into Fiona's beautiful eyes. Her heart belonged to Fiona and she wanted it to belong to her forever.

There were so many things Meg wanted to tell Fiona right then, but none of them would take form in her mouth. She simply stared at Fiona and drank her in, imprinting the picture before her in her mind forever; Fiona's beautiful eyes like liquid energy, the way the stray hairs around Fiona's face swayed gently in the breeze, and how the gold light shined through them, as if Fiona generated the vibrancy of the sunset from within herself. Meg knew she would never forget this moment.

Fiona must have sensed what was going on in her heart. Her face transformed into pure understanding. "I feel it, too." Her warm lips pressed against Meg's and she felt forever in their kiss.

71

FIONA AWOKE DISORIENTED IN A strange bed, a strange room, the warmth of a familiar hand on her back. Her skin beneath it tingled. She struggled to open her eyes.

"I'm sorry. I didn't mean to wake you." Meg sat on the side of the bed gently rubbing her back. "I heard CJ come in and I want to go see him before he goes to sleep."

"M'kay." She was so sleepy. When they'd arrived home, there had been dinner with Meg's parents. It had nearly killed Fiona to rein in the emotions and the aching need building within her since the moment on the cliff. When they'd finally found time to be alone, an incredible energy had flared between them in an unspoken demonstration of love, culminating in an emotional and physical union so intense it had depleted every iota of Fiona's energy, after which she had fallen into a coma-like sleep. Through the mists of fatigue numbing her mind, she wondered at Meg's ability to be awake, let alone lucid.

"Tell 'im I can't wait to meet 'im t'morrow," she mumbled, her head drooping as sleep tried to reclaim her.

"I will, baby. Go back to sleep. I'll be back in a few minutes."

Fiona snugged into the pillows and Meg smoothed the covers, gently kissing Fiona's lips. Her body tried to respond to the contact, but she couldn't manage to open her eyes. As she slipped into the soft velvet of sleep, she heard the door open and close quietly, then the sound of running feet. Meg's muffled hoot joined a male voice. The sound of mingled laughter rose and then abruptly stopped at the sound of a shutting door. Fiona smiled a sleepy smile and wondered what it would be like to have a brother, before the inky grasp of unconsciousness descended upon her.

* * * * *

THE NEXT MORNING, FIONA WATCHED Meg move enshrouded in the steam swirling against the glass shower door. Fiona had never witnessed a sexier scene. The sight of wet flesh moving in and out of the mist seemed to activate her every nerve. Desire initiated a slow pulse deep within her core. She could almost taste the water on Meg's shoulder, feel the slide of their skin as they moved together. Had they been home she'd have joined her, however she was slightly uncomfortable being so uninhibited in Meg's parents' home. Not that anyone had given any indication they were uncomfortable with their relationship. In fact, the opposite was true. Nevertheless, she wanted to be respectful while she was a guest in their home. The same feeling of respect compelled Fiona to get out of bed instead of sleeping in, and she had already showered and gotten dressed by the time Meg rolled out of bed, tired from her late night visit with her brother.

"I'm going to run downstairs and get a glass of juice; do you want me to bring you a cup of coffee?" Fiona's voice was thick. She needed to get out of there if she was going to refrain from jumping Meg when she stepped out of the shower.

Meg popped her head out the glass door. "That would be phenomenal. I stayed up later than I should have."

"Did you catch up with him and meet his friend?"

"His friend was already in bed. But CJ caught me up on all of his exploits and conquests of foreign women this summer. The jerk passed his bar and then went on a globe-trotting adventure. Must be nice!" Fiona couldn't tell if it was admiration or disparagement she heard in Meg's voice.

"Sounds like he's got a hard life, your brother." Fiona couldn't wait to meet CJ. So far, Fiona hadn't even seen a picture of him, and she was curious how closely he resembled Meg. Meg said they looked a lot alike, except he was blond, but she couldn't imagine Meg's feminine beauty in a man's body. She watched Meg wash her hair and the ache between her legs surged. She turned to leave the bathroom. "I'll be right back with your coffee."

Fiona left the room and the scent of fresh coffee wafted up the stairs. She imagined herself a cartoon character being led by a thin stream of smell as her toes dragged behind her on the floor. She giggled to herself and hoped they had decaf.

Reese was alone, sitting at the kitchen island with a scone and an enormous cup of coffee. The newspaper was spread before her.

"My, aren't you an early riser!" Reese said cheerily. "You missed CJ and his friend by a couple of minutes. He said he had Meg up until all hours last night. I didn't expect either of you to be up for a little while yet."

"I've been looking forward to meeting him."

"You didn't meet him last night? I assumed you joined the pajama party." Reese made drinking coffee look like a sacred act with the steam from the cup swirling up and her seemingly reverent enjoyment of it.

"I fell asleep almost as soon as my head hit the pillow." After they'd had sex, but she wasn't going to mention that. "Besides, they needed time to catch up."

"She probably told you they haven't been on the best of terms the last few years." Reese peered at her over the rim of her steaming vat of coffee.

"She mentioned something along those lines."

"Well, I certainly hope all of it's behind them now. It's true what they say about boys taking much longer to mature than girls. At least it's been true for my two offspring. Meg has hardly given us a squeak of trouble, while CJ, well… I'll say we've had to chase him down more than a few times to save him from himself. But he says he's grown up, and I want to believe him—for his sake and for all of ours." Reese chuckled. "I'm sure you'll like him. He's a real charmer. Both my kids are."

Fiona smiled to think how lucky Meg was to come from such a loving home. An unexpected pang of sadness flared within her.

Reese put her cup down. "Did I say something wrong, sweetie?"

Fiona smiled. "Not at all. I love how obviously you care about your kids. I was just remembering my own parents."

"You must really miss them." Sympathy flowed from across the counter. It was a good kind of sympathy. For once she didn't feel like shrinking away.

"Yeah. I guess I always will." She gave her a sad smile. "It makes me appreciate how your family has invited me to share in one of your special occasions."

"From the way my daughter looks at you, I have a feeling we'll be seeing you at a lot more of these." Reese gave her a playful wink.

"I hope so."

"You hope so, what?" Meg's hair was damp and she wore the jeans Fiona liked the most on her. She wanted to take her back upstairs. God. She was acting sex-starved. Meg seemed to read her mind and cracked a sly smile.

She whispered in her ear. "Where's the coffee you promised? Is my mom talking your ear off?"

Meg's voice tickled her ear and she squirmed, leaning into her.

"I was telling Fiona she has an open invitation to stay here any time she likes." Reese took a sip of her coffee.

"I guess you're stuck with me, then." Meg wrapped her arms around her waist from the back, and kissed her on the cheek. She let go as quickly as she had swooped in and walked over to a row of covered dishes. "Once the Jordan family collects you you're family for life."

Meg looked for her reaction as she casually lifted dish covers.

"A girl could do much worse, I suppose." Fiona joked.

She and Meg filled their plates, and she even went back for seconds. She was ravenous and she finally understood why they said pregnant women ate for two. It didn't help that the food was beyond awesome.

"So, what's the plan for today, Mom?" Meg asked, as she finished her second cup of coffee.

Reese looked up from her paper with a childlike grin and bounced in her seat. She bubbled with excitement as she filled them in.

"Your dad thinks we have reservations at seven for a nice quiet dinner at the country club. The caterers will set everything up here while your dad is in the shower and I hired a valet service to keep all the cars out of sight. Knowing your dad always waits until the last minute to get ready, I told everyone we invited to show up at precisely six-fifteen while your dad is getting ready. They'll congregate quietly in the family room, where CJ will help to keep them quiet. When we're about to leave, I'll ask your dad to get my bag from the family room. Then, 'Surprise!'"

Fiona watched Meg eye her mom. "He's going to flip out. You know he is."

"That's the point of it, honey."

Meg had told Fiona about how much her father hated surprise parties, but both of them seemed excited for this one.

Meg stood up. "Well, I can't stand the suspense. I think I'll take Fiona out to see the glorious sights of Seattle. We'll be back in plenty of time to get ready to 'go out.'"

Fiona eyed the potatoes left in the dish, but got up and put her plate in the sink.

72

SEVERAL HOURS LATER, MEG DROVE up the driveway, holding Fiona's hand in her lap, happy from their sightseeing adventures. She hoped for a lifetime of days like this. It had been perfect. The sun had shined brightly all day long, and the recent rains had made everything vibrant and crisp. Seattle had put on her best show for Fiona, and Meg couldn't have asked for a better day. Yet a small nugget of disappointment sat quietly in her heart.

When they set out that morning, Meg's primary goal had been to find the perfect backdrop against which to tell Fiona she loved her. She had taken Fiona to several of the most romantic spots she knew. Butterflies had mauled the inside of Meg's stomach each time as she anticipated the moment in which she would stand before Fiona, gaze deeply into her beautiful eyes, and let the words spill out. She wouldn't try to be poetic. She would be careful not to ramble on—something she knew she tended to do when she was nervous. She would simply tell Fiona she loved her, and then kiss her silly, showing her the content of her heart. The kiss would be easy. Hadn't she been showing her all along—every time they made love, with every look, every touch, and every kiss? She saw it in Fiona's eyes and felt it in her touch. Now she needed to give it voice.

But every time she had been about to say it, something would happen—a tourist asked her to snap a photo, a seagull swooped down and stole the churro right out of Fiona's hand, a band of rowdy kids invaded the area—and the chances slipped away.

It wouldn't be long, though. Meg could feel it swelling within her chest. The feeling was the purest thing she had ever known and she knew she wouldn't be able to hold it in very much longer. She wanted it to be special when the time came.

Meg parked the car under the portico and a young man in a jacket and tie came to the door to take the keys. Leave it to her mother to think of everything for the party. She gave him instructions to park the car in the garage with the family's cars, and Meg and Fiona went into the house so they could get ready for the party.

73

"MICKEY, CAN YOU CHECK THE family room to see if I left my bag in there?" Reese asked innocently as she bent to adjust the strap of her shoe. "It's either there or in our room."

Fiona and Meg stood next to her, presumably ready to go out to dinner. Fiona was impressed with Reese's acting abilities. At least a hundred people stood quietly, mashed together in the family room as she sent him unsuspecting into their midst.

"Sure, honey," he said, and headed toward the darkened room beyond the kitchen. Meg, Fiona, and Reese pressed in behind him. He looked over his shoulder. "I don't need an escort, you guys." He made a muscle. "Me big strong man. Dark no scare..."

A loud chorus of "Surprise!" nearly blew the foursome backward when Mickey flipped on the light.

Even with the knowledge of what was about to happen, Fiona was dumbstruck that all of the guests had fit into the living room and they had all been so quiet so as not to give the surprise away. She never heard so much as one sneeze or the clink of a key the whole time they had been upstairs getting ready, nor in the few minutes when they had stood in the kitchen waiting for Mickey to come down.

A rush of people came forward and surrounded the birthday boy who, against all predictions, smiled hugely. Fiona and Meg found themselves pushed gently aside by the throng of well-wishers, and Meg was relieved her father wasn't upset by the surprise. On the contrary, he absolutely beamed with happiness.

"You must be Fiona!" an unfamiliar voice boomed from Fiona's side. Fiona turned to face the man walking quickly toward her with his arms stretched out.

The man's resemblance to Mickey was uncanny, except for a few extra pounds, he could have been his twin. She smiled and stepped into a beefy hug.

"You must be Uncle Arthur," she said as he finally let her go.

"The one and only!" he said brightly. He lifted his shoulders with barely contained glee. "Meg already told you about me, huh? I hope she was kind. Did she also tell you about the first time she laid eyes on you? It was so cute. She spilled coffee all over the place. I think the hot liquid pouring over her fingers finally got her attention, but she didn't even bat an eye. Her eyes were glued on you. She set the overflowing cup down on the counter and told me, "There's my future wife, Arty." Isn't that right Meg?"

Two sets of eyes swiveled toward Meg. She opened her mouth as if she were going to say something, but nothing came out. She closed her mouth with a snap, turned a brilliant shade of red, and simply nodded her head. Fiona stifled a laugh over her lover's distress.

"Welcome to the family, Fiona, dear. I expect to see you in Ithaca more often." Then Uncle Arthur spotted Mickey, and excused himself to go congratulate the birthday boy.

"Did you really say that?" she asked, pressing in close to her blushing lover, pleased to see the red reignite across Meg's face.

"I honestly don't remember exactly what I said. I remember spilling the coffee, but I might as well have been alone, because all I saw was you." Meg slipped her arm around her and kissed her sweetly. The look in her eyes made Fiona's pulse race. Its intensity was off the charts.

She cleared her throat. "I like that story. We'll have to tell the baby when she's old enough to understand." Fiona stepped closer and grabbed Meg's hands, but she froze when it dawned on her what she'd said. There was the future again.

"Yes, we will." Meg smiled at her. Fiona's cold chill evaporated at the perfect response. Simple and sweet.

The two women gazed at each other while the rest of the room receded. They let their words sink in and Fiona wondered if it would be rude if they left the party. Just for a few minutes. Long enough for her to relieve some of the tension she was feeling. Good tension. Urgent tension.

Meg leaned forward, pulled by the tractor beams of Fiona's gaze. She opened her mouth to speak, but a figure appeared behind Fiona, and the moment was gone.

Fiona turned to see what had stolen Meg's attention. "What were you looking at?"

Meg swallowed her frustration and cleared her throat. "CJ. He was right behind you and then he suddenly turned away. Come on. I want you to meet him. I think he went into the kitchen." Meg grabbed Fiona's hand. When they entered the kitchen, there were several people in the room, but CJ wasn't in sight.

"I know he came in here," Meg sighed.

"Are you looking for CJ? He and his friend were here a minute ago. He's probably in the other room. Come here. You have to try the Swedish meatballs." Reese gushed as she pulled them toward a line of chafing dishes.

The next two hours were a whirlwind of introductions and party festivities. The more people Fiona met, the more she adored Meg's family. The gargoyle statue Meg gave to her father was a hit and Fiona lost track of how many times she gave out Tammy's website information for people interested in seeing more of her bizarre art.

Throughout the evening, Meg looked for CJ to introduce them, but it seemed they just kept missing him. When they asked where he was when Mickey opened CJ's present—a disappointing coffee table book of British barrister jokes—Mickey joked that his son was probably off canoodling with one of the pretty caterers. Meg seemed irritated at her brother, but Fiona figured she'd eventually meet him and shrugged it off to a house full of people, many of whom monopolized their time when they discovered Meg had finally brought home a girlfriend, which amused her.

The evening eventually wound down and Fiona was tired—in a good way. It was wonderful to get to know the people who had surrounded Meg through much of her life, but it was tiring trying to remember the names of so many new people

"I had a fantastic night, honey! Thank you!" Mickey turned to Reese when most of the guests had gone. "I'm sorry about the last time. I was a jerk." His expression was so earnest; he looked like a little kid and Fiona recognized Meg in him. She fell a little more in love with Meg's family because of it.

Reese simply smiled and put her forehead to his. "Obviously it didn't matter, sweetheart," she said with such affection everyone around them laughed.

When Mickey kissed Reese sweetly, Fiona had tears in her eyes. She wanted that with someone. She wanted it with Meg.

Suddenly a heavy hand with a pinky ring landed on Fiona's shoulder, and Uncle Arthur stood between her and Meg.

"We have to get going. Ricardo says I've had enough to drunk… drink." Arthur's eyes were glazed and he spoke with a slur, but his smile was bright. He winked and waggled his fingers at a good-looking man across the room—his long-term boyfriend, who Fiona now adored. They were a cute couple.

"I better make my exit before I do something he'll regret. I just wanted to say goodnight to the three loveliest ladies in the room, and to remind you two," he said looking pointedly at Meg and Fiona, "to come up to Ithaca and visit me before Meg moves back to Washington."

Arthur enfolded Fiona in a warm hug and she smiled over his shoulder at Meg, who watched with an amused expression on her face. Arthur held her for a moment too long, but Fiona didn't mind. She liked him. She liked all of Meg's family. When Arthur released her, he turned toward Meg for a hug, but stumbled into the glass of wine in Reese's nearby hand. Most of the red liquid splashed on the wood floor, but a few drops landed on the arm of Fiona's white shirt.

Ricardo rushed over and tried to move Arthur away, but he wouldn't have it. "Oh! S-H-I-T!" screeched Arthur, and he pulled at the cocktail napkin wrapped around Reese's glass stem, sloshing more of the wine onto floor. "F-U-C… oh listen to my foul mouth! I insist on paying for the cleaning bill. I'm such an ugly drunk. Ricardo was a prophet about this, as usual!"

Ricardo nodded his head vigorously, but he looked amused. "Look what you did, you brute!"

"I'm a clumsy oaf. How do you put up with me?"

Ricardo smiled and waved his hand in the air. "God, knows. I'm a saint. You need to fix this, though."

"Don't worry about it. If it doesn't wash out, you can give me free coffee when I visit you in Ithaca." Fiona gently pushed away Arthur's attempts to dab at the stains. It wasn't a favorite shirt.

"Free coffee isn't a fair trade. You will let me know if it doesn't come out?" Arthur asked, and she suppressed a laugh at his attempt to exact a promise with an intent stare under lowered brows.

"Yes, I promise." Fiona laughed and waved him off as Ricardo dragged

Arthur away with a faux disapproving "tsk-tsk".

"He's going to have a headache tomorrow. Guaranteed," Ricardo said over his shoulder with a laugh.

Promising them it wasn't a big deal, Fiona waved goodbye and turned to Meg and her parents, who looked like they were going to start apologizing all over again.

"Please don't worry about it. It's an old shirt. I should have worn the dress, anyway. Let me run upstairs to change and I'll be right back down."

Fiona tossed a smile over her shoulder as she took the stairs two at a time and rounded the corner at the top of the landing to head down the hall. Suddenly alone, her smile grew soft, and her eyes barely registered the rich colors of the rug running the length of the wide hall as she slowed to a walk. Fiona's thoughts were filled with the promises she had seen in Meg's eyes all evening. She wanted to turn around and call Meg up to her so she could give voice and touch to the feelings threatening to spill out of her. Images of Meg's skin and mouth filled her mind. Preoccupied with the thrill running down the back of her spine, she ran headfirst into a person exiting a room near the stairs.

"Oh! Sorry!" Fiona cried out, as she lost her footing and reached out to steady herself. Quickly regaining her balance, she let go of the stranger's arms and gasped when her gaze moved up and zeroed in on the face of the last person she had ever expected to see there.

"I'm sorry. I wasn't…" Mike's voice trailed away as his expression registered who she was. He held her elbows. "Fi? What are you doing here?"

"I was about to ask you the same thing."

Mike hugged her and smiled. "Charlie invited me out to meet his parents."

"Charlie? Here?" She had so many questions. Did Charlie's family somehow know Meg's family? Were they here for the party? She wasn't happy to know he was continuing to string Mike along, but it was interesting Charlie was introducing Mike to his parents. Was this just another build up to a big disappointment for Mike?

Mike was obviously excited to share his happiness with her. "This is his parents' house."

Fiona was confused. "This is Meg and CJ's parents' house."

Mike looked confused and shook his head. "Charlie is CJ. CJ is Charlie. They're the same person."

Things started to click, and not in a good way. She wrinkled her nose. "Charlie is Meg's brother?"

Charlie emerged from the room they were standing next to. "Hi, Fiona." He looked uncertain and wouldn't sustain eye contact. He wasn't acting like the cocky Charlie she knew from the study group. And now that she knew his relationship to Meg, she saw the uncanny shared resemblance. How had she not seen it before? But looks were as far as it went. His personality and the way he held himself were nothing like Meg.

"Hi, Charlie. Or should I call you CJ?"

He furrowed his brow. "My family are the only ones who call me CJ. I've been going by Charlie for years."

Fiona was still trying to come to terms with unexpectedly meeting Mike and Charlie here. Or CJ. Whatever his name was. She didn't answer. She looked back and forth between the two, wanting to go find Meg.

"I saw you downstairs. I mean, I thought it might be you, but I wasn't sure." Charlie shifted his eyes to a point next to her head.

Mike giggled. "I've been telling him he needs glasses. He's so vain, though."

Charlie made a face but ignored the remark. "So, um, Mike said you were, um…" His eyes drifted to her midsection.

Fiona's stomach dropped. This was not a conversation she wanted to have right then.

"Charlie…" Mike grabbed his wrist and shook his head.

"What?" Charlie laughed and he looked more like the guy Fiona remembered. "It's not like it will be a secret in a couple months when she…" Charlie put his hands before his belly and pantomimed a ball growing bigger until it popped."

She looked at Mike and tilted her head.

Mike had the decency to look sorry for Charlie making fun. "Hey. Come on, Charlie. We're still trying to get used to all of this."

Charlie laughed again. "I'll bet. Does Meg know?"

Fiona didn't answer. Meg and Mike were the only ones she'd talked to about it and it wasn't any of Charlie's business.

Charlie drew his head back with a smirk. "You haven't told her? You're not going to keep it, are you?"

"Charlie. Stop. Fiona and I need to talk about this first." Mike switched his attention to her and she took a deep breath, ready to hear him beg her to keep it. God, she couldn't do this. Not now. Not here. "Have you decided to get rid of it?"

Fiona cleared her throat, glancing at Charlie, wishing he wasn't there. "I'm keeping it."

Mike's face went pale. Not the expression she expected.

"Oh, wow. Um, if… if you decided to, um… because of me, well, um…" He scratched the back of his neck. "I… I changed my mind." He glanced at Charlie, who was watching with interest, and back to her. "I'm not ready to be a father. I don't know if I ever will be, but definitely not now. I think I was seeing a chance to prove something to my parents. I was grasping at straws. I realized it didn't change who I really am. All it would do is bring a kid into the world with a fucked-up dad." Mike laughed nervously. "Who needs another one of those?"

Fiona stared at Mike. She'd expected this conversation to happen so differently. She couldn't find words. She didn't even know how she felt. But it was starting to become clear. She was relieved. She was staring him with wide eyes and she could see him studying her face. She should say something.

"Fi…" Mike grabbed her hand. "Are you mad at me? Say something." He searched her face and shook her arm. "Tell me what you're thinking."

"I'm letting it sink in," she finally said.

"Is it a good sinking in or a bad sinking in?"

"A good sinking in, I think." She let the relief settle over her. She managed a smile. "It's good."

He looked relieved.

"I'm still going to keep it," she said.

Mike's face dropped and he looked like he was about to cry.

"Don't worry. You don't have to help."

He looked confused. "But—"

She raised her hand. "Seriously. No one needs to know you had anything to do with it."

The clouds started to shift away from Mike's face. "Seriously? Because I really, really don't want to be a dad."

She nodded. "Really."

"How's Meg going to react to this little development?" Charlie asked.

Both of them looked at her. "That's between Meg and me." She needed to go find Meg and tell her about the unexpected conversation. She turned to leave and there was Reese, standing at the top of the stairs. God. Had she heard any of the conversation?

Reese's eyes darted from her to the men standing behind her. Yes. She'd heard. Fiona felt like she was going to be sick. Embarrassment and disappointment bubbled in her stomach.

"I brought something—" Reese held up a bottle of soda water and a cloth.

She tried to smile. "Oh, um, thank you. I'll be right back." She needed Meg, so she pressed past Reese on the stairs to look for her.

74

"OH MY GOD, MEG. YOUR parents must think I'm some sort of… I don't know what." Fiona sat on the edge of the bed and buried her face in her hands.

Meg sat down next to her and stroked her back. When Fiona had come to find her, she'd been upset, and now, back in their room, she was getting even more upset as she explained. Meg was trying to figure out what had happened so she could fix it. "Are you sure she heard the whole conversation?"

"Enough of it to know I'm pregnant."

"I'll go talk to her and find out what she heard."

"Fuck!" Fiona's shoulders slumped. She shook her head. "Please don't. Your parents are going to loathe me."

Meg hated seeing Fiona like this. She'd begun to loosen up with her family and now this. Her parents would totally understand. It might seem like a weird situation at first, but they'd understand. At least she was pretty sure they would. "They're rational people. They don't live under a rock. They're not judgy. I'll tell them what happened and they'll totally understand."

Fiona looked up at her like she had two heads. "I got drunk and had sex with my gay best friend because he begged me to help him figure out if he was completely gay or only somewhat gay. Not only did we determine he was one hundred percent gay, I got pregnant from the experiment."

"If you put it like that. But if we tell them what you told me when you first told me, they'll understand. By the way, how is it Mike knows my brother? Don't you think it's a weird coincidence?"

"Charlie was in our study group."

"Charlie?"

Fiona shrugged her shoulders. "Your brother introduced himself as

Charlie in our study group."

"You're kidding me! He used to hate it when we called him that." Then it dawned on her. Charlie and Mike were… "Wait. Isn't Charlie the guy you said Mike was in love with?"

Fiona dropped her chin and looked at her. The new information about her brother threw Meg for a loop. CJ, using his childhood alias of Charlie, was dating men in New York. CJ—the guy she knew as a womanizer. The guy who used to make fun of her and call her a dyke. The brother who had made her life a living hell during high school, and off and on since then with his smirkiness and shitty barbs, was dating guys now? What the fuck?

Meg noticed Fiona watching her and remembered this conversation was about her, not her brother, even if this was a major deal. Or was it? The time she spent with CJ when he'd arrived the other night had been almost like old times. They'd had a good time. Maybe his shittiness had been about his confusion before he realized who he really was. Regardless, right now she needed to put this on the backburner and try to support Fiona.

She cleared her throat. "We can talk about CJ later. In the meantime, I want to assure you my parents are not going to hate you. It's all about how it's presented. We can tell them the story you told me and they'll understand like I did."

"I'm not sure you can spin it to make it sound less stupid." Fiona threw her hands up in the air. "To top it off, somehow the two of us—Mike and I—we both end up at their house! How are your parents not going to be horrified by this turn of events?"

When she put it that way, she could see Fiona's point. Her parents would probably be a little surprised, maybe even a little judgy—even though she said they wouldn't be. But she also knew they liked Fiona. She continued to run her hand in circles across Fiona's back. "Give them a minute to get used to it. I'm sure they'll understand."

Fiona fell back onto the bed and covered her face with her hands. "I'm not so sure. How can they understand if I don't even understand it most of the time?"

"You have to give them a chance."

"I don't know if I can survive feeling this mortified. How can I even face them?" Fiona spoke through her hands.

"Like you've faced everything in your life—head on. It will be okay. I promise. Let's get some sleep. I'm sure it'll seem a lot less awful in the morning."

75

FIONA FINISHED BRUSHING HER HAIR and watched Meg through the mist in the shower. She was right. Things didn't seem as bad in the morning. She was still embarrassed, but at least she didn't want to slink away in the dead of night. Maybe Reese hadn't heard everything. Maybe she was worrying about things to worry about, as her dad used to say when he was alive.

She put the brush down and backed toward the door. "Hey, I'll meet you downstairs in the kitchen."

Meg popped her head out of the shower. "You don't need to do it on your own, you know. Wait until I'm done here and I can go down with you."

The look of concern on her face was sweet. Fiona couldn't help herself. She kissed her. "Believe me, I'd rather jump into the shower with you right now. But I have to face the music sooner or later. I'll be fine. If it comes up, I'll just tell them what happened. Like you said. I have to give them a chance." She smiled, even though her courage was fading as each minute ticked away. There was only one way to move past this and it was to keep on doing what she'd normally do. Fiona shook her hair back and marched downstairs.

As she approached the kitchen, she heard Charlie talking. Who was he talking to? Who was in the kitchen? Her stomach lurched. She wasn't prepared to deal with a whole crowd.

"…knew Mike got Fiona pregnant, but I didn't know Fiona was dating Meg."

"Were she and Mike dating at the same time?" Reese asked.

Fiona stopped in the hall before they could see her. So, Reese must have heard at least something. At least enough to start drawing conclusions. The wrong conclusions. She wanted to go in and give them the truth. But was the truth any less embarrassing? Her face grew hot.

Charlie huffed. "I honestly don't know what they were doing. Mike calls her his best friend. Maybe it's a friends with benefits thing."

Reese made a sound like she was thinking it over. "Do you think Meg knows? She never mentioned Fiona was pregnant. I guess it's none of my business, but—"

"I don't know. If she does, she probably doesn't know the whole story." Charlie sounded so smug. She imagined his face cocked into the infuriating smirk he always seemed to wear. He was making everything worse. If she were Reese, she'd wonder what her daughter was doing with someone like her. What must Reese think of her?

"Poor Meg. She really cares about Fiona. This is going to destroy her. Knowing her, she'll probably try to take care of her and this baby." There was a sound of liquid and Fiona imagined Reese pouring coffee into her enormous cup. "She's just getting started. This will impact her whole life."

Charlie laughed. "And you always thought I was the fuck up."

Reese sighed deeply. "This isn't her fuck up, to use your vernacular. But I hope she knows what she's getting into. It's so sad. I liked Fiona. She seemed like such—"

She'd used the past tense. A surge of nausea lurched within her. She didn't wait to hear any more of the conversation. She couldn't. The pressure in her head deafened her and the mortification she'd felt the night before was back in full force, along with a burning anger and a sense of loss for the relationships she'd foolishly started to hope to nurture.

She barely remembered making the trip up the stairs and down the long hallway to the room she and Meg were staying in; Meg's childhood bedroom, the room where she'd explored Meg's trophies, posters, and childhood memorabilia. The room she'd hoped she'd visit many times more.

Meg started when she entered, jumping back from the suitcase she'd been bending over. She pulled her towel tighter around her and laughed. "You scared the shit out of me."

Fiona didn't respond. She put her suitcase on the bed and started throwing the few things she'd taken out of it back into it.

Meg came close. "Hey. Hey. What are you doing? Are you okay?"

Fiona wiped the tears off her cheeks, furious at herself for allowing them to fall. She couldn't look at Meg. "I need to leave."

"What happened?" Meg watched her press her stack of dirty clothes into the case, but when Fiona turned to go into the bathroom to get her toiletries, Meg grabbed her by the wrist. "Fiona, please. Can you hold on a minute and tell me what happened?"

She whirled and faced her. "Your family thinks I'm trash, that's what's happening. They wonder what you're doing with me."

Disbelief clouded Meg's face. "What?"

She dropped her head and stared at her feet. The pain in Meg's eyes was too hard to look at. "They think you're ruining your life by being with me and, and, and…" She wiped at her tears again and used the collar of her shirt to wipe her nose. "…and I agree with them. I don't know why I didn't think about it before. Just because this is my path, it doesn't have to be yours. I took you for granted, which was selfish of me. But—"

"But nothing!" Meg was still holding her wrist and she took the other. Her towel began to slip and she cursed. She grabbed a zip up hoodie from Fiona's suitcase and put it on and grabbed her wrist again. "No one took anyone for granted. I knew exactly what I was getting into and—"

"There is no way you know what you're getting into. I don't even know what I'm getting into."

"Fiona, don't use semantics on me. Please. Let's—"

A knock sounded at the door. Meg let out an exasperated sigh and Fiona pulled her hands out of her grasp. She backed toward the bathroom.

"Meg? Are you awake in there? I thought I heard you talking."

Meg took a step toward Fiona, who raised her hands in a silent request for her to stop. Meg did so, but her eyes were pleading. She turned toward the door, but her eyes never left Fiona. "I'm getting out of the shower, Mom. I'll be down in a few minutes."

"Can I come in? I have—"

Meg balled her hands into fists. "Mom! No!" She shook her head. Fiona hated to see the stress in Meg's eyes as she stared at her, but she continued to back into the bathroom. "I'll be down in a little while."

"Okay, honey."

They both stood quietly in the room, searching each other's eyes. At one time the connection would have felt intimate, in sync, but now it was cold and distant—a search for something neither of them could find in one another. Fiona dropped her head and turned toward the bathroom. There was no way she could stay here.

76

MEG DIDN'T KNOW WHAT TO do with herself after Fiona got into the Lyft and left. She hadn't listened to any of her attempts to get her to stay, and now she was gone. Meg's entire world had turned upside down in a matter of minutes and she didn't know what to do. She sat on the steps under the portico and watched the car drive down the long driveway. She tried to make it turn back around with her mind, but it kept on going until it was through the gate and gone. The warm Seattle day did nothing to warm her cold fingers and the chill in her soul. What the fuck had just happened? What had her parents said to Fiona? The deadness in her chest was soon replaced by a fiery anger.

She walked into the house, accidentally slamming the door as she entered. She found her mother and father sitting in the kitchen, drinking coffee. They were speaking in quiet voices and immediately stopped when she walked in.

"Was that you at the front door?" her mother asked, putting down her coffee cup.

Her father picked up the newspaper.

She nodded her head, afraid her voice would betray the anger boiling in her heart. She was sure her eyes showed it anyway.

"I thought it might be CJ and his friend Mike. They went out for a walk." Her mother's eyes darted away. It was so unlike her. She was usually direct. Meg wondered what she was thinking. Or was it shame? Was she sorry for something she had said? "Where's Fiona?"

"She just left."

Her mother's brow furrowed. "Left to go where?" Her mother looked at her father and back at her.

"For the airport," she said between clenched teeth. "What did you say to her this morning?"

Her mother looked confused. "I haven't talked to her, honey."

"That's not what she said. She told me about your conversation."

"Seriously, honey, I haven't even seen Fiona this morning."

Meg switched her gaze to her father. "Dad? Was it you?"

He lowered the paper. "I got back from my golf game about fifteen minutes ago. I haven't seen anyone except Ted and Frank at the club this morning."

Frustrated, Meg sat down at the barstool at the end of the kitchen island. She drummed her fingers on the tile surface. "Okay. I'm super confused. Fiona stormed out of here saying someone said they didn't know what I was thinking getting mixed up with her and she was ruining my life. Sound familiar to either of you?"

A look of understanding swept across her mother's face before it went passive. Meg had seen it before—her mother was using her court face to mask her expression. Meg's anger turned into something almost physical. She didn't trust herself to be reasonable and concentrated on her breathing.

Her mother tilted her head. "I think Fiona overheard something."

"Overheard what?" Meg's patience was getting thin.

"A conversation between me and CJ. Here in the kitchen."

Meg splayed her fingers on the counter top. "She came down here to get a cup of coffee for me and then came back crying."

"Oh dear."

Her mother looked at her father who sighed and pushed the newspaper aside to be more fully in the discussion. "You know your mother and I do our best to never meddle in you or your brother's lives, but—"

"What about my life?" CJ's voice echoed in the hallway leading toward the garage door. No one had heard him or Mike come in and they both entered the kitchen. As keyed up as Meg was, she noticed CJ looked relaxed like he'd been the night he'd arrived.

"We think Fiona may have overheard the conversation you and I had in the kitchen this morning," her mother explained.

CJ looked confused. "We talked about a lot of things. What part of it?"

His mother swiveled to face CJ. She hesitated, and Meg knew she was trying to be delicate in front of Mike.

"She heard you explaining what you knew about Fiona to me."

The cocky smugness CJ'd worn so much lately rose up. "I'm not sure how that pertains to me." Meg tried not to roll her eyes.

Her father looked at her brother. "I wasn't talking about you specifically. I was simply making a statement about how your mother and I try to stay out of your business. However, it seems we've had a rash of overheard conversations lately. You mother heard you and Mike talking with Fiona last night up on the landing. It was none of her business, but what she heard gave her a considerable amount of concern for your sister."

Meg was confused again. "Why are you concerned about me?"

"Maybe I should leave and let you all talk," Mike said. He started to leave the kitchen.

"Mike, wait," her mother said. "This is awkward. What we're talking about is yours and Fiona's business, but it affects Meg, too, which makes it our business as well." Mike stopped and stood self-consciously about a foot away from CJ.

"Okay," he said, chewing on the corner of his mouth.

Meg felt sorry for him, and she wanted to tell her mother it wasn't her business. But then she remembered how he'd badgered Fiona throughout the summer. He wasn't blameless. He needed to face whatever came of all of this.

Her mother looked at her. "Meg, we aren't sure you know exactly what's going on, and we're afraid to see you hurt."

Both of her parents turned toward her as if they expected something. "Why are you concerned about me?"

Her mother took her hand. "Honey, Fiona is pregnant."

Meg blinked a couple of times. "I know."

It was her mother's turn to blink. "And you know it's Mike's baby?"

She glanced at Mike, who looked like he wanted to crawl into a hole in the ground. "Yes, Mom. I know. I've known almost as long as Fiona has." She didn't want to explain how she'd found out, but she wanted her mother to know this wasn't at all new to her.

"Oh." Her mother looked like she had a lot more questions. Getting things out in the open was probably the best thing to do. But how could she get things out in the open without outing people. She looked at CJ and Mike, both of whom looked nervous. Mike actually looked like he might throw up.

Speaking of outing people. She held her breath. What about CJ? She didn't know how to even go there. She'd try to stay away from it. As far as she was concerned, CJ would have to bring it up, if he ever would. He so owed her, she thought, feeling like a jerk for even thinking it.

She looked at Mike. "Mike, not that it's any of our business, but it looks like people are making assumptions about things, and they may not be completely accurate. Do you want to explain what's going on? You don't have to, but it might clear things up and we can all get out of your business."

Mike looked like a deer in headlights. The chewing on the corner of his mouth grew more vigorous.

"Way to put him on the spot, Meg." CJ laughed. She could tell he was trying to lighten the mood, but it was a struggle.

"It's the last thing I want to do," Meg said, and her anger crept up a notch. "Fiona left this morning to go back to New York because she believes everyone in this room thinks she's trash. I don't know if those are the exact words she heard you say, but that's how she feels. The thing is, getting pregnant by her best friend was the last thing she ever thought she'd do, and now people are judging her without understanding." She tried to keep her voice steady. "I thought if Mike could explain some of it to the rest of you, maybe some of the judgement would go away and then we could figure out a way to prove to her no one thinks she's anything but amazing for dealing with all of this the way she has."

Meg wasn't too surprised when Mike was silent as he stared at his shoes. What she didn't expect was how CJ started to get uncomfortable. Was he afraid Mike would reveal something about their relationship? Because as far as she could tell, her parents hadn't put two and two together. Hell, she wouldn't have either, except for what Fiona had told her.

Mike's voice was barely above a whisper. "She left? Was she okay?"

Meg nodded, feeling all of the pent-up frustration and anger coming to a head. "About a half an hour ago. And no, she's not okay. She's dealing with a lot of stuff, trying to figure out how to manage this huge thing that got dumped on her for the crime of trying to be a good friend." She let her eyes shoot to CJ briefly and then back to Mike. She didn't want to put Mike on the spot with her family, but he'd been pressuring Fiona about the baby for weeks now and maybe it was time for him to take a little of the pressure. "Not only is she carrying a baby she never planned on, she's been dealing with the pressure you've been putting on her about whether she should keep it or not. She's also trying not to burden me with anything, even though I want the burden. And, now, she thinks my family hates her for possibly ruining my life. What a joke! She's worried about me and you," she pointed at Mike, "when she's the one everyone should be worrying about! I want to help make this gargantuan mistake into a good thing for her—for us! And right this minute, she's all alone." Her throat grew tight. "She's by herself at the airport, thinking everyone in the world who means anything to her has abandoned her."

Mike looked like he'd been punched in the gut. Suddenly, she didn't care at all about putting him on the spot. Some best friend he was!

"Oh my god. I never thought—" Tears rolled down Mike's face. He looked at CJ, at her, and then her parents. "It's all my fault. I begged her to sleep with me. I knew she was drunk. I knew she would say yes if I kept asking. It's… it's… my parents don't understand. No one in my family understands. My friends don't understand." He was sobbing now.

She wanted to tell him his friends did understand, if he'd at least talk about it.

"Don't understand what, son?" her father asked.

Meg was so tired of him making it all about himself all the time. It was time he took responsibility for himself. But she'd let him explain.

He took a deep breath and she expected an answer making him the victim, yet again. Instead he surprised her. She wished Fiona was there to see it.

"I'm gay. My family won't have it. They told me it's all in my head. If I tried dating women, I'd change." He looked at CJ, as if for confidence. "But it proved the opposite." He rubbed his red-rimmed eyes. "I know. It sounds messed up. And what's even more messed up, I tried to convince Fiona to keep the baby so I could prove to my family I at least tried. I don't know what I was thinking. Instead of hurting only me, I'm hurting other people now, too. I'm such a freaking idiot!"

Meg was surprised when her mother got up and hugged Mike. She barely knew him, but she tried to comfort him. "I'm sorry you're going through this, Mike. Not every family is supportive. And even the most supportive families have their issues." Meg wasn't sure, but she thought she saw her mother look at CJ when she said the last thing. She wondered if her mother knew something about CJ, or was it a response to some of the anti-gay things CJ had said to her in the past. "If it ever helps, I'll be happy to talk to your parents, as a parent who has been there when their child has come out."

Mike let her mother hold him, and when she let go, he looked a little better.

"Some of this is my fault," CJ said, surprising everyone.

"How's that, son?" her dad asked.

"Um, well," CJ seemed at a loss for words. He cleared his throat. "I wasn't very nice to Mike about it, either. I was part of the reason he turned to Fiona to help him deal with his… his… issues."

Mike grabbed his arm. "Charlie, you don't have to—"

CJ stepped closer to him. "I do, though."

Meg had never in her life seen her brother look so vulnerable. All her life, in any situation steeped in any kind of strong emotion, he'd always resorted to anger or belittling those around him. What had changed?

CJ blew out a big breath and furrowed his brows. He shifted his weight and his eyes grew distant as he seemed to be looking inward. For a brief moment, the old smirk flashed across his face, before he shook his head and it disappeared.

"I… I… messed with him. Made him think I cared about him and then… sort of pushed him away. That sort of thing." He had trouble meeting anyone's eyes.

Her mother rubbed his arm. "I suppose you weren't a very good friend, but I'm not sure it could be construed as—"

He interrupted her. "Not as a friend, Mom."

"I'm not sure I understand," she said.

CJ raised his eyebrows to underscore what he was trying to get across. The expression of confusion on her face grew more pronounced. "Mike and I are… we're… um, oh God." He took a deep breath and blew the breath out through clenched teeth. "Mom. Dad. Mike's my boyfriend. We're together."

Her father froze and his eyes darted around the room as the words sunk in. Her mother cocked her head to the side as if she might have heard it wrong, and then her eyes went wide and she stared at CJ for a moment.

"Honey, are you sure?" She stepped toward him, stopped and shook her head. Meg had never seen her mother so unsure of herself. "I'm so sorry. Of course, you're sure. What a stupid question." She finished going to him and held him by the arms. "Oh, honey. Thank you. Thank you. I don't know why I'm thanking you, but… oh, come here!"

She pulled him to her and he looked like he would faint with relief. Meg was stuck to her chair, completely blown away by what had just happened. Suddenly her father was there, next to CJ, wrapping his arms around him and her mom. She felt kind of left out, but this was her brother's moment. More than anything, she was relieved.

Finally, her mother and father let him go.

He laughed self-consciously. "See? This is why I never said anything." He dropped his head. "Actually, I'm a coward and didn't want you to think I was trying to be just like my sister."

Everyone looked at her.

She raised her hands. "What? I'm just enjoying the show," she said.

Her mother touched her arm. "What are we going to do to fix things with Fiona?"

There was only one thing Meg could do. She needed to go to her. It didn't matter that Fiona had asked her not to follow her. She needed to get to her and repair this.

77

FIONA SAT IN HER FIRST-CLASS seat and pressed her forehead against the uncomfortable plastic wall of the airplane as she gazed out through the round portal at the tarmac passing swiftly below. She had no idea how she'd managed to call a Lyft and change her flight to an earlier one back to New York, but she somehow made it and the plane was on its way. Now, she had nothing to do but think.

She ached to be with Meg, but she knew she would never be able to look into her eyes again and not see the potential she'd have stolen if she stayed.

Tears rolled down her face as the world beneath her fell further and further away.

78

MEG WAS FRUSTRATED. FIONA WASN'T answering her phone and she'd missed the plane Fiona had probably boarded to go back to New York. She'd spent the entire drive to the airport hoping she'd meet Fiona at the gate and be successful at convincing her everything had been cleared up. Instead, she was told by the ticketing agent she'd missed the cut-off time for booking by minutes. Impotence ran through her blood like acid. She arranged for a seat on the next flight and sat at the gate with a mass of anxiety pressed against her ribcage. She could only imagine what Fiona was going through.

Now she stood in front of the door to Fiona's apartment, and as the minutes ticked away with no answer to her knocks, Meg had to wonder if Fiona was running from her as much as she was running from her family and Mike. She rested her forehead against the hard metal surface and hoped the door would swing open and everything would be right again, but it didn't happen. Meg pulled out her phone, and called again, not caring that the last fifty calls she'd made were sent directly to voice mail. Her heart skipped a beat when she thought she heard the faint sound of a cell phone ringing deep within the apartment. She envisioned Fiona standing on the other side of the door and it made her crazy.

"Pick up. Pick up. Pick up," she chanted while she also knocked. The ringing stopped, and the recorded sound of Fiona's familiar voice asked her to leave a message. Meg hesitated a moment before speaking. The first thing she could think to say was that she loved her. The words tumbled over themselves in her mind. But she didn't want the first time Fiona heard them to be in a phone message, so she cleared her throat and told Fiona she was back in town and to please call her. She turned and slowly began walking to her own apartment.

As she jaywalked across the street, Meg imagined Fiona watching her. She turned to look, but the curtains hung, unmoved. The door stayed shut. A car blasted its horn and she dared it to hit her without even looking at it. The driver screamed an epithet out the window as he swerved past, but again, she didn't even look. She was going home, but her home felt like it was behind her, and every step she took was a step in the wrong direction.

79

FIONA STOOD NEXT TO THE window and watched as Meg crossed the street. Her heart flew into her throat. She knew she should move away, but she couldn't. If Meg looked a little to the right she would see her, and then Fiona would have no choice but to go to her. Fiona dared Meg to see her. Willed her to turn her head, just a fraction. But Meg's eyes stayed trained on the window of Fiona's empty apartment. They never even glanced toward Mrs. Rickles' window.

She flinched when she heard a horn and the screech of tires. Her heart raced in her chest.

"Get out of the fucking street!" She clutched her shirt in her fist, watching Meg stand there. Her heart ached at the despair written on Meg's face. When Meg finally turned and disappeared from view, she dropped the curtain and turned back to face Mrs. Rickles' knowing eyes. Her heart tried to resume its normal beat, but she was sure it was damaged for good. Fiona sat quietly back down at the table and mindlessly stirred her tea. A cookie sat untouched on the table next to her cup.

The flight back to New York had arrived very late. The city had been drowsy and dim as the cab rolled through the lonely streets. Infinite variations of the color gray greeted her bloodshot eyes and complemented her broken-hearted mood. The cabbie must have sensed her emotions because he didn't try to talk to her. She tossed some cash over the seat as she got out of the cab, and thought she couldn't feel much worse, but a wave of overpowering sadness nearly sent her to the ground when she opened her front door.

She left her bags where she dropped them and fell onto the couch, where she curled up into a little ball and cried until she could barely breathe. She longed for her bed, but the solace she needed wasn't in there. What was there was the unmade bed she and Meg had made love in, right before they'd rushed to make their plane to Seattle on time.

She hadn't thought it possible, but somewhere in her grief, she found a dark space that could block everything out, and the next she knew, a knock at her door pulled her from her sleep. The light in the room said it was mid-morning and the vague scent of fresh baked cookies told her the knock was Mrs. Rickles. Fiona would have left the door unanswered to anyone else, but she needed the comfort, so she unfolded herself from the couch, stretched her stiff limbs and back, and walked slowly to the door.

If Mrs. Rickles could tell Fiona had been crying, she didn't let on, and she didn't comment when Fiona guided them both over to the older woman's apartment rather than stay in the apartment which held too many memories. She simply shuffled back alongside Fiona and made a pot of vanilla lavender tea—Fiona's favorite.

Mrs. Rickles was pouring the tea when Fiona heard the first faint knock. Her heart moved to her throat when the cell phone she had left on the floor next to her couch started to ring a few minutes later. Barely audible, she recognized Meg's ringtone. She had no recollection of moving, but suddenly she was at Mrs. Rickles' window. The main stairway to the building stood between the two apartment doors, but she willed her vision to bend corners. When the familiar form finally came into view, she wanted to go to her, but instead, she only watched as Meg crossed the street, heedless of traffic.

Once Meg had disappeared from view, and Fiona somehow found her way back to her chair, any life in her heart had left. She was grateful Mrs. Rickles wasn't a nosy woman.

"To use the lingo of you youngsters, it must suck to want something so much and be too afraid to go after it," the old woman said simply, and then took a sip of her tea.

Fiona just nodded and sampled the tea she couldn't taste. She ached to go to Meg but she was afraid of who she would see looking out from Meg's eyes.

"For a long time, I thought I'd never eat another chocolate chip cookie," Mrs. Rickles said.

Fiona shook her head to get out of her own thoughts. "Huh?"

"This diabetes is a real pain in the patootie," the older woman said. "When you moved in and we started our lovely Sunday tea ritual, I thought I could at least bake them, enjoy the smell of them as they cooked, and think about the happiness you would have when you ate them. Then I found a recipe for diabetic-friendly carob chip cookies. It's not the same, but now I can eat cookies with you. And they aren't half bad."

Fiona studied her cookie. "I had no idea these weren't real chocolate chip cookies. They're delicious."

"Oh, the ones I bring you are the real thing. I only make a small batch for myself and bring one over for me when I come to call. I can tell the difference. But, if you want to continue enjoying your cookies, sometimes you have to work with the limitations life throws at you, sweetie."

Fiona studied the cookie she held and thought about limitations.

80

MEG PRESSED THE SPEED DIAL she'd restricted herself to calling only once a day. For the first few days after Fiona left Seattle, she'd called repeatedly hoping to wear Fiona down. But when she started to get the recording saying the voice mailbox was full, she realized how fruitless the calls were, and how much each of them took out of her. This call was no different and, once again, went to voice mail.

"It's been a week, Fiona. Please call me. I miss you."

Meg lowered the phone and was about to toss it onto the bed beside her when it rang in her hand. It was Fiona. Her hand shook as she pressed the button.

"Hello?" No answer. Her stomach was a knot. "Fiona? Are you there?" She waited for a moment. Hell, she'd wait until the call disconnected, no matter how long it took.

"Meg?"

Her name was said so quietly. Meg's throat tightened at the sound of Fiona's voice, small but real on the other end of the connection.

"Fiona, are you okay?" Meg's voice wavered. Was Fiona sobbing? The sound tore at Meg's heart. "Fiona. Please. I need to see you. Can I come over?" She stood and walked to her bedroom door, wanting to see her so badly. The pain she felt across the line sliced her open. "If I can't come over, will you come here? Or maybe we can meet someplace?"

There was silence on the line and Meg had to look to make sure the call hadn't failed… or been disconnected.

"Helga's," Fiona whispered.

Meg's heart was beating so loudly and she was having a hard time breathing. "Oh God, Fiona. Thank you. When? Now?"

Fiona cleared her throat. "Yes. I'll see you soon."

Meg stood where she was and stared numbly at the phone. She was about to see her. Fiona. The one thing for which she'd longed for over a week. It didn't seem real. She had to make her legs move. All she could think about was seeing her. She didn't remember leaving Vi's apartment, or crossing the busy street. Suddenly, she was in the coffee shop looking at all the tables, scanning faces for the one she needed to see. Fiona wasn't there. Not yet.

Taylor and Karma were at the table in the far corner looking at a laptop together. They both looked up and waved her over. She scanned the room once again, returning Noel's wave, as she made sure Fiona wasn't already there. Thankfully, Noel was waiting on a customer, so she didn't need to make small talk with him. She approached Taylor and Karma, both of whom stood and gave her their enormous hugs.

"Hey, Meg! We haven't seen you in a couple of weeks. How are you?" Karma pushed her white hair behind her ear.

It was true. Meg hadn't had the heart to visit the coffee shop since she'd returned. She didn't know what to tell anyone if they asked about Fiona. "I've been out of town," she said, forcing a smile and stretching the truth a little. She didn't want to have to explain why she'd locked herself in her room since she'd come back from Seattle.

"Oh yeah. Seattle, right?" Taylor said. "Did you have a good time? Did your dad enjoy the statue?"

"It was a hit. I'm not sure he'd use the word 'enjoy', but he appreciated the craftmanship." She tried not to be obvious about watching the door, which was hard since it was behind her.

"There she is," Taylor said, nodding toward the door. She wore a knowing smile, but Meg didn't have the heart to explain she didn't know what she thought she knew.

She backed up toward the door. "It was great seeing you two." She didn't wait to hear their goodbyes.

Meg saw the longing and pain in Fiona's eyes and she wondered what Fiona saw in hers. The same? Maybe with a little hurt and frustration.

"Excuse me?" a voice said through two inches of cracked open door.

Meg shook herself from her trance. They were blocking the doorway. She hurriedly moved aside and Fiona followed. When she looked back at Fiona, she was looking away. Meg wondered if she would ever see her beautiful eyes untouched by the memory of the last week again. Fiona didn't try to hug her hello and Meg was unsure if she should try.

Fuck it. She reached for Fiona and held her. Fiona held her, too, tighter than usual. That was a good sign. But it was over too soon and Fiona stepped back.

"Hey," Meg said.

Fiona's hazel eyes studied her and the guarded look in them made Meg feel cold inside. She looked tired. Maybe it wasn't distance in those pretty eyes. Maybe it was lack of sleep. God knew she hadn't been sleeping very well herself.

"Hi." Fiona looked around. "Should we get a table?"

"Oh. Yeah. Sure. How about on the patio? I know it's hot, but there's shade." She wanted to say it was less crowded and less people would see her cry if she wasn't able to keep all of her bound up emotions in check for much longer.

Noel approached and handed them each a cup of iced coffee. "Good to see you two are back in town. No time to talk. Gertie called in sick, so it's me and Leo right now, and you know how that goes. I do all the work, he sits on his ass doing 'inventory.'" Noel did air quotes as he backed up and then spun around to get back to the register. "At least Betty will be here in a few."

He was gone before Meg could thank him for the coffee. She turned back to Fiona.

Fiona shrugged. "Hope you don't mind. I ordered online while I walked up here."

"Ah. Thanks."

They walked past the line of customers waiting to be helped, and out onto the patio. Fiona walked over to the table the furthest from the door. They sat down. Meg sipped her drink, while Fiona fiddled with the straw in hers.

Meg cleared her throat, though she couldn't think of anything to say. She had a universe full of unstructured questions and feelings whirling around inside of her, but she couldn't seem to form a sentence.

"You and your brother have the same eyes," Fiona said, her eyes riveted to the straw in her drink.

"Yes," Meg traced the pattern on the top of the metal table top.

"I'm sorry I left," Fiona said.

Meg sat forward in her chair. "I don't blame you. I would have probably done the same thing. Did you listen to my messages? My family doesn't think you're trash. They aren't judging you at all. Mike and I explained what happened. They get it. They really like you. They like Mike. Hell, they even like CJ again." She hadn't expected everything would be back to normal after she explained, but the lack of response was hard to take. The guarded look in Fiona's eyes was killing her. She laid her hand on the table between them and almost said she loved her. But she stopped herself. Now was not the time. "Tell me what you need, Fiona. I… I'll do whatever it takes to make us work again."

"Meg…" Fiona put her hand over Meg's hand.

Meg stared at their hands. Tears pooled in her eyes. She watched Fiona's eyes fill, too, and a warm trickle ran down her cheek. Fiona slowly pulled her hand away and Meg had to fight from grabbing it.

"I don't know what to do." Fiona sat back in her chair.

"What are the options?" Meg's stomach clenched, afraid of what Fiona might say.

Fiona stared into the middle distance. "All I know is I've been selfish, Meg."

Meg scoffed. "You're the least selfish person I know."

Fiona tilted her head and watched her before she answered. "I was ready to steal your future and I barely even thought about it." The look on Fiona's face was almost one of disgust. Was it with her or herself? Meg didn't like either option.

Meg was confused. "We haven't even talked about our future. Besides, you can't steal something I'm beyond happy to give freely."

Fiona studied her fingernails. "I think there was a reason we never talked about our future, Meg."

"I don't think I follow you."

"We never talked about the future because the possibilities don't intersect."

That was an interesting and incorrect assessment. "Are you trying to say we don't have anything in common? It seems like we have a lot in common. In fact—"

Fiona stabbed her finger into the table top. "Meg, my future is pretty obvious. I'm having a baby. Once it's here, my life will be chaos. I don't know how it will affect my career or anything else. A baby takes over your life. Everything revolves around a baby. This is not what you signed on for. You have—"

Meg waved a hand in the air. She had to make Fiona see. "I've known almost from the start what I was getting into. I figure we can figure it out together."

"How? You have a career starting up in Okanogan. I live here."

Meg tried to understand what she was trying to say. "It sounds like you've made some decisions already. You and I haven't even talked about the possibilities. Why are you so certain your life is here and mine is in Washington?"

Fiona looked at her like she didn't believe what she just heard. "Because they are."

"Things change, we can—"

Fiona shook her head. "I don't want you changing your plans because my path forward has suddenly become narrower. I don't want to be the reason why you disregard the future you've been dreaming of since you were a kid to try and fit into a future neither of us can even predict. It's not fair to you."

"Don't I get a say in this? Don't I get a chance to determine what's fair for me?"

Fiona looked at her hands in her lap and it was a moment before she responded. When she looked up, her eyes looked cold and hard. "You're right. You get to determine what you do in your life. I'm not going to let you determine what I do with my life. Or my baby's life. I need space to figure things out without having to worry about how it's going to affect you, too. It's too much for me to try and navigate your life in addition to mine and my baby's."

Meg felt like she'd been slapped. Anger rushed toward the surface and she had to remind herself Fiona was upset. This wasn't like her. She sat forward. "Wait. Wait. That's not what I meant."

"Maybe not. But it's what I meant." Fiona blew out a breath and sat back. "I told you I was selfish."

"Fiona. Please. We can figure something out." Meg didn't care if she was begging.

"I don't see how we can," Fiona whispered. She didn't try to meet Meg's eyes.

An ache began in Meg's chest. Fiona needed some time. She could give it to her. "Fiona, let's wait a little while before we make this decision. Okay?" She scooted her chair over and pulled one of Fiona's hands into her lap. "I don't want to lose you. Why don't we give it some time? I can give you space in the meantime. You can let me know when you're ready. But… let's not end it, though. Okay? Because it sounds like you want to end it. Let's just think things out a little more."

She clutched Fiona's hand and Fiona nodded her head. She sighed with relief. The tightness in her chest eased up a little. She could almost breathe again.

"Thank you. I won't pressure you. I won't call you. You decide the next step, okay?"

Fiona nodded again. Meg stood up. She didn't want to leave, but there wasn't anything else to say. She still held Fiona's hand and Fiona stared at their entwined fingers. Fiona slowly leaned into Meg. The familiar smell of Fiona's shampoo wafted up and she breathed it in. Meg stroked her hair and pushed her fingers through it. Fiona wrapped her arms around Meg's waist.

Meg was scared. Her legs felt as if they might give way beneath her and she clung to Fiona.

The sound of metal dragging across cement pierced their cocoon and a woman cleared her throat loudly. They reluctantly pulled apart.

"This is a PG establishment, ladies," laughed Betty, as she pushed another chair under a nearby table and then opened the door to the café. Before she went in, she said, "Can't have you drawing a crowd out here, can we?"

Meg stepped from Fiona's embrace.

"I'll wait for you to call, Fiona. Please call," she whispered.

Fiona didn't say anything as Meg walked away.

Leaving was the hardest thing she had ever done, but if she turned around, she knew she wouldn't be able to give Fiona the space she needed. To keep her sanity, Meg kept on walking, but as she rounded the corner of the building, she wondered if sanity was worth the ragged hole she felt in her heart.

81

THE DAYS BEGAN TO BLEND together for Meg as she battled the growing emptiness she felt at receiving no word from Fiona. Without work or a regular schedule to keep her busy, she slept in late and went to bed early, which did little to ease the constant yearning that threatened to tear her apart when she was awake. Fiona monopolized her dreams and every time Meg woke with the apparition of Fiona fading behind her eyelids, the realization that Fiona was gone made the sadness only anchor itself deeper. No amount of sleep seemed to push away the fear that she had lost the woman she loved forever.

In an attempt to break free of a spiral into depression, after a week of waiting, Meg forced herself to go running. If nothing else, it got her out of her room, where she had started to feel caged in and restless.

The running helped. The exertion and rhythmic movement lulled her into an almost meditative state. Each day, her runs became longer, and she was finally able to see more of New York City, even if it was only from the perspective of the sidewalk. Soon, she found herself running in the mornings and again in the evenings. Once, when her loneliness threatened to crush her, she even found herself running in the middle of the night.

A little over three weeks into not hearing from Fiona, Meg picked up her paintbrushes, which helped in the same way the running did—by allowing her to go to a place where she could escape the loneliness threatening to choke her.

At least once a day, Meg stared at her phone desperate to call Fiona. She ached to hear her voice. She'd promised to wait, though, and she didn't intend to break her promise.

As September drew close, Meg's fear that Fiona would never call grew stronger, and despair began to squeeze her heart. If she left the city without seeing Fiona, she feared she'd lose her forever.

82

"DANNY, YOU DON'T NEED TO come down." Katie spoke into the phone as she smiled at the woman standing next to her. She rolled her eyes. "We have it completely under control. The boys are out back moving the bales and they're doing a great job… I know they'll slack off if we don't keep an eye on them… yes, I remembered to grease the lift on the pallet jack… I put dirt in the little holes, just like you instructed… I'm kidding… I said I was kidding… I grease gunned the zerts… I'm not a complete idiot… I know, it wasn't funny… oh, now you can't stop laughing?… Okay, I'll call you if anything comes up… You, too, Danny… You know, the fish won't bite if they hear you yammering away on the phone… Alrighty then… 'Bye, Danny."

"Danny checking in again?" Fiona neatly folded another pair of Carhartt work pants and added them to the display table. With fall coming on, the warm and durable pants were selling like hot cakes.

"The third time today," Katie sighed. "At least he called from the river."

"He's nervous because it's delivery day." Fiona straightened the piles of pants.

Katie sank to the floor cross-legged and picked up the pricing gun. She affixed a price to the pants coming out of the box sitting on the floor at Fiona's feet. "At least this week, he didn't just come down."

"I kind of like his checks-in." Fiona smiled down at Katie. "I've never worked in a store before, let alone owned one. I'm glad he's watching over us."

"Yeah, it makes me feel good, too, actually," Katie admitted. "I've worked here for ten years and could probably do it all myself, but it's nice to have Danny around."

Meg put her hand on her barely round belly. Those who didn't know her wouldn't know. A faint bubbly feeling in her belly held her attention.

"Is the baby kicking?" Katie quickly stood up. She always kept a watchful eye on her new boss. She didn't have any children of her own, but she was a natural nurturer. Fiona didn't know what she would have done without her.

"I can't tell." Fiona chuckled. "It seems a little early."

"Ooo! Let me feel!"

Fiona laughed. She loved Katie's knack for being refreshingly direct. "I can't feel it from the outside yet. Hell, it might be gas. But as soon as I know, I'll let you know."

Katie smiled at the promise, and Fiona stood for a few more seconds trying to tell if the little flutters were the baby or not. After a minute, they went away and she began to fold clothes again. The women worked in easy silence, except for the country music playing over the store speakers. In some ways it felt like she'd been there much longer than six weeks, but Fiona wasn't sure she'd ever get used to listening to country music.

Two months ago, if someone had told Fiona she'd be working in a store in Winthrop, Washington, she would have laughed in their face. But here she was, folding shirts. Of course, the law practice she'd bought from Danny was her primary job and it was a lot of work coming up to speed with the caseload, but she found she enjoyed some of the retail stuff, too. Especially when she got to spend time with Katie, who was quickly becoming a good friend.

Adjusting to life in Winthrop was easy. It was the memories she left behind that were hard.

83

ACROSS THE CONTINENT, MEG ONCE again stood at the door of Fiona's apartment. It was the middle of October and she'd come back to New York to pick up a few things she'd left at Aunt Vi's, knowing full well it was only an excuse to try to see Fiona again. It had been nearly two months and she'd kept her promise not to contact her. Starting her job at the clinic had helped to keep her mind off of things, but leaving New York without a single word had been one of the hardest things she'd ever done. Now she was getting ready to head back to the airport and the draw toward Fiona's apartment was too strong. She adjusted the large backpack she had slung over one shoulder and hitched up the long flat package wrapped in brown paper she had clasped under her arm. Her knocks on the door went unanswered.

The taxi she'd called pulled to a stop in front of her building across the street. It was time to go. She knocked on the door again and waited. She didn't expect Fiona to be home. It was the middle of the afternoon on a Wednesday, so she was probably at work. When no one answered the door, Meg propped the flat package against the door and walked slowly up the steps to the sidewalk. She waited for a break in traffic, then jaywalked over to the taxi and got in.

84

SEPTEMBER, OCTOBER, AND NOVEMBER HAD flown by for Fiona, and between getting herself settled in a new town, taking over an established law practice, learning how to run a thriving retail store, and keeping up with the corporate cases Frank continued to send her way from Threadlocke and Guernsey, Fiona had very little time to dwell on how much she missed Meg.

Deciding to actually leave T&G in New York had been difficult, but when she had told Frank what was going on, he'd asked her to continue doing the legal research and case prep, since much of it could be done remotely. While she'd wanted a clean break, she found having the link to her old life was comforting, and she was able to keep her medical insurance, something she hadn't even considered when she decided to leave. And when she'd discovered Katie was a certified paralegal, she was able to delegate most of the research as she got up to speed on everything else. Things mysteriously seemed to be falling into place. It didn't make her heart feel any better, though.

Every day had been a new experience since the day Fiona had called Danny to discuss buying his practice. Between Danny's eagerness to retire and Fiona's sudden lack of ties to New York, it had only taken a couple of weeks for her to get moved out to Winthrop, and she hadn't had a chance to take a breath since.

Danny was a good businessman and Fiona was fortunate to walk right into a well-run situation. Nevertheless, there was a steep learning curve, and Fiona didn't want to drop the ball on any of the clients Danny had been taking care of so well for so many years. On top of everything, she also had a retail store to learn how to run. Coming up to speed was time consuming— she was busy from the minute she woke up until the minute she dropped exhausted into bed every night.

It was mostly at night when the yearning took over.

It was Thanksgiving evening; Fiona was snuggled in her bed in her quiet little house amid stacks of unpacked boxes, listening to the unfamiliar creaks and groans of the old house settling under a fresh blanket of snow. She tried to push away the inevitable thoughts that always led to longing and tears. Tonight she wanted to think about what she was grateful for.

She was thankful she'd had a good day, her first real day off since she had moved to Winthrop. After calling Mike and Maureen and Josh to wish them a happy Thanksgiving, Fiona had spent the day at Katie's house, where she had watched football and eaten way too much food. It had been a cozy day. Danny had been there, as had Rickie the yard manager from the store and Jocelyn from the diner. She was thankful that, in the few short months she had lived in Winthrop, she had made a good friend in Katie and she'd built an eclectic little family of new friends. Only Katie knew her entire story, but the rest of them knew the gist of it. Fiona didn't know what she would have done without them.

Shortly after her arrival in town, one of the delivery drivers had asked her on a date. She'd been flattered but politely declined, providing a vague excuse about not dating people she worked with. She wasn't exactly hiding who she was—she just didn't have the energy to explain her situation yet. The town would know at least some of her troubles soon enough, when her pregnancy became evident. The driver took it easily enough and she thought that was the end of it.

However, she quickly discovered that even the most inane news spread like wildfire in the small town. Less than an hour later, Katie had walked into her office, shut the door, and demanded all of the details. Katie had a well-deserved reputation for knowing everything that went on in Winthrop, so rather than deny anything, she told her the truth—she was a lesbian, had recently ended a relationship, and she didn't have plans to date anyone for a long, long time, if ever. She hadn't known she was on the verge of tears, but as soon as she said the last part, she wasn't able to hold anything back. Mortified and sobbing, she didn't know what to do when Katie stepped around the desk to give her a hug. But Katie was a good listener and she proceeded to tell Katie her entire story. She left nothing out while Katie rubbed her back and smoothed her hair. The exchange was a short one since they had a store to run, but afterward, Fiona had felt so much lighter. Confiding in Katie hadn't fixed the hurt, but knowing she had someone to talk to had made living with it a little more bearable.

She smiled when she thought about the exchange.

Katie had made to leave the office but hesitated at the door. "For the record, boss—I'm a lesbian, too." Katie had winked, kicked up her foot, and walked out the door.

And because news traveled so quickly, the next day, Fiona discovered, one by one as they came to visit, that Jocelyn from the diner was a lesbian, and handsome, quiet Rickie was gay. Not one to be left out, Danny said he was so old and out of practice he couldn't remember if he was gay or straight, so the little group just sort of adopted him.

Alone in her bed, months later on the cold and snowy Thanksgiving night, Fiona thought about how lucky she was to have found such a great group of friends in the new town. She gave thanks for not being alone, yet the sadness was like a relentless river that threatened to overtake her. She tried to push it away by acknowledging her wonderful new friends, her health, the health of her unborn baby, and the perfect set of circumstances that brought her here. But there was a coldness in her, howling through the enormous hole in her heart, and she wondered if it would ever go away. She rolled onto her side and the hot tears came, as they did every night when the quiet reminded her how lonely she was without Meg.

85

IT WAS THE DAY AFTER Christmas, and Meg stood under the portico in front of her parents' house. Her hands were pushed deeply into the pockets of her coat as she stood next to her idling Jeep. She wasn't dreading heading back to Okanogan—in fact she was looking forward to burying herself in work at the clinic—but she was lonely, and the holidays made it worse. Specifically, her loneliness for Fiona. She hadn't heard from her since the meeting at Helga's and she'd almost lost hope she ever would.

"Will you call when you get home, honey?" her mother asked, as she pulled Meg into yet another goodbye hug. "The weather is supposed to get nasty tonight."

"I will." Meg gently acknowledged her mother's concern. "I'm going to stop and do a little snowshoeing on the way home though, so give me a few hours before you send out the patrols, okay?"

"Don't go too far off the trails. And be sure to sign in at the trail head. I worry about you going out by yourself."

"I will, Mom. Don't worry. Today will be a short one."

"Have fun. Stay warm, and call me when you get home. I love you, honey."

"I know. And I love you too, Mom. Give Dad my love, too, okay?"

Mickey and CJ—she kicked herself, Charlie—had left for the country club to play cards with the guys, as Mickey did every Sunday when the golf course was closed. Charlie had started going once he'd moved back home. Mike sometimes went, too, when he was visiting, which was often. It was weird watching CJ—ugh! Charlie—morph into this man she'd never known, who wasn't always snide and secretive. A man who was happy and almost sweet. It was great to see him like this, but it took some getting used to. Mostly because Mike was still close to Fiona. Except for when she dropped off the painting, and one other time of weakness when she'd called Mrs. Rickles just to make sure Fiona was okay, she refused to break her promise about giving Fiona the space she'd asked for. It was hard not to beg Mike for information, but she'd made a promise.

She hugged her mother one more time and climbed into her Jeep. A thin blanket of snow from one of the infrequent snowfalls Seattle had each year coated the sides of the quiet highway, though the lanes were dry and clear. Meg had the hardtop on the Jeep, but even with the heat turned all the way up, the inside was cold, and she could see her breath in the air. She pulled her beanie down more snugly on her head, and looked out across the landscape. It reflected her mood. A wall of gray clouds was moving in from the northeast. Snow was definitely coming. It was sure to be worse on the other side of the mountains. She loved the muted beauty of the falling snow when she snowshoed, but she suspected the pending storm would make her excursion a short one. A heavy storm was predicted, and she didn't want to take any chances. The outfitter in town would tell her what was safe.

✱✱✱✱✱

SHE PULLED HER JEEP INTO a spot along the curb next to the bright red building of the country store and outfitter. She jumped down from the driver's seat and stretched while she looked around. Snow was more frequent on this side of the mountains, and a thick layer coated everything. She loved the little town. It was small and rustic, and the community was tight. The sidewalk and parking spots were clear, but a tall bank of icy snow stood along the edge of the raised plank sidewalk. Meg walked around to the street corner to get to the sidewalk. She tried not to remember the last time she had been to Winthrop, even if they'd only passed through. She missed Fiona too much to think too long about the last full day they had been happy together.

The scent of freshly ground coffee drew her back to the present, and Meg stomped the snow from her feet on the steel grate placed before the door. An eerie sense of anticipation turned in her belly. She pulled off her gloves, unzipped her parka, and pushed the door open to the jingle of a little bell. The old barn was brighter than she remembered and the stacks of feed were more neatly stacked than usual. She was glad to be back. Something about the place filled her with comfort, which she attributed to its unchanging charm. The rich smell of brewing coffee led her gaze to the back of the store, where the clothing and outdoor equipment was displayed. She hummed along to the country song playing in the background as she walked through the stacks of feed and seed, stuffing her gloves into her jacket pockets. She smiled when she caught sight of a familiar form in front of the shiny espresso machine. She snuck up behind her.

"Guess who," Meg said, as she placed her hands over the woman's eyes, careful to do so only after she had set the cup of hot coffee down.

The woman stood up straighter, and laughed when she recognized her voice.

"Meg! I was wondering if I'd see you sometime this year." The woman spun around and gave her a hug. "Holy shit, you're so skinny!"

"Um… thanks?" Meg looked down at herself. "I've been running a lot. You look great, though."

"Sorry. I meant to say, you look skinny, but you're as gorgeous as ever." Katie laughed and rolled her eyes. "I'm just jealous. I always pack on the pounds in the winter."

Meg knew she'd dropped a little too much weight, but she teasingly waved a finger at Katie. "Good save. Can you make one of those for me?" She pointed at the steaming cup. "Where's Danny? I want to ask him about the storm coming in."

"Vanilla latte, coming right up! I'd give you this one, but it's decaf for the new boss. I know you take yours fully loaded." Katie winked, and she hit the switch on the espresso grinder. "Danny retired. Not sure why, because most of the time he's here, drinking coffee and getting underfoot. The new owner's over there doing inventory." Katie waved toward the far corner of the store.

"New owner, huh?" So much for things not changing around here.

"She's great. Why don't you take this over to her and introduce yourself?" Katie suggested, and she handed Meg the two lattes.

"I thought the place looked a little different." She backed up and looked around.

"It's cleaner with a couple more light fixtures, but everything else is pretty much the same."

"Maybe you could get her to change out the twangy country music."

"And have the town revolt? Hell, no!"

Meg adjusted the cups in her hands and laughed. "I'll be back in a few. You need to fill me in on any gossip since the last time I was here."

"You're on, girl!"

She went in the direction Katie had pointed, though she didn't see anyone. A head in a beanie bobbed between two rows of stacked feed near the front of the store. Meg wended her way in that direction. The new owner crouched with her back to Meg, intent on scanning a tag nailed to a pallet. Meg cleared her throat when she was a few feet away. The woman, who wore jeans and a loose blue work shirt with the sleeves rolled up, pushed herself up with some effort, and wrote something on her clipboard as she turned around. A double shock of recognition flared between them when she finally looked up.

The eerie sense of anticipation Meg had felt when she entered the store blossomed into an explosion of emotions. The hazel eyes that had haunted her dreams for more than four months were staring back at her. Was she real? If she hadn't been holding coffee in each hand she would have reached out to make sure.

Fiona looked shocked. She pulled off the beanie and smoothed down her hair, which was in two cute braids. They faced one another silently. Neither of them knew what to say, although a thousand emotions caused a tornado of feeling to spiral dangerously between them.

Meg remembered the coffee in her hand.

"Katie made this for you," she said stupidly, holding out the cup.

Fiona simply stood there, staring. What was she thinking? Was she angry? Would she ask her to leave? Meg suddenly felt as if she were intruding, so she sat both cups down on the nearest pile of sacks and started to turn away. She needed to leave on her own, because if Fiona asked her to, she'd break into a million pieces.

Suddenly, Fiona was in motion, and Meg found herself being held in her arms. It didn't seem real.

"I've missed you so much." Fiona whispered into Meg's neck, and Meg buried her face in Fiona's hair. God, this better be real. The scent of Fiona surrounded her and she closed her eyes. An unfamiliar bump, partially disguised by the oversized shirt, pushed against her. A mix of emotions swirled within Meg, and she didn't know which one to address, so she simply stood there and breathed Fiona in. The herbal scent of skin and hair made Meg's head spin in a fury of remembered feelings. She kissed the side of

Fiona's face before she knew what she was doing and a knot of uncertainty lodged in her stomach.

"Um… do you two know each other?"

Meg hadn't heard Katie approach.

Slowly, Meg and Fiona stepped apart, while Fiona wiped her eyes with the back of her hand.

"Yes, we're…" Meg wasn't sure how to describe them. What were they? She settled on something safe—she hoped. "We're old friends. We haven't seen each other in a while."

"I can handle it out here if you want to catch up." Katie studied Fiona.

Fiona seemed to shake herself. "Thanks, Katie. We'll be in the office."

Katie trailed them toward the back of the store. Meg followed Fiona into the office.

Fiona held the door as Meg moved passed her. When she closed the door, she faced Meg who stood in the middle of the small room watching her. Fiona clutched the door knob behind her as if it was her only tether to safety. She wanted to be Fiona's safety.

Without a thought, she crossed the space between them and wrapped Fiona in her arms. "God, I've missed you," she whispered into her hair.

Fiona didn't reply, but she let go of the door knob and held onto Meg. The closeness of their bodies was both familiar and foreign, causing Meg's heart to break. It took a moment for Meg to realize they were both crying.

After several minutes, Fiona lifted her head and looked at Meg. Meg had to blink a few times to make the blur of her tears subside.

"I can't seem to pull myself together." Fiona smiled self-consciously and ducked her head as she moved away. Not far, but any distance was too far. Meg missed her touch immediately.

She watched Fiona turn and lean against the edge of the desk, where she gripped the edges of the desk so hard, her knuckles turned white. The roundness of her belly was more pronounced with the shirt pulled across it. She was so beautiful.

They stared at one another intently for a moment before Meg broke the silence.

"You have no idea how much I've missed you." Meg's voice broke on the last word and she cleared her throat, though she couldn't look away from Fiona.

"Seeing you here—I can't remember why… I mean, I know why, but…"

Fiona said. Her voice started to drift away as she continued to gaze into Meg's eyes.

"You had good reasons," Meg offered.

Fiona's eyes searched hers. "Do you hate me?"

Meg was shaken by the question. "Hate you? How could I hate you?"

Fiona swallowed and looked down. "For leaving like that. For pushing you away."

"Never." Meg took a step closer to her and Fiona looked up. Meg couldn't read her expression, but it didn't look angry or scared. She took another step so she was right in front of her. "I never hated you. I hate what happened. But I understood. I still understand."

"I thought I had gotten used to missing you." Fiona's voice was a whisper. "But you're here… and I don't know what to do. How did you know I was here?"

"I didn't. I came to snowshoe. Please don't ask me to leave." The thought of leaving again killed her. Fiona shook her head and Meg was relieved. They stood quietly for a few minutes before she found the courage to touch Fiona's hand. "I never expected to find you here."

"I couldn't raise a child in the city. Once I made the decision, it seemed like the universe conspired to send me here. I looked all over, but nothing captured me like this place. I thought it would be too close… but… in the end, Winthrop chose me as much as I chose Winthrop."

"When Mrs. Rickles told me you moved, I thought I would never…" Meg began, but her throat tightened up and she couldn't finish. She remembered the day after Thanksgiving, when she had broken down and tried to get in touch with her. Her life was upside down and she needed to talk to her. When the message on the other end of the line said it had been disconnected, she had tried the only thing she could think of without interrogating Mike, which she refused to do. Her heart had shattered when Mrs. Rickles told her Fiona had moved. After that, it was easy to not ask Mike. By moving without telling her, by disconnecting her number, Fiona had made her intentions very clear.

Fiona touched her face. "I'm sorry, Meg." Fiona was crying again. "I never wanted to hurt you."

"I know." Meg kissed her hand. "Maybe it would have been easier if I thought you hated me, but I never thought you did."

"Maybe I should have keyed your car or thrown a drink in your face?" A trace of a smile warmed Fiona's face.

"Or a scathing note. Maybe one of those." Meg teased Fiona weakly as she wiped her eyes with the back of her hand.

Fiona's face turned serious again. "I'm so sorry, Meg. I wish I could take away any pain I caused you."

"And I wish I could make you happy again."

"You've always been so good to me." Fiona tugged on Meg's hips and Meg moved to stand between her legs as Fiona slid her arms under Meg's open winter coat and laid her head against her chest. Meg wrapped her arms around Fiona's shoulders and rested her chin on the top of Fiona's head. The warm smell of Fiona filled her senses, making Meg melt.

"Can you stay for dinner?"

The invitation made Meg's heart speed up. "I can stay as long as you want me to." She pulled back to see Fiona's face, afraid to get her hopes up.

"I think we should keep it at just dinner tonight." Fiona gave her a hesitant smile. "I can't bear to see you leave, but I'm not sure what's up or down right now."

"Dinner is more than fine." Meg would take whatever she could get. She saw Fiona scanning her eyes and wondered what she was trying to see. "We should make it an early one, though. The weather is going to get dicey tonight and I'll need to leave for Okanogan before it gets too bad."

"Let's go now, then." Fiona stood and Meg reluctantly let her go. "Katie can finish up here. We close early in the winter, anyway."

Meg followed Fiona out of the office.

"Katie, I guess I don't need to tell you I'm leaving for the day." Fiona called over to Katie, who sat innocently on her stool by the cash register. "Can you close up?"

"Huh? Did you say something?" Katie lowered the book she was reading.

"It's upside down…" Fiona said.

Katie looked confused. "What is?"

"The book you're reading…" Fiona tilted her head to read the title. "How to Lasso a Cowboy… Seriously? Katie…"

Meg hid her smile behind her hand.

"Uh… I'm thinking to get it as a gift for Rickie." Katie closed the book and looked away.

Fiona rolled her eyes and Meg laughed out loud.

"I told the boys to go an hour ago. Why don't you close up now? It's dead here."

Fiona led Meg to the door and shrugged into an oversized coat she pulled off a coat rack near the store's front door. When Fiona struggled to pull it closed, Meg finally realized how pregnant Fiona was. Up until then, she had been too preoccupied with the shock of seeing her to really take it in.

"Wow. Look at you."

"I'm enormous." Fiona frowned and buttoned the coat. "I feel like an elephant."

"You look beautiful." Meg held the door open.

Fiona blushed. "Thanks." She didn't look like she believed her.

The door shut behind them.

"The diner across the street?" Meg asked.

"Dinner's already started at my house if you're up for beef stew. It's less than a block away."

"Sounds amazing. With biscuits?"

"Close. Fresh baked bread."

Meg pretended to think about it. "I guess it'll do. You know I'm a real fan of your biscuits, though."

Fiona's face broke into the first real smile Meg had seen on her since before everything fell apart. Fiona took Meg's hand and led her around the corner and down the street that ran beside the feed store.

It had started to snow and they walked in silence until Fiona turned them onto the little path leading up to a yellow two-story house with white trim. The house looked warm and cozy against the gray backdrop of the sky. Meg could envision kids making snow angels and building snowmen in the front yard. Someone had recently shoveled the walk and scattered rock salt on a patch of ice at the foot of the porch stairs. Meg wondered who the someone was with a pang of jealousy.

"Danny's such a sweetheart." It was as if Fiona had read her mind. "I haven't had to shovel a single sidewalk since the snow started."

"Katie said he was still around."

"He lives next door." Fiona pulled keys out of her coat pocket as she mounted the steps. "Everyone says I don't need to lock it out here, but it's a habit."

Meg rarely locked her own doors in Okanogan, but she was relieved to see Fiona took her own safety seriously. Meg shuddered to think of Fiona all by herself with a baby to take care of.

Fiona pushed the door open. "Has Claudia had the babies yet?" Meg reached past and held it open so Fiona could precede her.

Meg nodded. "Exactly a month early. December 4th." Fiona shut the door and struggled with the deadbolt. Meg remembered another day in another city. "She was on bed rest for a month with preeclampsia, but everyone is doing well now. Two girls and a boy."

"What did she name them?"

Meg smiled. "Kayden is the boy, and the girls are Tristin and Fiona."

Fiona stopped and looked over her shoulder at Meg. "Really?"

Meg shrugged. The name had given her mixed feelings.

"Huh…" Fiona pushed the door open.

Meg watched a parade of emotions flit across Fiona's face, but she didn't say anything.

Fiona led Meg into the house, turning on lights as she went. Meg helped Fiona with her coat and then shrugged out of her own, hanging them on hooks next to the door. Following Fiona's lead, she kicked off her damp boots.

"I started the stew this morning and the bread machine should have kicked on a minute a go." Fiona unwound her scarf. "I didn't expect to be home so early. The stew is probably done, but the bread won't be done for another hour. Can you wait?"

"I'm not sure, but I'll try my best," Meg joked. "It smells great. This is a domestic side of you I never suspected. I like it."

"It's sheer necessity. Takeout's a little scarce around here," Fiona said with a smile. "However, Boonjira did give me her recipe for Pad Thai before I left. I think I've almost got it."

Meg hadn't had the heart to eat at Boonjira's restaurant since the last time with Fiona. "I definitely miss her cooking."

They both fell silent as they remembered. Fiona absently rubbed her pregnant belly, and Meg looked around, noting all the familiar furniture and a few extra pieces she had never seen.

"I guess you had to go out and get some new things to fill up this place, huh?"

Fiona shook her head. "I had a lot of stuff in storage. Most of it's from Aunt Corny. I can't seem to part with any of it. I have more out in the garage. I don't have room for it all, even here."

"I like it." Meg followed Fiona into the kitchen, where she checked on dinner.

A large window looked out on the backyard. Like most of the houses in the area, there was no fence to delineate where one backyard ended and another started, but the landscaping provided a good point of reference. The yard boasted a large sandbox with a setup worthy of a public park. It had swings, teeter-totters, rings, bars, and slides. A tire swing hung from a cottonwood tree in the corner. Next to the play area was a picnic table, and Meg envisioned a spring afternoon and kids from the whole area coming over to play.

"The backyard was one of the reasons I bought this place." Fiona came up behind her without touching her. "That and the short walk to the feed store. The place needs some serious renovations, though."

Fiona's proximity was like an electric current. Moving away to keep her wits about her, Meg took in the kitchen furnishings. Aside from the refrigerator and stove, which looked brand new, the countertops and cabinets were probably as old as the house. The windows even had manual storm windows on them.

"It's very cozy," she said.

"I had all the wood flooring and stairs redone before I moved in, but I figure I'll wait until next spring to get started on the rest. The house is old, but livable. Want the grand tour?"

Meg nodded and they started with the ground floor. There was the open foyer they had entered through, a large family room, the kitchen and dining area, a small bathroom tucked under the stairs, two large rooms connected through a set of French doors and a double-sided fireplace, and a mudroom with a washer and dryer. One of the rooms looked like Fiona's office. She envisioned a blazing fire, while Fiona worked at the huge cherry wood desk covered in law books.

They took a peek from the top of the stairs into the basement, which was dark and musty, even when the light was turned on. "I don't go down there," Fiona said with a shiver Meg thought was cute. "Thank goodness the washer and dryer are on this floor."

Fiona led her up the shining wood staircase. As they climbed the stairs, Meg couldn't help but worry about Fiona slipping on the smooth risers.

"The riser rug is in the closet ready to be installed, but I'm helpless with tools." Fiona, mysteriously read her mind again. "I wish I was as good with my hands as y… you are."

Meg noticed the stutter and thought about a similar conversation from months ago. She didn't feel it was appropriate to remind Fiona of the moment, although she probably didn't need to, based on the stutter.

Upstairs, Fiona showed her the spare room, which was full of boxes and disassembled furniture stacked against the walls. Next to it was the nursery. The only thing in it was a crib. The mattress was bare and several department store bags and online store packages with crib linen and baby clothes with tags still on them were stacked in it. In the corner were several gift bags. It looked like she'd recently had a baby shower. She wondered what friends Fiona had made in Winthrop and the thought of the life she wasn't part of made her sad.

Fiona stopped next to the crib. "My mom saved my crib. It's the only thing I've been motivated to assemble so far. They say pregnant women are supposed to get a nesting thing in the last trimester, but I think mine is broken." Fiona looked absently around the room. "I need to get to work on the rest of the room. The baby is due in a month."

Meg wished Fiona was excited about becoming a mother. Although she had no reason to believe she'd be asked to help, part of her was happy Fiona hadn't already finished the room. Maybe she could be a part of it. Stop it. She didn't need to get her hopes up like that.

She cleared her throat. "When's your due date?"

"January 27."

All of the months she had missed with Fiona immediately caught up with her. She wondered who had gone to all the doctor appointments with her, and who had been in the room with her when she heard the baby's heartbeat for the first time.

"Have you taken any ultrasounds?"

"I have some pictures in my room, the final stop in our grand tour," Fiona said.

She followed Fiona across the hall, but she was reluctant to enter Fiona's bedroom. She stood in the doorway and looked in. The furniture was the same, though the new room was much larger. A hand squeezed her heart when she recognized the comforter on the bed. How many times had it covered them? She had a visceral urge to pull Fiona down upon it. Her thoughts began to wander to when she used to lie next to Fiona, skin-to-skin, kicking off its soft weight during the New York summer. She'd appreciate it more when there was snow falling outside.

"Meg?" Fiona's fingers touched her hand, which was on the footboard of Fiona's sleigh bed. Somehow, she had moved into the room. She looked up from their hands and was riveted by Fiona's hazel eyes. "Where did you go?" Fiona asked.

"Thinking about how warm feather comforters can be in the winter." It was partially true. Fiona's eyes told her she had already guessed the full truth.

"I was telling you how much I love the painting." Her eyes followed Fiona's gaze to the wall above the bed, where the painting Meg had left at the door to Fiona's apartment hung.

Suddenly, she was back in her room in New York, painting feverishly. It was the middle of the night. A blank canvas stood before her, and all she wanted was to capture the look of Fiona happy. If she could paint it, she could make it happen, she thought, while images of them together shuttled through her mind. But the perfect expression eluded her as she tried to define Fiona's happiness with her brush. She had almost given up. She was tired, with morning around the corner, when the memory of Fiona in the park had suddenly flooded her mind. Fiona's head was thrown back, her eyes were closed, and a smile played across her mouth. It was that moment, when Fiona opened her eyes and looked at her. Joy had vibrated through her. That was it. Meg had finished the portrait as the sun started to ignite the neighborhood with its signature glow. When she stepped back from the canvas she had known she had captured it.

She stared at the painting. She wanted to look at Fiona, but it was almost too much to bear.

"Mrs. Rickles found it outside the old apartment a week or so after I left and she sent it out to me."

"I hadn't known you'd moved yet." She didn't mean to make it sound like an accusation.

Fiona faced her. "You don't know how hard it was for me to not run to you, Meg. The day I left was one of the hardest days of my life. The only thing comforting me was knowing I'd be closer to you."

Meg had so many questions. She let her eyes move from the painting to Fiona. It hurt to see the pain in Fiona's eyes. She saw a stack of photos in Fiona's hand. "Are those the ultrasound pictures?"

Fiona handed the stack to Meg, who moved over to the bedside lamp and sat on the edge of the bed to look at them. Fiona sat next to her and watched over her shoulder. The closeness was almost more than she could bear.

"Wow. It's amazing how much detail they can get." She'd seen Claudia's ultrasound images, which were just as detailed. But these were Fiona's.

"Yeah, it's crazy." Fiona smiled.

"Oh my God. I see a foot." She peered at the sepia colored photos, and glanced over her shoulder at Fiona. Fiona's body heat distracted her, although Fiona didn't touch her. She looked back at a photo. "It sort of looks a little like an alien, but you can definitely see parts. There's all five toes. And there's the ankle." She looked up incredulously. "Aw! Look at the hand all balled up in front of… the face? And the little mouth. It definitely has your chin. What's this one?" She squinted at it. "It kind of looks like… wait… it's a girl! You're having a girl. Oh, Fiona. She is right now inside of you listening to this conversation." She pulled the photos to her chest. "I bet you can't wait to hold this little girl in your arms." She was surprised at her excitement. She had never been a huge baby fan. She loved her new cousins, and she held them and cooed at them out of genuine affection when she was around them. But babies in general weren't her thing.

She snuck a glance at Fiona and saw she was crying. Fiona tried to smile, but it trembled and Meg's heart broke.

"Oh, baby. What's wrong?" She put the pictures down and pulled Fiona into her arms. She smoothed her hair. "It's okay. It's going to be okay."

Fiona clung to her and cried. As she pressed her cheek to Fiona's, Fiona's tears wet both their cheeks.

"Did I say something wrong?" She rubbed small circles on Fiona's back and kissed her wet cheek.

Fiona sighed. "Just the opposite."

"Why the tears then?"

"I didn't realize how much I needed to share this with you."

"Have you been doing this all alone?"

"No. Maureen went to the first appointment with me before I left New York. She's come out for a couple since I've been here. Otherwise, either Katie or Danny goes with me."

"I'm sure they're as amazed as I am."

Fiona waited a beat before responding. "It's different with you."

She couldn't imagine loving anyone more than she loved Fiona, and she wished she could tell her. All she could hope was Fiona could feel it in her touch and see it in her eyes. "You don't know how much that means to me." She leaned her forehead against Fiona's.

"I think I do." Fiona cupped the side of Meg's face with her hand. Her thumb gently stroked her cheek. Their lips were a breath apart. "I love you, Meg. I always have."

The words were a warm rush against Meg's soul. She took in the meaning of Fiona's words and cradled Fiona's face between her open palms. "I love you, too. I've wanted to tell you for so long. I love you so much, I think it might destroy me," she whispered and gazed into the hazel eyes she saw every time she closed her own.

Fiona bridged the gap between them and kissed her. Her lips were as soft as Meg remembered, sending a rush of heat throughout her body. Her lips parted and she tasted the mouth she had craved for months. The kiss deepened. An urgency of desire took over and an aching need to express her love flamed through her. She kissed Fiona's neck. The rapid pulse beat beneath her lips and her passion soared. When Fiona's hand slid under the hem of her shirt, she held the back of Fiona's head and lowered her to the bed, kissing her, feeling her, wanting her. She wasn't thinking, only doing. It felt so right to be in Fiona's arms again.

Fiona's lips were on her throat and her voice was low, causing shivers to ripple down Meg's back. "God, Meg, I want this. I want you." It sent flares of desire to her center. "I want you so bad, but…" When she heard the word "but", Meg stopped moving and dread seized her heart. She'd lost control. Out of breath, she touched her forehead against Fiona's, squeezing her eyes tightly shut.

Fiona stroked her back. "I'm sorry. So sorry."

She shifted so Fiona's leg wasn't pressed against her center. She was trying so hard to be respectful, but her body was well beyond its limits of control. Fiona had kissed her, true, but they hadn't talked about being together again. What about all the things that had made her run away before? And they needed to talk. Fiona had hurt her, and she needed to protect her own heart. All of that needed to be acknowledged before they got carried away physically. She tried to gently pull herself off Fiona, but Fiona held her close.

"I'm scared, Meg. God knows my heart wants to be with you, and my body is screaming to keep going, but my head is telling me we need to slow down."

Meg's body was on fire, but she'd heard Fiona. They both needed a little time. She moved Fiona's arms and rolled to her back.

Fiona rose up onto her elbow. Her eyes were soft. "I'm sorry." Fiona stroked her cheek and kissed her. "Just a little more time."

Meg knew it was the right thing to do. "I totally get it. We got a little carried away." She pulled Fiona's head to rest upon her chest.

They lay there tangled up together for a few more minutes. Meg wasn't ready to let go—she fought with her body's need to seek more intimate contact. She was slightly ashamed about her single-minded desire. Fiona's heart was far more important to her than physical release, but her body seemed to have one focus. She knew it would be fast for her, all she needed was a little…

"Are you ready for dinner?" Fiona's voice was low, and she knew Fiona was wrestling with her own desire. It was dangerous for them to stay on the bed like this. "The bread should be done by now."

"Sure." She tried to make it sound light, but she reluctantly rolled away. Once up, she helped Fiona, grinning at the floundering induced by the baby bump. A few minutes earlier, that roundness hadn't seemed so in the way. "I'm going to use the bathroom first. I'll be down in a minute."

Fiona smiled and started down the hall. Meg wondered if the look Fiona gave her was because she knew what she was about to do. It wasn't what she wanted, but if she had to give Fiona the space she needed and remain in the house with her, she had to do something about the throbbing between her legs.

She shut the door and splashed a little cold water on her face to see if it would help, but she couldn't stop thinking about Fiona's lips against her throat and Fiona's thigh pushed firmly between her own. She shut her eyes and slid her hand down the front of her pants. Even with a belt, they were loose on her. She slid her fingers beneath the waistline of her panties and a shuddering throb pulsed between her legs as she spread them a little more and skimmed the wetness coating her swollen clit. She was so ready. An image from the summer of Fiona lying naked across the bed filled her mind and her fingers stroked more firmly…

"Meg?"

It was almost a whisper. At first, she thought the voice was part of her memory, but the light tap on the door told her otherwise. She pulled her hand out of her pants. When she opened the bathroom door, Fiona stood there with an expression she had seen before. Raw longing and fierce desire met her eyes. A current of anticipation shot down her spine.

They stood less than six inches apart and she watched Fiona's chest rise with each breath. Goose bumps rose across her skin.

Fiona grabbed her hand and brought it to her mouth. She saw Fiona's pupils dilate as she took a finger into her mouth. With heavy-lidded eyes, Fiona gently sucked her finger, then gently raked her teeth across the tender skin of the knuckle. The throbbing in Meg's core turned into a slow, convulsive roll. She was about to explode merely from the sensation of the warm, wet feel of Fiona's mouth around her finger. Fiona slowly withdrew the finger from her mouth causing a gush of fluid to drench Meg's panties.

"I had a feeling you were going to take care of things yourself," Fiona said in a low voice. She closed the inches between them, kissing her with the intensity of a starving woman. Meg returned the kiss with equal fervor, their mouths working feverishly as Fiona walked her back into the bathroom and pressed her against the countertop. The thoughts that had stopped them before, as noble as they were, were no longer guiding them; their raw passion was. Meg's hands were everywhere and she began to remove Fiona's clothing with blind abandon. No patience was wasted on buttons. She unceremoniously yanked Fiona's shirt up and over her head before Fiona lifted Meg's shirt and moved aside the fabric of her bra to take an erect nipple into her mouth. Fiona's lips wrapped around her sensitive skin, her teeth grazing it before she sucked greedily on the firm flesh. A jolt of electric pleasure sped directly to Meg's clit. She gasped and arched back involuntarily holding Fiona's head to her chest. Fiona moved to the other nipple, while impatiently unbuckling and unzipping Meg's pants before pushing them down to her thighs. When Fiona's fingers slid into her, Meg's muscles pulsed rhythmically. She'd been on the verge and she came instantly. Her scream of pleasure surprised her. She couldn't have muted it if she'd tried. All she could feel was Fiona inside of her and she came again, and again, as Fiona continued to thrust into her, until she slumped against the cold marble behind her, unable to take any more pleasure. She wrapped her hand around Fiona's wrist and gently stilled her. Fiona wore a victorious smile before she kissed her mouth.

"God, Meg. You are so beautiful when you come for me," groaned Fiona next to her ear. The vibration of Fiona's voice traveled down her spine making her shudder. Her legs were rubber.

She took Fiona's head between her hands and kissed Fiona hungrily while she caught her breath, tracing a trail of kisses down her neck. Fiona's full breasts arched against her and she licked one of her nipples.

"I need to be inside of you, Fiona. I've missed you so much."

Fiona took a step back, capturing one of her wandering hands, and pulled her into the bedroom. As she walked, she stepped out of the jeans that were now around her ankles. Meg pulled her shirt over her head and threw it to the floor and Fiona pushed her own pants off. By the time they entered the bedroom, they were both naked. The sight of Fiona's unencumbered figure was breathtaking. Her body had grown absolutely sensual with the swell of her belly and the added heaviness of her breasts. Meg's desire surged again as she ran her hands across Fiona's soft skin.

At the side of the bed, Fiona pushed Meg onto her back, leaving her legs dangling over the side of the mattress. In a smooth motion she would never have expected from a woman so pregnant, Fiona was straddling her. The wet heat of Fiona's center pressed against her belly, and she cupped Fiona's swaying breasts as she rocked above her. Fiona held herself above Meg with one arm, and with the other took one of Meg's hands from her breast, thrusting it between her legs, hungrily pushing Meg's fingers inside herself. Meg surged in response to the feel of the silken folds as they slid around her fingers. The rhythmic compression fluttering around her fingers told her Fiona was close, and she hooked her fingers forward, applying pressure to Fiona's inner wall. Meg knew a little more pressure would send Fiona over the edge, so she alternately pressed and eased up on the spot to keep Fiona there for as long as she could. Fiona's grind against Meg's hand became frantic, the swell of her clit pushing against the sensitive skin of Meg's inner wrist.

Unable to look away, Fiona kept her eyes fixed on Meg's as the moment of her release grew inevitable.

Fiona bit her lip as she almost always did right before she came, and Meg gently pinched the nipple she held. Fiona groaned and threw her head back, arching into Meg's hand, a rush of moisture filling it as Fiona came. The warm fluid dripped onto Meg and it trickled down, blending with her own. Her sensitive clit twitched in response. She spread her legs and Fiona's fingers slipped inside of her as Fiona's grind became more intense and she rode out her orgasm. Fiona released a keening half-scream as she cried out Meg's name. At the sound of her name crossing Fiona's lips, Meg's orgasm exploded through her. Fiona froze, arched above Meg, rigid with her orgasm as her muscles fluttered around Meg's fingers. When the contractions began to subside, Fiona carefully eased herself from Meg's hand and curled up next to her, pulling Meg's arm tightly around her.

Trembling from emotion more than the exertion, Meg pulled Fiona toward her, and without warning, began to cry.

"What's wrong, baby?" Fiona asked. She looked frightened when she pulled back to look at Meg, but Meg buried her face into Fiona's neck and sobbed. Fiona held her tightly, gently brushing the damp hair from her face. "It's okay, honey. I've got you. I'm not going to let you go."

Several minutes later, Meg pulled herself together and they lay as one, their legs tangled, Fiona humming in her ear.

"Hey, Molly Malone is my song," Meg teased with a sniff, when she finally trusted herself to speak.

Fiona ignored the teasing and stroked her face. "What happened, baby? Are you okay?"

Meg took a deep breath. "I don't know. I think I got a little overwhelmed. Everything welled up inside." She stopped for a second, and tried to fend off the tears threatening to fall again. She cleared her throat and went on. "I don't want to lose you again. But it's not my decision. It's scary, you know?"

"I know," Fiona said, pulling Meg closer to her. "I guess we should talk about it."

"I don't want to push you," Meg said, but she needed to know if this was a new beginning or another goodbye.

Fiona shivered. "Let's get under the covers. I want to keep you close."

Once they were warm under the covers, Fiona began to speak. "I've been seeing a therapist."

Meg caressed Fiona's arm, but didn't say anything.

"I went to the therapist I saw after my parents died. Right after I deserted you in Seattle—"

Meg tried to interrupt her. "You didn't desert me—"

"Yes. I did." Fiona's tone was firm. "You have every right to feel abandoned. It was something I had to do at the time, but I take full responsibility for disappearing without a word. I was a coward."

"Sounds like therapy talk to me." Meg said. "But, I get it. I never felt like you did anything you didn't have to do."

"Listen to you trying to make me feel better, but it doesn't." Fiona gave a grim smile.

"Do you want to tell me what you're learning in therapy?"

"In addition to finally dealing with a lot of issues stemming from my parents' deaths, I realized I'm a bit of a control freak. And when I was faced with the very real possibility you might be with me out of some sense of chivalry—"

She sat up. "What? That's absolutely not the case. I'm with you because—"

"Wait." Fiona pushed Meg's hair behind her ear. "When I thought you might be with me out of some sort of chivalry, I couldn't stand it. There you were, with your life stretching out before you; and here I come and throw a baby into the mix to jack it all up."

Meg wanted to argue, to say it wasn't true, but she waited for Fiona to finish.

"The thought had crossed my mind before we ever went to Seattle, but all it took was your mother putting it into words for me to realize how selfish I was being. I couldn't let you make the life I was facing become your life out of a misguided sense of responsibility."

Meg almost did interrupt then. Fiona couldn't have been further from the truth. But Fiona held up her hand.

"My therapist helped me understand it wasn't my job to manage your decisions, though."

Fiona was quiet for a moment after she finished.

"Is it okay for me to respond now?"

Fiona nodded.

"I respect what you've gone through to figure this stuff out. I really do. And your therapist is right. I need to make my own decisions." Meg shifted so Fiona could see her face. "I never thought I would want kids. I didn't think I was the nurturing kind of person it takes to successfully raise a kid. But, honestly, I never thought the decision would come up either, because, you know, the lesbian thing. And then I met you. At first I was all "Hell no!" when I found out you were pregnant. My intent was to help you out with the kittens and then maybe we would be friends or something. But something changed. I fell for you. Hard." She traced her fingers down Fiona's face. "And then I realized I kind of was the nurturing type. To be a good vet, you sort of have to be. And the more I thought about it, the more I knew it didn't matter if I was the nurturing type. I wanted to be with you. I loved you. A kid is just a bonus, now. So, there you have it. I love you. I want to be with you. I need you to let me make the choice."

Fiona's eyes filled with tears, but Meg didn't know if they were good or bad.

"Can you let me take the chance with you?" she asked.

Fiona nodded. "I don't think I have a choice. I love you too much to not try. It would kill me to lose you again."

Meg's heart soared at the words. At the same time she hated to see Fiona look so fragile. "I've been so empty without you."

Fiona gave her a half-smile. "Somehow, I've managed to continue getting out of bed—most mornings—but I haven't been living. I always planned on seeing you again. You don't think I'd move forty miles away and not come to see you, do you? I didn't expect it so soon, but not a day has gone by since I moved here, that I haven't had to talk myself out of getting into my car and driving to see you. But you're here now. And I haven't felt this good since the last day I saw you. You being here is… I can't describe what I feel… it's so big. Nothing can diminish what I feel for you, Meg… nothing." Fiona's voice was thick with emotion when she finished, and she gripped Meg's arms so hard she left indents from her nails.

Fiona moved into her arms. "Where does all this leave us, Fiona? What do you want?" Meg whispered into Fiona's hair.

"I want to be with you, Meg. I want to do whatever it takes to make us work," Fiona said. "I hope you do, too."

"Are you kidding?" She squeezed Fiona so hard, she was afraid for the baby and had to let go. "Yes, I want it. I want it more than anything." Elation spread through her like sunshine. She shut her eyes and strummed her fingers over Fiona's smooth skin, basking in the sheer happiness of it all.

She nearly jumped out of the bed when a heavy mass fell squarely onto her legs. She looked to see what was moving stealthily across the foot of the bed. A black cat with vivid green eyes stared warily at her from its crouching position tucked in the valley of bedding between hers and Fiona's legs.

"Is that who I think it is?" she asked.

Fiona nodded. "Cardboard." Fiona gently pulled the cat up to lie between them. The cat immediately shut his eyes and stretched out, unabashedly luxuriating in the feel of long scratches on his tummy while Fiona kissed his nose. "He's normally a lot shier than this. He must remember you. His sister Molly is around here somewhere. She'll be here soon. She can't stand it when I give her brother any kind of attention… ah… there she is!" Fiona laughed as a white cat jumped onto the bed and walked over Meg to push her way between Fiona's hand and the furry black tummy she was petting.

"You kept the kittens!" Meg took over the petting of Cardboard as Fiona nuzzled Molly.

"Just these two."

"I think about them all the time. I wondered what happened to them,"

Meg said, pushing her face into Cardboard's belly. He purred contentedly.

"Betty adopted one, Maureen and Josh have two, and Tammy has another one," Fiona explained. "Betty and Maureen were easy marks, but I almost had to threaten Tammy to take Venus de Milo. It was only a day or two before Milo became the center of her universe. Tammy's finally fallen in love!"

Fiona and Meg played with the cats for a little while, before going downstairs to have some stew as the forecasted storm started to shake the storm windows. Meg called her mom, who was about to call the forest service, and told her she was home safely. She didn't tell her mother where she was because she wanted to savor it for herself for a while before she got her family involved again. There would need to be some resolution in that area, but the main issue had been fixed.

After dinner they went back upstairs and made love until they were exhausted. Finally, the emotional impact of the day took its toll on them, and they fell asleep in one another's arms.

✳ ✳ ✳ ✳ ✳

SOMETIME DURING THE NIGHT, FIONA rolled over and Meg spooned her. Fiona relished the feeling of Meg being curled against her back with a hand protectively holding her belly. She placed her hand over Meg's and savored the embrace she had gone to sleep craving for so many nights. She smiled as the baby kicked Meg's hand so hard it moved under her own, and she almost giggled when Meg sleepily rubbed the spot where the baby had kicked, murmuring something unintelligible. When the baby's kicks found her bladder, she quickly used the bathroom and came right back to snuggle in Meg's waiting arms.

Meg's voice was slurred. "I love you so much."

"I love you, too."

Meg squeezed her and a warm sense of peace settled over her as she drifted back to sleep.

THE END